PLAY YOU

REBEL INK #4

TRACY LORRAINE

Copyright © 2020 by Tracy Lorraine

All rights reserved.

No part of this book may be reproduced in any form or by any electronic or mechanical means, including information storage and retrieval systems, without written permission from the author, except for the use of brief quotations in a book review.

Editing by Pinpoint Editing

Proofreading by Sisters Get Lit.erary

Photographer Wander Aguair

Model Jonny James

NOTE

Play You is written in British English and contains British spelling and grammar. This may appear incorrect to some readers when compared to US English books.

Tracy xo

Andy and Amelia x

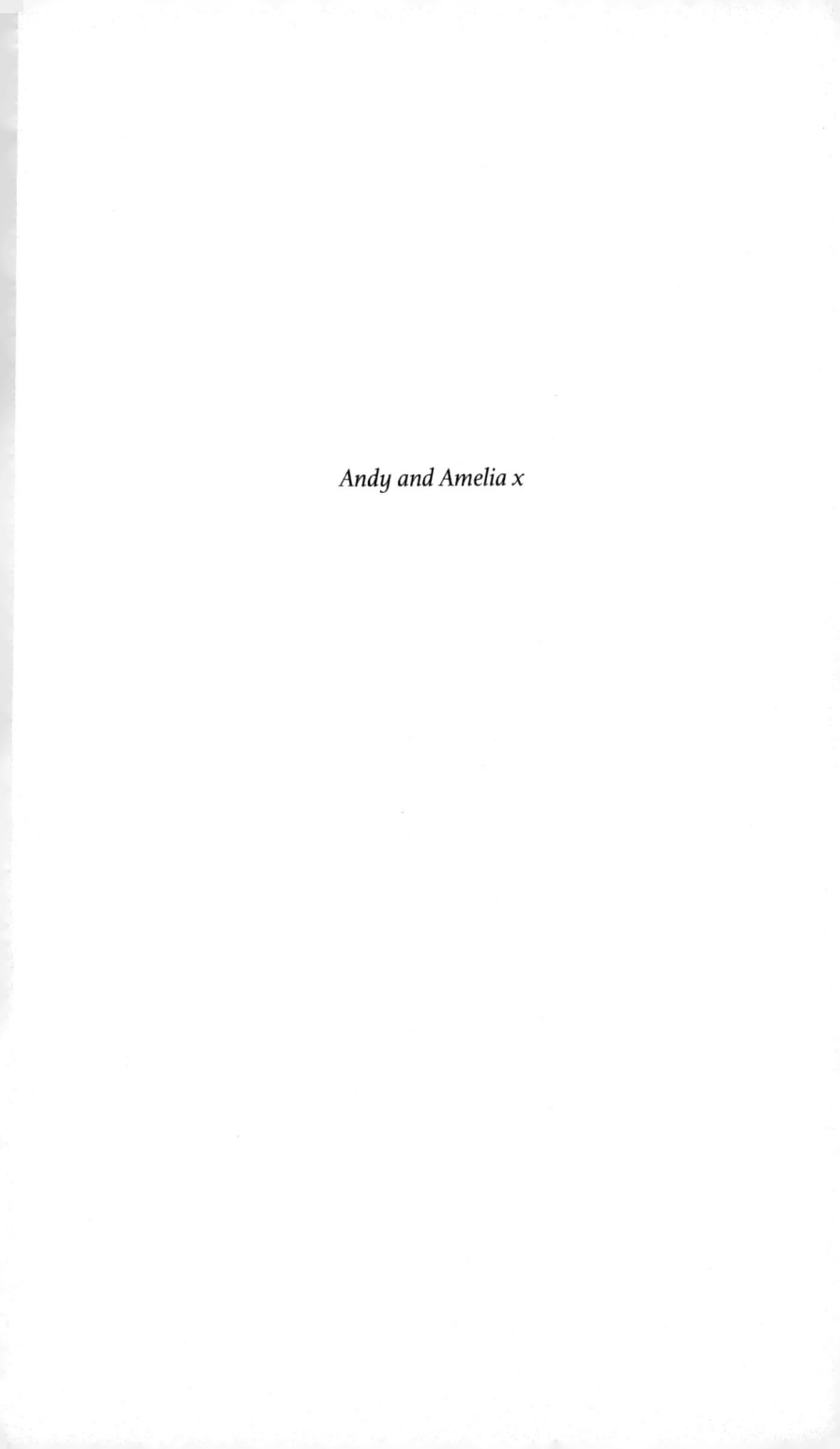

PROLOGUE

Dawson

Five years ago...

"Stop that, you've already done enough today," Gran says, coming to a stop beside me and resting her cool hand on my forearm, halting me from clearing up any more of the abandoned glasses scattered around her living area.

"It's okay. I don't want to leave you with all this."

She lets out a sad sigh. Today has been hard enough on her as it is; the last thing she needs is to be alone to clear up the mess left by all the people who came back here for my grandad's wake.

"Please, just go and sit down. I'll make you a cup of tea."

"Dawson, you don't—" I pin her with a look that cuts off what she was about to say. "Okay, I'll be in the summer room."

With her shoulders slumped in defeat, she heads toward her favourite room in the house.

My heart aches for her. She's lost her best friend, and although she had many people here with her today to celebrate his life, I was the only member of our family.

I wish I could do more, but I think we've been broken for too long now to try to fix it.

I put the kettle on and fish out her favourite teapot and cup we'd kept hidden in the cupboard, as well as some shortbread biscuits. I place everything on a tray with a bowl of sugar cubes and carry it through to her.

I find her staring out at my grandad's beloved roses with her eyes full of unshed tears.

"He'd have liked today," I say softly as I place the tray down on the table in front of her.

"He would," she agrees. "Thank you, Dawson. You're a good boy."

I smile at her. Only my gran could call me, a twenty-nine-year-old man who's covered in ink and rocking a beard, a good boy.

"I just wish—"

"Please, don't. I can't think about that right now."

I nod, giving her what she needs. But it doesn't stop me wishing that she had at least tried to reach out to my mum. I know it's been over thirty years, but it wasn't just Gran who lost someone she loved. My mum lost her dad. It might have been the perfect time to reconnect—or at least attempt to bridge the gap.

"I need... I need to talk to you about something," she

says after pouring herself a cup of tea from the pot and adding one sugar cube and the perfect splash of milk.

"Okay, I'm listening," I say, leaning forward to rest my elbows on my knees, sensing she's about to tell me something important.

"Your grandad's will."

"Gran, you don't need to do this. Not now. It's not important."

"It is," she says firmly, the tears and sadness of the day giving way to the strong and independent woman I'm more used to. Gran might have spent her life as a housewife, but you'd be a fool to think that's all there is to her. She's a force to be reckoned with. Hence, why my mother never fought all those years ago.

I nod, letting her say what she needs to.

"He's left everything to you."

My chin drops. "I-I'm sorry. What was that?"

She sighs, probably trying to refrain from correcting my English.

"After... everything, we'd both written your mother out of our wills. Your brother too. You're our family, Dawson. You're the only one who understood our decision but fought your way through anyway. It belongs to you."

"N-no. It belongs to you. You're his wife, it should be yours."

"Oh, my boy," she says, taking a sip. "I have more than enough for my last few years. You don't need to worry about me."

I'm not surprised by her words. It's no secret that my grandparents are very wealthy. The size of the house we're currently in is evidence enough. But their money was never the reason I reached out to them all those years ago.

The reason was Emmie. My daughter.

Thanks to the feud between my mother and grandparents, I'd grown up without them. I wasn't allowing them to miss out on anything with Emmie. I knew the second I turned up and saw the wide smile on my gran's face that I'd done the right thing. She's doted on Emmie ever since.

"There's one stipulation."

"Oh?" I ask, my brows lifting in curiosity. My grandad was... quirky. She could be about to say anything.

"The inheritance will only be released once you're engaged."

"Engaged?" I ask, frown lines forming on my brow. "Why?"

My gran and grandad's traditional views aren't news to me. I guess I should have seen something like this coming. They didn't agree with my mother's choices, and although they love Emmie with all their hearts, they're not happy that her mum and I aren't together and that we had her out of wedlock. I guess this is their weird attempt to get me to do it right the next time around.

They're missing something, though. I'm not money-orientated, and this isn't going to make me move any faster in terms of settling down. I've only been in love once, and after the way that ended and the pain it caused, I'm not sure I'm really willing to give all of that another shot. Being single with a few regular hook-ups when I'm feeling lonely is much simpler.

No promises, no commitment, and most importantly, no broken hearts when it all comes crashing down around our feet.

"We just want to see you happy, Dawson."

"I can be happy, single, you know."

She sighs, sadness washing over her. "Your grandad

was my best friend. Meeting him, creating a life with him, it was..." She stifles a sob. "It was everything. I want that for you. I want you to find your soulmate and create a life together."

"And you think the offer of money will make that happen quicker?"

"Consider it encouragement."

I laugh at her. I want to tell her their actions are misguided, but I can't. Hope fills her teary eyes and all I can do is thank her.

"Can I just ask one thing?"

"Sure, Gran."

"Try to make it happen while I'm still around. I'd love to see you get married."

Reaching over, I take her hand in mine. "I'll see what I can do."

1

DAWSON

"Emmie," I call up the stairs, "we need to leave. Now."

Reaching up, I run my hand through my hair as my frustration at my defiant teen begins to get the better of me.

One of the clauses of her coming to live with me was that she enrolled in sixth form. I wasn't having her move in here and dossing around. She had to finish her education, and that was the end of the discussion.

She needs it. Her results two weeks ago didn't exactly fill me with joy. It's time to sort her out and ensure she has some prospects for the future—a few more than her mum was providing her with, at least.

"Emmie," I bark once more before her bedroom door finally opens and her footsteps head my way.

Her legs appear at the top of the stairs, and my teeth start to grind as her ripped jeans and biker boots come into view.

She might be her father's daughter as far as her dress

sense goes, but it's not exactly appropriate for where we're going.

"Whoa, you going to a funeral or something, old man?"

"No, I'm taking you for an interview. I suggest you get back up those stairs and get changed. I can see your bra, Em."

"It's just sixth form. No one cares."

My fists curl in frustration. "Where we're going, they *will* care."

"And where *are* we going exactly? You've been a little too secretive about this for my liking."

"For a very good reason. Now go and find a pair of trousers that don't have more rips than fabric and a top that doesn't show what you've grown beneath."

"Jesus, you're such a prude."

"I am not—" She cuts me a look that has my words faltering. "You're my baby girl. I'm sorry if I want you to dress appropriately. Now, will you *please* go change?"

"Ugh," she sasses, moving toward the stairs again. "But only because you asked so nicely."

She stomps back up, huffing as she goes just to nail home how unhappy she is about this.

"Be quick. We're already late."

Fifteen minutes later than I wanted, Emmie finally climbs onto the back of my bike and we set off.

I fly us through the city in record time. I had to pull some serious strings in order for her to even be considered, so the last thing we need is to be late.

As we approach the entrance to the school, Emmie's grip around my stomach tightens. I can imagine how her face looks right now, and I can't help but smile.

I kill the engine and lower the stand to allow her off.

"What the actual hell, Dad?" she seethes the second

her helmet is off her head. "I can't go to school here." She waves her arm to the huge, elaborate building behind.

"You can and you will." I lock our helmets in the bike before taking a step toward the entrance. "You coming?"

"No." She stomps her foot to the ground like a toddler about to have a tantrum.

"Okay, I'll just guess what classes you want to do then."

I take off, leaving her sulking behind me.

I start counting in my head and can't help smiling to myself when I hear her feet against the gravel after only three.

"I'm not happy about this," she mutters once she's caught up with me.

"I know."

"I don't belong in a place like this," she murmurs to herself as I pull open the huge door that leads us into the reception.

"That's all in your head, Em. You're as worthy as anyone else here."

"Sure, you keep telling yourself that, old man. Just one question..."

"Shoot."

"How exactly are you planning on paying for this? You do know you have to pay, like, thousands a term for a place like this, right?"

"Yes, smart arse. I'm aware."

"I wasn't aware that you're a secret millionaire."

"Let me worry about that. You just need to get in and come out the other side with some decent grades and a bright future ahead of you."

"Yeah, so you've said. You're starting to sound like a broken record."

"Don't care. I'm not allowing you to have a life without

options. And this place will give you the most, so suck it up and plaster a smile on your face."

She rolls her eyes at me but continues forward beside me as I walk up to the immaculately dressed lady sitting at reception.

"Good morning, sir." Her eyes linger on my face for a second too long before she looks at Emmie. I have no idea what she sees on my daughter's face—probably a scowl—but her eyes widen slightly. "How may I help you?"

"We've got an appointment this morning for Emmie Ramsey about her enrolling."

"Okay, great. Mr. Davenport is actually in an urgent meeting right now, so Miss Hill will be meeting with you. If you can both take a seat, I'll let her know you're here."

"I can't believe you actually think this is a good idea," Emmie sulks the second we sit down.

"I warned you that living with me came with conditions."

"Yeah, I thought you meant a curfew or something, not that I'd have to attend a posh school. You know everyone will hate me here, right?"

"You won't be here to be liked, Em. You're here for your future."

"Jeez, could you sound any more like a father?" She rolls her eyes at me so hard I can't help but wonder if it hurts.

"Just doing my job, baby."

"Really?" she snaps, narrowing her eyes at me.

"Just trust me, yeah?"

"We'll see."

My phone pings in my pocket and I quickly pull it out to silence it before we go into this meeting. Unfortunately, the woman we're about to meet walks toward us as I'm distracted.

"Emmie Ramsey?" she asks, her soft voice ringing in my ears and sending shivers down my spine.

That voice.

Pushing my phone back into my pocket, I look at the woman standing before us. Her body is encased in a red wrap dress, the top half covered in a fitted black blazer. Her blonde hair is hanging straight around her shoulders and her face...

Holy

Fucking

Shit

"Piper," I breathe. It's so quiet that I don't think either of them hear me as Emmie stands to greet her.

"Hi, I'm Miss Hill, I'm the Student Welfare Director here at Knight's Ridge College. Would you like to follow me, and we can discuss your enrolment here?"

Emmie stands while my eyes are still locked on Piper.

Why is she here?

How is she here?

And why is she called Miss Hill?

Her name is Piper Collins, and I thought she was... *fuck.*

"Mr. Ramsey," she says, turning her violet eyes on me. The second I look into them, it's like someone takes a baseball bat to my chest.

As our connection holds, it's like the years just fall away again. Suddenly, I'm eighteen years old, staring into the eyes of the girl who's been the only one to ever hold my heart in her hands.

My chest constricts as I fight to drag in the air I need. My head spins as memories hit me.

I remember standing on the street and watching the house burn. I remember my father telling me to look closely because that's what happens when someone crosses us. I remember him telling me that he'd had it confirmed that all three of them were already taken care of before the fire started. It didn't matter on that day that she'd betrayed me; the girl I loved more than anything had burned in that house, and I'd never get to hear her beg me for forgiveness after using me the way she did.

No one messes with the Royal Reapers and gets away with it. I hear my father's voice as if it were only yesterday.

That was the day I decided that the lifestyle I'd been brought up in wasn't for me. It was that day I watched my father's hope of me following in his footsteps die when I handed him my cut and walked away. If he wanted one of his sons to take over one day, then he was going to need to look to Cruz, my younger brother.

"We're just down here." She points down the hallway and takes a step in that direction.

"Dad, are you okay? You look like you've just seen a ghost."

Yeah, because I have.

"I'm good. Let's go and get you in here, yeah?"

I stand and follow my daughter down the hallway, but my eyes don't leave *her* back.

Miss Hill...

I think Miss Hill and I have plenty to discuss.

2

PIPER

"Hey, your appointment is here," Lisa says, poking her head into my office.

"Okay, great."

"I'd sound a little more enthusiastic if I were about to sit opposite this guy. He is fine with a capital F."

"Oh yeah?" I ask, knowing that Lisa isn't exactly choosy when it comes to men.

"Yeah, and there's no woman. I'm thinking... rich, hot single dad who's looking for a good time."

"You're insufferable, you know that, right?" I ask with a laugh.

"It's been two weeks, Piper. Two freaking weeks. I'm dying over here."

I shake my head at her as I reach for my lip gloss.

"I don't know how you survive," I mutter. I might have had it more recently, but I can't say it was anything to write home about. In fact, I'd say it wasn't worth wasting my time with, but it's all I've got right now and I refuse to play the Tinder game as Lisa does. I'd much rather have a bad experience than meet a serial killer who'll off me in my sleep. I've already dodged that bullet once in my life. I don't need a repeat.

"I know, right? The pain is real."

I roll my eyes at her as she flounces out of my office and back to reception while I smooth down my hair and grab my blazer.

Walking out, I look straight down the corridor to see just how hot this dad is... only, when my eyes lock on him, it's not his insanely good looks that make my breath catch. It's the memories that slam into me like a fucking truck.

Dawson Ramsey.

My teenage crush and the only boy I've ever loved.

I slip back into my room as my heart pounds in my chest and my hands tremble.

"Fuck," I breathe into the silence.

I knew there was a chance this day would come. I knew moving back to London was a risk, but I missed my hometown. I thought I'd be safe here. Clearly, I was wrong.

I take two minutes to compose myself before I smooth my dress down my thighs, hold my head up high, and walk straight down to him.

If he's here to finish the job his father started all those years ago, then there's no point in running. He's just proved that they'll catch up with me eventually.

I made a mistake all those years ago, and I escaped. It's time for me to pay the price.

Sucking in a deep breath, I square my shoulders and walk toward where he's sitting with a young girl. His daughter? Maybe. Or just a pawn in his game to get to me? Much more likely.

I might have had a heads-up, but that doesn't mean my body doesn't react the second his eyes lock on mine. I keep my focus on the girl, Emmie, too scared to meet his eyes. My temperature soars and my stomach tumbles with a mixture of nerves and fear. My fingers itch to do something, to expel the energy racing through me, but I have nothing other than the edge of my blazer.

He was always able to disarm me with one look into his dark, mysterious eyes. I can't imagine anything has changed, especially knowing just how strongly I react to just being in the same vicinity as him.

And I'm right, because the second I turn to him, my breath catches in my throat and it feels like the world's just been swept from under my feet.

Dawson was always good looking—hell, he was better than good looking—but the years have been good to him. His frame is wider now, his face rougher, but in a good way. His chin is covered in a thick layer of scruff that has my thighs clenching just looking at it, and he has ink peeking out from the neck and cuffs of his black button-down shirt.

Just saying his name feels all kinds of weird, and the second I look into his eyes, I realise that I was wrong. He's not here to kill me. He wasn't expecting to see me.

This is as much as a shock to him as it is me.

Our eyes hold for a second too long before I rip myself away and gesture for Emmie and him to follow me.

My legs feel weak as I make my way back down to my office.

Is this really just a total coincidence? Is he really just here to enrol his daughter?

Fuck. He has a daughter, which means he might be married. He might have the two-point-four kids, be happy and have a white picket fence. Or he could have taken his rightful position and replaced his father as Prez of the

Royal Reapers, and although he didn't come here for me, he could be leaving with very different intentions.

My head is spinning with a million possibilities by the time I push my door open and wait for them to enter.

Emmie walks straight in as if she's been here a million times before. Her dad, on the other hand, stops right in front of me. His eyes flick over my face as if he can't really believe it's me. I guess that's to be expected when you stumble across someone you thought was dead.

He shakes his head before continuing into the room and dropping down into the chair beside Emmie.

I try to take a breath, but as I shut the door, it feels like he's sucked all the air out of my small office.

"So, Emmie. You'd like to enrol at Knight's Ridge for sixth form?"

"Apparently so," she says, shooting her dad the evil eye.

He takes a breath and leans forward in his seat, making me press back into mine to keep as much space between us as possible.

"Emmie didn't have the best secondary school experience."

"Pfft," she scoffs, rolling her eyes.

I have to fight my smile. I like her already. She reminds me of me when I was younger.

"As far as I'm concerned, she's got two years to turn it around and open up as many opportunities as possible. She's a bright girl, but her previous school failed to inspire her. I'm hoping that Knight's Ridge might just be the place for her to discover her potential."

"I'm sure it could." I keep my eyes on Emmie. If I so much as look at her father then I fear this whole meeting will turn to shit.

I already know I'm going to approve her application. Not only did Henry tell me to offer her a place when he bailed on this meeting, but there's no way I can refuse Dawson's kid. That could only make things worse for me.

"So, Emmie, tell me about yourself and why you think Knight's Ridge would be a good fit for you?"

"Because *he* thinks it's a good idea. Honestly, I won't fit in here. I'm not rich. I don't come from money. I come from a council estate where people spend their days getting high instead of thinking about their prospects. I think this is a terrible idea."

This time, I chuckle at her. "I like you, Emmie. I like your honesty."

"What's the point in lying? Where's that going to get me in life?" she asks innocently.

My eyes fly to Dawson's as his narrow in accusation. I swallow down my nerves before turning back to Emmie to talk about subject choices.

Throughout my conversation with his daughter, Dawson's gaze never leaves me. My skin continues to tingle and my blood races through my veins at just below boiling point.

I fill out the paperwork needed for her application before I get to the part I need to discuss with Dawson.

"So, in regard to the fees..." I slide a piece of paper toward him, but his eyes don't drop to it. Instead they just hold mine.

I can see a million and one questions spinning in his dark depths. I'm not surprised. If I were in his position, I'd have questions too.

"I've got the money. You don't need to worry about that."

Movement in the corner of my eyes catches my

attention, and when I look over at Emmie, I find her staring at her dad with narrowed eyes. "How?" she breathes.

He shakes his head. "I have the money. You don't need to worry about anything else other than getting the grades I expect from you."

She pales and sinks down in the chair a little.

His eyes return to me and I gasp. They're darker than previously, even more dangerous, and it's in that moment I figure that he must have taken over. How else would he be able to get his hands on the kind of money he needs for tuition here?

His family never had all that much growing up, but as the Prez of an MC, the world is your oyster and you can pull in money from whatever avenue you wish. If you've got the balls for it, which I've no doubt Dawson has.

"Well," I cough, trying to clear my throat. "That's good. D-do you fancy a tour?"

"I can't wait," Emmie says sarcastically, earning her a warning stare from her father. She seems totally unaffected by it. I'm not sure I'd feel the same if he were to turn that warning on me.

There are only a couple of people I've feared in my life.

Dawson is one of them.

As we walk around campus and I point out all the different buildings to Emmie, Dawson trails behind, his eyes burning into my back and making my skin tingle with awareness.

"Do I really have to wear that?" Emmie sulks when I point out one of our upper sixth students making her way out of the library. "I thought sixth form meant embracing who you are and being yourself."

"No," Dawson barks, proving that although his eyes might be elsewhere, he is actually paying attention. "Sixth form is about finding out who you are and what you want from life."

"Sounds like fun," she mutters much to my amusement. "You'll be telling me there aren't any parties next."

"I should hope not. I'm not paying for you to continue fucking up your life."

Emmie shakes her head but doesn't say any more as we follow the path back to the admin building and my office.

I talk through everything she's going to need to know, handing over reading lists, uniform requirements and all the other important information for her starting here in a week. The entire time, just like when we were outside, Dawson's dark stare remains on me. It's totally unnerving, and every time I risk glancing up at him, I find his face a mask of indifference and totally unreadable. I have no idea if his constant attention is because he's interested—probably not after everything that went down—or just because he's figuring out the quickest and easiest way to kill me—definitely more likely.

"You're talking like I'm in," Emmie says, shifting through all the paperwork I've passed over.

"You are."

"Haven't taken in enough charity cases to fill your quota this school year, huh?"

"Emmie," Dawson scolds, his voice so deep it has tingles heading south of my waist. I don't remember his voice being quite so gravelly and, well... hot, before.

"We're thrilled to have you, Emmie. I think, despite your reservations, that you'll do really well here."

"We'll see."

We finish up and Emmie reluctantly places everything I've given her inside the folder before pushing to stand, ready to run for the door.

"It was lovely to meet you, Emmie. I'll look forward to seeing you around campus."

She grunts at me as she reaches for the door handle.

"Emmie," Dawson growls, once again doing things he shouldn't do to my insides.

"Thank you, Miss Hill. It was a pleasure meeting you." Contempt drips from every word, but all I do is smile at her. She's not the first kid I've met who hates the hand they've been dealt. Hell, I was one of them only a few years ago.

"Emmie, please go and wait outside."

My entire body jolts as his words hit me. I can't be alone in a room with this man. It's dangerous, potentially in more ways than one.

Silence surrounds us before the click of the door shutting makes me almost jump out of my skin.

"What time do you finish tonight?"

"Um... What?"

"You heard me. What. Time. Do. You. Finish?" he spits at me, barely able to control his irritation.

"Um... I'll probably be done by four. Four-thirty at the latest. W-why?" I don't know why I ask; I already know the answer. Since his daughter walked out, his mask has slipped a little and I can read a little more into his intentions. Although being able to do so doesn't settle any of the unease that's bubbling away inside of me.

"I'll pick you up." He pushes to stand, his scowl still firmly in place as his eyes drill into me, daring me to defy him.

"I have plans."

"Cancel them. You owe me, Piper."

"I can't just—"

"Yes, yes you can. Cancel your plans. I'll be waiting."

My lips part to argue, but he's quicker, because by the time I look up, he's pulling the door open and walking through it.

"Don't let me down, Piper. It seems you were lucky the first time. I'll ensure that won't happen again."

As the door closes behind his warning, I fall down into my chair and drop my head into my hands as fear shoots straight down my spine.

I always thought I was lucky, that for some reason I was meant to survive the wrath of the Royal Reapers, but right now, I'm thinking dying that day alongside my family might have been the best option.

3

DAWSON

"Let's go," I snap at Emmie when I approach where she's standing with the Knight's Ridge folder under her arm, staring at the array of photographs and certificates of students' achievements.

"I thought you'd never ask," she mutters, not helping with my frustration levels.

"Was it too much to ask for you to keep your smart mouth shut?"

"You bring me to a place like this, expect me to be happy about attending with all these rich pricks, and think I'm going to keep schtum about how I feel about it? Yeah, it's like you don't even know me at all."

I blow out a breath, trying to get the events of the last hour to align in my head.

It was meant to be a simple meeting to enrol Emmie and to talk about her future. I wasn't meant to walk headfirst into my past. A past I thought was long dead.

"I think we should go and celebrate," she announces once we're standing beside my bike.

"Celebrate? Celebrate what?" All I want to do right

now is go home and drown in a bottle of Jack, but seeing as I've got a daughter to look after and a woman to interrogate in a few hours, I can hardly do that.

"I got into a posh school. It's not every day a girl like me manages that."

"Oh, so now you're happy about it?"

"Err... no, but any excuse for pizza. Come on, I'm starving."

She nods for me to climb on my bike, and I do so. Not because my sixteen-year-old daughter says so, but because she mentioned pizza, and I'm really fucking hungry.

I drive us back into town and pull up down the street from our favourite pizza place.

"So, how'd you do it?" she asks, her eyes narrowing in suspicion as she sips on her glass of Coke. "Pops had something to do with it, I'm assuming."

"No, actually. I sorted it. Pops isn't the only one with connections."

"But ultimately, it's from him, right?"

I blow out a breath. "Fine. Yeah. Happy now?"

She smiles at me, but it's totally fake. "I'd be happy if you let me go to a normal college with all my mates."

"And fuck around for two years and not come out of it any better off? Not a chance, Em."

"You know, I thought moving in with you would be fun," she sulks, "but so far, you're just a hard-arse."

"Never claimed to be anything else, kid."

We spend the afternoon at the uniform shop getting everything Emmie is going to need to start school. We end up having to order most of it, seeing as she's a short-arse, but it still costs me an arm and a leg. I knew this idea was going to be expensive, but I have every confidence it'll be worth it. She needs it. She needs the challenge and the focus, and I need to feel like I've done the right thing by her at last. I've tried since the day she was born, but most of my efforts have been blocked by her mother—a woman I really wish I could regret, but sadly, due to the awesome outcome of that less than memorable night, I can't. I just wish that I'd chosen a slightly more relaxed and less psychotic woman to use in my need to drown my sorrows back then.

Thoughts of what I was running away from the night I met Emmie's mother leads me straight back to my current issue.

Piper Collins. The girl I handed my heart to, only to have her stomp all over it with her lies and betrayal, isn't six feet under like I was led to believe. She's walking, talking, and breathing the same air as me, and has been this whole time.

My fingers twitch to pick up my phone and ask my dad about it. He never gave me any reason to believe that he thought Piper had escaped his wrath after he found out the truth about what her old man was up to. But if I start asking questions and he really doesn't know she's alive, I could send him right to her door. And now I've found her, I'm not giving up that easily after the way she played me.

It's time for me to have a little fun.

I shower, change, and am heading out the door well before she said she'd be finished for the day in case she decides to slip out early and give me the run-around.

The sun is still beating down when I pull up in the school car park. I bring my bike to a stop right by the entrance and only a couple of windows down from where her office is. Her window is open, so there's no chance that she hasn't heard my arrival, should she be inside.

I kill the engine, rip off my helmet, and put my Aviators on. Throwing my leg over, I rest against the bike with one ankle crossed over the other, and my arms folded across my chest.

Each second ticks by like it lasts five minutes. My watch taunts me as the time passes and she doesn't emerge.

I'm at the point of storming inside to drag her out myself when it gets to quarter to five, but just as I'm about to push from my bike, a figure appears behind the doors.

I watch, my eyes trained on her as she says something to the lady who greeted us earlier before she turns my way and walks through the doors.

"You didn't forget then?" she asks, coming to a stop in front of my bike.

My fingers twitch to remove my glasses so I can get a better look at her, but I don't want her to read what I'm thinking. It was hard enough keeping a neutral mask on my face this morning.

I drop my eyes down her body. She's dressed the same as this morning in that red, figure-hugging dress that does nothing to hide the curves she's developed since the last time I saw her. Only I swear her makeup has been freshly applied.

A smirk tugs at my lips that she's gone to the effort for me.

By the time I make my way back up her body, I find her standing with her hand on her hip and a brow raised, as if I'm boring her.

"Get on." I throw my leg over my bike and wait for her to join me.

"You're kidding, right?"

"Does it look like any of this a joke?"

Dropping my glasses into the neck of my t-shirt, I pull my helmet from the handle and drag it over my head.

"But—"

"I said, get the fuck on my bike, Piper," I growl.

Her eyes widen, a mixture of shock and fear passing through them, and I fight my smile. At least I'm not the only one who's been thrown for a loop today.

"Helmet is in the top box."

Turning away from her, I start the engine, allowing the rumble to settle me as I wait for her touch.

I tell myself that it won't be the same as all those years ago. She won't make my body burn with need with the simplest and briefest of touches. We're both different people now. Too many years have passed for that connection to still be there.

But it is. You felt it the moment you heard her voice earlier.

I force away the little voice and grit my teeth as the bike shifts when she puts her weight on the step.

A gasp escapes my lips as her thighs encase mine.

I lower my head, fighting my need to turn around and find out just how she looks with her dress hitched up around her hips.

I wait for a beat to see if she's going to wrap her arms around my waist, but when she doesn't, I assume that she's opted for the handles instead. Disappointment floods me. I'll just have to come up with another way to test my theory about our connection later. There's no way it can still exist. No way at all. It will have died like she should have that day.

I don't bother saying anything; I just assume that after all her years of being around bikes she knows what's expected of her.

We fly out of the school car park, the gravel kicking up behind us.

My body burns to feel her wrap her arms around me, but at no point does she move to do so.

I'd spent all afternoon trying to decide the best way to play this. But even now with her sitting behind me, I have no clue what the right thing is.

I need her. Enrolling Emmie at Knight's Ridge was a huge risk. I might have inheritance sitting waiting for me to claim, but I don't have my hands on it, and I certainly don't have the necessary requirements to get a hold of it right now either.

Gran's words from all those years ago fill my mind.

"The inheritance that's due to you will only be released once you're engaged."

When Emmie's mum decided that three weeks ago was the perfect time for her to give up all responsibilities of our daughter after years of fighting with me, I knew I needed to step up my game if I wanted Emmie to have the best shot at life.

I'd had no reason to need that inheritance before now. I have everything I need; I work for everything I want. I've never been the kind of person to rely on handouts from my wealthy grandparents. It's their money, not mine. I have no ownership over it.

But suddenly, I could put some of it to very good use, so I figure I may as well try.

All I need is a ring and a woman who's going to play the part. If my gran was still alive, then I might feel guilty about deceiving her, but she passed only two years after my grandad. But my daughter can use this money, and I know my gran would never deny Emmie anything.

Despite my words, a shiver of guilt still runs down my spine. I'll deal with it if it means Emmie doesn't end up following a similar path to her mother: a part-time job in the corner shop with no prospects, and the only thing to look forward to is the drinks and drugs that await her after her shift.

I shake my head. Why did I ever think that was a good idea?

I know the answer. I was young, stupid, and heartbroken. Still no excuse, but it is what it is.

I pull the bike to a stop a little down the street from where I've booked a table for this evening and kill the engine.

She's off and standing on the pavement faster than I thought possible. Pulling my helmet from my head, I reach out to take hers but freeze as she starts adjusting her dress.

"What?" she snaps when she realises I'm staring.

"N-nothing."

"Where are you taking me?" she asks, looking down the street for clues. She might be standing with her shoulders wide and trying to look confident, but I can see fear lingering in her eyes. It seems she's forgotten her mask, because back when we were kids, she was the expert at hiding the truth.

I had no idea that she was playing me.

I always thought I could read her. I believed every lie that fell from her lips when we were kids.

Well, not now. I'm older, wiser, and a hell of a lot more tainted by the bullshit that is life, especially one connected with the most notorious MC in the city.

I lock the helmets away and secure my bike before turning to her.

She swallows nervously and I fight my need to smile, knowing just how anxious she is right now.

"Let's go." I press my hand to the small of her back and push her forward, unable to miss the shudder that rips through her at my touch.

4

PIPER

My legs are so unsteady as Dawson guides me down the street that I fear I'm about to crumble to a pile on the concrete at any second.

His large hand burns through my blazer and dress, which makes my temperature soar. His freshly showered, manly scent that's assaulting my nose doesn't help either.

He doesn't smell like the men I spend my days with at the school. He smells like... man. Like my past. It floods me with conflicting emotions. A part of me wants to feel safe with him. It's how he always made me feel: secure and protected.

But I know it would be foolish to allow that to happen.

He might still be Dawson, the boy I fell in love with all those years ago, but I can't forget that I betrayed him. That I took every ounce of trust we'd built together and shattered it.

I'm pretty sure there's no coming back from what I did, which is why I'm so scared about where he's leading me. I guess the only good thing right now is that we're not walking toward his father, because as influential as he is, I'm pretty sure he wouldn't be waiting for me in one of the bars and restaurants that line this street. When—not if—he gets his hands on me, then it will be somewhere much less populated to reap his revenge.

My stomach turns over at the thought. I know all too well the kinds of things that go on behind closed doors at their clubhouse with the likes of our fathers and their acquaintances.

My eyes widen in surprise when he turns me toward a steakhouse and guides me inside.

The scent of the flame grill makes my mouth water and my stomach grumble.

I didn't eat at lunch. I couldn't. After having Dawson in my office, it was all I could do to breathe properly as memories of our time together played out in my head like a fucking movie.

"W-what's this?"

"A steakhouse."

"Smart-arse," I mutter as he steps up to the waiter who greets us.

"I've got a table booked for Ramsey," he says quietly, so quietly that I almost miss it. Although what I don't miss is the quick movement of his hand as he slips the waiter a note.

My stomach tumbles, my earlier appetite disappearing in the blink of an eye.

"Of course. Please follow me."

Dawson doesn't move. Instead, he waits for me to step forward and once again places his hand against my back, guiding me through the restaurant and out the door at the far end of the vast room.

"W-where are we going?" I ask hesitantly, unsure if I actually want the answer to that question or not.

"I've organised a surprise."

"Fuck," I mutter under my breath.

He can't kill you in a busy restaurant, a little voice pipes up, but it does little to settle the unease swirling around inside me.

We walk down the bright corridor before the waiter pushes another door open and gestures for us to step through.

Inside is a small room with a laid-up table in the centre. Soft music plays from the speakers and candles flicker on the mismatched pieces of furniture.

It would be a great place for a romantic date. Only, that can't be what this is, can it?

"Here you go. Freya will be your server tonight. Get yourselves settled and she'll be through to take your drink order shortly."

The guy leaves as I step into the doorway, feeling more confused than ever.

"W-what is this?" I stutter as Dawson pushes me farther into the room.

"A surprise. Come and sit."

He walks around me and pulls a chair out.

Apprehension races through me, and I fight the need to turn to look back at the door so I know I've got an escape route.

My heart beats wildly in my chest as I hesitantly step toward him.

"What's wrong, Piper? I don't bite. Well, not hard."

I swallow, although the lump that's been sitting in my throat since I first heard his bike rumble to a stop at school doesn't move.

"Water?" he asks the second he's in his own seat opposite me.

I nod, and he lifts the jug of water and starts pouring into two glasses.

Knowing that I need to be sensible, I wait for him to take a sip before I do. Although, he's hardly going to kill me this early into our evening by poisoning my water. He probably wants to enjoy his meal first. To grill me about what happened when we were kids. It's dessert I should be watching out for.

My hand trembles as I reach out for my glass, but before my fingers connect with something cool, they find his.

"You're shaking. Am I really that scary?"

"Dawson," I breathe. As terrified as I am, I can still hardly believe this is happening.

The first few months of being back in London, I looked over my shoulder every few minutes, thinking that he or one of the other Royal Reapers would appear. But they never did. So at some point, I stopped looking. I never totally let my guard down, and I certainly never forgot. But things became easier.

"I... um... You've just blindsided me, that's all," I admit, snatching my hand back and this time making sure I get my glass.

I lift it to my lips and swallow the contents. The cool water feels good, but it's not enough of a distraction.

"More?"

I nod, and he refills my glass.

His eyes don't leave me the entire time I drink it. It's as unnerving as it is familiar. He always used to disarm me with just one look; it seems that might be one thing that hasn't changed.

"So," I start, needing to end this oppressive silence that's fallen between us. "How are you?"

"How am I?" he asks like it's the most absurd question he's ever heard.

His eyes hold mine, but what I see within his has me looking away despite the pull I feel. The anger that's shining back at me every time I so much as glance at him is too much.

He should have just put me out of my misery when he first found me.

"So, you've got a daughter? Married?" I ask, glancing down at his bare ring finger.

He's wearing huge rings on the other fingers, along with ink covering every single one. Heat washes through me as I run my eyes over the patterns.

We were at the point of making some serious decisions about our lives when our time together ended. I wonder what he went to do. Or if his father put him straight to work for the Reapers. The rings sure point in that direction.

I bet they cause some serious pain to any guy on the other end.

He clears his throat, successfully dragging my eyes up to his dark ones.

Staring into them is like watching a storm approaching. Only, I could weather a storm. Dawson? Not so much.

No matter what happens between us now, I already know I won't survive him a second time.

"No, I'm not married. Never have been. Emmie was a happy accident a little over seventeen years ago."

Thankfully, his eyes soften a little as he talks about her. Something inside me relaxes. Maybe there is still a bit of the sweet boy I remember all too well beneath the hurt and anger.

"She's really quite something."

He chuckles, and the sound does weird things to my insides. Things I want to keep feeling around him instead of the constant fear.

"She is. She's got so much potential—"

"Hence Knight's Ridge."

He nods. "She's lived with her mother up until a few weeks ago. She wasn't the best influence."

"She'll have all the opportunities available to her now."

"That's my plan. Assuming I can make her attend," he mutters, much to my amusement.

Something tells me that the small amount of sass I experienced from her earlier is nothing compared to what she's capable of.

"She seems thrilled by the prospect; I can't imagine she won't want to attend." My sarcasm is loud and clear, but it doesn't seem to hit the spot with Dawson because his eyes just narrow on me. And they remain there as a soft knock fills the room and we're joined by our server.

"Hi, I'm Freya, I'll be serving you tonight. Can I take your drink orders?"

Unable to rip my stare from the piercing one before me, I keep my eyes locked on Dawson's.

"Just sparkling water please," I whisper.

"Sir?"

"Coke."

"Very well, I'll be right back."

She leaves us alone once again, and I swear she takes all the air with her.

"What do you want from me, Dawson?" I ask, unable to sit here and play this game with him any longer.

He sits back and stretches his long legs out beneath the table. One of them rubs up against my bare calf and I gasp as electricity shoots through me at the simple touch.

A wicked smile pulls at one corner of his lips.

"I guess you'll just have to wait to find out."

Dread and fear swirl around me like a storm, but I refuse to let him see that he affects me.

"Very well. I'm just going to use the bathroom."

He nods and watches me as I walk toward the door. It's not until I step out into the hallway that I manage to drag in a massive lungful of air, and I feel the world right itself once more.

I can't be in a small room alone with that man. It's dangerous.

The temptation to run is high, but as I stand staring at my flushed skin and wide eyes in the bathroom mirror, I realise that in my haste to get away, I left my bag hanging over the back of the chair.

"Fuck," I whisper-shout to myself.

Thankfully, the bathroom is empty, giving me a chance to have my little freak out alone.

He's brought me to a restaurant and arranged for us to have a private room. What's he playing at?

My head spins as I try to predict what his next moves are going to be. But so far, he's shocked me at every turn.

I still haven't even worked out how he feels about finding me. He's angry, sure. But there's more to it than that. I just can't quite put my finger on it.

Damn him and his mask.

It was never there as a kid. He was a get-what-you-see kind of boy. It's one of the reasons I was drawn to him. Everyone else in my life was always playing a game. But

Dawson, despite his upbringing, was just Dawson. The happy-go-lucky, slightly brooding artist.

He made my job too easy. He let me in without questioning it, and we helped convince each other that what we were doing wasn't wrong and potentially going to get us both killed.

We might still be breathing, but I fear the Dawson I knew is long gone.

I killed him, and in his place, he's erected that mask. The exact one I saw on my dad daily, and the same one I'm sure Dawson experienced from his as a child—possibly does even now, assuming he didn't end up with the same fate as my father.

I shake my head. There's no chance. Charles Ramsey was too powerful. Even back then. I used to shiver in fear just being in the same room as him. No one, aside from my own power-hungry father, would be stupid enough to go up against him. He was born to rule. It's just yet to be seen if he instilled that same control and power into his eldest son.

I really fucking hope not. Because if he's anything like his father, then I really don't want to be in that room alone with him tonight.

The urge to run washes through me again when I get to the door, but I swallow it down, throw my shoulders back, and hold my head high.

I might not know what game he's playing, but I do know that I'm stronger than to back down.

I'm Piper Collins. My father raised me to never bow down to a Ramsey.

So what, he stole my heart at eighteen and never returned it? He's still the enemy.

As I push the door open, I discover he's on his phone.

His eyes find mine the second I step inside before they drop down my body.

My temperature soars as his eyes eat me up and his full lips wrap around the words he's saying into his phone.

I don't hear any of them. I'm too lost to the sensation. Until one name brings me back to reality.

"Cruz, don't sweat it, bro. I got this." His words are like a bucket of ice-cold water over me.

My eyes hold his, and I swear I find excitement dancing in them.

"Yeah, bro. Tell him not to worry. I've got a plan."

He nods as Cruz, his younger brother, says something before he says his goodbye and hangs up the phone.

"Sorry about that," he says, pocketing his phone and gesturing for me to sit back down. "The waitress will be back shortly. She wants to take our orders." He pushes the menu closer to me, but there's no way I could read it now even if I wanted to. My head is still repeating the things he said to Cruz. He was talking about me, that much was obvious.

5

DAWSON

I fight my need to smile as all the blood drains from her face the second I say my brother's name.

It amuses me that she thinks I'd hand her over to Cruz and my father quite so quickly. I thought she'd know me better than that. That she'd expect me to have a little fun before the real pain begins. Because it will happen, there's no doubt about that. I just need to make sure they don't find out about her until I've used her for what I need.

She stares down at the menu, but I know she isn't seeing it. The thing could be written in Japanese and she wouldn't notice right now.

She's scared, on edge, exactly where I want her.

Cruz's call couldn't have come at a better time even if I'd planned it myself.

Her fear is the reminder I need for what's happening here. I need to think of the endgame, because after only a few minutes together, I can feel myself beginning to fall under her spell again.

When I caught her hand trembling, all I wanted to do was reassure her that I'm not going to hurt her, that she's safe with me. But I can't.

Because she isn't.

"Are you ready to order now?" The waitress walks toward the table when I nod and pulls out her notepad.

"Oh um..." Piper hesitates. "Err... sirloin, please. Medium."

I study her as she rattles off the rest of her order. She's so familiar yet so different at the same time. It's a head fuck.

She's got the same unique violet eyes that I used to stare into for hours, but there's something darker within them now. She's got the same slightly crooked nose from where she broke it falling off her bike as a kid, but her freckles are much fainter. Her lips are still the same—plump, kissable, probably sweet—only now they're stained a dark red.

I shift a little in my seat, becoming uncomfortable as I think about how those dark lips might look wrapped around my cock.

"And, sir. What can I get for you?"

Feeling two sets of eyes staring at me, I drag my head from my dirty thoughts and back to the here and now.

I look up—not at the server who's patiently waiting for me, but at the woman opposite me.

"Ribeye, rare."

She holds my stare, her earlier hesitation dissipating before my eyes. Surely, she doesn't feel safe right now. I might not be my father or Cruz, but I'm hardly a fluffy fucking teddy bear.

"Oh," I say when Freya is about to disappear from the

room. "And a bottle of..." I trail off, hoping that Piper will fill in the blank for me.

"Shiraz," she says, reading my silent order.

"You've got it."

Silence descends, although it's heavy with the millions of questions we both have.

"Not married either then, I see." I nod to her bare left hand.

"N-no."

An uncomfortable silence falls over us. Piper squirms in her seat as my eyes remain on her despite the fact that she can't hold my stare.

"Are you scared of me?"

Her eyes fly up and her lips part, but she must think better of her response because whatever her knee-jerk reaction was going to be is swallowed.

She squares her shoulders, trying to look brave, but I see the chink in her armour. "Should I be?"

"After what you did? Yeah, you should."

She visibly shudders, but before either of us gets to say any more, Freya reappears with Piper's bottle of wine.

"Just pour it," Piper snaps when she's offered to taste it. Freya pales slightly but does as she's told.

"Sir?" she offers, turning to me.

"No, thank you. Another Coke would be great."

"You ordered a bottle knowing you weren't going to have any. Why?"

"Why not? Why do we do the things we do?" I raise a brow and Piper fights to keep her eyes locked on mine.

Reaching out, she takes her glass and swallows down two huge gulps of wine. I'm sure she doesn't even taste it.

"Taking the edge off?"

"I'm not sure anything could do that right now," she mutters, much to my amusement.

A part of me is glad she's scared. Another part, the naïve eighteen-year-old boy who still lives inside me, wants to kick my own arse for doing this to her. But I need to keep my head. I'm no longer a young boy handing his heart to someone for the first time. I'm now a man, staring at the woman who betrayed him in the most deceitful way.

Was my father right to go after her and her family the way he did after the truth was out? No, probably not. But having stepped down from his MC, I'm not exactly in a place to argue with how he handles his business.

A small smile curls up at one side of my lips, but she looks anything but happy about this situation. If anything, the longer we sit here, the more terrified she gets.

I study her as she shifts in her seat and sips her wine. What I wouldn't give to know her thoughts right now. To know what really happened and how she feels sitting before me once again.

I could demand answers, but I fear she wouldn't open up. Not yet, anyway. In the end, I go with another pressing question.

"Why'd you come back?"

"You're assuming I left," she sasses, tipping her glass once more and emptying it.

"Well..."

"Yeah, I left. But London is my home. I couldn't see myself being happy anywhere else."

"Even with the threat of being caught?"

"It appears so, doesn't it?"

"You're aware of what will happen when my father catches up to you?"

She shrugs. "I refuse to spend my life running from my mistakes, Dawson. This place is my home. It's where I'm happy. I'll just have to cross that bridge when it comes to it." She swallows nervously, both of us more than aware that the bridge is closer than ever. All I've got to do is mention her name to my father and he's going to be out for blood.

I'm still trying to formulate a response that doesn't give away my intentions of not going straight to the old man about this when we're interrupted once more by Freya delivering our dinner.

I thought securing a private room here would mean we'd get time alone; I wasn't expecting to have our server join us every few minutes. Maybe I should have just taken her home where I really could have dragged the information I need out of her. *And scare her shitless in the process.*

You need her, Dawson. Keep her on your side.

"Would you like anything else?" Freya asks politely before backing away from the table.

"No, thank you," Piper answers while I just nod in agreement.

"Okay, well... enjoy."

The second the door closes behind her, the tension becomes heavy once more.

Piper's stare burns into me, but in my need to appear unaffected by her presence, I pick up my knife and fork and dig in.

The steak, as always in this place, is perfect. It's almost good enough to distract me from my company. Almost.

"Are you going to eat?" I ask when I'm halfway through and she's still sitting there, staring at me with an unreadable expression on her face.

"I... um... yeah," she stutters before picking up her own cutlery and delicately cutting a piece and placing it into her mouth.

I watch as it passes her lips and she chews. Her eyes roll back slightly as the flavour hits her, but it's not until her tongue sneaks out to lick away the juices from her lips that I realise I may have a problem.

———

I shut down any chance at a dessert—not that I think Piper could stomach one, seeing as she left half her dinner—and instead request the bill.

We might be more alone back here, but the interruptions are beginning to annoy the fuck out of me.

"Ready?" I ask once I've paid, pushing my chair out behind me.

She finishes her current glass of wine before pushing to stand with me. "Sure. I'll just call an Uber."

The second she has her phone in her hand, I snatch it away from her and slide it into my pocket.

"What the fuck?" she gasps, her eyes flitting between my hand and my pocket.

"You don't need an Uber. Tell me your address. I'll take you home."

"N-no. I really don't think—" I step right up to her, our bodies only a breath apart.

"Tell me your address," I grate out. "I'll take you home." My voice is low and leaves little room for argument.

"Dawson, I—"

My hand lifts, and she drags in a surprised breath when my fingers wrap around the nape of her neck. A shudder races down her spine at the contact.

Lowering my head, I allow my lips to brush her ear. "Do you really think you're in any kind of position to argue with me right now?"

She swallows loudly as her trembling begins to get more violent.

"Scared, baby girl?" I whisper, using the name I used to call her back in the day.

"No," she spits.

"Funny, because your body is telling me something else."

Without waiting for a response, I spin her around and direct her through the tables and diners out in the main restaurant until we come to a stop beside my bike.

"Here." I hand her my spare helmet.

She looks over her shoulder back at the restaurant before gazing down the street.

"If you're waiting for someone to rescue you, I think you're going to be bitterly disappointed."

"I'm not..." I raise a brow, and it successfully cuts off her argument.

"Helmet, then I need your address."

Thankfully, she does as she's told, and after doing the strap up, she rattles off her address.

"Brilliant. I can't wait to check the place out," I say as she climbs on the bike behind me. She stills at my words, but she doesn't try to argue. "Hold tight. All that wine might have loosened your grip."

I regret the words the second her hands brush my sides. Electric bolts explode around my body from the contact, but none stronger than the ones that shoot directly to my cock.

"Motherfucker," I mutter as I turn the engine.

Her arms wrap around my waist, her breasts pressing into my back and her thighs gripping my hips tightly.

My fingers tighten around my handlebars until my knuckles turn white.

Her touch shouldn't feel this powerful after all this time. After all the years I've spent hating her.

6

PIPER

I shouldn't have drunk the wine. I knew that before the first drop even hit my lips. But I did it anyway, because Dawson's presence is too much to handle sober. The way he looked at me... It was disarming. I have no idea if he wants to fuck me or kill me. And the longer I sat there, staring into his dark eyes, the more I was realising that I wasn't really that bothered with which way he went with it, if it meant getting to spend more time with him.

He might think everything that was between us was a lie, that it was all fake so I could do my father's dirty work. But it wasn't. Everything I felt for him was real. Too fucking real, which is why I now feel like my entire world has tilted a few degrees.

I also shouldn't have got on the back of his bike. Or wrapped my arms around him like I once used to. But I knew he was right. The effects of the wine are starting to hit me full force, and I'd be stupid to trust myself to cling onto the small handles by my sides. I might be okay with Dawson ending it all for me, but my imagination has that happening while his hands are on me. Falling off the back of his bike and getting squished by a London bus isn't my idea of a good way to go.

He flies through the streets, heading toward my building.

Part of me wanted to give him a fake address. It would have been so easy to give him Lisa's and to pretend I live there with her. But I don't want to drag her into this. The Royal Reapers wouldn't think twice about hurting an innocent in order to serve their vengeance.

In what feels like only a few short minutes, he's pulling the bike toward the parking outside my building. The vibrations of the bike disappear the second he kills the engine, and every muscle in my body locks up.

What happens now?

He's already alluded to the fact that I'm going to allow him upstairs.

Is that where he's intending on ending this? Leaving me dead in my flat for Lisa or Henry to find in a few days when I don't turn up to work?

My stomach is doing somersaults as I climb down from his bike and pull the helmet from my head.

I haven't been on the back of a bike in years, but it feels as natural as if I only did it yesterday. I guess that's what happens when you spend your childhood on one.

I stand awkwardly as I hand the helmet back to him once he's removed his own, indicating that he wasn't lying about seeing where I live.

"Are you going to invite me in for coffee?" he asks, his tone a little lighter than the one he used as we left the restaurant... the one that had tingles erupting in my lower stomach.

I remember him using that deep tone to whisper in

my ear as he made love to me. He used to tell me that it didn't matter what my surname was, that once we'd finished school we'd run away and be together like we were meant to be. But that was then, back when he thought my intentions with him were entirely honourable. Now he knows the truth, and I know he isn't about to start whispering any promises other than where he might hide my body.

"I wasn't aware you needed an invite. I thought you just took what you wanted," I shoot back over my shoulder as I head for the entrance.

He chuckles behind me, and it makes my thighs clench with desire. I'd be lying if I said I didn't think once or twice about how his beard would feel down there while he stared at me over the dining table in the restaurant.

Fuck, I really shouldn't have drunk that wine.

"Good to know that you're learning, baby girl."

I shiver at his nickname for me but swallow down the feelings. The teenage girl it awakens within me needs to stay asleep. There is no young love or promises of a happily ever after anymore.

We're adults full of hurt and betrayal, and loneliness, although I can't speak for Dawson on the last one, but it's a bad mix, and one that I already know shouldn't be combined with us alone in my flat.

I've already made enough mistakes today, what's one more?

I don't bother looking back to see if he's following me or if he's going to catch the door I just walked through. I know he's right there. I can feel his presence, his stare.

I decide against the lift, telling myself that the extra few minutes walk up the stairs might help clear my head and allow me to formulate a plan, but really all I'm doing is putting off the inevitable.

Lift or no lift, we're about to be alone in my small flat. Anything could be about to happen.

He's had ideas spinning around his head since the moment he saw me at school earlier. I just wish I knew what they were.

"This is... cute," he says as he follows me into my small open plan living area.

I stifle a laugh. Hearing his deep, rough voice say the word 'cute' is comical.

"Yeah, I guess." I didn't rent the place for the inside space. I chose it because of the small balcony and the view over the park beyond. The lack of outside space is the only thing I didn't miss about London in my time away.

Movement behind has me spinning on my heels to see what he's doing. I find him lifting, studying, and then putting down the photo frames that sit on my dresser. His shoulders visibly tense as he stares at the photograph of me and my parents. I don't need to get closer to see that his eyes are trained on my father. He might hate me, but I know it's got nothing on how he must feel about him. None of this would have happened if it wasn't for his need for power and control.

"He's gone." I don't mean for the words to come out loud, and I gasp when I realise that they did, effectively turning his dark stare on me.

"Is he, though? I thought you were, and yet here you are standing here before me and breathing the same damn air as me."

"They both died that day," I confirm, trying to keep the emotion from my voice. It might have been years ago, but whenever I think about how my parents went out it threatens to consume me.

I should have been there with them. I was meant to die that day at the hands of Dawson's father.

Not wanting him to see the tears burning the backs of my eyes, I spin away from him and walk to my kitchen.

"Coffee?" I ask over my shoulder.

"Sure. Black, no sugar."

"Sweet enough, huh?"

He laughs, although I don't hear any actual humour in it. "I think we both know that's not true, don't we, baby girl?"

"I don't know. I remember a little sweetness." I regret the words the second they pass my lips. Damn wine loosening me up.

"Maybe back then. I was young. Naïve. Easily played."

I swallow the lump of fear that climbs up my throat as his footsteps begin to get closer.

Hitting start on my coffee machine, I shrug off my jacket and throw it onto the counter, suddenly feeling like I walked into a sauna, not just my flat.

The noise of the coffee machine fills the small space, but it's not enough to cover his footsteps or the tingles that race around my body at his proximity.

Time seems to slow almost to a stop as he gets closer, but finally, the heat of his front burns down the length of my back.

His hand lifts and he sweeps my hair away from my neck, tucking it over my shoulder. His breath caresses my sensitive skin as he drops his lips to the shell of my ear.

"They might have indeed died that day, but what I want to know is why didn't *you*?"

I swallow, desperately trying to get my brain to

function and not just focus on how good his body feels pressed against mine.

"He... he knew it was coming."

"How?" he breathes, but despite the softness of his voice, it's impossible to miss the demand in his question.

"I-I don't know. But that morning... he made me pack a bag. He gave me an address to put into my GPS and told me to never look back."

"Where'd you go?" I tense at the question, not wanting to drag the woman into this who held me while I cried for my parents and the boy I loved but had wronged. We might not be blood-related, but for all intents and purposes, she's my family. She's all I've got.

"Does it matter?"

"I guess not."

Silence stretches out between us for a few seconds as Dawson's fingers splay across my stomach.

Oh God. How does this still feel so good?

"I stood there and watched that day. Dad told me what you'd done, and he forced me to stand there and watch as your house burned."

A whimper falls from my lips as his hand begins to move upward.

"I watched as they carried three bodies from that building once the flames were under control."

His hand continues to rise, and I can't fight the gasp that rips past my lips as his fingertips brush one of my nipples.

At my reaction, his hips push harder against me until my hip bones collide with the edge of the counter so I'm pinned between the two with no means of escape.

His ascent doesn't stop until his hot, rough fingers wrap around my throat.

Another whimper rumbles at his possessive move. I should probably find it threatening, but I don't.

"Who was the other body, Piper?" His voice is barely audible as he breathes the question into my ear.

His fingers tighten around my throat when I don't answer immediately.

"Oh God," I moan. His grip, his heat, his scent. It's too much. My brain is misfiring when I know that I should at least attempt to have some control in this situation. But that's the thing about Dawson, the exact thing my father underestimated when he sent me in on my mission. He calls to me like no other. He *affects* me like no other.

"Piper," he warns, "are you going to tell me what I need to know, or do I need to find another way to get it out of you?"

"I-I don't know who it was. I had no idea what was going on until it was over."

"Liar," he booms, making me startle.

"I'm not. I'm sorry. I have no idea."

"Always fucking lying," he murmurs. His hand that was wrapped around my waist, helping to hold me in place, moves until he pulls at the knot holding my wrap dress together.

"Dawson," I half-warn, half-moan when the fabric parts. My arms lift in an attempt to cover up, but his fingers wrap around my wrists to stop me.

"You want me to stop, baby girl?"

Do I? Do I want him to stop?

I should. This is fucked up. But his touch, his scent, even his vicious words... I crave all of them. I have since the day I left, and now he's here, his hard body pressed against mine, I need it—him—more than ever.

"Yes?" I don't mean for it to come out as a question, but

the battle between my head and my heart confuses me too much. Not to mention the wine.

"Hands on the counter. Don't move them."

He chuckles as his fingertips connect with my bare stomach. I suck in a sharp breath.

Just one touch and the entire world ceases to exist.

It's a heady feeling, and one I've only ever felt with him.

The first time I was with someone else, I thought it was just because he was useless in bed. But then I met someone else, then someone else, and I soon came to the decision that it wasn't the guys. It was me.

I was broken.

He broke me, and I was never going to be the same again.

"Your lies are going to land you in even more trouble." His hand cups my lace-covered breast as his fingers around my throat tighten a little. "Why did you do it?"

"D-do what?" I ask, my head spinning, my grasp on reality vanishing fast as he circles my already peaked nipple through the fabric of my bra.

"Play me. Why did you do it, baby girl?"

"B-because I didn't have a choice," I admit.

"Better. See, I knew we'd finally start getting the truth out of you. And I'm not opposed to a little... *persuasion*."

"Shit," I squeal when the lace covering me is ripped away and the cool air of the room surrounds my bare breast.

His fingers pinch until it hurts, sending a bolt of lust between my legs.

"Dawson," I moan, shamelessly grinding my arse back against his length. He groans at my movement. I'm affecting him just as much as he is me right now.

"Did you enjoy it?" he asks, his hand leaving me and making me want to beg to have it back. "Did you get some sick fascination out of watching me fall for you, knowing that you were going to rip my heart out?"

"What? No, no, Dawson. Never."

"Bullshit," he spits as the familiar sound of a flip knife opening hits my ears.

Fear rips through me.

"Dawson, what are you..."

He brings the knife in front of my face.

"You remember this?" he asks.

"Y-yes." I swallow harshly as my eyes run over the Royal Reapers crest engraved into the handle. It's almost the same as the one I have, only that's got my father's MC crest on it.

I was handed it at thirteen, just like Dawson would have been, in order to protect myself, if necessary. I've never used mine. I know that when we were eighteen Dawson hadn't either. I wonder if that's changed.

"Good. So you know just how sharp it is. Just how... *deadly* it can be."

I nod as the tip presses against my collarbone.

Oh shit. This is it. This is where I die, and at the hands of the only man I've ever loved.

He lowers it down my chest, the blade barely kissing my skin until he hooks it under the centre of my bra and tugs until the fabric falls away from my body.

Heat floods my core as he growls in my ear, his length growing impossibly hard against my arse.

"You always did like to experiment," he murmurs, his teeth sinking into the shell of my ear until I cry out. "We never did move onto pain though, did we?"

"Dawson, whatever it is you want to do to me, just get it over with."

"What's the fun in that, baby girl? You know as well I do that most of the fun is the anticipation. The thrill of the chase."

The tip of the blade circles my nipple before moving to the other. My breaths race past my lips as my heart thunders in my chest, but I fight like hell to keep still, not ready to feel the blade making easy work of my skin.

"Is that what you enjoyed? Knowing that you were betraying me and just waiting to be caught?"

"No. It wasn't like that," I cry.

"Really?" he barks, moving the knife away. I sag in relief, but his grip on my throat tightens for a beat before it slips around the back of my neck and I'm pushed forward until my cheek presses against the counter before me.

The coldness of the marble bites into my sensitive skin, but it does little to cool the inferno raging inside of me.

7

DAWSON

The need to cause her some pain, to get even a small taste of revenge for what she did to me, burns through me so strong that it's impossible to ignore.

I press down on the back of her neck, forcing her to remain bent over the counter as I move my other hand to pull the fabric of her dress from her body.

I discard it on the floor and run my eyes over her porcelain skin. It's as flawless as it always was, and my fingers itch to mark it, to brand her so that she never forgets who she belongs to. She may never have been mine, not really, but she does belong to me. Her pain, her pleasure, her possible future are all in my hands right now. One way or another, she's going to learn just how wrong she was to play me like she did back then.

With her cheek crushed against the marble, she watches me over her shoulder.

"Go on then," she taunts. "Punish me. Hurt me. Break me. I deserve it," she seethes, her eyes narrowed on mine.

"Shut up," I bark, lifting my knife once more and

making quick work of slicing through the thin band of lace at her hips.

Her knickers float to her ankles before she kicks them away and widens her stance, arching her back as much as she can and wiggling her arse at me, tempting me.

"Will it make you feel better about this whole thing if you fuck me like an animal? Will it settle the beast inside you?"

"You have no idea what it'll take to settle my need for revenge, baby girl. A quick fuck will barely scratch the surface."

My knife clatters to the floor as I rip open my fly and push the fabric of my jeans and boxers down just enough to free my aching cock.

"What you deserve, I don't think I'm capable of," I admit. She must hear my warning loud and clear, because a shudder rips through her. "But I know a few men who would love nothing more than to teach you a lesson you'd never forget. Once I've finished with you, that is."

I don't bother checking to see if she's ready. I already know she is. I remember her tells all too well. And I'm proved right when I push the head of my cock against her entrance and find her wet for me.

"Just like back then, you try playing innocent, baby girl. But your lies will always be exposed."

I surge forward, filling her to the hilt. She rolls her hips as she adjusts to my invasion, but I only give her a second before I pull almost all the way out and slam back in. The head of my cock hits her cervix and she cries out in pleasure, her walls gripping me so tight I worry that I'm not going to be able to last.

I want to draw out every second of pleasure from this. I fucking deserve it.

"Fuck," I bark, unable to keep my mouth shut. I don't want her to think I'm enjoying this more than she can feel. I slam my lips shut before I give too much away and focus on my restraint so I can hold off a little longer.

My fingers tighten on the back of her neck as I pound into her. Sweat begins to glisten on her skin as she moans under my hold.

Needing more, I slip my hand back around the front of her throat and pull her from the counter so her back hits my chest.

"Does it feel like you remember?" I grate in her ear.

"No," she confesses.

"Good. That boy you played? He's long gone, baby girl. The man in his place is going to fucking ruin you."

"Oh God."

A low chuckle falls from my lips. "God? Nah, baby girl. You might need to reconsider. You're headed straight for the devil."

My hand slips down her stomach until I find her swollen clit.

I pinch her hard and she immediately falls over the edge.

"Dawson," she screams, her head falling back against my shoulder as wave after wave of pleasure rips through her.

Her pussy clamps me so tightly as she loses herself to the sensation that I have no choice but to let go.

The roar that spills from my lips doesn't sound like my own as I allow the pleasure I've been craving since my father discovered the truth to consume me.

I've hated her since that moment, but I also can't deny that she affected me like no other woman I've ever met.

My chest heaves as I drag in the air I need, my release beginning to subside.

"Dawson?" she whispers through her own increased breaths.

"Don't," I snap. "Just because I let you come, don't think this is anything more than a cheap fuck. You were just easy. Here. Begging for it."

She tenses in my hold before I push her back down on the counter and pull out of her, watching as the evidence drips out of her.

I release her and stand back to right my clothing, but she doesn't move. Not that I'd allow her to.

I can't look into her eyes right now. I just can't. And it seems on some level she knows that because she remains exactly where she is as I reach down and collect my knife, tucking it back into my pocket.

I run my eyes down the length of her spine, over her slim waist and full arse, and down to her swollen pussy, still glistening with our releases.

My muscles ache to take more. To give her more. But I know I can't.

Not tonight, anyway.

This woman completely disarms me. One look in her eyes, one whiff of her sweetness, and I forget everything.

It's dangerous. *She's* dangerous, which is exactly how I fell for her games in the first place.

I need to remember that she's not the one in charge this time. I'm the one with the game plan, and I intend on seeing it through before handing her over to someone who will be more than interested in her reappearance.

"This isn't over," I warn, marching toward her door, needing to get away from her before I do something I'm going to regret.

I'm about to step through when her voice rings out through the silent flat.

"It's okay, I'm on birth control, you arsehole."

I don't respond. I can't. The thought of her pregnant with my baby does weird things to me, things eighteen-year-old me would have got excited about. I need to remember that everything is different now.

8

PIPER

The second the door slams shut behind him, my legs give out and I collapse to pile on my kitchen floor. I'm so numb that I don't even feel the cold biting into me.

Tears stream down my cheeks as ugly sobs rumble up my throat. They're not because of what he did, they're because he just walked out.

I should be relieved, not devastated that he couldn't even look at me as he backed away and disappeared out my door.

I have no idea how long I sit there, drowning in my guilt and my loneliness, but at some point, the coldness seeps into my bones and my shivers get so violent that I have to move.

I kick off my shoes, allowing them to collide with the wall at the other side of the room before sweeping up my discarded and ruined clothes. I drop my underwear straight into the bin. I'm tempted to put my dress in there as well; I'm not sure I'm ever going to be able to wear it again and not be confronted with memories of tonight.

Tonight might have been all kinds of fucked up, but I don't want to throw away the reminder that he was here, that he touched me, that our connection—for me, at least—burns as strong as ever.

I pad through to the adjoining bathroom and run the bath, my body aching in a way I haven't felt in years. And as good as it might feel, I'm not sure the memory of his rough touch is what I need right now.

I pour in some of my favourite bubbles before turning to the mirror hanging above the basin.

I gasp as I take in the faint red scratch marks that run down from my collarbone to my breasts. Lifting a finger, I trace the marks, remembering just how the cool, sharp blade felt.

Heat floods me once more and my cheeks flame with embarrassment that just the memory of his brutal visit turns me on more than any of the guys I've been with over the years.

Dropping my hand and attempting to push the memories away, I reach for my cleanser and set about removing my makeup.

The heat of the water stings as I step into the bath, but as I sink down into it, I realise it was exactly what I needed.

I rest back, allowing the soothing water to seep into my muscles and the scent of shea butter and ginger fill my nose. I sink down lower until it's only my face and the top of my head above the water.

I close my eyes and try to relax, but the only thing I can see in my mind is him. The only thing I can feel is his touch.

It's only a few minutes later when I decide the attempts are futile and I pull the plug and get out.

It's a school night; I should be getting ready for bed so I'm fresh in the morning, but instead, I fear that I'm going to spend the entire night with my head still in the kitchen.

It's the beginning of a new year, which means new students, fresh starts, and clean slates.

It should be an exciting time. It usually is, but my first day back after the summer off and everything has already gone to shit.

I angrily rub myself with some moisturiser before pulling on a clean pair of pyjamas and going back to the kitchen for a drink.

Needing something comforting, I dig around in my cupboard for a tub of hot chocolate and make myself the biggest mug I can.

The coffee I started for Dawson taunts me from under the coffee machine, and in a moment of madness, I take it from under the spout and launch it at the wall where my shoes met the same fate not so long ago.

The ceramic shatters and the dark liquid coats the cream wall before running down to form a puddle beneath.

The moment my hot chocolate is ready, I turn my back on the mess—and hopefully the memories—and lock myself in my bedroom.

As predicted, I toss and turn all night. I wake up covered in a sheen of sweat and with vivid images of Dawson in my head more times than I care to count.

By the time my alarm goes off the next morning, I'm exhausted and frustrated. The last thing I want to do is go to work, but nevertheless, I drag my arse from bed and just hope that I don't get any unexpected visits from a member of the Royal Reapers. Or worse, a Ramsey.

"Two things..." Lisa starts as she falls into the chair in front of my desk barely two seconds after I walk inside. "One, please tell me that exhausted look on your face has something to do with the hot daddy who was waiting for you on his motorcycle yesterday. And two... please, tell me the reason you never responded to my message was because he was banging your brains out."

"Well... it sure wasn't Henry," I mutter, dropping my bag into my drawer and following her move as I fall into my chair.

She snorts a laugh but claps her hands together. "OMG, tell me everything."

Guilt ripples through me, but I already know I can't dive into things between me and Dawson. They're too... fucked up.

"It's nothing like that."

"So, you didn't spend the night with that beard between your legs?"

"Uh... no," I say honestly. It's probably the only thing I can be honest about, because that particular act didn't occur. Although now she mentions it... my mind wanders off into dangerous territory. "Yesterday wasn't the first time we met, Lis. We knew each other as kids," I admit with a wince.

"Oh, okay. It was just a catch up then?" she asks, looking totally disappointed.

"Of sorts, yeah. We didn't exactly end things on good terms back then."

"So, you *have* been with him?" Her eyebrows wiggle in excitement.

"We were eighteen, Lis. He was different... we were different people."

She opens her mouth to say something but changes her mind and blows out a long breath instead.

"Spit it out." Reaching forward, I power up my computer so that I can get started once Lisa finishes with her little fishing quest.

"Can I..." she trails off. For a second, I don't know what she's getting at, and then all of a sudden realisation and a wave of jealousy hit me like I've never experienced before.

But I have no right to feel that way.

Dawson isn't mine; he hasn't been for... Hell, he was never really mine. Everything we had was founded on a lie. I might have been myself while I was with him, I might have been honest about who I was, about my hopes and dreams for the future, but the truth is that if it weren't for my dad, nothing would have happened between us.

We were—we still are—forbidden.

"Sure," I say, although the word tastes bitter as it passes my lips.

"Sweet. Besides, you've got Henry. You can't steal all the hotties." Guilt twists my stomach despite the fact that what she's saying is wrong. I don't *have* Henry. There's nothing serious between us, and there never will be. We just... lean on each other when we need it.

"Right." I fight to keep my eye roll in. Lisa knows the deal between us, yet she likes to believe that Henry could be my knight in shining armour and the two of us can ride off into the sunset together. For someone who claims to only want men for sex, she sure is a romantic. "I'm sorry, I really need to..." I point at my computer and she pushes from the chair.

"Yep, duty calls. Got to get all those little monsters

settled in." I watch her walk to the door before she turns back around, deep in thought and chewing on her bottom lip. "Any chance I could get his number?"

"Err... no." Dread settles in my stomach as her earlier words come back to me about not replying to her message.

He has my phone.

"I don't actually have it."

"You're really not seeing him again?"

"We made no plans." I smile at her, but it's forced at best. We may not have made plans, but he clearly has ideas because I can't imagine he's going to send my phone back to me in the post.

"Jesus," I mutter, falling back in my chair and allowing it to spin around of its own accord.

Movement out of my office window catches my eye, and when I focus, I find Henry sitting at his desk, smiling at me.

"Fucking hell," I whisper to myself, forcing a smile onto my face.

Our offices are part of the same building, but there's a small courtyard between us that's attached to our staff room. There have been many times that I've felt secure knowing that there's always someone keeping an eye on me—when he's not teaching, that is—but right now, I have the burning desire to pull my blinds down and hide.

What I said to Lisa is true. The thing between Henry and me is just fun. We're both single and not looking for anything serious, but he's a good friend, so knowing what I did last night still has guilt lacing through me. I have no idea if Henry has been with anyone else while we've been sleeping together, we've never had a serious conversation like that, but now I've been with Dawson, all these questions are starting to spin around in my head.

Sucking in a deep breath, I turn away from him and flip my diary open.

I've got meetings with our new students all week, along with a couple of group sessions with some of our more vulnerable kids.

My eyes lock on what I've got written down for Friday. *Lisa's birthday.*

She hasn't told me the plans, aside from demanding my entire Friday night and warning me that it'll come with a hangover the next day.

Forcing myself out of my own head, I open my emails and dive into my day, hoping that if I focus on something else hard enough then my memories of Dawson will eventually fade to nothing.

It's wishful thinking.

"What's happening Friday?" I ask when Lisa joins me in the afternoon sun warming the courtyard to eat lunch.

She pulls the lid off last night's leftover pasta and I stare longingly at it. It looks, and smells, much more appealing than the few leaves I threw in a tub before I left home this morning.

"Uh... drinking? What else needs to happen?"

I shake my head at her, a genuine smile pulling at my lips for the first time since I discovered Dawson in reception yesterday morning. Lisa and I are similar in so many ways, but when it comes to our need to party, she's like a teenager while I'm more like a granny who's happy at home in her slippers, stroking her cats.

"How about where? Are we going to eat first? What should I wear?"

She rolls her eyes at my need to know all the details. "Dinner, yes. I'll book a place once I have the final numbers." There are a handful of staff here at Knight's Ridge who are single or just can't turn down the opportunity to party; we end up doing this most weekends. It's almost becoming a tradition. "Not sure about after, probably the usual. And, as for what to wear, you already know the answer. Something sexy, P."

"You want me to shoot out an email?"

"Nah, I messaged everyone last night. You would know if you weren't too busy with your—"

"Ladies, how's it going?" Henry asks, sitting down on the picnic bench we've taken over.

"Great," I mutter while Lisa dives into her Friday night plans once again.

"You're in, yeah?"

"Hell, yes. It's not every day you turn thirty, pup." He winks at her and her cheeks brighten.

We chat away until someone pokes their head around the door and calls Henry away for something. Our sixth form students aren't back from their summer break yet, so as Head of Sixth he's quieter than usual. That's all going to change in the coming days as our boarders start to reappear.

"You gonna call it off with him?" Lisa asks once he's out of earshot.

"There's nothing to call off. And even if there was, there's nothing going on. I told you that earlier."

"Yeah, but I didn't believe you. Something," she starts waving her finger around in front of me, "is different about you this morning, I just can't put my finger on it, although I know it has everything to do with motorbike man."

"Enough, okay? There's nothing to know." She stares at me for a few seconds as if the truth will magically appear on my face, but finally, she averts her gaze.

"If you say so. I gotta go, shit to do." She stands and collects her stuff.

"Hey," I call out once she's at the door, "if I see him again, I'll give him your number, yeah?"

A smile pulls at her lips, but it doesn't meet her eyes. She knows I'm lying to her, and I hate it. But what am I meant to do, tell her the truth? I shake my head. I lived through it and I still don't believe it all happened most days. That life seems like it happened a million years ago now.

It's in the past.

And it's best it stayed there.

9

DAWSON

"Biff said you've turned us down tonight. Hot date?" Spike asks, inviting himself into my room and flopping down on my leather couch.

"Nah, nothing like that."

He stares at me for a beat, almost as if he can tell I want to say more, but he doesn't press me for information.

"How's the kid doing?"

"Ugh, don't," I moan, thinking of my first few weeks as a full-time parent to a gobby almost-seventeen-year-old. "I don't remember being that much of a pain in the arse at sixteen."

"Might have something to do with the fact that your dad is scary as fuck."

I laugh. Yeah, that might have something to do with it. Aside from the club's illegal activity, and all-around fear factor, Dad is a good man, a good father. But that doesn't mean he didn't raise a hand to me should he think I deserved it.

The worst two times were after I was a little shit to my

teacher. After those two beatings I sure thought twice about my actions.

"So I need to be harder with her?" I ask.

"How the fuck should I know? I have no experience with this shit. I don't even have actual parents. Just do what feels right, I guess. She's going to fuck up, it's part of being a teenager."

"I guess. I just don't want her to ruin her life before it's even begun."

"She won't, man. Not while she's got you watching her back."

"This is all her mother's fault," I say, sitting forward and placing my elbows on my knees. "She let her run wild and refused to involve me."

"What changed?"

"Fuck if I know. Neither of us has heard from her since Emmie packed her stuff and turned up here. She didn't even call her on results day."

"That's cold, man."

"Em said she didn't care, but I can see it eating at her. I'm just worried she's going to act out instead of deal with it."

"Then you need to let her. Like it or not, she's practically an adult. There's only so much you can do."

"I've enrolled her at Knight's Ridge," I admit.

"No fucking way. How'd she take that?"

"Exactly as you'd expect. Her uniform turned up this morning. You should have seen her face."

"It'll be good for her."

"That's what I keep saying. She doesn't agree."

Spike chuckles. "What does she want to do?"

"No idea. I'm hoping this will help her figure it out."

"It won't hurt, that's for sure."

"She's starting Monday. If I can get her there."

"Rather you than me, man. You want coffee?"

"Yeah. I've got a client in five, then I'm out of here."

I stretch my legs out and pull Piper's phone from my pocket. I've been keeping tabs on her messages all week after I discovered I still had it. It certainly wasn't my intention to not give it back, but it turned out pretty perfectly because not only do I now know her plans for the night, but she doesn't have a passcode on the thing, so I know a lot more than I'm sure she'd want me to.

By the time I've finished working on the back piece for my evening client, I'm more than ready to head out and get a drink.

I swing by home, check on Emmie—who's watching some series about a girl playing chess who really needs a new hairstyle—shower, change and head out to the club Piper's friends discussed going to tonight.

The guys and I are at The Avenue pretty regularly. I have no idea if Piper goes a lot, but it makes me wonder if we've been under the same roof numerous times over the years and had no idea.

The queue outside the club stretches well down the street, but, much to everyone's annoyance, I walk straight up to tonight's security, fist bump Jamie and walk straight inside. Tattooist perks.

Unlike usual when I get to the stairs, I don't go down. Instead, I head up.

The floor is laid out exactly the same as the basement, but instead of the garage music that pumps through the speakers down there, up here is all dance.

I look around as I head to the bar. Despite the fact that there's a crowd gathered, I get served almost instantly.

With a glass of whiskey in my hand, I rest back against the bar and scan the crowd.

I don't find anyone even remotely familiar for the longest time, and I'm at the point of wanting to give up when a flash of blonde catches my eye in the middle of the dancefloor.

My grip on the glass in my hand tightens to the point I worry it's about to shatter under the pressure as I watch her dancing with a guy.

She has her back to him as she throws her head back and laughs like she has no cares in the world. I can only see to their shoulders, but I can imagine his hands possessively on her hips as they move together to the beat.

Slamming my glass down on the bar, I order another two, needing something to settle me before I march over there and rip her from his grip.

"Fancy seeing you here," an unfamiliar voice says behind me before a warm hand lands on my upper arm.

Spinning, I run my eyes up the woman's barely-dressed body before they land on her blown ones. She's off her arse drunk and swaying on the spot. I recognise her, but I have no idea who she is.

She's pretty, sure. Not really my type, but then I've never been known to be picky when it comes to a willing woman.

She doesn't let my silence deter her because she steps closer, the scent of her perfume and whatever she's been drinking filling my nose.

"You were at Knight's Ridge on Monday with your daughter, right?" she asks as realisation hits me. She's the woman from reception.

"I was. My daughter is starting on Monday."

"We should totally get to know each other then..."

"Dawson," I add, although I really don't want to get into a conversation with her when I could be planning my move with Piper.

"Dawson," she says as if she's trying it out for size. "It suits you."

"Well, that's a relief, seeing as it's my name."

She throws her head back and laughs at my non-joke.

"It was nice talking to you," I say, tipping the remains of my glass into my mouth and pushing from the bar.

"Lisa. My name is Lisa."

"Great." I smile at her before walking away. When I glance at the dancefloor, I find Piper alone for the first time.

After a few seconds, my eyes pick out the guy heading for Lisa, so I take my chance.

"That was quick," Piper shouts when I step up behind her and drag her arse back into my crotch.

I keep my lips sealed, not wanting to give myself away yet, although all it would take is one look at my hands and she'd soon realise that her little posh boy is gone.

Lowering my head, I run my nose up the length of her neck. She shudders in my hold and pushes her arse back harder.

My cock swells as we move together in time with the music.

I step us forward, needing to move away from where her friends are expecting her to be if—when—they return.

The song changes and the beat drops.

"I love this song," she declares, lifting her arms above her head and moving faster. Her head falls back on my shoulder and her arms drop as she loses herself to the beat.

My hands lift from her hips and drift up to her waist. With my lips pressed against the glistening skin of her neck, I feel more than hear her moan of pleasure as my thumbs brush the underside of her braless breasts.

My cock aches, knowing only a thin layer of fabric covers her.

Parting my lips, I lick up the column of her neck, her taste exploding on my tongue.

"Henry, what the hell?" she half-shouts, half-moans. She twists, but I'm quicker. One of my hands splays across her stomach, keeping our bodies connected, and the other slips into her hair, my fingers twisting in the soft lengths and holding her in place.

"Your posh boy has gone," I growl into her neck.

"D-Dawson?"

"The one and only," I whisper. "Miss me?" My teeth sink into the shell of her ear and she sags in my hold.

"What are you doing here?"

"I was invited," I lie.

"H-how?"

"Okay, so I wasn't technically invited, but you were, and I have your phone. So..."

"You were waiting for me?"

"Waiting. Watching. Same thing. Who's the guy, Piper?"

"N-no one."

Pushing her forward, I ensure we're in the darkest part of the dancefloor, surrounded by others. I spin us around and look out over the crowd once more.

I find her friend not far from where I first saw Piper, dancing like nothing else exists, and after a few seconds she's joined by him, but not before he obviously looks around for Piper.

"Really?"

"Y-yeah."

"Okay."

She stills in my arms before turning to look at me, but with my grip on her hair she's unable to move more than an inch.

"You believe me?" Disbelief coats her words.

"I fucked you Monday night. You didn't even so much as mention him. I'm thinking he's... *insignificant*," I growl in her ear. "Let's go."

"Where?"

I ignore her question as I push her toward the stairs.

"I can't just leave. My friends—"

"Fuck them. They're distracted."

"Dawson, I can't—"

"Arguing will get you nowhere, baby girl. The easiest thing is to just do as you're told."

She struggles against my hold but soon must realise that she has no chance, because she gives up and allows me to lead her to the basement.

The familiar music hits my ears, and I feel more at home than I did upstairs.

I walk her straight to the bar and order four whiskeys.

"What if I don't like whiskey?" she sasses, flexing her neck now that I've released her, although my hand is still clamped around her hip, reminding her that she's not going anywhere.

"Drink up. You're probably going to need it."

I lift the first glass from the dark wood bar and knock it back.

Keeping my eyes on her, I widen them and nod toward the drinks.

Her teeth grind as she stares back at me, but she doesn't say whatever is on the tip of her tongue. Probably for the best, because I suspect it's an insult.

She reaches out and takes one of the glasses, lifting it to her red lips before seductively licking away the excess.

My cock jumps at the sight.

"Bottoms up, Dawson," she smiles wickedly before downing the second. She winces as it burns her throat before stepping into me and running her hand up my chest.

It's the first time she's touched me, and it burns. Capturing her wrist, I pull it behind her back. I don't need a reminder of what it used to be like when we connected. I need to keep my head.

With both her arms pinned behind her back, she presses her breasts against my chest instead and reaches up on her tiptoes. For a second I think she's going to try to kiss me, but at the last minute she moves to the side instead.

"Dance, fuck, or kill? What's it to be?"

"How about all three?" My arm tightens around her body and she gasps as my length presses against her stomach.

"Sounds like a game I could get on board with. Don't forget, though. You're not the only one with a knife."

"I'm aware. I'm also aware that only one of us has ever used theirs."

"Are you sure about that? There's a lot you don't know about me these days, Dawson."

"That may be true, baby girl. But you're no killer. Shall we?" I ask, stepping away from her and leading her toward the dancefloor as if we weren't just talking about murder like it's normal.

I come to a stop in a bit of space and pull her into my body once more. She tries to spin so we're face to face, but I stop her and pull her ass back into me.

"You know," she shouts, resting her head back against my shoulder, "I'm starting to think you don't like looking at the front of me."

"Something like that."

"Why is it?" She wraps her hands around mine, dragging them up her body. "These not big enough?" she asks, forcing me to squeeze her tits.

"It's more your face that I have an issue with. It's easier to forget I'm touching a liar when I'm not looking at you."

"Ouch," she says, but there's no hurt there. She knows exactly what she is and what she did. "I didn't have you down as a coward, Dawson."

"What makes you think I am?"

"I thought you'd look me directly in my eyes as you fucked me over."

I have her front against mine in a second. One of my hands squeezes her arse—hard—while the other wraps around her throat.

"Trust me, baby girl. You'll know all about it when I fuck you over."

She swallows harshly at my threat, but her body betrays her because it leans into me.

"Kiss me," she demands.

I chuckle. "You really think you're in any position to make demands? You're at my mercy now. I say what happens, and I say when. You got that?"

She nods once, her eyes boring into mine.

"I think I'm done with the dancing portion of the

night. Shall we move onto the second?" Her lips part and her pupils dilate.

I'll take that as a yes.

Spinning her in my arms once again, I walk us toward the stairs and then this time, the exit.

10

PIPER

The second the fresh air hits me, so does the whiskey. My head spins and my legs shake as Dawson guides me out onto the pavement and to an awaiting taxi.

He steps forward, but it's not enough for me to miss his words.

"I'll pay you triple if you don't look in your rearview mirror."

I swallow roughly as heat descends to my core.

What the hell is he planning to do?

The driver agrees, and in seconds I'm being ushered into the back while Dawson barks out my address as confidently as if it's his own.

I've barely put my arse on the seat before he leans over me and pulls the seatbelt across my body.

"I'm more than capable of doing that myself," I hiss as his knuckles brush over my nipple before he buckles it in.

"I'm sure you are." His whiskey-scented breath caresses my lips and my mouth waters to get a taste of him.

I want to demand he kisses me again, but I still

remember the sting from his rejection inside the club. I don't need that again. Instead, I swallow the words and bite down on my bottom lip.

His eyes focus on it, but he doesn't do anything. He just sits back and puts his own seatbelt on.

"Can I have my phone back now?" I ask, holding my hand out impatiently.

"No."

"N-no?"

He turns to me, his knee bumping into my thigh and his upper body shielding me from the driver.

His eyes search mine for a beat before they drop to my lips. It's the first time he's given me any indication that he might want to kiss me, and I can't help the smile that pulls at the corners of my lips.

I startle when his large palm lands on my bare thigh.

The dress I'm wearing tonight isn't one that emerges from my wardrobe all that often, but Lisa was adamant that I had to wear it, and seeing as it's her night, I went along with her plan. I regretted it when Henry's eyes almost popped out of his head when we arrived at the restaurant. I'd felt naked and uncomfortable as he took in all my bare skin on show.

"This dress," Dawson murmurs as if he can read my thoughts. "It shouldn't be allowed out in public." His finger trails down the low neckline and caresses the exposed swell of my breast, making my nipples pucker.

Tucking his finger under the fabric, he exposes my left breast.

"Dawson," I gasp, partly in shock, partly in desire.

"Let's not pretend like you're all innocent." His fingertip flicks my nipple and a bolt of lust shoots straight to my core.

My thighs tense and he smirks, clearly not missing the move.

His thumb and forefinger pinch down on my peak and he twists, hard.

I cry out before slamming my hand over my mouth when I remember where I am.

"You n-need to stop," I beg.

"Where would the fun be in that? How wet are you for me right now?" he asks, his dark eyes full of heat.

I slam my lips shut and swallow.

"Now's not the time to deny me, baby girl. You know I'll just have to find out for myself."

"Like you wouldn't anyway." I narrow my eyes at him in challenge.

"You're mine now, Piper. I know it, you know it. The taxi driver knows it. And at the first possible opportunity, the guy you were dancing with tonight is going to know it. You got that?"

"Why? You hate me."

"Because you owe me, remember?"

He twists my nipple again, only harder this time, and I sink my teeth into my cheeks to stop from screaming.

"Do you understand me?"

I nod at him and he releases my burning nipple, but I don't get any reprieve because he lifts the already insanely short hem of my dress and peeks underneath.

"Lift up."

"What?" My heart pounds in my chest and my stomach tumbles. He's not really going to remove them, is he?

"Lift, or I'll just rip them off."

Holy shit. I'm amazed they're still there, because from the way he's looking at me, talking to me, touching me, I'm surprised they're not melted right off me.

I shouldn't be turned on by his dirty words or his threats, but I am. More than I ever have been in my life.

I should be running scared when he says he owns me, but instead, I'm falling further under his spell.

He's going to ruin you, break you, and then spit you out, the little voice in my head warns, but I don't listen, I can't. I'm too lost in him.

Both his tattooed hands disappear under the fabric, and before I have a chance to make a decision, my body acts on instinct and rises from the seat.

"Good girl." He pulls my thong down my thighs before dropping it to my ankles and unhooking it from my shoes.

"What are you... of course you are." I chuckle as he stuffs them in his pocket. "Memento?"

"It's better than what you left me with last time."

Regret swirls around me like a storm cloud, but no matter how much I might want to take back what happened, I can't.

I have to embrace it, accept it, attempt to make up for it.

I certainly didn't do it by choice. It was through necessity. If I didn't agree, Dad would have found me something much worse to do to earn my place at the club.

A shudder runs through me at the thought.

"I never—"

"No," he barks, placing a finger over my lips. "I don't want to hear your apologies, your excuses. The time for talking and trying to explain is long gone. You had your chance to come clean, to tell me the truth, and you didn't. Now, I'm in control."

His hand presses between my thighs and pushes them open.

"Let's see just what a dirty little slut you are."

"Oh shit." My head falls back in pleasure when his fingers connect with my sensitive, swollen flesh.

"Oh," he all but laughs, a smirk pulling at his lips. "You like belonging to me, don't you, baby girl?"

"Dawson," I breathe as he circles my clit before pushing lower and finding my entrance.

"You like being at my mercy? Knowing that I can have you whenever, wherever I want you?"

"Oh God," I whimper as he pushes a finger inside me.

"He's not going to save you this time, baby."

He pushes deeper, and my eyes roll to the back of my head. My release is already within reaching distance, despite the fact that he's barely touched me.

He adds a second finger, stretching me wide and making the sensations even more intense. He curls them both, finding that sweet spot inside me that makes me sees stars, and he rubs at me as my muscles lock up with pleasure and my wetness drips down his fingers.

"Dawson," I whisper when I'm right on the edge, my body just ready to fly, to forget reality and just focus on the pleasure.

But then... it's gone.

"What the—" My head flies forward, my eyes opening to find him grinning at me.

Lifting his fingers, he pushes them past his lips and sucks.

"Jesus, fuck, Dawson."

"You taste too sweet for someone so bad."

"Takes one to know one," I spit at him before ripping my eyes away and looking at my surroundings.

I find my building outside the window and my brows pull together. "How long have we... doesn't matter," I mutter, reaching to cover myself up and undoing my seatbelt.

I climb from the car without looking at the driver, I'm too ashamed of my actions. With my head lowered, I pull my dress down my thighs as far as it will go and march toward the main entrance.

I'm lifting my key to the lock with unsteady hands when it's ripped from my fingers.

I look back over my shoulder at Dawson, who's seemingly just inviting himself up. I mean, I'm not surprised after what he said just a few minutes ago in the taxi, but it doesn't stop anger swelling in my belly.

"Do you mind?" I snap, turning my back to the door and glaring daggers at him.

"No, I really fucking don't."

I squeal like a little girl as my feet leave the floor and I find myself staring directly at Dawson's arse.

"Put me down, wanker," I shout, kicking my legs and pounding my balled fists into his solid butt.

He laughs, a full-on belly laugh as he pushes through the door and starts jogging up the stairs as if I weigh nothing more than a feather.

"Dawson, put me down."

"It's cute that you think I'm going to listen, baby girl."

Crossing my arms, I huff out a frustrated breath as his large palm burns my bare arse cheek beneath my dress. It's the first time I remember that I'm not wearing any fucking knickers.

"I swear to God, Dawson, if I flash any of my neighbours, I'll—"

"You'll what?" he taunts before his heat leaves me seconds before it cracks against my skin.

"Ow, that fucking hurt."

"Good. It might stop you complaining."

I snort. "Unlikely."

He comes to a stop at my door, but I don't bother fighting. Instead, I just hope that once we're inside he'll release me.

It's wishful thinking, because he lets the door slam behind us before walking straight to the kitchen and pulling open the cupboards.

"Where's the alcohol?" he asks after a few seconds of coming up empty.

"Top right."

"Ah-ha. I'm going to need this if I've got to put up with your smart mouth."

"You could leave. I'm sure you've got a perfectly good bed at home waiting for you."

"Yeah, it's damn comfortable too, but it's missing one thing."

"Oh yeah?" I ask, trying to sound as bored as possible.

"Yeah, you."

He turns around and my head spins before marching through my flat like he's been here a million times before and finally depositing me on my bed.

"Better?" he quips, watching me bounce with my dress up around my waist.

"I would be if you'd leave."

"Aw, you don't mean that, baby girl." He twists the top off the bottle of vodka he found in the cupboard and lifts it to his lips before swallowing down a generous gulp.

"Don't I?" I seethe before reaching for the bottle. He isn't the only one who needs something to take the edge off.

Thankfully, he hands it over, but he only allows me one mouthful before he rudely snatches it back.

"We both know your fingers wouldn't give you what you need tonight." He swallows down more as my eyes find their way to his throat, his inked skin rippling.

My mouth waters and every muscle below my waist tenses.

"My fingers, no. But I've got a pretty fantastic vibrator that does the job better than any man I've ever met."

"Any man?" he asks curiously.

"Yep," I state proudly.

"I've not got much to live up to then."

"Who says I've been with anyone aside from you?" I sass.

I hoped he might look offended, shocked even by that comment, but all he does is smile.

"Fuck you," I mutter, once again holding my hand out.

"Strip," he demands, clutching the bottle to his chest.

"I'm sorry, what?"

"I. Said. Strip."

Something explodes inside me, and I jump from the bed faster than my alcohol-fuelled brain can seemingly handle because the room spins and I sway on my feet.

"Fuck you, Dawson. You don't get to march in here like you own the place and order me around. This is my home. My life."

I'm in his grasp faster than I can compute and he stares down into my eyes.

"Don't I? I gained the right to do whatever the fuck I want the day you decided to betray me. So fuck you, Piper. You thought it was a good idea to mess with me? Let me show you just how wrong you were."

The sound of ripping fabric fills the room a second before my ruined dress flutters to the floor.

"Better, now get on the bed. Spread your legs."

I narrow my eyes at him, my need to stand my ground strong. But the second he growls at me, my inner rule follower jumps into action and I crawl back onto my bed until I'm resting back on my elbows with my feet wide, showing him everything I've got.

My heart races, my chest heaving at an alarming rate as he just stares back at me with nothing but an intense expression on his face. I have no idea if he's going to dive at me or just turn his back and walk out.

The feeling is exhilarating, although I must admit that if he decides on the latter then there's a good chance I'd chase after him and demand he finish the job he started.

The silence echoes around the room. The only thing I can hear is my own breathing as tension crackles between us.

After long, excruciating minutes, he finally moves. My heart jumps into my throat when he turns his back on me.

My lips part, ready to say anything I can to make him stay, but I relax when he pulls open my wardrobe door instead of leaving.

I breathe a sigh of relief, but it doesn't last long. Confusion swamps me as he begins rummaging through my clothes. What the hell is he looking for?

"Dawson, what are you..." I trail off when he turns toward me, and I gasp.

Unlike earlier, I can read every one of his intentions, and it makes my core tighten with desire. His eyes are dark and full of wicked thoughts as he laces one of my scarves through his fingers.

"Lie back, arms above your head," he demands. Without instruction from my brain, my body complies.

The soft pink fabric is wrapped around my wrists before being tied to the posts of my headboard.

"Better," he mutters, coming to the end of the bed, taking my ankles in his hands and tugging until my bindings are pulled tight.

"How's it feel after all these years to be totally at my mercy?" he asks, slowly walking around the bed like a lion would his prey, his eyes locked on my body.

My back arches and my thighs clench under his heated stare.

I don't respond. I can't. My brain is misfiring as I watch him stalk me.

"I should just leave you here like this. I should walk out and never come back. Do you think someone would find you?"

I shake my head. No one would even bat an eyelid until I didn't turn up to work on Monday.

"There's just one problem."

"W-what?" I whimper, sounding needy and pathetic. What is it about him that makes me lose all sense of myself and turn into a mess of need, despite the fact that I know he's only doing this to hurt me.

He lifts his arm, his hand disappearing behind his head.

"I can't." His eyes flash with something, but I can't get a read on whatever internal decision he's just made.

The next thing I know, the fabric of his shirt is lifting and my eyes get to feast on the skin he reveals.

His abs are cut to perfection, but they're nothing compared to the ink.

"Fuck," I breathe once he drops the shirt to the floor and takes a step toward me.

The lanky, virgin-skinned teenager I knew is long gone, and in his place is this incredibly toned, strong, vicious man.

My eyes fly around his broad shoulders, trying to take everything in but failing. Until he reaches into his pocket and pulls out his knife.

I visibly swallow as images of what he did with it last time we were together slam into me.

He doesn't miss my reaction, and a smile twitches at his lips as he looks between me and the deadly blade.

But instead of flicking it open and putting it to use, he places it on the bedside table, just in reach should he so wish to use it, before lowering both our phones beside it.

I watch as his fingers make quick work of his belt before he flicks open his fly and pushes his jeans down over his hips. After toeing off his boots, he kicks them to the floor, leaving him standing in just a tiny pair of black boxer briefs that leave very little to the imagination.

My mouth waters and my core floods, knowing just how good he feels inside me. He just hit something, did something, that no other man has achieved since I was forced out of his life.

"Please." I don't realise the demand has fallen from my lips until he pauses with the bottle of vodka halfway to his mouth.

"Baby girl," his words are like silk wrapping around me, and my skin prickles with goose bumps, "you are in no position to make demands."

"Oh God."

He hasn't touched me in what feels like hours, yet I still feel like I'm right on the edge of the cliff, ready to dive off, consequences be damned.

He continues with his earlier quest, and I watch as the bottle presses against his full lips, he swallows down the liquid, and his muscles ripple down his neck.

"Want some?" he asks, turning his eyes on me.

I nod, my mouth suddenly dry and desperate.

"Open," he demands, standing beside me with the bottle hovering above my face.

I do as I'm told, and in a second the cool liquid is trickling both into my mouth and down my cheek.

"Whoops," Dawson says jokingly before dropping to his knees and licking the small river of vodka from my skin.

It's the closest he's got to kissing me, and I shamelessly turn my head in the hope of catching his lips. But unsurprisingly, he's faster than me.

The bottle lands on the bedside table before the mattress dips as he kneels on it. He lowers his head, but it's not to my lips, although I can hardly complain when he sucks one of my nipples into his mouth and teases it with his tongue.

My back arches as a needy cry falls from my lips. I tug at my restraints, desperate to thread my fingers through his hair, to scratch my nails across his shoulders, to just feel the heat of his skin, anything, but they're too tight, too secure.

"Dawson," I moan when he lifts up a little, although his lips don't leave me. Instead his teeth sink into my sensitive flesh. "Ow, shit." My nipple burns for a beat before his tongue licks around it and an even stronger bolt of lust shoots straight to my pussy.

His eyes find mine and I gasp. They're so dark, full of lust, hunger and anger. I swallow, my fingers clenching and my nails digging into my palms as he switches to the other side.

When I first saw him on Monday and assumed he was there to kill me, this was not what I was expecting. I thought it would be painful, and although my nipple still throbs, this isn't how I thought he'd end me.

Our eyes hold as he descends my stomach, his beard scratching down my sensitive skin and driving me to the point of insanity.

My core throbs and my entire body tingles with my need for release.

"Please, Dawson. Please."

He pauses—not what I was hoping for—before his tongue licks along his full bottom lip.

"Please what, baby girl?" A smirk pulls at one side of his lips as he waits for my response.

"Please... break me," I taunt, narrowing my eyes at him.

"Fuck."

His large palms spread my thighs as wide as they'll go before his face lowers and he sucks my clit into his mouth.

I thrash about beneath him, but I'm hardly able to move with my hands bound and my hips pinned to the bed.

He releases me, his tongue taking over. He circles my clit before dropping lower and spearing it inside me. My muscles contract around him, desperate to pull him deeper inside.

Every single one of his movements is controlled, planned, and executed with perfection. It's like he's got a fucking road map to my body, because everything he does hits the exact spot he wants it to and drives me higher and closer to a mind-blowing release that I know is coming.

"Fuuuuck," I cry out when one of his fingertips circles my entrance.

"Greedy, baby girl. Look at you, trying to suck me inside your body. You think you deserve the release?"

"I don't care, Dawson." My voice is rough, and the words come out between heaving breaths.

It's only as he says those words that I realise he hasn't been keeping me on the edge for pleasure. He's torturing me. Hurting me. Breaking me. Just like I asked for.

"You're an arsehole, you know that?"

"Oh, baby girl. You don't know the half of it."

He sits up and wipes his mouth with the back of his hand. His eyes roam over my body, burning a trail wherever he goes.

One second I'm lying there with my chest heaving and him between my thighs, and the next he's got my hips in his hands and he's flipping me over.

"Arse up," he barks before his palm connects with my skin with a loud crack.

I groan through the pain, pushing my arse into him in the hope he finally gives me what I need.

The seconds feel like minutes without his touch. I'm about to start begging when he pushes the head of his cock through my folds, teasing my swollen clit.

My head hangs as I bite down on the inside of my cheeks.

"You won't come. Not until I say you can."

"Fuck you," I seethe, but all he does is chuckle before surging forward.

His hand grips my hip just in time to stop me flying headfirst into the headboard. The pinching pain of his fingertips digging into my skin only heightens the sensation of his length inside me.

He pulls almost all the way out before his palm lands on my arse again. It's the same place as last time and it burns even more than before as a rush of heat floods my core.

"Fuck, baby girl. You like that, huh?"

"Dawson."

His hand skims up my spine, his touch almost too gentle compared to his grip and the slap. It makes me shudder before his fingers sink into my hair and he pulls my head back.

He turns my head so I have no choice but to look over my shoulder at him, and I'm so fucking glad he does, because the sight of his inked bare chest and abs pulled tight and his groin hidden by my bare arse is something I'll never forget.

"Watch," he demands, thrusting back in with such force that white spots appear in my vision.

His grip on my hair tightens until it starts to pinch, but I barely feel it as he continues to slam inside me. My body jolts forward with every thrust of his powerful hips.

My lips part, but I can't find any words. I'm too lost to the sensations, too lost to him.

"Don't you dare come," he warns, his low, gravelly voice only pushing me closer to the release I'm not allowed.

"Fuck. You," I spit, forcing every ounce of anger I possess into my tone.

"Oh, baby girl, I am. You need it harder?"

My brows pull together as he leans over me and, in one quick move, releases my bindings. My arms ache as they move, but I soon forget about it.

"Dawson," I cry out as he pulls my body up by my hair and laces an arm around my waist. My head falls back against his shoulder and my eyes slam shut as the angle change makes everything so much more intense. His touch, the feeling of his skin against mine makes everything just so much more.

Reaching behind me, I slide my fingers into his hair.

"Did I say you could touch?" he grates out.

"You didn't say I couldn't." Twisting my head, I find the soft skin of his neck.

He tenses beneath me as my tongue laves right above his pulse point. It thunders beneath, almost as erratically as mine, before I sink my teeth in.

"Bitch," he grunts, but he does nothing to pull away, and I'm sure his cock only gets harder inside me as the sting of pain hits him.

His hand skims down my stomach, stopping when his fingers connect with my clit.

"Oh fuck," I shriek.

There's nothing soft or gentle about his touch. In fact, it's utterly brutal as he rubs at me, sending my world spinning out of control. The second he pinches my clit, I lose any control I had over doing what I was told and I fall headfirst into the most mind-blowing release.

Not even a second later, Dawson's cock jerks inside me, filling me with hot jets of his cum and ensuring my release goes on for excruciatingly blissful long minutes.

"Never could do as you were told, huh, baby girl?" He pulls out of me and I'm pushed down to the bed.

I flip over, just in time for him to cage me in, his hands on either side of my head. My legs wrap around his waist, ensuring his semi teases me.

"You know I have a thing for rebels."

His eyes search mine as if he's finally trying to discover the truth about what happened before they drop down to my lips.

"Go on," I taunt. "Kiss me."

His dark, intense stare comes back to mine.

"Why? Because you want me to?"

"No, because *you* want to. You can't lie to me, Dawson, I can see it. You still want me, no matter how much you might hate me." Honestly, I have no idea if those words are true. The boy whose thoughts I used to be able to read as if they were my own is now so closed off with walls built so high I fear that I have no chance of being allowed back inside again.

"You got one part of that statement right." With one more quick glance at my lips, he pushes off me and stalks across my room to the bathroom door.

I want to snap at him, but I damn near forget words exist as I watch his arse tense and flex as he moves.

It's the first time I've seen him naked in years, and damn, it's one fine sight. Those years sure have been good to him.

The second he disappears into my small bathroom, I glance down at myself. I try to keep myself in some kind of shape, but honestly, I prefer lifting a glass of wine than I do weights. Dawson, on the other hand, looks like a real gym bunny.

The sound of my shower starting forces me to swing my legs off the edge of the bed and pad over. The evidence of what happened in here only moments ago slips down my thighs.

I never allow guys inside me unwrapped. Ever. Yet he crashes back into my life and every rule I live by seems to fly straight out the window.

I know I shouldn't, but I trust him. Actually, I trust him with my life, which in itself is ironic because he could very well be the one to end it when he gets fed up with this little... whatever this is.

I come to a grinding halt when I get to the doorway, because the sight of Dawson standing behind my glass shower screen with bubbles running all over him renders me speechless.

"Make yourself at home, why don't you?" I sass, resting my hip against the frame to shamelessly continue watching him. I have no idea how long he's going to allow this to continue, so I need to get my fill while I can. He could turn me over to his father at any moment, and any pleasure he's given me will be long forgotten.

"I couldn't walk out of here smelling like you." His words cut. I wasn't really expecting him to pull me into his arms and drift off to sleep together, but hearing that he's already regretting it makes my chest ache.

I'm treading on thin ice here. But as much as I can tell myself that I shouldn't have allowed him back into my life and that I'm going to be the one broken and bleeding out when it's all over, I can't stop. Not that he's really given me a chance to say no. He's barrelled his way in and planted himself firmly in the middle of my life, whether I want it or not. It's why it's going to hurt that much more when it's over.

"Silly me," I mutter, ripping my stupid tear-filled eyes from his delicious body and walking to the toilet before dropping down.

I'm not really a fan of peeing in front of the guy I'm seeing, but right now, I don't have a lot of fucks to give about the situation. I have a feeling that Dawson is going to see me in a worse position than sitting on a damn toilet in the near future.

"Love Hearts. Really, Piper?" he asks, dragging my eyes up from the tiled floor, to where he's holding my bottle of shower gel with a raised brow. "Feeling nostalgic?"

"Don't flatter yourself. It was on offer."

"Sure it was." He squeezes another generous amount

on to the pink puff in his hand and begins rubbing it over himself once more.

"You really want me off you, huh?" I comment bitterly.

"You have no idea."

"So that's it, is it? You fuck me into oblivion, wash me off and what, walk out of here like it never happened?"

"Yep, that's pretty much the long and short of it. Why? Did you want to cuddle?"

"You know, you've turned into a right arsehole, Dawson."

Standing, I press the flush with more effort than is necessary. I'm back in the bedroom and pulling my robe on when he calls out.

"Fucking bitch."

A wicked smile pulls at my lips. I know all too well how hot that shower runs when the cold is pulled away from it.

"You're welcome, arsehole," I shoot over my shoulder, heading for the kitchen for a drink.

I want alcohol, but I've already had enough of that, and look where it led me.

That had nothing to do with the drink.

I shake the thought from my head and grab a mug from the cupboard.

My coffee is almost done when he joins me in the room.

Sucking in a steeling breath, I turn around.

As expected, I find him fully dressed and ready to leave.

"Well, thanks. I guess."

"Don't think that me walking out right now means we're done."

"Wouldn't dream of it. I want to say it was fun but..."

He chuckles, and the sound washes over me like melted chocolate.

Our eyes hold and something crackles between us. The tether that was always pulling us together is back with a vengeance, making me desperate to step up to him.

My eyes drop to his lips and my tongue sneaks out to wet my bottom one. I want him to kiss me so fucking bad.

With a simple nod of his head, he spins away from me and walks out.

The second he's gone, a violent shiver rushes through me, and I can't help but wonder if I imagined the whole thing.

I spin to collect my mug, and my muscles pull, evidence that it was all very real.

He worked me over in a way that was so needed, but now I've had it, I know I'm only going to crave more.

He gave me everything I needed and more. I blow out a breath, suddenly feeling exhausted. I dump the mug in the sink and go back to my bedroom.

His scent hits me almost immediately, and the loneliness I've become all too used to over the years slams back into me, making tears burn my eyes.

Just for those few stolen minutes, I felt like I belonged once again.

11

DAWSON

The second the main door to the building closes behind me, I fall back against the wall and pull my phone from my pocket.

I've got a stream of messages from the guys talking about their night out and inviting me to join them if I'm not otherwise engaged—or, in Titch's words, balls deep in pussy. The temptation to agree, call an Uber and join them is strong. Although not as strong as my desire to head back upstairs and take Piper again.

"Fuck," I growl, the image of her spreadeagled on her bed not so long ago burned into my brain. There were only one or two things that were missing from that scene. Things I plan to do to her at my first possible opportunity.

My fingers twitch to get her in my chair in the studio and set to work on her.

She's a virgin, a blank canvas. My fucking kryptonite. Especially when she needs a permanent reminder of who she belongs to. Seems like the perfect way to ensure she remembers.

Closing down their messages, I pull up the Uber app and call a car to take me home instead.

It would be so easy to spend my Friday night out getting drunk and pulling an easy woman or two like I used to, but my life is different now.

I've heard nothing from Emmie, so I can only assume that's because she's fine at home. She hasn't really gone out much since she moved in with me. I was worried about her leaving friends behind and completely starting over. I was expecting her to want them to come around, to be forced to endure nights of girls sleepovers. But as of yet, I haven't even learned any of their names, let alone met them.

It makes me wonder what her life really was like with her mother.

She always puts on a brave face whenever we've spent time together, which admittedly, isn't as much as we should have thanks to her vindictive mother. I gave up everything to be the father Emmie deserved, but even then she threw it in my face. It's why I couldn't really argue when Emmie decided to call it quits on her mother and move in. I just still can't believe she allowed it.

My eyes are heavy by the time the car pulls up in front of my place. The lights in the living room are still on, and when I walk inside, I find Emmie exactly where I left her: under a blanket, surrounded by snacks, and watching something on the TV.

"Hey, good night?" she asks without taking her eyes from the screen.

Something twists in my chest at her question.

"Uh, yeah, it was okay," I lie. In truth, it was fucking incredible, and I wish it was still continuing.

The way Piper's eyes burned into me while I was in

her shower, I knew all I had to do was call her over and she'd have joined me in a heartbeat. I could have had her against the wall and been inside her again in seconds.

But I couldn't.

I've been with her twice in a week, and already I crave her more than any other woman I've spent time with in the past seventeen years.

I didn't understand the connection we had when we were kids, and I sure as fuck don't understand it now.

I put it down to us being young and in lust back then. I was a horny teenage boy who finally had a girl all to himself. I was in my element, because she was as insatiable as I was.

It seems that may have been one thing that's not changed.

I slam down thoughts of what she's been doing for the past few years. I don't need images of her with other guys in my head or I'll likely end up locking her up in my bedroom to stop it ever happening again.

It's bad enough that she's out there where my father, Cruz, or any other guys could recognise her. I don't need to be worrying about other men too.

I think back to the posh guy she was dancing with earlier. The two of us are like night and day. He looked like a snooty private school toff, and I'm... well, me.

"You good? I'm gonna head up."

"Yeah, yeah," she waves me off.

"You know this has to change come Sunday night, right? I'm not having you staying up late and turning up to school exhausted."

"Sure thing," she agrees, but I don't think for a second that she heard a single word that just came out of my mouth.

We've lived together pretty seamlessly over the past few weeks, but I fear that could all be about to change when I start expecting her to actually do something and be responsible.

I scrub my hand across my face as I walk from the room and climb the stairs. Piper's lingering scent along with the fucking Love Hearts fill my nose and sends me back a few years.

"Love Hearts, really?" I ask as she snatches them from the shelf.

"Yeah, I love them."

"But we're at the cinema. You have popcorn."

"You might. I have Love Hearts."

"You're weird," I say lightly, wrapping my arm around her waist and pulling her into my body.

"You're weirder," she whispers, staring up at me, her violet eyes sparkling with lust and excitement.

We don't get to spend much time together out in public for fear of being spotted. We should be mortal enemies due to our surnames, not devouring each other at any chance we get. But I wanted to treat her right, like any girl deserves. So we'd both made up some bullshit story to our parents about spending the weekend with friends, hopped on my bike, and got the hell out of the city.

Thankfully, Justin, my best friend's parents are never home, so hopefully there will be no reason for my parents to suspect anything or for anyone to tell them differently.

I couldn't even remember the name of the place I'd booked, but I didn't care. I was too excited to spend the entire weekend with my girl without constantly looking over our shoulders. We both knew what the consequence would be if we were caught; it was a constant weight pressing down on our shoulders. But being away together without that pressure? It was everything.

Together we'd handed our ticket over to the guy at the stand, her clutching her Love Hearts and me, my giant tub of popcorn, and we found ourselves seats at the very back of the movie theatre in the shadows and got comfortable.

Sadly, it was a little too full to do any of the wicked things I wanted to do to her in my head, so I was forced to be satisfied with resting my hand on her upper thigh and watching the film she'd chosen.

It was okay, I guess. But nowhere near as fun as getting between her legs while she tried to keep quiet like I was desperate to do.

"Here," she says without looking over at me.

Glancing down to her hand, I find a Love Heart sitting in her palm. Reaching out, I lift her hand closer to my face so I can see what it says.

Be mine?

Glancing over at her, I find a sly smile playing on her lips. We hadn't talked about us being anything serious since it started. We both knew we were playing with fire, but in that moment, I knew that I'd deal with anything either of our fathers could throw at us if it meant we could be together.

"Always," I whisper before lowering my lips to her palm, flicking the sweet into my mouth with my tongue and licking across her skin before placing a kiss to the centre.

She looks over at me, and the smile that lights up her face damn near knocks the wind out of me. We've only been messing about for a few months, but already I'm fighting to keep those three little words inside me. I have no idea when I fell, but I did. And hard. And despite the fact that I already know we have no future, I also know that I'll never regret this. I will always look back on our time together fondly because of all the things she gave me.

I was so fucking naïve back then, I think, dragging myself from the memory of that weekend. It was by far the best few days of my life. It was a hell of a lot better than what was going to happen in the coming weeks when I was to learn that every second we'd spent together had been fake and based on a lie.

Stripping out of my clothes, I throw them at my laundry basket and walk into my en suite. The shower calls to me despite the fact that my hair is barely dry from the last one, but the need to rid myself of that scent is almost too much. It makes me want things I know I can't have. Things I shouldn't crave after everything that happened.

I fall into my cold bed, wishing that I was in another, and stare up at the ceiling, desperate for a distraction from the memories running around my head at the speed of light. Images from when we were kids start merging with the two from this week and mess my head up more than it already is.

At some point, they must send me to sleep, because darkness fades in.

Although at no point do I stop thinking about her.

In my slumber, I never left her flat. Instead, I caved to my need to kiss her before I left and ended up spending the night devouring her, which is exactly my fear.

I cannot become more attached, more infatuated than I already am.

She's part of a game to secure my daughter's future. I need to keep that front and centre of my mind, and once that's done, then I need to do what I should have done the second I saw her.

Tell my father.

A pain lances through my chest at the thought of doing so. I know it's what has to happen. She betrayed him. She betrayed *me*. It's the way it has to be, despite what my heart is trying to tell me.

I'm already tempting fate by keeping her a secret. It won't just be *her* head on the chopping block when I hand her over if he discovers that I've known for a long time.

He won't understand that I needed to make use of her first.

When I wake, it's with my cock tenting the sheets and the image of having her body pressed up against mine in my head.

I groan when I see the sun is already streaming through the cracks in my curtains. I throw the covers back ready to start the day, but my phone on the bedside table stops me in my tracks.

Sitting on the edge, I swipe it up and find the new app I downloaded.

It takes about a minute to load, but when it does, I find exactly what I need.

I shower and dress in record time, not wanting to miss my opportunity.

Emmie is still sleeping when I poke my head into her room, so I leave her a note for when she eventually emerges and head toward the address on my phone.

A smile twitches at my lips as I climb on my bike and start the engine.

She has no idea what's in store for her. The thought causes more excitement to explode in my belly than it should.

12

PIPER

It takes me longer than usual to drag myself from the sleep fog that surrounds me to figure out what the noise is.

I crack my eyes open to find the morning sun illuminating the room, along with the insistent buzzing that woke me.

Pushing myself up on my elbow, I look at my bedside table.

My phone?

My brows pull together. I don't remember seeing it there last night. But then I guess I wasn't exactly with it after Dawson turned me into a sex-crazed mess.

My cheeks heat as I think about what went down between us. I squirm, my thighs clench, and my temperature spikes.

Damn him. He shouldn't still have this power over me.

My phone stops ringing, reminding me that I should be doing something other than reliving last night, and I reach over for it.

Seeing as it was Lisa, I call her back.

"Have a good night?" Curiosity drips from every one of her words.

"Err..."

"Breakfast. Right. Now," she demands, making my eyes roll.

"Lis, I've just woken up," I whine.

"Don't care. Meet me at our usual post in forty-five minutes and not one more. I will come and find your arse."

"Ugh, fine. See you there."

I hang up before she has a chance to say any more.

Throwing the covers back, I strip out of my pyjamas on the way to the bathroom and turn the shower on to warm up the second I walk in. My body aches with every movement and step.

I lock down my thoughts, not needing to remember how he looked standing on the other side of that glass barely a few hours ago.

I pee and brush my teeth, and I'm about to turn to the shower when my reflection in the floor-to-ceiling mirror on the door catches my eyes.

"Holy fuck," I gasp, inching closing to get a better look.

My neck, chest and boobs are covered in red hickeys and bite marks, but even more shocking are the almost purple fingerprints on my hips.

"Motherfucker." I twist this way and that, finding that the bruises cover my arse as well as my inner thighs.

Well, I guess there will be no forgetting about him for a good few days. If he was trying to ensure I wouldn't sleep with anyone else, then I think he's probably achieved that.

Ripping my eyes away from the evidence of our time together, I walk straight into the shower and allow the heat of the water to wash away the tension in my muscles.

"It took you forty-seven minutes," Lisa mutters when I fall down in the chair beside hers at the back of our usual cafe.

"You were timing me?" I ask, although I don't know why I'm surprised.

"You have juicy gossip and I need it, seeing as I went home alone last night and had to make do with my friend in my top drawer."

"Shush, there are kids over there."

"They don't know what I'm talking about," she says, rolling her eyes and waving me off. "Anyway. Spill, girl."

"I need coffee," I mutter, pushing to stand while she whines behind me. "The usual?"

"Please."

Lisa sits with a scowl on her face and her arms crossed while I queue up to place our order.

"So, I know he was there because I saw him, talked to him," she starts the second I'm in hearing distance once again.

"You spoke to him?"

"Spoke to... chatted up... same thing."

"Jesus, Lisa," I mutter, hoping like hell it covers up the wave of jealousy that washes through me.

"What? He is smoking hot, and you seem to think you're not interested."

"I'm not."

"Which leads me to my next point... where the hell did he take you, and what happened next?" Her eyebrows wiggle in delight. "And don't lie to me, I saw you dancing. I could feel the chemistry between you two from the other side of the club."

"You were wasted, Lis. I doubt that."

"Drink makes my chemistry-o-meter better, thank you very much. Thank you," she says, looking up at the server when she lowers our plates with breakfasts wraps onto our table.

"Fine, we danced. Then he took me down to the basement for some more dancing."

"Wanted you all to himself, huh?"

"I don't know what he's playing at," I admit around a mouthful of my wrap.

"You took him home though, right?"

"Um..." I decide to go with honesty. Well, as much as I can, at least. "He didn't give me much choice."

"Oh my God," she squeals in delight. "I just knew he'd be the ultimate alpha in the bedroom. It's in his eyes. You see it, right? So what happened next, did he bang you all night long until you could barely stand?"

"Yeah, did he do that?" a deep, very familiar voice asks as the spare chair beside me is pulled out and spun around.

Oh my fucking God.

Lifting my eyes, I watch as he throws his leg over the chair and sits on it with his arms on the backrest in front of him.

"What the hell are you doing?" I snap, narrowing my eyes at him when a smug smile pulls at his lips.

"Joining your stimulating conversation. Please don't let me stop you. I want to hear just how good it was." He winks, and my face burns with mortification. "Something tells me it was wild."

Lisa smothers a howl of laughter while I pray for the ground to swallow me up.

"What do you want, Dawson?"

"Thought I'd come for breakfast." Without asking, he reaches out and snatches up what's left of my wrap and stuffs it in his mouth.

"You did not... oh my God. You need to leave."

"But things were just about to get interesting. Did you tell your friend here yet how you ended up tied to the bed?"

I don't need to look at Lisa to know she's got a shit-eating grin on her face.

"No? What about how I ate you out until you shattered, crying my name like I was God?"

"Okay, enough. You need to leave," I snap, standing with such speed I send my chair crashing to the floor behind me. All eyes in the café turn to me, and my face burns bright red at the attention.

Totally ignoring my words, the cheeky fuck reaches out for my coffee and takes a sip. His lip curls in disgust. "Caramel? And here I thought you were already pretty sweet."

If it were possible, I swear steam would be billowing out of my ears as I grit my teeth and stare daggers at him.

"You need to leave," I repeat, despite the fact that he makes no move to do so.

"Sure, it looks like you're finished here, anyway." He stands, and I breathe a sigh of relief... until he wraps his hand around mine and pulls me into his body. "Missed you, baby girl," he whispers, although he makes sure it's loud enough that Lisa hears. My eyes find hers as she practically melts into a puddle on her chair.

"Go with him right now, but I will be calling you later."

"She might be otherwise engaged."

Lisa smiles at me, totally ignoring my pleading look as Dawson drags me from the café and out onto the street, where I now see his bike is parked.

"What the fuck was that? And how did you know I'd be here?"

"Lucky break?" It comes out a question, so his innocent face and the shrug of his shoulder do nothing to convince me.

"You're becoming a real pain in my arse, you know that, right?"

"No, but I'm sure it could be arranged." Before I can step away, his arm snakes around my waist, effectively pulling me into his body as his hands squeeze my arse. "I'm more than willing to claim all of you, if you are?"

"Oh, so you *can* ask for permission?" I sass.

"You're cute. Get on."

"No." I place my hands on my hips and stare at him.

"No?"

"Exactly. No." Taking a step back, I prepare to walk away from him. "This was fun and all, but I've got shit to be doing."

I make it two steps before I'm hauled back against his hard body.

"Whatever shit you've got to do can't be as fun as the shit I've got to do, so you really should just come with," he growls in my ear. Goose bumps race across my skin as my fight begins to leave me.

I want to stand my ground and walk away. He did just ruin my morning and eat my breakfast after all, but a part of me wants to know what his plan is.

"Are you going to kill me?"

He laughs, and I can't help but wish I was facing him so I could see him smile.

"No, baby girl. Not today."

A shiver runs down my spine at the silent warning in his words.

"I had something very different in mind."

"Okay." The word falls from my lips before my brain has even registered the thought.

He stills for a beat, I assume shocked at how easily I agreed, but I'm too curious to walk away now.

He hesitantly releases me before opening his top box and retrieving a helmet for me.

"How convenient," I mutter, pulling it on my head while he does the same thing.

Sensing someone watching me, I look over my shoulder to find that Lisa has moved to the table in front of the window and practically has her nose pressed up against the glass.

"Your friend is..."

"Crazy?" I finish for him.

"Yeah, something like that."

I stand on the pavement as he throws his leg over his bike, then waits for me to join him.

He stills the second I climb on, but unlike the first time I sat behind him earlier in the week, I can't restrain myself and wrap my arms around his waist, resting my palms against his abs. With him refusing to allow me to touch him when we've been together, I figure I might as well take what I can get.

"I haven't been on the back of a bike since you." My lips slam shut the second I realise I said it out loud. His body tenses under my hold, so I know he heard me, but he doesn't respond. Instead, he starts the engine and kicks the stand. In a heartbeat, we're flying through the city. I hold tighter and let the vibrations rumble through me as I think back to us doing the very same thing all those years ago.

I have no idea where we're going, and every time he slows, I look around, thinking that this might be the place he thought he wants to take me.

When he finally brings the bike to a stop in a car park, I look around with frown lines marring my brow. At least it's not an empty warehouse—or worse, the Royal Reapers clubhouse.

"The cinema?" I ask once we've both pulled our helmets off.

"Yeah. Problem?"

"No, it just wasn't what I was expecting."

"What were you expecting?"

My thoughts dive straight into the gutter, and from the smirk that appears on his face, I assume he can read them.

"Not today, baby girl. Something tells me that you're still sporting the evidence from last night."

My cheeks flame.

Reaching up, I open the top two buttons of my blouse and pull the fabric aside.

His eyes immediately darken as they lock on the swell of my breast.

"Keep showing those off in public and I'll have to kill any motherfucker who looks this way."

"I'm not flashing anyone. Jesus, caveman," I mutter, buttoning back up and righting my clothes.

"Good." After locking up his bike, he takes my hand and leads me toward the cinema.

"What are we watching?" He shrugs, looking at what's on offer. "I don't mind."

"I thought you wanted to come."

"Not really. It's more of a spur of the moment kind of thing."

"Riiight."

"So shoot 'em up or chick flick?"

"Your choice, but choose wisely," I warn.

"Why? Will the wrong choice result in me not getting inside you again?"

I want to say yes, but I think we both know that I'm unable to do so around him.

"I'm sure we could negotiate."

"You mean like I say what I want and you say yes."

Something like that, I think to myself as I follow him over to the machine to get tickets.

He stands in front of the screen so I still have no idea what we're watching as he leads me over to the snacks.

"Popcorn?" The moment that one word falls from his lips, I'm hit with a wave of nostalgia so strong that it threatens to buckle my knees.

"N-no." I glance around at what's on offer before my eyes land on something I haven't eaten for years, despite my shower gel choice.

"Love Hearts?" he asks, reaching out and picking up two packets from the shelf.

"Two?"

"You might need the extra sugar for later." His eyes trail down my body. I might be fully dressed, giving nothing away in my attempt to hide all the love bites this morning, but still, I may as well be naked from the heated look in his eyes.

A desire-filled shudder rips through me before he grabs my hand, places my sweets down on the counter to pay, and orders the biggest tub of popcorn they offer.

He passes the tickets to the young guy who directs us down to screen four.

The name of the film he chose shines brightly on the screen above the door and I smile.

As we walk up the stairs toward the back of the theatre, we only pass one other couple who are sitting silently, stuffing their faces.

"Here's fine," I say, tugging on his arms as we get to a row of seats, a few from the dark ones in the back.

He chuckles but pulls harder, ensuring I follow him all the way to the top.

I feel like a naughty teenager when he encourages me to walk down to the darkest part. We all know the kinds of things that happen back here, and my blood turns to lava at the thought of him touching me again.

He falls down into the seat beside me, stretching out his legs and widening them enough that one of his thighs brushes mine.

"So... you thought against a chick flick, then?" I ask, not really knowing how to break the weird tension that has fallen over us.

He stills with a handful of popcorn to his mouth before lowering it back down and leaning over to me. His lips brush my ear, the caress of his warm breath down my neck making my skin prickle with awareness.

"You grew up in an MC, baby girl. I know a chick flick wouldn't get your engines revving." I gasp as his giant hand lands on my thigh and skims up until his little finger is teasing the seam directly in front of my clit.

"Dawson," I warn, but all it makes him do is chuckle.

"Don't try to pretend like I don't know you. This isn't actually our first date, remember."

A weird cough rumbles up my throat. "T-this is a date?" I ask, my eyes wide as they turn to take him in.

He shrugs nonchalantly. "Two people in the back of a cinema not having a fucking clue what they're watching because all they can think about is when it's over so they can go home and fuck? Yeah, sounds like a date to me, baby girl."

"You want... you think..." I stutter, his finger never once pausing at my core.

"I don't think, Piper. I know," he breathes.

My head falls back against the chair and my eyes close as he presses harder.

"But not yet," he announces, ripping his hand away and leaving me feeling cold.

"Arsehole," I mutter, much to his amusement as he resumes eating. The prick doesn't so much as look over at me as I silently fume, waiting for the film to start.

I've seen adverts on the TV for it, and it's pretty good. He was right in what he said; I'll always choose action over anything that might have a sappy happily ever after.

We're getting toward the end of the movie when I pull the last Love Heart from my packet and turn it over.

Kiss me.

Glancing over at Dawson, I find him lost in the movie. The action is ramping up, ready for the final fight before we race toward the end, and while I might want to know what happens, I've got other things on my mind right now. Like the slow thrum of desire that's been coursing through me since he last touched me.

I elbow his arm to get his attention before handing the Love Heart over. He takes it curiously, ripping his eyes away from the screen to look down at it.

His entire body tenses as he reads those two words. He

doesn't move for a solid two seconds before he turns to me.

"Not gonna happen, baby girl."

"Why?" I ask, hating the vulnerability that creeps into my tone.

"I have my reasons," he growls out. I expect him to pass it back and really stomp on my heart, but at the last minute, his lips part and he throws it into his mouth. I watch his lips as he chews, then his tongue sneaks out to lick up the sweetness, and I damn near melt into a puddle.

"Problem?" he asks, looking back at me.

"N-no." I hate that he knows I'm lying. I hate that he has this power over me.

I slump down in my chair and focus back on the film, although I don't see any of it. I'm too busy sulking.

"Stop pouting, baby girl," he whispers in my ear, making me jump out of my skin. I was so lost in my own head that I didn't even feel him move closer. It's not even been a week and he's already screwing with me. "It doesn't suit you."

I would say I should have walked away, but seeing as I didn't plan any of this today, I don't think it's very realistic. It's clear that he's got a game plan here. The question is if I actually want to be a willing player. The fact that I'm probably going to end up just as broken, if not more so, than the last time should make me run, but I can't help myself. I know the flame is going to burn me, yet I can't stop myself from getting closer.

His lips press to the side of my neck.

"This what you wanted?" he murmurs, brushing them against my sensitive skin.

"Not exactly, but I'm assuming it's all you're going to give me."

He chuckles before his tongue sneaks out and licks up the column of my neck.

"Are you wet for me?"

"Screw you. You won't give me what I want, so why should I do anything you want?"

"Because you don't have a choice."

"And you do?" I snap, turning my head toward him. Our lips are so close I can feel the heat of his burning mine, yet he still doesn't move.

I edge forward, but he clocks the move and retreats a little.

"Why?" I ask, my brows pulling together.

"I can't, baby girl."

My eyes search his, desperate to find the answer to my question. He'll do all the things he's done to me willingly, yet he won't kiss me. It makes no sense.

"Stop overthinking. Just..." he reaches out, tucks his fingers under the fabric of my blouse, and finds the button on my jeans.

"Dawson, you can't distract me with..." My words trail off as his fingers push inside the fabric.

I fall back into my seat, stretching out a little to give him more room.

"For someone who wants to fight, you're sure being compliant," he mutters, amusement filling his voice.

"You owe me." My eyes lock on his.

"Is that right?"

I gasp when his rough fingers find my clit.

"Baby girl, you're going to need to be quiet."

I nod eagerly, not willing to let him stop now that he's started.

He circles my clit a couple of times before pushing lower. A low growl rumbles up his throat.

"Fuck, you're soaked."

"It's all the action," I mutter, nodding toward the screen. "Gets my engine revving."

He shakes his head at my joke. His lips part as if he wants to say something, but no words pass his lips.

"Go on," I encourage as his finger dips inside me, making my head spin, but I focus on his dark eyes, desperate for him to open up to me, even just a little bit.

"I... fuck," he snaps, looking away from me.

"No, don't hide." I reach out and take his cheek in my hand, pulling his head back to me. "Tell me."

"I missed you, okay? I fucking missed you. All right?"

His jaw clenches the moment the words have passed his lips, and his shoulders pull tight.

A second passes between us, and it's not until he moves his finger once again that I realise he's stopped and what position we're in.

"I missed you too, Dawson."

His breath catches at my words, his eyes darkening. But he soon covers it, bringing his sky-high walls back up and focusing on the job he started.

With one hand cupped over my mouth, my other claws at his forearm as he works me. I come just at the same time a car explodes on the screen, so when I do cry out into my hand, it's lost.

My chest heaves, my skin covered in a sheen of sweat as I continue to lay there limp as my body tries to recover.

"You're welcome," comes from beside me as he tugs his hand from my clothing.

"Am I? You should know that I'm not returning the favour."

"Did I ask you to?"

Lifting his fingers, he pushes two past his lips and sucks. His eyes roll a little as he tastes me.

"Better than the popcorn?" I ask as I sit up and put myself back together.

"You've no idea, baby girl."

13

DAWSON

By the time the film is over, not only am I hard as fuck for the woman whose sweet scent filled my nose through the entire thing, but I know I've only got an hour to get to work and I'm not going to be able to have time to rectify the situation.

"What now?" she asks as we emerge from the dark theatre.

"I need to take you home."

"Oh." The disappointment in her tone makes me smile. For some insane reason, and despite her argument earlier, she actually wants to spend time with me.

It's perfect. It's exactly what I hoped for, although totally not what I expected.

"I've got to go to work."

"Okay."

I pass her my spare helmet as we get to my bike and she quickly pulls it over her head. I'm surprised—I was expecting one hundred and one questions about what I do, amongst other things. But instead, she just waits for me to throw my leg over my bike and climbs on silently behind me.

Her arms once again come around my waist, and I have to fight the wave of desire her touch causes.

The drive back to her building is tense. We might not be looking at each other or even able to speak, but that doesn't mean I can't feel her pulling away.

"Well, thanks, I guess," she says, pulling the helmet off and passing it over once I've killed the engine and climbed off.

"You make out like you didn't enjoy yourself." Her cheeks heat as the memory of what happened in the cinema hits her.

Reaching down, I rearrange myself in my jeans, a move she doesn't miss. Not that I expected her to.

She quirks an eyebrow.

"If you think I'm going to—"

"I don't think anything, baby girl," I say, stepping up to her and pushing her back until she hits the wall beside her main door.

I don't stop until my hips are pinning her in place and her breath catches from our closeness.

"Dawson, please, don't."

She turns her head away from me, refusing to allow me to look into her eyes.

"What are you afraid of, baby girl?"

Reaching out, I press my knuckle to her jaw and twist her head back.

"You," she breathes. "I'm afraid of you."

"You think I'm going to hurt you?"

"Well... aren't you? You want revenge. I get it. This thing between us, it's not real, and I'd be stupid to think it was."

Clever girl. Pride for my girl swells inside me, but I can't let her read it. She might be suspicious, and she might just have every reason to be, but I need to squash it.

She's right, I do need my revenge. I need that and something else alongside it. And am I going to hurt her? I sure fucking hope so, because she shattered me all those years ago and she needs a taste of her own medicine.

"It's real, baby girl."

"But," she starts, tears pooling in her eyes, "you... you won't even k-kiss me."

"Trust me, it's not because I don't want to."

"So why, Dawson? Talk to me."

I can't tell her the truth, that if I allow myself to kiss her then I fear all of this, my resolve, my need for revenge, will come crashing around my feet.

"I-I want it to be special."

She swoons at my words, her eyes softening.

"Things between us have been..."

"Intense?" she adds.

"Yeah. Seeing you at Knight's Ridge, it was a shock. I was angry. I thought you were dead, Piper. Then there you were, standing in front of me. It fucked with my head, baby."

"I'm... sorry."

"Fresh start?" I ask, watching her eyes sparkle.

"For real?"

"Yeah, baby. For real. However," I add, needing her to know the reality. She must sense what I'm about to say because she tenses beneath me. "We can't just forget about the past." Fear rushes back through her eyes. "You will tell me the truth about what happened."

"O-okay." She swallows nervously.

"I know you're worried that I'm going to hurt you or

tell my father, but equally, right now, I have no idea what you're planning. If this is going to work, we both need to lay all our cards on the table."

"I'm not planning anything. I didn't think I'd ever see you—"

I press my fingers to her lips, cutting her off.

"Not now. Soon. I'll be in touch." Tilting my head up, I press my lips to her brow, lingering for just a second before spinning away from her and marching back to my bike.

I don't look back. I can't. I've lost myself enough in her in the past week. I need to turn things around, put my plan into action and my need for revenge on the backburner, because that time will come.

I head to the studio via home so I can check in on Emmie. She's awake and back under a blanket, curled up on the sofa again.

"Your arse is going to fuse to that thing if you don't do something else, you know?"

"Ha, funny," she mutters without taking her eyes from the screen. "I'm just enjoying my freedom while I have it."

"Good, make the most of it. Tomorrow is a school night."

"Yeah, yeah."

"I'm serious. I'm off tomorrow, and we're going to make sure you're all set. I won't have you behind before your first day." I'm not doing all of this to pay her tuition for her to just fuck it up before she's even donned the uniform.

"I can't wait." She rolls her eyes.

"Great. I knew you'd be excited."

"Oh yeah. I can hardly sleep."

"I'm trusting you, Emmie."

"I know, Dad. I'm not going to screw this up, I promise."

I roll my eyes at her. I know she's not thrilled about the idea of attending Knight's Ridge, but I also know she understands what I'm trying to give her. I'm pretty sure she even appreciates it, in her own unique way.

"Okay. I'm going to be at the studio all afternoon and evening. If you need me, call me, yeah?"

"Will do."

"The fridge is stocked, or you can order dinner. Whatever."

"I know, Dad. I've got this. It's not the first time you've gone to work since I've been here."

"Okay, well... be good."

"When aren't I good?" she calls as I head back to the front door. Shaking my head, I make my way to work, ideas flitting around in my head for what I'm going to do to start over with Piper.

I want her to believe that I'm serious, so I want it to be something a little more creative than taking her to a fancy restaurant and trying to impress her with my choice. She knows me well enough to know that I'm not an expensive meal kind of man.

With a sigh, I pull the bike up outside the studio and make my way inside.

The guys are nowhere to be seen, but Biff and Kas are sitting on the sofas, drinking coffee as if they're in a café.

"Afternoon," Biff says, nodding her head at me.

"Hey, how's it going?" I drop down onto the sofa opposite them. I could use their advice right now.

"Same old, same old."

"Spike's got a client who's having a... personal tat." Kas

winks. "Pussy didn't want me watching." She rolls her eyes, and I can't help but laugh.

"Gotta love those. Listen, I need some advice."

They both lean forward a little. I understand why they're intrigued; I've never asked either of them for anything before, despite their offers to help with Emmie should I need a woman's touch.

"I need to plan a date."

Biff's chin drops. She's known me for long enough now to know that I don't date. "Go on..."

"I need something thoughtful, something... memorable."

They both think for a few seconds. "I'm assuming a restaurant is out?"

"Yup."

"Okay. What's she like?"

"Um... she's... just normal, I guess. Not flashy, not impressed by money, if that's what you mean. She's... kinda like you. Down to earth."

"I think there's a compliment in there somewhere," she whispers to Kas. "Okay, leave it with me."

"Thank you."

"You want a coffee?"

"That would be awesome." I disappear down to my room to set up for my first client of the day, hoping it's something big enough that I can lose myself in it.

By the time I'm done for the night, my desire to go back to Piper's building and take what I need is almost all-consuming. But I know I can't. I told her we were starting over, and that needs to include everything. I want her to believe I'm being sincere, so I need to treat her right. Show her that we could be real.

In the end, I opt for shooting her a message before I leave the studio. Something that I hope will remind her of what's happened between us this past week and ensure she falls asleep thinking of me.

Dawson: Your scent is still on my fingers.

I smile to myself as I picture her eyes widening as she reads it.

Her response comes faster than I was expecting. I don't even get out of my room.

Piper: You really should wash your hands a little more often.

I'm still smiling when I walk out to reception.

Biff is sitting behind the desk, tapping away at the computer. Zach might be training her up as an artist, but he still has her doing all his dirty work.

"D," she says, ripping her eyes away from the screen, "I've got a few options for you."

"Awesome."

"You got time now?"

"Yep, hit me with them."

"Okay, so... get her out of the city; take her to the beach; moonlight walk on the sand? A picnic somewhere with a view. Hiking." She rattles off at least ten ideas, one of which I know she'll love but would require waiting until next weekend to plan it. I need more if I want Piper to believe that I can't stop thinking about her.

"So, who is she?" Biff asks, leaning forward on her elbows and looking up at me excitedly.

"No one."

"Bullshit, D. You haven't dated anyone in the entire time I've been here. She clearly means something if you're going to this much effort."

"She's just..." I swallow down a few of the words I could use to describe Piper. Most of them I don't want to accept, let alone say out loud. "Someone from my past."

"Oh, ex-girlfriend?"

"Something like that," I mutter. "Thanks for the ideas, I really appreciate it."

"Oh, uh, yeah. Any time. You know where I am."

I nod at her before dumping my mug in the kitchen and heading out.

My head is spinning with ideas as I make the short journey home.

Nerves flutter in my belly as I think about what I'm trying to achieve. On paper, it seems like a really good idea. Use her, get what my daughter needs, and then drop her like she did me years ago.

There's just one problem...

Every second I spend with her, the more I remember just how incredible our time together was. And the more the thought of handing her over to my father and Cruz terrifies me.

I know my father is still out for Collins blood. This means he won't think twice about taking his revenge the second he locks eyes on her.

Not three minutes after I walk through the front door do the credits roll up on the program Emmie is watching. I snag the remote before she gets a chance and turn it off.

"Hey, I was watching that."

"You're in exactly the same place as you were when I left." The only difference is the pizza box on the coffee table.

"So?"

"Tidy up and go to bed. You need a routine."

"No, what I need is to watch another episode. I'm not even tired."

"I don't care, Em."

She crosses her arms over her chest and stares at me. If she thinks I'm going to back down on this then she clearly doesn't know me very well.

"Okay, fine," she huffs after long, silent seconds, throwing the blanket off and collecting all her crap.

"First thing in the morning, Em, we're tackling what's left of that school stuff."

"Whatever," she mumbles from the kitchen. All I do is smile.

She might be a pain in the arse when she wants to be, probably my genes, but I love having her here. I love having this time together. It's something I never thought I'd get.

Not long after, she stomps up the stairs like a toddler having a tantrum.

"Night, Emmie," I sing with a laugh.

"Night, Dad." I swear I hear a smile in her voice. She might pretend to hate me, but I know deep down she's craving the routine and rules I'm forcing on her. Hell knows her mother never did.

I find the kitchen spotless as I walk in—aside from the pizza box. Okay, so she didn't spend all day on the sofa. I know it didn't look like this earlier.

Reaching into the top cupboard, I pull a bottle of Jack down and tip a generous measure into a glass.

I watch as the amber liquid swirls around for a few seconds, its scent permeating the air before I knock it back.

Flicking off the lights, I make my way up. Soft music plays from Emmie's bedroom as I pass, but I don't say anything. She's up here and in her room; there's only so much I can demand of her. She's sixteen, a young woman. It's easy to forget and think she's still my little quirky six-year-old.

Making my way to my room, I close the door behind me and look around.

Piper might never have been here—no woman has, actually—but still, it feels empty, cold.

Stripping out of my clothes, I drop them into the laundry and walk straight into my en suite and turn the shower on. I make quick work of cleaning up before whipping a towel around my body, brushing my teeth and falling into my bed.

I grab my phone and respond to the couple of messages I had that I ignored when I sent one to Piper earlier. I confirm with Mum that Emmie and I will be there for Sunday lunch tomorrow and barely crack a smile at the meme Titch sent.

I find myself staring at Piper's reply from earlier. A few responses float around my head, but in the end, I decide that actions speak louder. Pushing the sheets as low as possible without exposing myself—one step at a time—I snap a selfie of my tense abs, chest, and up to my chin.

Dawson: What are you wearing in bed?

I attach the picture and stare at the screen, waiting to see if she's awake.

The little ticks alert me to the fact that she is, and in another second, the dots start bouncing.

Piper: Nothing, and I'm cold ;-) Night, Dawson x

Dawson: You can't say things like that to me. Now I'm anything but cold.

She sends back three sleeping emojis, effectively cutting off our conversation. Closing down my apps, I place my phone on the charger beside my bed and lay staring at the ceiling while my cock tents the duvet.

She's teasing me, I know that. But damn, the idea of her lying there alone and naked does all kinds of crazy things to me. Things I've not felt in years, and most definitely things I should not be feeling now. She's the one who's meant to fall under my spell. It's not meant to be the other way around.

By some miracle I manage not to spend the night reliving my moments with Piper, and, not long after I switch the light out, I fall fast asleep.

The sun is bright when I next open my eyes, although when I look at the alarm clock sitting on my bedside table, I find it's only eight AM.

Dragging my arse from the bed, I get ready for the day before heading down to make coffee. The house is in silence. I assume that Emmie is still sleeping, but that's not going to last very long.

With a steaming mug of coffee in hand, I climb the stairs once more and knock on her door.

"Em, it's time to get up," I call through.

"Go away."

"No can do. We've got work to do."

She groans. "I hate you." Her voice is muffled, as if she's pulled her pillow over her head.

"I can cope with that. I'm coming in. I've got coffee," I say as a peace offering.

I push the door open. Her room is in total darkness, not helped by the black paint she insisted on covering the walls in the first week she moved here.

As expected, I find that she's just a lump under the duvet.

"I'll just leave this here, but if you're not down and ready to work in thirty minutes then I'm coming to drag you down there myself."

"I think I made a mistake. Can I go back to Mum's?"

I laugh at her, because we both know she's joking. And not just because neither of us knows where her mother is right now.

I might be hard on her, but I know she's desperate for rules and routine. Deep, deep down. She just doesn't want to admit it.

"Okay, kiddo. Twenty-eight minutes now." I leave her room and head back toward my own coffee.

To my amazement, twenty minutes later Emmie appears with an empty mug, dressed in an oversized hoodie.

"Well, aren't you a sight for sore eyes." I watch as she pads over to the coffee machine for a refill.

"This school had better be really bloody good, Dad. It's not even nine AM on a Sunday morning."

"It will be worth it. You got everything we need?"

She nods toward a folder on the bookcase, and I reach

over and grab it, flicking through all the information that Piper gave her.

Turns out that she's already done most of it.

"Em, why didn't you tell me?"

She shrugs. "I don't just stare at the TV while you're not here, you know."

"I know, but I didn't think..."

"Dad," she sighs, turning to look at me and resting back on the counter with her fresh coffee in her hands. "I'm not a complete fuck-up."

"I know that, Em. Come sit with me," I say, ignoring her language.

We go through everything and look at the emails I've received this week with her timetable and other information. I know she doesn't need me to do this. She's a bright young lady, but she humours me, nonetheless.

Once we're done, I convince her to come for a run with me, which she reluctantly agrees to before we get ready to spend the afternoon with my parents.

We don't often do the family thing, but every now and then Mum insists on having us all together. She also attempts to ban Dad and Cruz from talking about business, but that's yet to happen. As long as none of their conversations have anything to do with Piper, then I'm happy.

I glance at Emmie as she shoves her feet into her boots, ready to leave. A warning about not saying anything about Piper is right on the tip of my tongue, but as of yet, she has no idea there's anything between us. I really hope I can keep it that way so Emmie doesn't get dragged into this mess.

"Everything okay?" she asks, looking back at me with her brows pulled together.

"Yeah, just looking forward to an afternoon with your grandparents."

"I think I might be more willing to go to school a day early." I want to chastise her, but to be fair, I'm not exactly looking forward to this afternoon either.

14

PIPER

Thankfully, Lisa is already on the phone when I sneak past reception Monday morning, but I know I'm not going to be able to hide from her forever. I'm amazed I got through yesterday without an inquisition after the way I was rudely dragged away.

I slip into my office and close the door behind me.

I want to put him out of my mind, but with the image sitting on my phone that I've stared at for entirely too long since he sent it Saturday night, and the knowledge that he's going to be here today dropping off and picking up Emmie, I can't.

I didn't want to allow him back in. I *shouldn't* allow him back in—it's dangerous, and not just for my heart—but I don't seem to be able to keep him at bay.

Those things he said to me outside my flat on Saturday afternoon... I can't stop thinking about them. Does he really want to give us a second shot?

Or is this just a game, so he can hand me over to his dad?

He'd have done it already, a little voice says in my head.

If he wanted revenge, if he wanted to see me pay even more for the mistakes I made, then surely he'd have already handed me over to the devil himself?

Fear races through my veins as I think of Charles Ramsey. My father was scary when you got on the wrong side of him, but he was nothing like Charles. It's why Dad was so desperate for some inside information. He knew he'd never be able to touch him without it. He's too powerful, too much of an enigma.

I blow out a breath and fall down onto my desk.

I have two choices.

I either believe him and allow myself to be swept away by the one man I've ever loved. Or I stand firm and walk away from what could be the best thing that ever happened to me. I mean, how many people really get a second chance like this?

My head is still spinning when my door opens and a familiar head pokes inside.

"Nice try, bitch. You can't get away from me that easily."

I groan as she drops her arse into my chair.

"Don't you have new kid drama to deal with or something?" I ask with a roll of my eyes. I reach forward and turn my computer on so I don't have to look at her.

"So..." she starts.

"So we went to the cinema. Then he took me home because he had to work."

"Piper, don't. Don't do that."

"Do what? It's what happened," I say innocently.

"And you're just going to ignore the fact that he turned up and went all alpha on your arse."

"Um... yeah?"

"Girl, it was so fucking hot. How you didn't jump him right there on the street, I don't know."

"Jesus, Lis. I'm not an out-of-control hormonal teenager."

"With a man like that following you around, you should be."

"Things aren't that simple."

"Really? Seems that way from where I'm sitting. You're single, he's single. I assume. What's the issue?"

"It's... it's nothing," I say with a sigh. I can't talk about what happened back then. Not only would Lisa probably not believe me, but I don't want anyone knowing. The risk of being found is too huge. "How often do second chances really work out anyway?"

"With chemistry like you two are rocking, I'd say you've got a very good chance, Piper."

"We'll see."

"When are you seeing him again?"

"Um... I don't know. He said he'd be in touch."

"Oh, mysterious. Maybe he'll walk in here and throw you over his shoulder."

"I really hope not. Did Henry say anything about me leaving on Friday night?" I ask, realising that I didn't get to ask her on Saturday morning.

"He looked pretty disappointed for a bit, but he soon found a replacement."

I nod and force a smile onto my lips. I don't want to hurt Henry. He's been a good friend to me since I started here. Not that I have a lot of choice in how things played out on Friday night.

"Do you mind? I really need to..." I point at my now awake computer, hoping that she'll get my not-so-subtle message.

Our sixth formers are starting today, which means I've got a full day introducing myself and welcoming our new students. The majority of our cohort are returning after doing their GCSEs here, but there are a few, Emmie Ramsey included, who are starting fresh.

I go through my emails, pull up the files on all our new students, and familiarise myself with their names and photos before heading out to find Henry ready for his inspirational 'this is the first day of the rest of your lives' assembly that I'm sure is to come.

"Hey," I say, finding him at the entrance to the sixth form common room, welcoming everyone in.

Cars are spilling in and out of the car park, but as of yet, I haven't heard the rumble of Dawson's bike. Assuming he doesn't also have a car, of course.

"Hey, how are you?" I have no idea if it's my imagination or not, but his voice seems a little clipped.

"I-I'm good thanks. Did you have a good night Friday?" I ask with a wince, not wanting to pussyfoot around the situation.

"It was... fine."

Ouch.

His eyes turn on me, and all I see is disappointment in them.

Fuck.

"He's an old friend," I blurt out before kicking myself. I really don't want to talk about this, especially with Henry.

"Didn't look very old to me," he mutters, nodding at a group of students who walk our way.

"Yeah, well..."

"It's fine, Piper. This," he says, gesturing between us, "was just a bit of fun. We both knew that."

Did we?

"I-I know. I wasn't expecting him to be there on Friday. It was as much as a surprise for me."

Someone calls my name, but not before I hear Henry mutter, "I'm not so sure about that."

My stomach twists as one of the students I spent a lot of time with last year bounces up to me to say hello. I don't want to hurt him, and I fear that I might not have been clear enough about the fact that there really was nothing between us but a bit of easy fun.

I glance back at him once I'm alone again, but he's been swallowed up by the football team.

I watch them for a second before a familiar rumble shakes my body.

I tell myself not to turn around, but it's pointless. The pull I feel to him is already as strong—if not stronger—than it ever was.

My eyes land on him as he flies into the car park and pulls into the bike parking, which unfortunately is the closest possible place to where I'm standing right now.

The second he brings the bike to a stop, he rips his helmet from his head, his eyes already on me.

Fire burns through my veins as our eyes lock. A smirk pulls at his lips as we watch each other.

It's not until he turns to Emmie, who is now off the back of his bike, that our connection is broken.

"Well, I guess that answers the question of how you reconnected," a familiar voice whispers in my ear. His heat burns into my back, telling me that he's entirely too close. Not just because students are around, but because Dawson is right there.

Something tells me he won't take too kindly to Henry starting a pissing contest. I'm also pretty sure who'd win said contest.

"Yeah, it was a shock. If you did your own meeting, then maybe it wouldn't have happened," I snap. I know that wasn't his fault—he was called away on an emergency—but still. I remember all too well how terrified I was the moment I saw him there.

"It's time to get started, Miss Hill. Please ensure your personal life doesn't impact your ability to do your job."

My lips part in shock that he'd ever assume I would put my job second. I've worked my arse off for him and our students since the first morning I started here.

Arsehole.

I'm just about to turn to follow him inside when Dawson's burning stare stops me in my tracks.

I look up at him. His eyes are narrowed, and even from this distance, I can see they're darker than usual. He shakes his head slowly before his lips part.

"Mine," he mouths, causing butterflies to erupt in my stomach and desire to head south. What is it about his caveman act that hits me quite so hard?

Lifting my hand, I wave at him, attempting to ignore what he's trying to get at.

His lips curl into a small smile at my move.

I'm still rooted to the spot as he pulls his helmet on, revs the engine, and flies from the car park.

"Hello, Emmie. All ready for your first day?" I ask when she gets to me.

"What's the deal with you and my dad?" she asks, diving straight into the deep end.

"Oh... um... nothing."

She narrows her eyes at me as if she's seeing much more than her sixteen-year-old self should. But then I guess she is Dawson's daughter, so it stands to reason that she might possess the same power to get under my skin.

"Really? Something tells me that you didn't just meet last week."

"You would be correct. We knew each other as kids."

"Right."

"Mr. Davenport will be waiting for you. I'll catch up with you later to see how you're getting on, okay?"

"I can't wait, Miss Hill." She smiles sweetly, but it's all an act. I've met her twice, and I'm already learning that she's as much as an enigma as the other Ramseys I know.

Fucking hell.

After rounding up the few lingering stray students, I head inside and close the doors behind me.

Glancing around the room of students, I find Emmie sitting right in the back at the corner, hiding. I'm not surprised; she doesn't seem like the kind of kid who'll throw herself straight into the popular crowd.

Henry stands on the stage, commanding everyone's attention. All the students silently stare at him, waiting for him to launch into his speech.

"Today is the first day of the rest of your lives..." *How did I know?* I roll my eyes and stand at the back of the room as he continues.

———

A light knock sounds out on my door.

"Come in," I call out, but I already know who it is. I called for her ten minutes ago.

"Hi," Emmie says nervously, stepping into my office. She might think I'm doing this because of her dad, but it's not true. Throughout today, I'm meeting all our new students before I start making my way through our long-term ones.

"Come and take a seat."

"Sure." She drops her bag to the floor with a thud and flops down.

"Have you not found your locker yet?" I ask, wondering just how heavy her bag is with the sound of the bang.

"No, not yet."

"Okay, well I can show you where it is if you're not sure."

"I'm sure I can cope." She tilts her chin and stares at me.

"I'm sure you can. But the offer is there if you need it." Silence falls between us before I turn to my screen and open her file. I know most of it; I studied it after she and Dawson left last week.

"This isn't a special meeting, Emmie. Over the coming days, every lower sixth student will sit in that chair."

"Good to know." She has zero expression on her face. She's even harder to read than her father, and that's saying something.

Okay.

"Let's start with your grades. They—"

"Were shit, I'm aware. There's no need to beat around the bush here. Dad thought this place would sort me out. It might. You know the school I've come from, and I'm sure you know its reputation. The fact that I finished with any grades and didn't end up stabbed or shot is a miracle."

"Yes, it's not one of the city's finest."

She snorts. "Look," she says, sitting forward in her chair and resting her elbows on my desk. "I don't know what you think of me. Quite frankly, I don't care. I don't care what anyone thinks. They can stare at me all they like. I know I don't fit in, and I don't want to.

"But, despite what those grades say on your computer, I'm not stupid. I might think my dad has lost his mind, signing me up here, but I know he can see my potential and just wants the best for me. I appreciate that. It's more than my mother ever did for me."

"I'll do what's required of me. I'll work hard. I'll try my best, but I'm not suddenly going to turn into some pretentious rich kid to fit in. I like rock music, the colour black, and as soon as I can convince my dad to do it, I'll have ink and a bike."

"O-okay. I wasn't going to suggest you do anything to fit in, Emmie. You are your own person and I'd only want you to embrace that."

"Great. I just thought I'd get that out now before you start talking to me about Oxbridge or some other crazy shit."

My lips part, but I soon find I have no words to respond.

"Was that all?"

"N-no. So, no Oxbridge," I smile, "but do you have any idea what you might like to do in the future?"

She shrugs. "I dunno. Not thought about it."

"That's fine. It's still early days. Knight's Ridge will open up opportunities for you, opportunities that you really should embrace."

"We'll see," she says, pushing from the chair. "That it?"

"Um... yeah. Unless you wanted to talk about anything else."

"Nah, I'm good." She's at the door with her hand on the handle when she turns back to me. "I forgot. Dad asked me to give you this." She digs about in her bag for a bit before revealing an envelope.

"Oh, t-thank you." She's almost disappeared before I gather my senses. "Have a great day, Emmie. I'm here if you need anything."

She doesn't respond. I'm not even sure if she hears me.

Holding the plain white envelope in my hand, I turn it over, looking for clues as my heart begins to race.

I should put it in my bag until I'm home later, because I just know that whatever is inside has nothing to do with Emmie attending Knight's Ridge. Everything we do here is electronic, so it's unlikely it's an old-school permission slip.

I pull my drawer open and drop it in, but despite the fact that it's out of sight once I close it, it's never out of mind.

I see three more students with it taunting me.

By the time I say goodbye to the last, I can't wait any longer and pull it out. I make quick work of ripping the flap open and pulling out the contents.

I unfold the piece of paper and something falls onto my lap.

Dawson's messy handwriting is scrawled across the paper.

The best day of my life.

My brows pull together at his cryptic message until I pick up what fell onto my lap and turn it over.

My breath catches as I stare down at younger versions of the two of us at a fairground.

A wide smile forms on my lips as I remember that weekend we skipped out of London. We weren't heading for a fair, we just happily stumbled across it where we'd booked a B&B for the night.

He's not wrong, it was incredible.

Before I can control it, my memories get the better of me.

. . .

"Come on, don't be a scaredy-cat," Dawson taunts as I slow to a stop in front of the Ferris wheel.

"Dawson, I really, really don't want to go up there."

"Why, what's the worst that could happen?"

"Oh, I don't know. We could plummet to our deaths."

He laughs at me. "Piper, you get on the back of my bike without so much as batting an eyelid. I can assure you that there's more chance of dying on that than there is on a Ferris wheel."

"Bikes don't scare me, and I trust you. Heights, however..."

His arms wrap around my shoulders. "Baby girl, I'll never let anything happen to you."

He stares down at me with so much love in his eyes that I have no choice but to nod and allow him to lead me over to the ticket booth.

My entire body trembles in fear as we wait for our car. It swings when I step on, but that's nothing compared to what it does under Dawson's weight.

"I'm going to fucking die. It's not funny," I snap when all he does is laugh at me.

"I'm not going to let you die, Piper." He pulls me close and holds me tight.

"Oh my God. Oh my God," I whisper to myself as we start moving. I squeeze my eyes shut tight and cling onto Dawson for dear life.

"You're cute."

"I'm not cute, I'm terrified."

"Come here, let me distract you." His warm fingers tilt my chin up before his lips brush over mine.

In only two seconds I forget where we are as his tongue sweeps into my mouth.

A moan rumbles up my throat as my reason to cling onto him changes.

His hand tenses at my waist as his kiss gets even deeper.

I have no idea if he was aware, but when he pulls back, we're right at the top. My heart jumps into my throat as I stare at the sky above me, desperately trying not to look down.

"Piper," he says, his hand cupping my cheek and his thumb running over my skin.

My eyes find his and I gasp at the look in them. They're dark, hungry, and full of emotion.

"Piper, I... I think I've fallen in love with you."

15

DAWSON

"I need to talk to you about something," Emmie says the second we're back in the house after school.

"I'm not going to like this, am I?" I knew delivering that little memory to Piper via my daughter wasn't the right way to go about it, but I needed to do something. Sunday is a long time away; I need to ensure I'm in her head. And I'm hoping that the photo was perfect.

I almost burned everything from our time together. The day I learned of her betrayal, I shoved everything into a box and vowed to watch it go up in smoke just like our relationship. But I couldn't do it.

What I thought was exciting and pure was in fact all fake and based on a lie.

She told me she loved me back, that day up on the Ferris wheel. It was the single most important moment of my life. I thought I'd found it all in Piper. I knew we shouldn't have been together, but the naïve boy thought we'd be able to get around it. That we could just sit our fathers down, explain how we felt, and it would all be okay.

How wrong I was.

My fists clench as I think about her saying those three little words. I believed her. Not once did I ever question her intentions. I was blinded by her. Totally fucking blinded.

"When can I get a bike?"

"Fucking hell," I mutter to myself, rubbing my hand down my face.

"What? You told me that—"

"I know what I told you, but I didn't think you'd actually want to."

Emmie has been talking about having a bike of her own since she was old enough to know what one was. I told her that when she was sixteen I would buy her one. I paid for her CBT for her birthday in the hope that she'd get on a bike and be scared witless and never want to ride one again. It backfired, because now she wants one more than ever.

It utterly terrifies me.

"Can't you just wait to get a car?" I ask, walking through to the kitchen to start the coffee machine. Although I'm not sure there's enough caffeine in the world for this conversation.

"No, I don't want a car. I want a bike, and I'm seventeen in a few weeks, which means I can get a 125cc."

"Emmie," I groan.

"Dad," she sasses. When I turn to look at her, I find her standing with her hands on her hips and her brow quirked. "I've done everything you've asked of me since I moved here. I'm going to that bloody school. And, if you agree, then I won't even give you the twenty questions you deserve about Miss Hill." Her eyes narrow in my direction.

"Whoa, who taught you how to barter?" I mutter, almost impressed with her attempt. "First, you do what you're told because you're a child—"

"Wow, are you really going to hit me with that bullshit? I'm sixteen. I can have sex, get married, buy a lottery ticket. I can even move out if I so wanted." She tilts her head to ensure I hear that last one. "I can also legally ride a bike, as you well know."

"Okay, you're not having sex under this roof." My eyes widen in horror, but all she does is laugh.

"What, you really think I'm going to pull one of those rich pricks at school and sneak him here to fuck him on your bed?"

"Emmie," I warn, my blood starting to boil.

"Relax. If there's one who's not a total prick, then I'm sure his mummy and daddy have a mansion we could make use of."

"Christ, give me strength."

"How about we cut a deal?"

"Sure, hit me with it."

I swallow down my nerves because I really don't want to have this conversation with my sixteen-year-old daughter, but I know it would make me an irresponsible parent if I didn't.

"We can go and look at getting you a bike if..." Her brows rise as she waits for me to finish my sentence. "If you get yourself to the doctor and on birth control just in case what you threatened me with becomes reality. What? Why are you laughing?"

"Aw, Dad. I love you, but you really are clueless sometimes."

My lips part to ask what the hell she's talking about, but I can't find any words.

"I've been on the pill since I was fourteen."

"Oh."

She must see the horror on my face because she quickly adds. "It's okay, originally it was for heavy periods."

I relax for a beat. "Originally?"

"So, when can we go shopping?" she asks, swiftly changing the subject.

I stare at her for a beat in her Knight's Ridge uniform. She might have heavy eye makeup and almost purple lips, but she's right, she's done nothing but comply with all the changes in her life the past few weeks, despite a bit of sass about school.

"Go and get changed."

"Oh my God," she squeals. "For real?"

"Yes. But be quick before I change my mind."

"Oh my God, I'm so excited. Thank you so much." She flies at me and throws her arms around my shoulder. "I love you. Thank you."

"I love you too, Em." I drop a kiss to the top of her head and watch her run from the room, wondering what the fuck I just agreed to.

At least I got out of having to explain to her why she was my unofficial postman for Piper.

We end up grabbing a burger for dinner after spending entirely too long at the garage while Emmie sat on every single 125cc bike they had.

I expected her to want a moped, but I shouldn't really have been surprised to discover she basically wanted a miniature version of what I ride. My girl is a bad-arse, after all.

So after ordering her new baby, we headed for food and then home so she could do her homework.

The purchase came with some clauses. No trouble and good grades. She eagerly agreed, but I guess only time will tell how both will go, because knowing my sassy daughter, two years at Knight's Ridge isn't going to pass without a little drama.

It's not until I fall into bed later that night that I realise I never heard anything from Piper. I was sure she'd reach out after seeing that photograph.

Grabbing my phone, I hit call on her number. I could text her, but a big part of me wants to hear her voice.

"Hey," she says happily.

"Hey. It's not too late, is it?"

"No, I'm still up."

"I... uh... was expecting to hear from you today," I admit, hoping that it makes me sound more interested than it does a pussy.

"Sorry, it's been a crazy day with the lower sixth starting."

"It's okay. I've got you now."

She sighs down the line, and it's all I need to hear to know that those words are true.

"Thanks for the walk down memory lane. I needed that."

"I'm assuming because you'd just had a delightful meeting with my devil child?" I ask with a laugh.

"She'd just left, yeah. But she's a good kid, Dawson."

"I've just bought her a bike," I blurt.

"As in, a pushbike?" Piper asks hesitantly, although I know she knows it's not.

"Nope. She kinda blackmailed me into a real one."

"Wow. I think I might need to spend some more time with her, find out her tricks."

"You're funny, but I'm pretty sure both of you have me wrapped around your little fingers."

"That right, huh?"

"What are you doing right now?" I ask, my voice getting lower with every word.

"Uh-uh, we're not going there, Dawson," she warns.

"Going where?" I ask innocently. "I was just wondering what you're doing... what you're wearing."

"Something really, really unsexy, I can assure you."

"I beg to differ. You could wear a sack and still turn me on."

"As nice as it is to hear that, I'm not entirely sure it's true."

"Try me."

"Maybe I will. You tell me when I'm going to see you again, and I'll prepare my sack."

"Shouldn't that be my line?" I deadpan.

She laughs but tries to cover it. "I thought you were planning on taking me out. Treating me right," she quips.

"Oh, I am. You don't need to worry about that."

"Are you going to tell me where and when?" she digs.

"Sunday. The where is under wraps right now."

"Is that because you haven't planned it?"

"That's for me to know and you to find out."

"Okay, well, as fun as this has been, I need to get to bed." Something sloshes in the background, and I'm instantly on full alert.

"Piper," I grind out, "are you in the bath?"

"I have no idea what you're talking about," she says sweetly, making me groan in pain.

"You're naked right now, aren't you?"

"Again, no idea what you're talking about. But I really need to go. I guess I'll see you Sunday."

"Assuming I can wait that long."

"You're a big boy, Dawson. I'm sure you'll cope."

"You're right there, baby girl. I am."

"Oh God. I'm going. Thanks for the picture today. I'll see you soon." She hangs up before I get a chance to say anything in response.

Chuckling to myself, I place my phone down and slip under the covers with images of her in a hot bubble bath as my hand descends.

———

With each day that passes, I find a way to show Piper that I'm thinking of her. On Tuesday, I send flowers to the school, and seconds after they arrive I get a message telling me how mortified she was when her friend proudly walked into her office with them, quickly followed by a thank you.

On Wednesday, I had a car waiting to take her home after discovering that she uses the tube, and we all know how much that sucks in rush hour.

Yesterday, I sent her lunch from what used to be her favourite restaurant when we were kids. I think she really appreciated that one because before I fell asleep, I received a message from her much like the one I sent on Sunday night, only her breasts were covered in silk, and her toned stomach was on full display with her hand disappearing inside her matching shorts. Safe to say I fell asleep with a smile on my face while deciding to up the ante for the final day of the week.

16

PIPER

"Your surprise is here," Lisa announces happily not a minute after the lunch bell has rung out through the building.

"Oh God."

"I think you're really going to enjoy today's."

"Tell me it's cake. Please tell me it's cake, or wine."

"You work in a school, Piper," she admonishes with a laugh.

"I have no student meetings planned this afternoon. No one would notice, I'm sure."

"What the hell has gotten into you?"

"Nothing," I mutter, but it's not quiet enough, because Lisa barks out a laugh.

"Well, you might be in luck with that little issue."

Tingles erupt in my belly.

"Is he—"

"Come see for yourself."

I push my chair out behind me with such force it clatters into the bookcase behind.

I shouldn't be this excited about the prospect of seeing

him, but after all his little gifts this week and our cheeky messages and phone calls, I'm damn near desperate.

I eagerly follow Lisa until I'm able to look out over the car park. My eyes land on him instantly. He's leaning back against his bike, wearing just a black t-shirt with his inked arms crossed over his wide chest and a dark pair of glasses hiding his eyes. I know the second they land on me, though. My blood heats and my skin prickles with awareness.

"Enjoy. You know the spot all the kids go to hide, right?" Lisa asks me with a wink.

"We're adults, Lis. We can restrain ourselves," I mutter, heading for the doors.

"I'll believe that when I see it."

I flip her off over my shoulder as I walk out toward him.

His lips twitch up into a wide smile by the time I step up in front of him.

"This is a nice surprise."

He pulls his glasses off and tucks them into the neck of his t-shirt, allowing me to see his eyes.

"I wasn't sure how to beat the last few days."

"I think you've managed it. Tell me you brought cake and it will confirm it."

"You might be in luck there."

He reaches behind him and grabs a bag that's resting on the seat.

"You know anywhere good for a picnic?"

"I do." I point toward some benches where the kids never go.

Reaching out, he grabs my hand before allowing me to lead the way.

"This place is a little different to what I remember

from school," he says, staring out over the rolling countryside.

"I know. It's not exactly your average inner city comprehensive."

We both take a seat before he silently reveals what he brought with him.

"Take your pick," he says, gesturing to the premade sandwiches, crisps, and, most importantly, cake.

"Thank you," I say reaching for one of the sandwiches and ripping the packaging open, my grumbling belly getting the better of me.

"How's Emmie getting on?"

"Ah, so that's why you're here," I joke. "You want inside information."

"You know that's not why I'm here. I'm just curious. All I've got from her this week is that it's fine."

"As far as I know, everything is fine. I haven't heard anything to the contrary."

"Good. That's good," he says almost awkwardly before falling silent.

"Can I ask you something?"

"Sure."

"How'd you get Emmie in here at such late notice? I know we've got a waiting list, but you seemed to jump it."

"Contacts."

That one simple word sends a shiver racing down my spine.

"C-contacts? Should I be worried?"

"Yes and no." I swallow nervously, because where he was a closed book those first few days after we found each other again, now he's relaxed, and I can read him. And right now, he's being totally honest.

"Who? Do they recognise me? Do they know who I am?"

"What do you think?" he asks around a mouthful of cheese and ham sandwich.

"I think I'm still alive, so that's a good sign."

"Just don't go around announcing your real surname."

"And what if they find out?"

"You know the answer to that, Piper. But you came back, so you must have thought the risk was worth it."

"It's my home, Dawson."

"I understand that. Others won't."

"Fuck," I mutter, suddenly feeling much less hungry.

I pick at my sandwich as a weird tension falls over us.

"I'm sorry, Piper," he says after a few seconds. "I hoped this would make you smile."

"It has. I'm sorry, I shouldn't have brought it up."

Reaching over the table, he laces his fingers through mine.

"I won't let anything happen to you, Piper."

My head spins with his promise. There's still so much I don't know about him. He keeps saying all these incredible things to me, but I'm still in the dark as to whether he's working for his father right now. It sure wouldn't be the craziest thing that's happened to us.

"Stop worrying, baby girl. You're safe."

I nod at him, wondering just how true those words are, but I have no reason not to believe him. Okay, so he was rough at the start, wanted to teach me a lesson, but since then I've believed everything he's said. I *want* to believe him. I want to believe that this is real and that second chance Lisa was talking about.

I'm terrified that this all might be a lie and I'm falling headfirst into it.

But what if it's not?

"Shouldn't you be at work right now or something?" I ask after a few seconds, needing to stop running around in circles in my head.

"I'm going after."

"What do you do?"

"What do you think I do?" he asks cryptically.

I think back to our time together as kids, but I don't remember us really talking about the future. We were too concerned about getting caught and neither of us having one.

I remember that he loved to draw and was obsessed with music.

"Umm... Work at a club or some sort? Events organiser?" I ask, thinking about his night-time hours.

"Good guess, but no. I'll show you one day soon."

"You'll show me?"

"If you're brave enough."

I swallow nervously. "Brave enough?" I croak out. As far as I know, I'm only afraid of heights. What the hell could his job be?

The bell rings out from the buildings in the distance, and we reluctantly start packing up.

"This was nice, thank you."

"Nice?" he asks, sounding offended.

"Yeah, it was a nice surprise, so thank you."

He smiles at me as I stand from the bench before he pulls me onto his lap.

He stares into my eyes as if it's the first time he's ever done so.

"Dawson?" I whisper, needing to know what his sudden intensity is about.

"No one is going to touch you, baby girl." He brushes

his nose against mine. My lips pucker for a kiss that I know isn't going to follow. He kisses my cheek before his lips brush my ear. "Unless I tell them to," he whispers, his voice so low it sends a shiver of fear and desire coursing through me.

I gasp and he laughs.

"Relax. You're safe with me."

I have no idea if I should believe him, but without my brain's approval, my body relaxes at his words.

"Come on, you need to get back to work."

Nodding, I reluctantly climb from his lap and help him tidy up before we walk back toward the main building.

"What time on Sunday?" I ask when we get to his bike.

"Ten-thirty."

"In the morning?"

"Yep. I don't want to waste the day."

I smile up at him, my heart beating wildly in my chest.

"I can't wait."

"Me neither, baby girl." He gathers me in his arms and drops a kiss to the top of my head.

"I'd better..." I flick a look over my shoulder and unsurprisingly find Lisa staring back at us.

"Yeah."

He watches me walk back to the building, where I stand inside and keep my eyes on him as he pulls his helmet on and throws one long leg over his bike.

"How the hell are you letting him go without jumping him?" Lisa says, coming to stand beside me.

"Because I'm at work. I've got cake," I say, holding up what remains from our picnic, much to her delight.

"I mean, it's not a hot biker with the skills to show me heaven, but I'll take it."

Laughing at her, I make my way to my office to finish the week off.

It's halfway through the last lesson of the day when a knock sounds out on my door.

I call whoever it is inside, but I don't look up from my screen straight away; I'm too lost in the email I'm reading.

"Have a fun lunch, Miss Hill?"

I turn to find Emmie leaning back against my closed door with a shit-eating grin on her face.

"I did, thank you. Have you had a good first week?"

"Meh," she says, dropping her bag to the floor and then falling into the chair opposite me.

"Shouldn't you be in class?"

"Should you have had a date at lunch?" She raises a brow at me.

"Your dad and I are friends, Emmie."

"Friends. Right. See, here's the thing, I might have only been living with him for a few weeks, but I like to think I know him pretty well. He never, and I mean never, makes that kind of effort for a woman. He's never had a girlfriend. I've never even met a female friend aside from those he works with."

"M-maybe he just likes to keep his lives separate," I state, not really wanting to talk about this with his daughter.

"Maybe, but I really don't think that's the case."

"What about your mum?" I regret the question the second it falls from my lips. I shouldn't be digging for this kind of information from Emmie.

"My mum?" she asks with a laugh that has my brows pulling together. "My mum and dad hate each other. They always have, as far as I know."

"Oh, okay so..."

"I think you're different."

You have no idea. "We're just friends. So how was your first week?" I try again.

"It's just school." She waves me off. "Are you seeing him again?"

"I... um..."

"I just think you should, that's all."

My lips part to respond, but I can't find any words.

"You make him smile, Miss Hill. It doesn't happen all that often."

"Okay... that's... that's good," I stutter, fighting a grin. "So, school. Everything's been okay this week? Teachers and classes all right?"

"Yeah, I never thought I'd say it but it's actually quite nice to be in a class where people want to learn and the teacher isn't spending the whole time firefighting... sometimes literally."

"That's good. I'm glad you're enjoying them. Friends?"

"I'm not here to make friends."

"Maybe not, but it will be a long two years without any."

"I'm sure I'll be fine. You may not have noticed, but I don't really fit in."

"I'll let you into a little secret." I lean forward and she does the same, intrigued as to what I'm going to say. "No one does. They're all playing a game."

She scoffs. "I've seen the boys who think they own the place and the girls who follow them around like lost puppies. They're not acting, their egos really are just that big."

"Like I said... games."

The bell for the end of the day rings and Emmie stands from the chair.

"Thanks for the chat, Miss H."

"I'm always here if you need me."

She stares at me for a beat. "Give my dad a chance. He's a good guy, under the scowl and scary ink."

I chuckle. "I know, Emmie. I met him before either of those emerged." Her eyes soften as she moves to the door. "See you soon."

She smiles and slips out of my office, leaving me a little bewildered.

It's Friday night, which means one thing: Lisa begging me to go out so she can attempt to pull. It takes a bit of argument, but, finally, she lets me off. I'm exhausted, I just want a night on the sofa with a bottle of wine to myself and a film or two. I also want to be able to hear should Dawson decide to call me later.

17

DAWSON

"I thought you'd be asleep by now," I say when soft footsteps join me in the kitchen.

It's long after midnight, seeing as I went out for drinks with the guys after work. I was waiting for them to roast me on the date I asked for Biff and Kas's help with, but to my surprise, no one even mentioned it. If the girls told their guys then they must have sworn them to secrecy, which I appreciate.

The last thing I need is everyone knowing before I achieve what I'm trying to.

The conversation we had at lunch earlier still plays out in my mind. I might have exaggerated when I suggested there was a threat to Piper at Knight's Ridge. There isn't anyone walking the halls who would know who she is. My connections to the school are behind the scenes, and they have no interest in who the staff are. But I wanted to see her reaction, to see if she was scared, in the hope that it might give me a clue as to where her head's at.

Right now, I feel like we're both dancing around each other, not knowing what's real or not. I know that's probably mostly my fault. The fact that I'm playing games makes me wonder if she is, if we're just using each other.

I want to say that's not the case and that she's just wary because she's smart. Even people who don't know me are cautious, let alone someone who has every right to be.

"I was doing homework."

"Who are you, and what have you done with my daughter?" I ask jokingly, looking over Emmie's shoulder.

"Shut up, you idiot. I was never that bad a student. I just got fed up with being one of the only ones bothering."

"Good to know. So you don't totally hate me for sending you to that place then?"

"Nah, I could never hate you, old man, even if you are basically banging one of my teachers." The water I'd just taken a sip of sprays from my mouth.

"I'm sorry, what?"

She hops up on the barstool and looks at me as if I'm an idiot as I reach for a tea towel to clean up the mess.

"You thought I wouldn't notice that you've got a hard-on for Miss H?"

"Emmie," I gasp. "I don't... can we not... fucking hell. I was not prepared for this. *Let my teenage daughter move in, it won't be that bad, they said,*" I mutter to myself as I try to figure out how to play this.

"Talking to yourself won't make this any better."

"No, but you going to bed and never mentioning me having a hard-on ever again would."

She rolls her eyes at me and reaches for an apple that's sitting in the fruit bowl.

"So, you and Miss H... serious?"

"We're just old friends."

"Funny," she mutters around a mouthful of apple. "She tried to feed me that line too."

"You've spoken to her."

"Yup. And you're welcome, by the way." She winks, causing my temperature to spike.

"Emmie, what did you do?" My voice is low, my warning clear.

"Just helping you out, old man. I can't imagine you've got much game, seeing as you're forever single."

"That's not through lack of skill."

"I should hope not. But I thought I'd give you a little help."

"What. Did. You. Say?"

Her top lips curls as she thinks. "Nope, can't remember." She hops down from the stool and is at the door before I can even blink. "Night," she calls disappearing before I can throttle her.

"Jesus fucking Christ."

Pulling my phone from my pocket, I find Piper's contact and my thumb hovers over her number.

It's late, the clock on the oven telling me that it's closing in on two AM.

I shouldn't call. I should wait for the morning.

Despite knowing it's what I should do, I hit call anyway. *She can just not answer,* I tell myself.

But that's not what happens, because it connects on the third ring.

"Hello?" Her voice is rough and husky and immediately has my cock swelling.

"You asleep, baby girl?"

"I was, yeah." I can almost picture her curled up in her bed. "Is everything okay?"

"Yeah. I was just learning that you had a nice little chat with my daughter this afternoon."

"Oh yeah, that. She spilled all your secrets, you know?"

"Yeah, that's what I'm worried about."

"If you think I'm going to repeat what she told me then you need to think again. There is such a thing as girl code."

"Jesus," I mutter, rubbing my hand down my face. "I'm going to be in trouble with you two, aren't I?"

"It's two against one, so I would say so, yeah." She yawns, and I instantly feel guilty for waking her.

"I'll let you go back to sleep."

"Hmm," she mumbles as if she already is. "My bed is cold," she whispers. "It could really do with another person in it."

"Don't do this to me, baby girl. You know I'd be there in a heartbeat if I could." I look up at the ceiling. I'm sure I could go out; Emmie is more than capable of being home alone, but I don't want to be that parent. Plus, I made Piper a promise, and a late-night booty call isn't it.

"But I'm wearing—"

"Don't," I warn. "Don't do it."

"You're no fun."

"I think you know that's not true, baby. I can be lots of fun."

"I remember well. Makes me wet just thinking about it."

"Piper, have you been drinking?"

"Might have had one or two. I was lonely, so I may have had a third. I can't remember."

"No Friday night out?"

"Nope, I stayed home, hoping I might get a visitor."

"Well, I'm sorry to disappoint. Now, tell me more about how wet you are..."

Saturday drags. I love my job and the guys I work with, but nothing can pull me out of my despondent mood as I impatiently wait for Sunday morning to roll around.

I shouldn't be this excited to see her. I shouldn't miss her so much, and I certainly shouldn't crave her the way I am.

I fear that my well-laid plans are going a little awry.

I wanted revenge. I wanted to give my daughter a future. At no point was I meant to become this invested.

I think back eighteen years and familiarise myself with the anger I felt when her betrayal was discovered. I need to hold onto that, I need to harness it to spur me forward to do what needs to be done. Because it doesn't matter how I feel; she wronged not only me but my family. Lessons need to be taught, and no doubt blood needs to be shed.

But this isn't just my fight. She took it beyond me when she agreed to go after my dad.

Actions have consequences, and no matter how many years have passed, they will always be remembered by those wronged.

I'm the last one in the studio by the time I've finished with my client. Zach and Biff are upstairs in the flat, and Titch and Spike both left a little over thirty minutes ago.

After seeing my client out, I clean up and get ready to head home. It wasn't so long ago that we'd be going out tonight as well as last night, but now the guys all have girls, everything has changed.

We once used to be four free and single guys up for as much fun as we could find every night of the week, but now, I'm the only one left.

Thoughts of how they're all moving on to the next stages of their lives makes me think about my future. Do I want to continue as I am for the next thirty-something years? Or do I want what they've got—someone to spend it with?

Images of Piper and me pop into my head, but it's pointless. I might be craving her, but I can't be thinking about anything past right now.

We don't have a future.

We can't.

———

I pull up outside her building ten minutes early and kill the engine. She told me she'd meet me down here, so I refrain from walking over and buzzing for her and instead climb from my bike and wait for her.

I don't have to wait very long; not three minutes later does the main door open. My eyes almost pop out of my head as I watch her emerge. She looks like my inner teenage boy's wet dream.

She's wearing a skin-tight pair of jeans with a fitted leather jacket zipped up to reveal her impressive cleavage.

My mouth waters as I take her in.

Lifting my eyes from her tits, I take in her flawless face and her long, blonde, wavy hair.

"Piper, you look... wow." A smile pulls at her lips.

"I figured I'd dress for the bike."

"You mean this isn't for my benefit?" She laughs, and the sound along with the wide smile on her face do something to my insides, something I know I shouldn't be feeling.

"So what's the plan? Where are you taking me?"

"Hop on and you'll find out."

Her eyes narrow at me as she silently tries to get me to

confess. She's going to have to try harder than that if she wants to know my secrets.

"Okay."

I pass her the helmet, and, once she has it secure, I climb back on my bike and wait for her to join me.

She doesn't hesitate to wrap her arms around me and I just about manage to catch the sigh of contentment that threatens to rumble up my throat as her warmth surrounds me.

I rev the engine and shoot off from her building and across the city.

I know exactly where we're going, but that doesn't stop me from taking the long way around so I can enjoy having her behind me. I also use it as an opportunity to discreetly go via Dad's clubhouse.

It's probably cruel and tempting fate, but I want to feel her reaction as she wonders if that's where we're going.

The second she registers the turn I take and where it could possibly lead, her arms tighten around my waist.

I can't hear anything she might say right now, making me wish I had microphones set up in our helmets.

Her grip only gets tighter the closer we get, and I swear I feel her tremble in fear at one point.

Interesting.

Before we get too close, I take a left and head in the opposite direction. Her hold immediately loosens, and I can practically imagine her blowing out a relieved breath.

It's only fifteen minutes later when we pull up to our destination for the afternoon.

"Borough Market?" she asks, pulling her helmet off and running her fingers through her hair.

"Yep."

"Not what I was expecting, I'll be honest," she admits.

Taking her helmet from her, I lock it up before doing the same with mine and pulling a bag out to take with us.

"Part of me thought you'd found a funfair and were going to torture me on the Ferris wheel again." I can't help but smile. I'm glad she's still thinking about that photo I sent her. I know I sure am. "But then you headed toward the Reapers clubhouse and I thought..."

I shake my head as fear washes through her violet eyes.

Reaching out, I take her hand in mine and pull her into my body. Her scent fills my nose and I almost lower my head to claim her lips right there. She knows it too, because her eyes drop to mine in anticipation.

"I wouldn't take you there, baby girl. Hell, I haven't been there in years."

"You haven't? So, you're not..."

"No, baby. I'm not associated with them. Well, aside from my name."

"Oh." Her body visibly relaxes with my confession.

"I was a mess after you... died. I'd already told Dad I was leaving, but then Emmie's mum announced she was pregnant, and I walked away for good."

"But you were due to patch in."

"I know. But after seeing the fallout of what my father did to you and your family, enemies or not, I just couldn't. I didn't want my daughter to be brought up surrounded by that life."

A sad laugh passes her lips. "I understand that."

"Dad was not happy. But I was almost eighteen; I was an adult, and he couldn't really do much about it unless he didn't want me breathing. I didn't talk to my parents for a long time after that. They missed out on Emmie being a baby. It's only in the past few years as Mum's health has declined that we've somewhat patched things up, although it'll never be what it once was."

"So you really don't want to kill me?"

I can't help but chuckle. "No, Piper. I don't want to kill you. Everything we went through as kids... it was fucked up. We heard too much, saw too much, experienced too much."

"We were forced to do too much." Our eyes lock as she says the words.

"Yeah, we were. Things could have been so different for us if we weren't born into the families we were."

"Right, we could be married with kids by no—" She stops herself. I'm not sure if it's because of what she can read on my face or what, but she panics. "Shit."

"Hey," I say softly, cupping her cheek. "We could have been. Hell, we should have been."

"You really think we'd have made it that far?"

"I really do, baby girl. I was so fucking gone for you back then."

She gasps at my honesty. "And what about now?" she asks hesitantly.

"Now?" I twist us until she's backed up against my bike. Resting my palms on the seat, I surround her, hovering my lips right above hers. "Right now, I feel like I'm eighteen all over again."

Her eyes shutter in preparation for my kiss, but it never comes. Not yet, anyway.

"Dawson," she complains when I take a step back from her.

"Good things come to those who wait."

"Yeah, assuming I don't combust first," she mutters, much to my amusement.

"Come on. We've got some shopping to do." I twist my fingers with hers and pull her toward the market.

"You brought me shopping for a date?" she asks, sounding totally confused.

"I did. I thought dinner and a movie were overrated."

"And out of all the other options you decided on shopping... in a market."

"I did. Now," I say, pulling her into my body and wrapping my arm around her shoulder, "what do you fancy for lunch?"

"Uh..." She looks up at me before glancing back at the food vendors surrounding us.

"We're going for a picnic, baby."

"Oooh. I guess that makes more sense." She looks around once more. "Bread, cheese... definitely cheese, olives, wine."

"Hungry?" I ask with a laugh.

"Yeah, actually. I was too nervous to eat." Her cheeks turn pink with her admission.

"What did I ever do without you?" I ask her. My voice is serious, too fucking serious, because despite everything, it's the damn truth.

"Made a child?" she asks, trying to lift the tension that's fallen over us.

"That didn't take more than four minutes tops."

"Oh my God, you did not just say that."

"It was a mistake. I was drowning and I made some very questionable decisions. Emmie's mum being one of them."

"She said the two of you hate each other."

"Ah, so that's what you were talking about, huh?"

"One of the things," she admits.

18

PIPER

Dawson tries to dig into what Emmie and I spoke about on Friday after my admission, but I don't give him anything—not that there really is anything, but I like to keep things mysterious because I can see it's driving him crazy.

We wander hand in hand, looking at everything Borough Market has to offer for our picnic.

If you'd asked me what I thought our date was going to consist of, this wasn't it. To start with, I'd got in my head that he'd take us out of town like he used to. I know we're not hiding anymore—well, he's not—but I still didn't think we'd stay in London.

"Happy?" he asks once he tucks our latest purchase into his bag.

"Yeah, I think we've got enough to feed the five thousand."

"You did say you were hungry."

"I am, but we have a lot."

"It can be dinner too," he says with a smirk.

"Am I still going to have to put up with you by that time?"

"Cheeky. You're not getting rid of me that easily. This picnic is only the beginning of my plans for you today, Piper."

My stomach somersaults and desire pools in my core.

We walk out of the market, the sun making me squint before Dawson directs us to a park where he pulls out a picnic basket and other useful supplies like plates, cups, knives and forks.

Amazed by his level of planning, I take a seat and wait for him to join me.

"I'm impressed," I say as he starts laying out the food we purchased.

"It's just a picnic. I wanted to do something that would give us time to talk."

I swallow nervously. I know there's still so much we haven't touched on since we reconnected, but I've been quite happy living in ignorant bliss. Although I can't deny that his confession that he's not part of the Royal Reapers helped me breathe a little easier.

"Help yourself," he says once everything is laid out before me.

"It looks so good. And that bread smells incredible."

We both dig in, enjoying the fresh, local, and homemade delights we'd picked up.

We eat in silence, and although it's comfortable, as the time creeps on I can feel the tension building.

He tips back his small glass of red wine before dropping down so he's lying on his side and resting on his elbow.

"Piper, I need you to be honest with me about a few things."

"I'll tell you anything you need to know, Dawson. I'm not hiding anything."

"Good." He nods for a second as he forms his first question. "Why'd you do it?"

I blow out a long breath. I knew he was going to start there. "Because my dad left me no choice."

"What did he want to know?"

"I don't know the details, only what I overheard. You know as well as I do that club intel was never shared with minors, Prez's kid or not." He nods, so I continue. "He thought your dad was doing something illegal. I have no idea what; drugs, guns, I don't know. But he was desperate to expose whatever it was and bring him down. I don't need to tell you how jealous he was. The Reapers were growing so much faster than the Brotherhood and he was obsessed with putting a stop to it. It was... stupid. A war he was never going to win, but one he thought was a good idea, nonetheless.

"I didn't want to do it. I refused. Argued. The last thing I wanted was to put myself in the middle of your family and the battle between our fathers, but he left me little choice."

"Did he... did he threaten you?"

"The details don't matter."

"Piper," he growls. "I need you to tell me everything."

My stomach knots. I haven't talked about this with anyone, and Dawson is the last person I want to know.

"He threatened to make me earn my keep at the club."

Dawson's eyes widen. He knows what goes on at MC clubhouses with the women. It is not pretty. His jaw pops and the tendons in his neck strain.

"It didn't happen."

"No, you took the other option."

"What choice did I have?" He shrugs. I know he understands this on some level.

"What if I didn't fall for you?"

"I honestly have no idea. I think Dad was just hoping that you were a red-blooded teenager and would go for any girl who showed an interest."

"I guess he was right. Only you weren't just any girl, were you?"

"You should have turned me away."

"Never."

"We never should have happened, we both knew that. I might have been placed in the situation, but you didn't need to accept it."

Moving the remains of our lunch out of the way, I lay down in front of him and stare up at the passing clouds.

"How was I meant to resist, baby girl? You walked into my life and turned my world upside down." His large hand curls around my waist and tugs me closer so the length of our bodies press together.

"You did mine, too. I thought I'd just do what I needed to, find out something my dad could use and get on with my life. I never expected to fall in lov—"

"You and me both, baby." His fingers slip under the hem of my t-shirt, his palm burning my skin and making my entire body tingle with desire.

"How did your dad find out?" I ask. It's my turn to get some answers.

"Turned out you weren't the only one with suspicions. Dad set one of his boys trailing your father. He saw the two of us together, reported back, and everything unravelled from there."

"Jesus," I sigh, watching one of the fluffy white clouds float through the sky. "Dad knew you were going to strike.

Someone leaked false information. He thought you were coming the next morning. He sent me away, and he and Mum were going to leave first thing the next day before the Reapers turned up. Only, that's not how it played out."

"I'm sorry you got dragged into it all."

"I guess I should just be glad Dad sent me away when he did."

"Don't," he warns. "For as much as I hated you back then, I never would have wished that on you."

"I almost reached out to you so many times after I left. I missed you so much. It felt like I'd ripped my heart out and left it in London."

"Where did you go?"

"Mum had a childhood friend who'd moved to Cornwall. She took me in. Lived in this tiny, quiet village in a cute little cottage. I hated it. I craved to be back in the city with the noise and the people. I went to the local college, finished my A-Levels, and then I went to university in Exeter. What about you?"

"I got drunk. Very, very drunk. I fucked anyone with a heartbeat and generally checked out on life for quite a long time." His admission makes my chest ache. "I didn't know how to cope, thinking you'd burned in that house. I hated you so much, yet I loved you just as fiercely. I didn't know which way was up."

"What do you think you'd have done if I did reach out?" I ask, trying to decide if I'd done the right thing or not.

"I don't know. At the beginning, I probably would have come and killed you myself. But as time went on, I was so lonely. Miserable. I probably would have been happy, I guess."

"Do you think you'll ever forgive me?"

"Baby girl," he breathes, cupping my face so I have no choice but to turn to look at him. "I already have."

He leans forward and my breath catches. Is this it? Is he finally going to kiss me?

My eyes flutter closed as his breath washes over my face.

"Dawson," I half-moan, half-beg when the heat of his lips hits me. He pauses for a beat before they brush across mine.

Oh God.

It's so gentle. So... opposite to everything else we've done together.

My heart beats erratically in my chest as I reach out and thread my fingers through his hair, although I don't pull him closer. I need him to do this of his own accord, because he's finished battling whatever inner war has stopped him so far.

"Piper," he whispers, his voice full of awe, "it was always you."

I gasp and he uses it to his advantage, plunging his tongue past my lips.

I greedily suck it into my mouth and brush mine against it.

His kiss starts out gentle, as if he's showing me just how true those last few words were, but then he rolls his weight onto me and things turn up a notch or two. His hand drops down my body before he cups my breasts, making my back arch from the blanket. It's entirely too erotic to be happening in a public park, but I really can't bring myself to care as his tongue continues to caress mine before biting down and sending a bolt of lust between my legs.

My nails scratch down his back and he stills, the bite of pain a reality check.

"We need to stop before I fuck you right here for everyone to watch." He presses his forehead to mine, his short, sharp breaths fanning my face.

"Almost as romantic as what you said at the beginning," I murmur, my voice deep with lust.

He laughs, and it makes my chest constrict.

"You know me. I have a way with words."

"I particularly like your dirty ones."

"That's good, because right now I have so many I want to say to you." He pulls my hip into him and rubs his length against me. "I need you so fucking bad, baby girl."

"Maybe we should get out of here then? I happen to know a flat that's empty right now." He groans, dropping his face into the crook of my neck.

"I knew kissing you would be dangerous."

"Dangerous how?" I ask, unable to wipe the smile from my face.

"Because I knew once I did it, I'd never want to stop."

"I don't have a problem with that. Let's go home and we can spend the rest of the day doing just that. It'll be like we're kids again."

"As incredible as that sounds, I've got other plans for the rest of the day."

"Oh?"

He pulls his head up and looks down at me, his eyes twinkling in delight.

"What you said earlier about us being married with kids if none of that bullshit happened... did you really mean that?"

I swallow nervously. It was an off the cuff comment, but I can't deny it was true. I might have had an ulterior motive back then, but what I felt for Dawson was real. The dreams I had for the future were real.

"Yeah, I meant every word."

He nods, lost deep in his thoughts. "You fancy finding out what I really do for a living?"

"Yes," I squeal, sitting bolt upright, excited to learn something new about the man my boy has turned into.

"Let's pack up then and I'll take you there... if you're brave enough."

"Any heights involved?"

He thinks for a moment. "You should be okay. But there is one thing..." I quirk a brow at him. "How high is your pain threshold?"

"Okay, now I'm worried."

Not long later, we're back on Dawson's bike and flying through the city. I have no clue where he's taking me, although I can't deny that his question about my pain threshold is playing on my mind somewhat. I wrack my brain to come up with the answer, but when he pulls to a stop outside of a tattoo studio on the other side of town, I feel stupid for not figuring it out. He's covered in enough evidence, after all.

Excitement zips through my veins as I think about what's to come in the next few hours.

I'd like to say that he's not crazy enough to get me under the needle on our first official date, but this is Dawson we're talking about.

Shaking my head, I climb off the bike and unclip the helmet.

"So this is what you do, then?" I ask, looking up at the pink neon Rebel Ink sign that hangs over the front of the building.

"It is. Are you ready? My chair is waiting for its client."

"You're really going to do this?"

"Yes," he states, taking my hand and walking toward the building.

All of the lights are on, and as we push inside, there are a couple of clients waiting on the sofas and a woman sitting behind the reception desk.

"Welcome to Rebel Ink, how can—oooooh," she sings once she's dragged her eyes up from whatever she was focusing on. "D, how nice to see you on your day off. And who is this?" she asks, glancing down at our joined hands

"Biff, this is Piper. Piper, this is Biff."

"It's so nice to meet you," I say genuinely, because the way she's studying Dawson right now makes me think they're somewhat close. I ignore the trickle of jealousy that threatens to erupt. They're colleagues; I'm sure they're just friends.

"You too. I'd like to say I've heard loads about you, but this one keeps things close to his chest." She narrows her eyes at Dawson, and I laugh. Yeah, she does know him fairly well.

"I knew this was a bad idea."

"No, no. You did the right thing. I hope you're prepared to meet everyone else, Piper."

"They can't be as scary as this one. I'm sure I'll be fine." Biff throws her head back and laughs. I'm not sure if it's because the others really are scary or if she thinks I'm lying. I'm not. Even knowing who our fathers are—were—and what they're capable of, Dawson still scares me more than anyone because he has too much power. He owns my heart—always has, which means he's capable of breaking me like no other.

"Oh, just you wait. They're going to love you."

I swallow nervously as Dawson tugs me toward a small hallway.

"You two want coffees or anything?"

"No, we're good, thanks. Probably best if you just leave us to it." My cheeks heat at the silent meaning in his words.

"You got it. My lips are sealed."

"Appreciated."

"So," I say, following him into a room that is just so... him that it takes my breath away. Everything is dark and leather. My entire body tingles as if I'm surrounded by him—well, I am, despite the fact that he's physically on the other side of the room. "You're an artist."

"Yeah, I'm surprised you didn't guess."

"Me too, to be honest. Seems pretty obvious now I'm here." I stare at the walls that display his work. "These are stunning. I knew you could draw but... wow."

"Thanks. After you... left, it was the only thing that would help. I used to sketch for hours when I wasn't drunk or high. Finally, I enrolled in art school and the guy who owned this place back then gave me a lucky break. I've never looked back."

"Who owns it now?" I ask, half expecting him to say that he does.

"Zach, Biff's other half. There are four of us who work here. Biff and my boy Spike's girl are training." I nod, continuing to take in his work.

Each and every single piece tells me something about him. I reach out and run my fingertip over a couple of the more poignant, heart-breaking designs. Until I come to a portrait of a girl.

"Holy shit," I breathe.

"I never could quite let you go." His heat burns my

back as he comes to stand behind me and wraps his arm around my waist.

"It's almost like a photograph." I stare in awe. He's captured every single one of my features.

"I used to draw you while you were sleeping, did you know that?"

I shake my head, too engrossed by the sketch to force out words. "You always looked so beautiful, so peaceful, yet tormented all at the same time."

"Now you understand why," I murmur. "I was falling in love with you but knew I was going to break your heart and in turn mine. I had no idea when my father was going to pull the plug, but I knew it had to happen at some point. It was either that or we get caught."

"I'm sorry he put you through that."

"Me too, but I often find it hard to hate him for it." He stills behind me. "He brought me you, Dawson. Despite the fact that it was based on a lie, you have always been the sole most important thing that ever happened to me. I might have wished for it to be on different terms, but I could never regret the time we had together."

I spin in his arms and look up at him, needing him to know that I mean every word I'm saying.

"You taught me so much." Sliding my palm up his chest, I wrap it around the back of his neck and pull his brow down to mine. "You taught me how to love. You taught me what true happiness was."

His breath catches as we stand staring at each other. My lips twitch to kiss him, to drown in him, but I still want him to take the lead on that. It seems like such a big deal to him.

"Get on the chair, baby girl."

My stomach explodes with nerves.

He stares at me for another few seconds, his eyes getting darker, hungrier until I do as I'm told and break our connection.

I climb up on his black leather chair and wait. He keeps his back to me for a few moments, as if he needs to compose himself, before he turns on me and stalks over. I can't help thinking that I'm his prey right now with his slow, haunting movements.

He lowers himself to a wheelie stool and moves closer.

"W-what are you going to do?" I stutter, my nerves getting the better of me.

"I've got so many ideas flying around my head," he admits.

"O-okay. I don't want anything big," I blurt, and he looks up at me with a raised brow.

"Oh, baby girl. I have it on good authority that you're very good with... big things."

"Yeah, two very different things there, Dawson." Although as I say the words, I wonder if he's right. Those couple of times we've been together, I thought they were about revenge, about him hurting me. Now I'm wondering if really he was claiming me, much like he's about to do by branding my skin.

"If you say so."

He pushes his hand into his jeans pocket and pulls something out.

"You remember this?"

I gasp as he holds his finger up and I find a very familiar black leather bracelet dangling from it. "I can't believe you still have this."

Gently, I take the piece of jewellery from him and hold it in front of me. We'd bought matching ones when we'd gone out of town so we could be together.

The piece itself is simple, just a piece of leather with an infinity charm sitting in the middle, but the meaning behind it is so much stronger.

I rub my thumb over the worn leather.

"I've got everything from our time together."

Emotion clogs my throat and tears burn the backs of my eyes.

"I've still got mine too," I force out.

His eyes find mine and something shifts between us. With that one look, any doubt or fear I had about his intentions and where this is going vanish, because I realise that I don't care. This could last two weeks, two years, or forever, and I could never regret having a second chance with him, no matter what the consequences might be.

"Do it," I say. "Whatever's in your head. Do it."

"You have no idea what you're asking for, baby girl."

"Maybe not. But I'm willing to find out."

"Fuck," he barks, startling me a little. "You're fucking perfect."

His eyes drop from mine and trail down my body. It heats under his stare, and I start to wish I wasn't here just for some ink.

"Anywhere you've always wanted one?" I shake my head. Like everyone I'm sure, I've thought about it over the years, but I've never been brave enough or come up with anything meaningful enough to permanently mark my skin with. But being here right now, I already know that anything that Dawson creates will mean the world to me.

"Your choice." The smile that curls at his lips would knock me on my arse if I weren't already sitting down.

He wheels himself to the end of the chair and reaches for my waistband.

I swallow the desire that threatens to bubble at the thought of him undressing me.

He pops the button open before I lift up to help him pull them over my hips. He peels the fabric down my legs, stopping to tug my boots off and drop them to the floor, then pulls my jeans from my feet.

He chuckles when he sees the little motorbikes on my socks, but he doesn't allow them to stay and they join my jeans on the floor.

"Now, that's what I'm talking about." He runs his eyes up my bare legs until he hits the lace covering me. Sitting forward, I pull off my jacket, suddenly too hot to stand having it on.

Reaching down, he rearranges himself, his eyes still locked on me.

"I really hope you don't have this reaction to all your clients."

"Only you, baby girl."

"Good to know."

"I should probably admit that I mostly work on ugly MC guys," he says with a laugh, but it cuts off as I tense. "Don't worry. It's my day off, and I know what clients the guys have. I wouldn't put you in that situation."

I nod at him, feeling myself relax at his words.

"So, what's the plan?"

"You want to see?"

"You've already drawn it?"

"Of course I have. Many times."

My lips part to respond, but I'm too shocked to say anything.

Standing, he leaves me sitting there speechless while he gets himself ready.

I don't come back to myself until he snaps some gloves on and settles beside me, wiping the skin of my thigh clean.

"H-here?"

"Yep."

"Is it... is it big?"

"It can be," he says cryptically. "But we'll start small and we can add to it if you wish.

"O-okay."

"Do you trust me, Piper?"

"I... I do. With my life."

He smiles for a beat before reaching out and making me squeal when he flattens the chair to a bed in one swift move.

"A little warning would have been nice," I grumble, my heart pounding in my chest.

"And ruin the element of surprise? Never. You ready?"

"Aren't you going to trace the design out or something?" The reality is that my knowledge of tattoo artists is limited to TV shows, so I don't really know what I'm talking about.

"I thought you trusted me." He winks before turning his machine on.

The ominous buzz fills the room and my body trembles.

"This is going to hurt, isn't it?"

"It's nothing you can't handle, baby."

I gasp the second the needle hits my skin.

My eyes lock on the patch of skin he's marking, unable to look anywhere else but the artist at work.

"It's not that bad," I admit after a few minutes.

"That's good, baby, because you've got a long way to go yet. Relax, just let me do my thing."

As much as I want to watch him, my eyes are heavy despite the pain radiating from his actions. I rest my head back and close my eyes.

I don't fall asleep—at least, I'm pretty sure I don't—but equally, I don't have any idea of how much time has passed when the buzzing stops and he wipes at my skin one last time.

"All done. You can look now."

Ripping my eyes open, I stare up at the ceiling for a beat. I'd be lying if I said I wasn't trying to imagine what he might have been inking on my skin. Thoughts of him getting his revenge on me almost had me looking down to ensure he wasn't writing 'traitor' or something equally as awful down my thigh.

I blow out a breath and swallow down some courage to look at his handiwork.

"Oh my God," I gasp, my hand coming up to cover my gawping mouth.

19

DAWSON

It's been years since I've felt this nervous about what my client might think of my work, but as I sit there staring at Piper, who gazes down at her thigh with her eyes wide and her hand covering what I hope is a happy-shocked mouth, my hands actually tremble.

"Dawson," she breathes after long, agonising seconds, "it's... it's... unbelievable."

The two of us stare down at the ink. I've been drawing the Ferris wheel design for years. Back in the months following what I thought was her death, I filled a sketchbook with drawings I did for her. I had no idea at the time that they would turn into artwork I wanted to paint on her skin. I never thought I'd get the chance.

The lines of the Ferris wheel are black, but it's surrounded by an explosion of colour, roses, and infinity symbols, along with a few other things I remember from our time together. It's only a part of the design I have for her. I could cover her entire body with images that remind me of her, but I'm happy to at least have started. It might take her a while to find it, but nestled in with all the ink is my name. Because she is mine. No matter what happens from here on out, she belongs to me. She always has and always will.

"I can't stop looking at it," she whispers, her hand hovering over it as if she wants to trace the lines.

"You like it?"

"Are you kidding? It's incredible."

When she finally lifts her eyes to mine, they're full of tears.

"Dawson," she sobs, lifting her arms for me.

Unable to resist, I stand and lean over her and press my lips to hers.

I knew that kissing her would only fuel my addiction, and it seems I was right. From the moment I brushed my lips against hers in that park, doing it again is all I've been able to think about. Well, that and a few other things.

Kissing across her jaw, I suck lightly on the soft skin of her neck, smiling when I find that she once again smells like Love Hearts.

"God, Dawson," she moans as I kiss down her chest. She's still wearing her t-shirt, but the V is low enough to give me a taste of what she's hiding beneath.

I lick over the swell of her breast and pull the fabric aside to get more of her.

One hand cups her other breast and I squeeze hard, making her cry out.

"You need to be quiet, baby girl."

"Oh God," she moans as I pull the fabric and lace of her bra away from her nipple, sucking it into my mouth. "Fuck."

"Hmmm... there's an idea." The vibration of my voice makes her squirm on my chair. I release her with a pop. "You need more, baby girl?"

Pushing her shirt up, I kiss down her stomach, dipping my tongue into her navel before going lower.

"Dawson, you can't—"

"Says who? This is my room, I get to make the rules."

"Please tell me you don't do this often."

"Never, Piper. No one has ever got off on this chair before."

"G-good."

"I'm pretty sure I'm never going to be able to look at it again the same though, after this."

Wrapping my hands around her ankles, I lift them, plant her feet on the edge, and push her thighs wide, careful of her new ink.

I hook my finger inside her lace knickers and pull them to the side, revealing what I want the most.

"Baby girl, look how wet you are for me."

Her pussy glistens in the harsh electric light above us and makes my mouth water.

"Dawson, please," she begs as I trail a finger through her wetness, dipping it into her just enough to drive her insane.

"Fuck, you make me crazy, baby girl."

I dive for her, licking from her entrance right up to her clit. I circle it a few times as she writhes against me.

"Soon," I murmur, replacing my tongue with my finger. "I'm going to pierce you... right... here." I press my finger to where it would sit.

"Oh fuck."

"You want that, baby?"

"Yes, Dawson. Anything."

A smile pulls at my lips at the thought of teasing it with my tongue, knowing that I'm the only one who knows it exists.

"Soon, baby. Right now, I need you in full working condition."

Dropping lower, I plunge my tongue inside her and pinch her clit. She cries out before slamming her hand over her mouth in an attempt to keep it down.

In seconds she falls over the edge as her thighs clamp me in place.

When she finally releases me, I sit up, wipe my mouth with the back of my hand and stare down at her. Her legs have fallen limp over the edges of the chair and her chest is heaving with exertion.

"You taste like heaven, baby girl."

"Hmm..." Her eyes drop down my body to where my cock is trying to punch through my jeans. "I'm still waiting to find out just how you taste these days."

"We should get out of here, and maybe I'll let you find out."

She looks around the room, but if she's trying to see outside, she'll be shit out of luck.

"What time is it?"

"Late."

"Jesus, how long have I been lying here?"

I pull my phone from my pocket. "About five hours."

"Five hours?"

"Let me wrap you up and we'll get out of here."

"Okay," she agrees, her eyes following me around the room as I tidy up after myself and grab what I need.

"You're not going to be able to wear your jeans, they're too tight," I tell her after finishing up.

"Err... I can hardly walk out of here in my knickers, Dawson."

"The guys have seen worse, I can assure you."

"Hey," she complains, swatting my shoulder.

"I'll see if Biff has anything you can borrow."

"N-no, I don't want—"

"It won't be an issue. Just wait here."

I sit the chair up, making it easier for her to get up and stretch her legs and then slip from the room, it seems at exactly the same time Biff emerges from Zach's.

"Have fun in there?" she asks me with a knowing wink.

"She wasn't quiet enough, huh?"

"Not even close, D. Tell me you got some ink on her first." She chuckles as I follow her down to reception.

"I did, which is why I need a favour."

"Shoot," she says, tidying up her desk, ready to close for the night.

"She can't wear her jeans, they're too tight. You got something she can borrow?"

Biff turns to me and places her hand on her hip, assessing me.

"On one condition."

"Oh?" Biff has never asked anything of me before, so this makes me very curious.

"It's Kas's birthday. We're all going out. You and your girl agree to come, and I'll sort her out with something suitable."

I want to say no, to take Piper home and finish what we just started, but there's something about the idea of us hanging out with my friends that just feels right.

Before I know what I'm doing, I've agreed. "We're only coming for food, though. She's got work tomorrow."

"Oh yeah, because that's the reason you don't want to spend all night with us."

She's off down the corridor to collect my girl before I have a chance to say anything.

They're deep in conversation when I join them.

Piper looks at me, concern filling her features.

"It's okay. You go. I'll tidy up and wait for you in reception. Are the others nearly finished?" I ask Biff.

"Yep, all done. Your girl here is our final client of the night. I don't think the others enjoyed their time quite as much, mind you."

Piper's face flushes red. "Don't worry, girl. We've all been there."

"My ears," I complain, walking around them to my desk.

"Pfft." I don't need to look at Biff to know she's rolling her eyes at me. "Come on, I think I've got the perfect thing for you."

I turn and watch them both leave, my eyes locking on Piper's almost bare arse in her tiny knickers. Reaching down, I once again rearrange myself. This is going to be the longest night ever.

When I look back up, she's smiling at me over her shoulder. She blows me a kiss before disappearing with Biff.

Have I just made a massive mistake?

Ten minutes later, I'm alone in reception, waiting for everyone else to join me.

"Ah, look who's here," Titch announces as he, Spike and Kas emerge from their rooms. "And to think, I assumed it was Spike giving the birthday girl here a special present. Rumour has it, D has a girl."

"Fuck off," I grunt. But all he does is smile. He is way too amused by this right now.

"He even took her on a date," Kas helpfully adds, making me groan.

"Whoa, so where is the brave woman who's trying to tame our boy here?" Titch asks.

"She's upstairs with Biff."

Titch's brows pull together as he drops to the sofa in front of me.

"I inked her. She needs to wear something different."

"You inked your girl? Sweet. Danni still won't let me anywhere fucking near her."

"She's pregnant with your kid, man. Give her a break."

"I know, but the thought of that belly and my ink... Fuck. I get hard just thinking about it."

"Okay, well that's great. I'm just gonna..." Kas nods toward the door that leads to Zach and Biff's flat.

"You fucking idiot, you scared her off," I mutter to Titch.

"Fuck off," Spike says, sitting beside me. "It'll take more than that. She's a bad-arse, remember?"

"We're not likely to forget anytime soon, don't worry."

"So where is Danni, anyway? She's coming, right?"

"Yeah, meeting us there. She's just called an Uber. You for real got a girl?" Titch asks, still seemingly flabbergasted by the idea.

"Seems that way."

"I didn't think I would see the day. You've always been so hung up on..." I shoot him a death glare, but I'm too late. Spike heard.

"Wait, D's been hung up on a girl all this time, and I didn't know?"

"Fucking hell, Titch."

"Sorry, man." He holds his hands up in surrender, but clearly he isn't really sorry, because he continues to run his mouth. "D has a childhood sweetheart. She broke his tender little heart and he's never got over it."

"How the fuck did I not know this?"

"It's not something I go around telling everyone

about." Titch only knows because he accidentally found himself in the middle of the Reapers world when he naïvely started fighting for Mickey all those years ago.

"So who is she? How'd you meet her? Give us all the juicy deets," Titch says, wiggling his brows and rubbing his hands together.

Thankfully, footsteps sound out from the flat, and in only a few seconds the girls emerge, Kas dressed as she was previously, Biff now in a pink dress that matches her hair, and my girl... fuck me.

My eyes run the length of her in a little black dress that does insane things to her rack and shows off every inch of her figure, along with a good portion of her new ink.

"Take her back up, she can't wear that in public," I say, standing from the sofa.

"See, I told you he'd love it." Biff laughs. "We're leaving."

My eyes hold Piper's in warning, but all she does is smile at me.

She steps forward and places her hands on my shoulders.

"All of this is your fault you know." She quirks a brow at me and smiles shyly.

"You are in so much shit when we get back to your flat."

"I know, I can't wait."

"D, man, you gonna introduce us to your gorgeous girl or what?"

Turning back to the guys, I reluctantly pull Piper from my side, allowing them to see her.

"Titch, Spike... Zach," I say with a tilt of my chin when he emerges from his room. "This is Piper."

Spike and Zach both smile at her and say hello, but as I feared, Titch's chin drops.

Motherfucker. I'd hoped he'd forgotten the name. It was years ago I reluctantly told him snippets of the story one night when we'd both been drinking, and I got a little more emotional than I usually would, seeing as it was the anniversary of her death. I even showed him a picture, a move that I'm now seriously regretting.

Everyone aside from the two of us seems to miss Titch's reaction, because they all start moving toward the door and Biff kills the lights.

"He knows who I am," Piper whispers beside me.

"He knows bits. And he thinks you're dead, so you can understand his shock."

"I guess, but... is he..."

"Titch isn't a threat, baby girl. Well, unless you fancy joining the Circuit and getting in a ring with him."

"Um... no, I think I'll pass, thanks."

Running my hand down her back, I squeeze her arse and push her forward.

Titch waits until I pass him to step up to me.

"I thought she was fucking dead, man," he snaps, his shock evident in his voice.

"You and me both. I need you to keep it zipped. We'll talk, okay?"

"Yeah, yeah. Whatever you need. But fuck, man. Is this a good idea?" His loyalty makes me smile.

"Fuck knows, but I need her."

"I get that. But we fucking need you too."

———

The Pear Tree isn't the most obvious of places to celebrate a birthday, but then I guess Kas isn't exactly your average kind of girl, and if this is what she wants then I'm all for it.

We find our normal booth. Danni is already waiting for us, and we have to pull up two chairs at the end seeing as our group keeps growing.

Our arses have barely touched the leather seats when a tray of drinks appears in front of us. We all take ours before Piper adds her order.

"Food will be right out."

"Thanks, man," Spike says as the server backs away from our table.

"So, D. A little birdie told me that you took your girl out on a date today. Fancy telling us how that ended with dinner with this bunch of motherfuckers?" Spike asks.

I chuckle, feeling at home around my family. I look to my left and pull Piper into my side where she belongs.

A lot of shit might be up in the air between the two of us, but I can't deny that this doesn't feel totally natural right now.

"He took me to Borough Market and we had a picnic in the park."

The girls swoon as the guys look at me like I've grown a second head.

"What? I can be romantic," I argue.

"How long have you been seeing each other?" Zach adds.

"I happened to find her by chance two weeks ago."

"I work at the school Emmie has started at."

They all nod before everyone's attention is captured by the plates and platters of food that descends on our table. My stomach rumbles, reminding me just how long ago it was we had our picnic, and I waste no time in digging into the tapas Spike pre-ordered.

"Umm... this is amazing," Piper mumbles around a piece of chorizo.

"Eat up, baby girl, you're going to need some energy for when I get you alone again."

———

"I'm just going to pop to the ladies' before we go," Piper says, nudging me to scoot out of the booth to allow her out.

"I'll come with," Biff says, followed by Kas and Danni.

We all watch as they make their way through the bar.

"What the fuck is it with chicks pissing together?" Titch asks, his eyes locked on his wife's arse.

"Fuck knows, but I need a slash too."

I don't realise anyone is following me until the door to the men's doesn't immediately close behind me.

"So, she looks good for a dead woman," Titch says.

"Funny that, I thought the same thing," I mutter as I turn my back on him.

"Do your father or Cruz know she's alive?"

"No, and I'd really appreciate it if you didn't go and shout it from the rooftops."

"Of course not. I'm just... what the hell are you playing at, D?"

"I'm not playing at anything." The lie tastes bitter on my tongue, although I'm starting to wonder if it really is a lie, seeing as this thing between us is moving faster and getting more serious than I ever intended.

"You could end up getting both of you killed."

"It won't come to that," I assure him.

"How do you know that?"

"I just do, okay?"

When I turn around, I find his narrowed gaze trained on me.

"You can't hide her forever, and if this is serious—"

"It is," I say with more certainty than I should, but I can't help it. Everything I used to feel for Piper is rushing back faster than I can control.

"Then you're going to have to introduce her to your old man at some point."

"I'll worry about that when the time comes. Right now, I'm just enjoying the fact that I've got my girl back. And I'd appreciate it if you could at least pretend to be happy for me."

"Fuck, D, I am happy. I'm fucking stoked for you. But I also would like you both to be alive enough to fucking enjoy it."

"I've got it covered."

I wash my hands and turn to face him once more.

"You don't need to lose sleep over it. I know what I'm doing."

"Do you?"

I flip him off as I walk out and head back to the table.

"You ready to go, baby?" I whisper in Piper's ear when she emerges with the others a minute after I get back.

"I sure am. It was nice to meet you all," she says politely to everyone. "And happy birthday again," she says to Kas.

They all say their goodbyes, and in only seconds I have her pulled into my side and walking out to the street.

She shivers the second the cool air hits us and pulls her jacket tighter around herself.

"You want me to call a car?" I offer. "I can pick up my bike tomorrow."

"No, I'll be fine. It's not far."

We walk up to my bike, and as I hand over her helmet I catch sight of her bare legs and realise my mistake.

"You can't ride behind me like that."

"Why not?"

"Because I won't be able to focus, knowing that every motherfucker is looking at your legs."

"S'all good, caveman. You're the only one who's going to be in my bed within the hour."

"But—"

She cuts off my argument by hopping up on my bike and spreading her legs to allow me space.

It might be fairly dark out, but that doesn't mean I can't see the scrap of lace covering her pussy. She leans back on the handles and waits for me to gather myself.

"Feel free to take a photo," she shouts through her helmet.

"One day, baby girl, I'm going to take you up on that offer. Right before I fuck you over this thing."

She squirms on the seat and I bite down on my bottom lip as I try to stop myself from stripping her naked and doing that right now.

"Get the fuck on the bike, Dawson. I won't wait forever."

Her warning snaps me from my trance and I throw my leg over, just about managing to miss her, and bring the engine to life.

With her heat burning into me and the promise of what's to come, I race toward her flat faster than I should.

By the time I let her off, her chest is heaving and her eyes are dark and hungry.

I lock up before taking her hand and leading her toward the entrance.

I go for the stairs like the last time I was here, and she happily follows.

"Everything okay?" she asks when I pull my phone from my pocket and start tapping out a message.

"Yeah, just checking in on Emmie. Hopefully she won't respond because she's already sleeping."

"She's a good kid."

"She is, despite her mother's best intentions."

"She's too headstrong to be influenced by others. She knows her own mind."

"Tell me about it," I mutter, thinking of the previous few conversations we've had.

"Okay, enough about your daughter," she says, pressing her back against her door and pushing it open.

My eyes run down the length of her. She's unzipped her jacket, allowing me to see her cleavage that I swear is bigger than before. I drop down her waist and to her hips. Her dress is sitting dangerously high on her thighs, exposing her new ink, then down her legs to her biker boots.

Stepping forward, I lift her into my arms, pull her from the door, and kick it closed behind me.

"Fuck, I need to be inside you."

"Dawson," she groans against my neck as she grazes her teeth down my exposed skin.

The second we're inside her bedroom, I throw her on the bed and start stripping out of my clothes.

She sits up on her elbows and watches me as I lose each item of clothing.

"Get on the edge of the bed," I demand as I take myself

in hand, stroking up and down a few times and she settles before me.

Her mouth is right where I want it and her heated eyes stare up at me, begging me to take what I need.

Stepping forward, I run the tip over her lip, coating them in the precum that's already beading at my slit.

"Open," I demand, pushing forward and slipping past her lips before she has a chance to move.

The heat of her mouth burns my skin, and my teeth grind.

"Fuck," I bark, threading my hands into her hair and holding her still.

I allow her a couple of minutes to take control before my fingers tighten and I take over, pulling her forward until I hit the back of her throat.

I stare down at her; the sight of her dark red lips around my shaft and tears filling her eyes has my release surging forward faster than I'm ready for.

"I'm gonna come down your throat, baby girl. You feel so good."

My hips start to thrust as I begin to lose control, but other than a couple of gags she takes it all, sucking me down like a champ.

"Fuck, Piper. Your mouth, fuck," I chant as my balls draw up. "FUCK," I growl as my cock jerks.

20

PIPER

Tears coat my cheeks and I fight the need to gag again at his size. My chest burns with my need for air, but I don't rush. I swallow everything he has as he holds me still, riding out his high.

I've never felt as powerful as I do in this moment as he stares down at me, his eyes black with lust.

"Fuck, that was good."

He lifts me from my seat on the edge of my bed and slams his lips on mine. He must be able to taste himself, but his kiss doesn't falter. His tongue sweeps past my lips, seeking mine and sucking it into his mouth.

He bites lightly and I shudder in his hold.

His lips rip from mine in favour of my neck. He kisses, sucks, nips all the way down to the fabric covering my breasts.

His fingers wrap around the straps over my shoulders and he pulls them down, dragging the dress down my body.

My breasts spill free, and he hungrily sucks one into his hot mouth while his hand palms the other.

"Dawson," I moan as my clit continues to throb and heat pools between my thighs.

"Are you wet for me again, baby girl?" His kisses drop down my belly until he's on his knees before me. It's a sight I don't think I'll ever forget: this strong, powerful man on his knees as if I hold all the power.

"Yes." My answer is simple and straight to the point.

He hisses through his teeth before reaching for my knickers and ripping them down my legs. He knocks my boots off my feet before throwing the scrap of lace over his shoulder, leaving me bare for him.

One second I'm on my feet, the next I'm flying through the air until I land on the mattress with an oomph.

In a beat, my thighs are spread as wide as they'll go and he's feasting on me once more while I pull at his hair in my attempt to get him closer.

I was already halfway to release from just sucking him off, so the second he pushes two fingers inside me and expertly locates my g-spot, I fall over the edge with a scream.

"Oh my God, that was intense," I manage to get out between my heaving breaths.

"That was nothing, baby girl. We've got a long night ahead of us yet."

My sensible side wants to remind me it's a school night, but the second he crawls over me, the evidence of my release glistening on his face, I forget all about reality and just focus on this, something I never thought I'd get to have or experience ever again.

He wipes his mouth before settling between my thighs and dropping his lips to mine.

"I can't get enough of you, baby girl."

"The feeling is entirely mutual."

Our hands are everywhere as we kiss each other as if it might be the last time again.

Fuck, I missed this. I missed him.

"Dawson," I moan when he pulls back for a second to catch his breath. "I need you."

Reaching down between our bodies, he takes himself in hand and guides the head of his cock to my entrance.

"Anything, baby girl. You can have anything."

He pushes inside me and we both moan, swamped by the sensation of us connecting once more.

It's mind-blowing, all-consuming. Just fucking unbelievable.

"You, D. I just need you."

He drops his forearms to the mattress at either side of my head and stares deep into my eyes, his cock barely moving inside me and driving me insane.

His eyes bounce between mine, and I'm not sure if he's trying to read something within them, or if he's trying to make some kind of decision.

"Daw—"

"Marry me?"

My eyes widen as my entire body tenses.

"W-what?"

He lowers down so our lips brush, but his eyes never drop from mine.

"I asked you to marry me, baby girl."

"I-I thought that was what you said," I whisper, totally shocked by this turn of events.

"We've wasted too much time apart already. We both know this is meant to be. I loved you seventeen years ago, and nothing has changed for me, Piper. Has it for you?"

I shake my head, struggling to form words. He's serious. He really did just ask me to marry him... while he's inside me. We'll have to come up with a new story to tell our grandkids one day.

The second I register that thought, I start laughing.

"What's so funny? This isn't a joke, Piper." There's an edge to his voice that cuts off my moment of madness.

"I know," I say, brushing my fingers through his hair, "I was just thinking about our grandkids."

"And here I was thinking I was the one rushing things. So what do you say? Shall we make things right, how they always should have been?"

People will probably tell me that I'm utterly insane, and to be fair I might be... but also, they may never have met their soulmate. I didn't need to meet Dawson again to know that he's mine. That first day I forced myself into his life, I knew there was something different about him. I knew the connection we shared was special. I just didn't know how to deal with that on top of the situation I was already in. Maybe both of us could have handled everything differently; who knows. Right now, who cares?

"Yes," I blurt out.

"Yes?" he repeats, the corners of his lips twitching up into what I'm sure will be a mind-blowing smile.

"Yes, Dawson. Let's make things right. Yes, I'll marry you."

His lips crash to mine in a bruising kiss as his hips start to move, reminding me that we're still connected in the most intimate of ways.

Goose bumps race across my skin as I replay the past minute or two in my head.

I just agreed to marry Dawson freaking Ramsey.

I laugh once again, forcing him to pull his lips from mine. When I drag my eyes open, I find him staring down at me with his own wide smile playing on his lips.

"This is insane."

"I couldn't agree more."

He rolls us so that he's on his back and I'm sitting astride his waist with his cock buried deep inside me. "Ride me, baby girl. Show me what you can do."

With his hands gripping my hips tightly, he helps lift me up and down on his length until I can no longer hold myself up and fall down onto his chest as my orgasm rips through me. Seconds later a growl rips past his lips as he falls over the edge once more, his cock jerking inside me and setting off little aftershocks around my body.

"I'm so tired," I whisper, resting my head on his chest and closing my eyes.

His arms close around me and he kisses the top of my head gently as I begin to drift off, but still, the smile remains on my face.

When my alarm goes off the next morning, I'm not ready for it. My body feels like it's sunk into the mattress and doesn't want to get out.

I reach my arm out to silence the irritating sound before rolling over to find Dawson—only when I slide my hand over the sheet, I find it cold and empty.

Disappointment washes through me. I'd have given anything to wake up to him this morning, to see his face, to have the reminder I need right now that last night really did happen.

That he really did ask me to marry him.

Butterflies erupt in my belly as I remember him staring down at me, asking me that question that turned my world upside down.

Despite the fact that I know it was real, it feels like a dream.

My fingers drift to my ring finger, wishing I had the accessory that usually comes with that question. It just shows how spur of the moment it was. I don't need the lack of ring to tell me that; the shock that flashed across his face the second the words fell from his lips was enough.

I smile to myself as I replay it over and over before my second alarm goes off, telling me that I really need to get moving if I'm going to get to work on time.

My muscles pull as I sit myself up. The first thing I notice when I push the sheets away is the ink on my leg. Seeing it this morning takes my breath away just as much as it did the first time I looked at it yesterday evening.

It's stunning, easily the best bit of skin art I've ever seen. He really is talented.

I want to pick the wrapping off to see it properly, but I figure I should probably shower first. I don't really know the first thing about aftercare; I kind of hoped that Dawson would be here to tell me, but I can't be too disappointed. He'll have had to get home for Emmie. I can hardly begrudge him for looking after his daughter.

Ripping my eyes from his handiwork, I find a note on my bedside table.

Baby girl,
Thank you for yesterday. It's made the top of my 'best day ever' list.
Don't prepare any lunch. I've got you covered.
I'll see you soon.
Dx

Despite the fact that the rain was torrential when I left my flat this morning, I couldn't wipe the smile off my face.

Somehow, by some miracle, I've managed to find everything I ever wanted.

I spent years wondering what Dawson was doing, wondering if he'd found someone else—I could only assume he had—and if he was happy.

I always hoped he was, although deep down there was a part of me that hoped he missed me as much as I did him. The day I walked away, it was like I left a part of me behind, and it's not since finding Dawson again that I realise just how huge that piece was.

When I smile now, it feels real. When I laugh, I mean it.

I'm not sure one person should hold that kind of power, but I have no control over it. Finding Dawson again meant finding a part of myself, and I'm whole again. Something I haven't felt for so long.

My smile is something Lisa notices the second I run into the building from the Uber that delivered me to school. I didn't have the energy after last night to even contemplate getting on the tube. I must have done a better job than I thought I did with my makeup, because she doesn't comment on my obvious lack of sleep.

The morning drags. With the memory of his note filling my mind, I not so patiently wait for the clock to tick around to lunchtime.

When the bell rings, I damn near bolt from my chair in my need to go and find him, but the second I stand, my phone rings.

Seeing Henry's extension, I reluctantly pick it up.

Movement out my window catches my eye, and, as he chats away about the antics of a few members of the football team, I find myself looking at him through our office windows.

I blow out a breath as he chatters on about the prank they played on a few unsuspecting students this morning.

On a normal day, I'd probably find it amusing, but right now, I've got a lunch date, and I'd much rather be listening to him than Henry.

A knock sounds out on my door, and my heart jumps into my throat. Looking over, I expect Lisa to come bounding in, but when the door opens I find another body filling the doorway—a much bigger, more ruggedly handsome one.

The smile that lights up my face makes his eyes twinkle with delight. I point toward the seat in front of me, but he doesn't take it. Instead, he walks around my office as if he's making himself at home.

"Who are you talking to?" he whispers.

Discreetly, I point to Henry, who I know is watching us curiously.

"Ah," Dawson says, walking over to the window. Henry pauses as they stare at each other. I know Dawson recognises Henry instantly from the way his shoulders tense. I can only assume Henry knows who he is too. Dawson doesn't exactly blend into a crowd.

My eyes widen when Dawson lifts his hand and waves at Henry before swiftly turning and dropping the blinds.

I gasp as Henry's voice gets deeper over the line.

"Well, it looks like you have a more pressing issue than what I'm telling you about. Just remember there are kids about."

"What exactly are you suggesting, Henry?" I snap,

irritated that once again he's questioning my ability to do my job.

"N-nothing. Bye."

He hangs up while my chin is still dropped in shock. What does he think I'm going to do? Let Dawson fuck me over the desk while the kids come and go?

I blow out a long breath and slouch back in my chair.

"Is he being a problem?"

"Henry? No, I think he's just... jealous," I admit with a wince.

"Hmm... maybe I should have left the blinds up, really give him something to be jealous about." Dawson steps toward me, cradles my face, and lowers his lips to mine. "Missed you," he whispers before plunging his tongue into my mouth.

I moan into his kiss, already desperate for more but knowing I can't have it.

He kisses me for long minutes, but, in the end, he breaks away and drops a kiss to my nose.

"I'm sorry I snuck out," he says, resting his arse back on my desk and tangling his fingers with mine.

"You had to get back for Emmie, I understand."

"I hated doing it, but you looked too peaceful to wake."

I smile up at him. "I'm assuming you brought food? I'm starving."

He chuckles before walking around my desk and lifting up a bag I totally missed when he first arrived.

"Sure did." He proceeds to lay out everything he brought.

"You really do have a thing for picnics, don't you?" I ask with a laugh as he pulls out a quiche, followed by sausage rolls, some salad, and a bottle of dressing.

"Yeah, but I like to think this one is a little more

sophisticated. I even have real plates," he says with a laugh, pulling them out of the bag.

"You're a nut."

Shaking his head at me, he sets about dishing up.

"A girl could get used to this," I say, accepting the plate he pushes my way.

"I'm not sure your boss could."

"Ignore Henry. He's a good guy really. You'll find out soon when you come in for Emmie's progress meeting."

"It's with him?"

"Well, it will be with her tutor, but he'll be there. And I have a feeling he'll want to talk to you."

"Great. I can tell him everything he's missing out on now you're mine."

"Dawson," I chastise him.

"What?" He throws a sausage roll past his lips and chews. I pause with my fork halfway to my mouth and watch his lips move, wishing they were on me instead. "You're the one who's going to get yourself in trouble if you keep looking at me like that."

"What? I'm not..."

"Sure."

Silence falls between us for a few minutes as we eat. Although every time I glance up at him, he's staring at me as if he can't believe I'm really here.

"Did last night really happen?"

"You mean, did I really ask you to marry me?" he asks, his lips pulling up at the side.

I nod.

"Then yeah. That was real."

"It's insane, Dawson. We only met again two weeks ago."

"Baby, are you trying to tell me you're changing your mind?"

"What? No. No way. I'm just saying we're crazy."

"Never claimed to be anything else."

I laugh at him lightly, but I can't help the weight of what's developing between us pressing down on my shoulders.

"Out with it," he demands, clearly sensing my concern.

"What happens now? This isn't as simple as us just getting engaged, is it?"

"Is this because I didn't have a ring?" he asks jokingly, but I know he's just trying to lighten the mood.

"You've got a daughter, Dawson. One who goes here. Your priority now should be her, not me. Then there's the small issue that your father will probably kill me the second he learns I'm breathing, let alone that I've agreed to marry you."

"We'll sort it," he says, reaching for another sausage roll like it's nothing.

"You make it sound so easy."

He blows out a breath and stares at me for a beat. "Piper, none of this is going to be easy. Honestly, I have no idea how I'll deal with my father, but there's no question about us not being together. He'll have to accept it, accept that you didn't do what you did out of choice, or..."

"Or..." I prompt.

"I don't know. We leave, maybe."

"We can't do that. Emmie has just started here. You can't pull her out before she's even settled because of me. I won't allow it."

"That's the worst case, baby. Dad wanted your father, not you. You were just caught in the crossfire. I'll talk to him. I'd like to think my happiness comes above the club."

I raise a brow because we both know all too well that often the club comes above all else. "We'll figure it out." He reaches across the table and takes my hand in his. "This is meant to happen, baby. We were meant to meet again."

"You really believe that?"

"I do. It's why we've never found anyone else. It was written in the stars."

I smile at him, my heart tumbling in my chest.

"I'll talk to Emmie. She already knows there's something going on anyway, and I'm pretty sure she won't care. Then we'll deal with my family in the next few weeks or something. I just want to enjoy you first."

"Okay." I want to say I feel lighter, but until we know which way it's going to go with his family, I know I'm going to be uptight about this.

Obviously, I don't want myself in any danger—but more than that, I don't want to cause Dawson or Emmie any issues.

"Stay with us this weekend?"

"You sure?"

"Baby, I want you to be my wife. Of course I'm sure. If I didn't already know that you want to take things slow for Emmie, then I'd demand you move in right now."

"I don't even know where you live, Dawson."

"Huh, I guess this was all a bit fast." He laughs, and I can't help but join in with him.

The bell rings out, signalling our time together is over.

"What are you doing for the rest of the day? I ask, knowing that it's his day off.

"I might head into town and start jewellery shopping."

"You are not," I joke.

"I guess you'll just have to wait and see," he says, pulling me into his hard body the second I round the desk

"I guess I will."

"I wish I didn't have to work every night."

"Me too," I say, sliding my hand up his chest and wrapping it around the back of his neck.

"Pack a bag and I'll pick you up the second I finish work on Friday night."

"Okay," I breathe, excitement already starting to swirl around in my belly.

Our noses brush and his lips press against mine a second before he captures them in a bruising kiss.

By the time he pulls back, I'm a panting ball of need.

"You don't play fair," I complain.

He takes my hand in his and slides it down his body until my fingers brush over his hard length. "And you do? I've got to walk out there and get accosted by your friend with this."

I can't help but laugh. Lisa would be all over that if she knew.

"Aw, she's harmless really." He raises a brow at me.

"If you say so. I'll call you later, yeah?"

"If I don't answer, it's because I've passed out. I didn't get much sleep last night."

"Is that right? Some hot man keeping you up?"

"Yeah, so hot you wouldn't believe. Now get out of my office, I have important work to do."

He shakes his head, drops a kiss to my brow, and then slips from my office.

It feels cold the second he closes the door behind him.

I finish up clearing my desk of the remnants of our lunch and pull the blinds back up. Henry is no longer in his office, but I'm sure he's got a few words to say when he catches up with me.

To my amazement, I have a quiet afternoon. Not even Lisa appears to find out some gossip, which I find odd.

The second the bell rings out at the end of the day, I discover why.

"That was the longest meeting I have ever been forced to sit through," she whines, inviting herself into my office and flopping down at the desk. "Oh, sausage rolls, can I?" Her eyes light up when they land on the tub.

"Of course."

"Finish up," she mumbles around a mouthful of food. "We're going for dinner. I want to hear all about yesterday's big date."

"He proposed," I blurt out.

"He what?" she squeals at a pitch I'm sure only dogs should be able to hear. "He actually asked you to marry him? Oh my God, Piper. That is epic."

"It is, yeah," I say, but apparently my face doesn't show the level of excitement it should.

"What's wrong? Don't tell me you said no."

"What? No, of course not. Things are just… complicated."

"*Things* that involve a man, of course they're complicated."

"It's more than that, Lis."

"Then even more reason to pack up your shit so we can go and hash it out over a cocktail or ten."

I'm exhausted, and all I really want to do is curl up on my sofa with a bowl of pasta, but I can't deny that a night out to talk through all of this doesn't sound good right now.

21

DAWSON

"You told her everything? How'd she take it?"

"Honestly, she was totally dumbfounded to start with. She had no idea MCs existed outside of TV dramas and novels."

I can't help but laugh, it's not the first time I've heard similar words. The way I was brought up, the way my family live their lives, is like an entirely different world sometimes. They have their own rules, laws and rituals. It's easy to appreciate how outsiders struggle to understand the reality of it.

"So what was her advice after she got over the shock?" I ask Piper on our late-night phone call.

I was half expecting the call to ring out after her warning that she might be asleep, but I was pleasantly surprised when she answered and explained that she'd actually only just got in herself.

"She told me to trust you. That if you care about me like you seem to then you'll ensure I'm safe." Guilt twists my insides as her words come down the line. The memory of my phone call to my grandparents' solicitor this afternoon to tell him about my engagement fills my mind.

I need to remember why I'm doing this. It's for Emmie. To give her the future she deserves.

"Maybe she's not so bad after all," I say, my voice rough with emotion and guilt. But thankfully Piper misses it—or at least, she doesn't comment on it.

"She's not bad at all, actually."

"That's because she doesn't look at you like a piece of meat."

"Well, she knows you belong to me now, so hopefully she'll stop it."

"I belong to you. I like the sound of that," I growl down the phone, imagining her squirming on the other end.

"How'd the shopping trip go?"

"I can't possibly say," I joke. Actually, I got exactly what I wanted in the first shop I walked into.

"Tease." I hear her move about on the other end. "What are you doing?"

"Just getting a drink."

"Boring."

"Did you talk to Emmie after school?"

"I did," I confirm.

"And..."

"She's fine about it, baby girl. Wants to know when you're moving in."

"Really?"

"Yeah, really. Despite appearances, she's actually pretty laid back."

Piper laughs down the line. "Why do I think I'm going to have a little visitor tomorrow?"

"She's already asked if she needs to start calling you Mum."

"You're kidding?"

"No, but I think she was."

"Jesus, I don't feel old enough to be called that."

"I hate to point out the obvious, baby, but you are."

"Yeah, yeah, whatever. I can barely look after myself, let alone a child."

"I think you'd be an incredible mother."

She sighs down the line, and I can't help the question that falls from my lips.

"Do you want kids, Piper?"

"Honestly, it's not something I've ever allowed myself to really think about. Since leaving you, I've been missing a pretty vital part of having a kid."

"You've been with guys though, right?" I hate to ask, but I do nonetheless.

"Yeah, but no one I ever really wanted a second date with, let alone a child."

"I could say the same thing about Emmie's mum. I never even considered a first date with her."

"You know, I kinda want to meet this woman."

"You'll have to find her first."

"Still no news?"

"Nope. It's like she's fallen off the face of the Earth. I mean, it's not a huge loss, but Emmie deserves to have a mother at least at the other end of the phone, should she need it."

"Yeah, she does." Piper yawns, and I feel guilty for keeping her up once more.

"You should head to bed."

"I know, but I like talking to you."

"You won't thank me in the morning when you're asleep at your desk."

"No, probably not. I'm never going to get any sleep if I

move in, am I?"

"What do you mean *if*? You *are* moving in."

"I meant when. Don't freak out, caveman."

"Good. Because it's happening. This. Us. It's happening."

I can almost hear her smile. "Yeah, it is. I can't wait."

"Okay, you need to go."

"Okay," she whines. "I'll talk to you tomorrow, yeah?"

"Yeah. Goodnight, baby girl."

"Goodnight, Dawson."

―――

The week passes slowly as I all but count down the hours until I finish work on Friday night. I've got a solid day of clients, my most recent one currently making himself at home in my chair, making me wonder if he's planning on leaving anytime soon.

"How's my niece getting on at that posh school you're forcing her to attend?" Cruz asks, putting his shirt back on after getting me to add to his ink.

"She's doing good. I think it was what she needed."

"I can't believe she agreed to it. Have you seen the uniform?" He pulls a face. "I thought the one we had to wear back in the day was bad, but that? Ugh."

"Have you finished?" I ask, making a point of tidying up, getting ready for my next client.

"You should have sent her to do an apprenticeship with me."

"Oh yeah, I considered it for all of about... zero seconds."

"What? She's going to need to know how to tune a bike one day."

"I've ordered her a 125cc," I admit, much to his delight.

"Yes, bro. Now you're talking." He snaps his fingers like he's still eighteen.

Rolling my eyes, I turn my back on him.

"When's it coming? She's gonna need some special Cruz lessons on how to ride that thing."

"She's done her CBT, she knows what she's doing. She doesn't need you to teach her anything."

"You're such a pussy. You want her to impress those rich fuckers, don't you?"

"No, not really. I just want her to get some good grades and make a life for herself. I'd rather she didn't die on her bike because you taught her some stupid trick."

"You used to be fun, you know?"

"Really? When was that?" I bark over my shoulder.

"You need some fucking pussy, man. When was the last time you got some?"

"None of your fucking business."

"Well, there are these new chicks at the club. I have no idea where they've come from, but fuck me, bro. You need to come check them out."

"I don't need to do anything. You know you're not going to tempt me there, even with the best pussy in the world."

"Yeah, well, that's where you went wrong, man."

"Whatever. Are you leaving yet?"

He doesn't get a chance to answer, because my phone lights up on the counter next to me and I snatch it up before he sees Piper's name.

"Sorry, it's Emmie's school. I need to get this." I expect him to leave, but the irritating motherfucker just settles back in my chair. Anyone would think he hasn't got a job or home to go to.

"Hello," I say the second I connect the call.

"Hey, it's me," she says as if I don't already know. "Emmie has had an accident."

"Shit, is she okay?"

"Yeah, yeah, she's fine. Hockey injury." There's something in Piper's tone that doesn't sit right with me, but I can hardly ask what's wrong with my brother's eyes drilling into my back. "Are you busy?"

"Yeah, I've got back-to-back clients all day. But I can cancel them."

"If you're happy, I can take her home. I'm pretty much done for the day anyway."

"Are you sure? I don't want to cause issues."

"What? Of course not. I'll make sure she's fine, get her some dinner or whatever. We're good. You don't need to worry."

"Not possible," I admit but regret it when I hear movement behind me.

"Okay, I'll pack my stuff up and call us an Uber."

"Thank you for letting me know," I say stiffly, more than aware that I've got an audience.

"No problem. See you later."

"Yeah. Thank you, bye."

I stare down at my phone for a second before the nosey fucker behind me pipes up. "Everything okay?"

"Emmie had a hockey accident at school." My stomach clenches as I say the words. I trust Piper, but still, my need to know she's okay and take care of her prevails.

"Is she okay? You want me to go and get her?"

"She's fine, and no, it's all sorted."

"You know, if you don't trust me with your kid, all you gotta do is tell me."

"Fine, I don't trust you with Emmie. Happy?"

"You're a prick," he mutters, finally getting up from the chair and putting his cut on.

"Don't care. I don't want her dragged into your world."

"Careful, bro. You're forgetting that it's your world too. You can only run for so long."

"Is that a threat, Cruz?" I growl, taking a step toward him. He might think he's the big man now he's Dad's VP, but he needs to remember who's the oldest and fastest out of the two of us.

"Nah, just reality, bro. You'll be back and you know it."

I narrow my eyes at him, wondering what the hell has gotten into him today. He often gives me shit about my decision to step away, but never like this.

"Whatever. I've got work to do."

Reaching around him, I pull the door open and gesture for him to leave.

"Nothing like a nice welcoming visit to family."

"It was fine until you started running your mouth."

"Biff, gorgeous, how's it going?" he sings the second he spots her in reception.

Not wanting to listen to him attempt to hit on her, I swing my door closed and give myself a few minutes.

Grabbing my phone, I quickly type out a message to Piper.

Dawson: Sorry, Cruz was here. Is she really okay?

Piper: Yeah, no broken bones or anything. We've got it covered. Enjoy the rest of your day. I'll be waiting.

Feeling a little better, I finish up and call in my next victim.

22

PIPER

I'm pointlessly staring at the clock, wondering if I can find an excuse to get out of here early so I can go and pack for the weekend at Dawson's, when a knock sounds out on my door.

"Come in," I call, turning that way when the door is pushed open.

"Oh my God, what happened?" I gasp, pushing to stand when Emmie emerges, half her face is covered in blood.

"I'm fine. It looks worse than it is."

"Emmie, there's blood dripping from your chin." I scrabble about and pull a packet of tissues from my bag and hand them over. "Sit. I'll go get the first aid kit."

"I'm fine. It'll stop in a bit."

"Sit," I repeat before racing from the room, glad I did my first aid training when I started here.

I'm back in a matter of minutes to find she has at least done as she's been told and taken a seat. Crouching down in front of her, I begin wiping away the blood in an attempt to find the cut causing the issue.

"What happened?"

"Hockey got a little rough."

"A little? Jesus, were you all fighting or something?"

"Pretty much." My eyes widen, because I wasn't exactly expecting her to agree. "Some of the girls don't like me very much," she admits quietly as I work.

"They did this to you?"

"Yeah but..."

"But..."

"I might have started it."

"Emmie," I warn.

"What? They were chatting shit. They deserved it."

"Em—"

"You're going to tell Dad I've been fighting, aren't you?"

"No." Her eyes widen in shock. "You are. I'm not getting in the middle of you two. Working here and being involved with you is a predicament, but I will not go behind your back, just like I won't go behind his."

"Fair enough," she mutters before wincing when I find the cut just above her eyebrow.

"Let's get this patched up and get you home. I don't think going to your last class is a good idea. Where have the others gone?"

"No idea. Miss Peterson was dealing with them. I walked away."

"Emmie..."

"I wasn't standing there listening to them tell her how it was all my fault. She loves them, she'll never take my word over theirs. I'm just the new girl from the rough side of town."

"Em—"

"Don't. Don't try to tell me that's bollocks, because we both know it's the truth. I don't fit in here and I never will."

"Have you been having other issues?"

"Some stuck-up bitches can't touch me, Miss Hill. They think they're better than me? Fine, let them. It's water off a duck's back."

"It shouldn't be. Give me their names, I'll make sure..." She stares at me, and my words trail off.

"You just said you wouldn't get in the middle."

"Yeah, of things with you and your dad. But this is my job. I'm here to make sure you're happy, that you're settling in okay. This," I say pointing to her head, "is not settling in okay."

"It's fine. They'll get over it. Or they'll learn I can throw a harder punch. Whatever. Don't give me that look."

"Okay," I say, placing a couple of butterfly stitches over her cut. "Let's see how that does. I'm going to ring your dad."

"Great," she groans.

"I could have come back on my own, you know," Emmie says once we're both in the back of an Uber, heading toward their house.

"I know, but I told your dad I'd look after you, so here I am. Plus, if I'm honest, I was more than ready to finish for the weekend. This is just a good excuse," I admit, much to her delight.

"Here?" the driver says, pulling to a stop on the side of the road.

Dawson lives a little more out of town than I was expecting on a really nice, homely looking street. I immediately feel at home, which is weird seeing as we're not even inside the house yet.

"Great, thank you." Emmie hops out and, after also thanking the driver, I do the same.

I follow her to a house on the opposite side of the road that has twisted wrought iron railings out the front and a black front door with chrome fittings. It couldn't be any more Dawson if it tried, and I find myself smiling as Emmie unlocks the door.

The sound of a deep, rumbling bike engine has me looking over my shoulder. I feel ridiculous as disappointment flows through me when he doesn't appear. He just told me he's got clients all afternoon and evening; I know he's not coming.

I follow Emmie inside and find pretty much what I was expecting: a bachelor pad.

The walls are all painted a soft grey and the hallway has dark wooden flooring with just one unit against the wall with boxes in it, I'm assuming for shoes.

"Living room." Emmie points through a door and I find another grey room with two huge black leather sofas and dark furniture. There's a pink blanket on one that looks totally out of place. I don't need to ask who that belongs to. "Kitchen. Garden." She points out to a small gravel courtyard-style garden beyond the sliding doors at the other end of the room.

"Are you hungry?" I ask, studying his elegant kitchen. The units are—unsurprisingly—grey, but he's added a teal accent which is really quite stylish.

"Yeah. You know what I really fancy?"

"Go on..."

"Nachos. Loads of cheese, guacamole, sour cream, jalapeños." My stomach rumbles as she rattles it all off. Knowing that Dawson wasn't going to appear with a picnic today, I was forced to put up with the salad I threw together before leaving the house this morning. Needless to say, it didn't really hit the spot.

"Do you have everything for it?"

"No," she says with a wince. "There's a corner shop right down the street. Let me get changed and we can walk down."

"No, I'll go. Just point me in the right direction. You take some painkillers for that and clean up." I did the best job I could with some wipes in my office, but she's still covered in dried blood. "Just be careful of the stitches. I'll pick up some more if they have some so we can redo it, or we'll get your dad to grab some on his way home."

"Are you sure?" she asks. "I don't mind coming. You've already done more than enough."

"Yeah, I'm sure."

"Okay, turn left out of the house and just keep walking, you can't miss it. It's not even a five-minute walk."

"Okay, cheesy nachos coming right up."

I leave her as she pulls the fridge open and grabs a can of Coke.

I collect my bag from the unit in the hallway, along with Emmie's key, and head out.

The second I step onto pavement, the feeling that I'm being watched washes through me. I look over my shoulder, but the street seems to be abandoned.

I look into Dawson's house as I pass and find Emmie standing there. She gives me a small wave before she turns, and, I assume, heads for the stairs.

I look around at the rows of houses, but nothing seems out of the ordinary. Tugging my bag a little higher on my shoulder, I pull my phone from the side pocket and look down, ready to shoot Dawson a message, knowing that he'll be worrying about Emmie. Only I don't get a chance to even unlock it because an arm wraps around my waist as a hand clamps over my mouth and I'm hauled backward and into the darkness of the back of a Transit van.

I struggle in the man's hold, but my strength is no match for his.

"You really are a stupid fucking bitch, aren't you?"

"Cruz?" I ask when he releases my mouth.

"You remember me. I'm honoured, snitch."

I don't get to say any more, because a length of tape is slapped across my face as whoever is driving the van floors the accelerator and I stumble backward until I collide with the backdoors, my shoulder burning in pain.

His hands land on my upper arms and he spins me until my front is pressed against the cool metal as he binds my wrists behind my back.

"That's it, snitch. Be a good little girl now."

"Fuck you," I shout, but with the tape covering my mouth all he gets is a muffled scream.

His nose runs up the column of my neck and he breathes me in as I retch. "You always were a feisty little bitch. Probably how you got my dumb-arse brother under your spell so easily."

I suck in as much air as I can through my nose, but my head spins.

Cruz turns me again, his evil eyes landing on mine and his fingers wrapping around my throat, squeezing enough that I start to see stars.

"You thought you could just walk back into his life and there would be no consequences? How stupid are you?" Tears spill from my eyes. "Aw, you really think he loves you, don't you?" He chuckles, but there's zero amusement in it. "He's been playing you, baby *girl*."

"No," I scream, my tears coming faster as a sob rumbles up my throat. My stomach turns over at his use of Dawson's nickname for me.

"Karma is a bitch, right? You're nothing to him aside from the huge cheque he gets to cash in. You mess with the Royal Reapers, you can bet your arse we're going to come for you eventually. Well, baby girl, my father and I have been waiting for today for a very, very long time."

My stomach turns over.

But I never get to find out if I throw up, because pain radiates from my temple before everything goes black.

Every part of my body aches when I start to come to, and I'm cold. So fucking cold. My entire body trembles and my teeth chatter despite the gag that's now between them.

I want the darkness to claim me again. At least there I can pretend that none of this happened. I can pretend that I'm still in Dawson's house with Emmie, waiting for him to come home.

Cruz's words come back to me.

"He's been playing you, baby girl."

No. No. That can't be right. What we've had these past few weeks, it's been real. I know it has.

I try to move to ease the ache in my shoulder and hip, but nothing helps. In the end, I'm forced to open my eyes and succumb to reality.

Ripping them open, I find I'm in a room so dark that I can barely make out my own legs, let alone anything else.

A cold breeze continues to blow over me. Originally, I assumed it must be a window, but it's September. It's too cold to be coming from outside.

As I lie there, my eyes eventually begin to get used to the blackness surrounding me and I'm finally able to make out the white box in the corner. It doesn't take a genius to work out that it must be an air-con unit.

I shift again, desperately needing to sit up, to do anything.

I try to move but my arms are still tied behind my back. My ankles are now also bound, but I can breathe easier and I soon realise the tape has been replaced in favour of a scrap of fabric.

"Motherfuckers," I scream around the gag, knowing that no one will hear me but feeling better for at least trying.

After what feels like a year, I eventually manage to sit myself up and shuffle back until I hit a wall.

I pull my legs up to my chest, wishing that I could wrap my arms around them in an attempt to keep warm.

Dropping my head forward, I run through what I remember from the moment Cruz snatched me from the street, but all I can think about are his words.

"He's been playing you, baby girl."

I tell myself time and time again that it can't be true. The way he looks at me, the way he touches me. All the little things he's done over the past two weeks. It can't be fake. He's not that good an actor.

Is he?

Reality slams into me. Really, I don't know him anymore. The boy I fell in love with is not the man I met again by surprise two weeks ago.

Fuck. Was it even a surprise?

Has all of it been fake? A game to get revenge on what I did to him all those years ago?

No. No.

I shake my head, refusing to allow the thoughts to linger as tears burn my eyes. I don't want to cry; nothing good can come from my tears, but I'm powerless to stop them. Faster than I can control, they spill from my eyes and soak into the fabric that's cutting into my mouth.

I cry until I have nothing left. My body is spent, my head aching. I've no idea how long I've been in this dark and cold room for, but no one else has visited. No one cares.

A sob rips from my throat.

I thought I'd found everything that was missing from my life the day Dawson walked into Knight's Ridge, but I fear that the reality is very different.

It was just the beginning of the end.

23

DAWSON

"Is everything okay?" I ask Emmie when I return her missed calls while I'm between clients.

I might get one missed call from her when I'm working—she knows I'll call her back when I can—but to find five from her? That gets my hackles up.

"Um..." she hesitates. "I... I don't know."

"Emmie," I warn, needing her to spit out whatever it is.

"Piper left to go to the corner shop almost two hours ago." I instantly sit up straighter on my stool.

"W-what? Are you sure?"

"Yes, Dad. I can tell the time."

"Sorry, that's just..."

"Weird. I know. I told her I fancied nachos and she said she'd go and get the stuff. She took off but hasn't reappeared."

"Have you tried calling her?"

"I don't have her number. I've been calling you."

Guilt washes through me that I didn't just apologise to my client and answer. I'd just assumed that Piper was there and things would be sorted.

"Shit. Okay, I'm sure everything is fine," I tell her, but as the words fall from my lips, I know they're not true.

Piper wouldn't just disappear. Especially not when she's looking after Emmie.

"Are you okay?"

"Yeah, Dad. I'm fine. It was nothing. I'm more worried about Piper."

"Yeah, you and me both. I'm going to find her, okay? Call me if she reappears."

"I will. Is this my fault?" she asks hesitantly.

"What? No, of course not." *It's mine.* I sigh, pinching the bridge of my nose. " Order yourself some dinner. I don't know what time I'm going to be home."

"Okay. Love you, Dad."

"Love you too, Em."

My blood races past my ears as I scroll through my phone and hit call on her number. It doesn't even ring.

"Fuck."

Leaving my room as it is, I rip the door open and race down to reception.

"I need you to cancel all my clients, probably for tomorrow too," I bark at Biff as I pass.

"Is everything okay?" she shouts back as I push through the front door.

I pause, wishing I had an answer for her. "Honestly, I have no idea."

"If you need us, just call." I don't hang around long enough to respond.

I'm on my bike and flying toward her flat in the blink of an eye.

I manage to blag my way inside when someone leaves and run up to her door.

I know deep down that she's not here. I feel it in the dread that's wound its way around my entire body.

Cruz has her. I know he does. It's why he was so weird with me earlier.

He knows.

And that phone call about Emmie played right into his hands.

"Motherfucker."

Despite knowing that, my fists rain down on her front door in the hope that she got side-tracked and ended up here.

As suspected, there's no sign of life inside her flat.

Spinning so my back rests on her door, I open the tracking app I synced her phone to.

The last time it was seen was on my street, presumably as she left to go to the shop.

I might be playing right into their hands if my suspicions are correct and Cruz and Dad are behind this, but right now, I don't give a shit.

Climbing back on my bike, I head for a place I swore I'd never go again.

The Royal Reapers clubhouse.

The prospects at the door give me a double take when I pull up. I might not have been here for a long time, but that doesn't mean they don't know who I am.

They both nod and open the gates for me.

Driving inside, it's like I've been transported back to my childhood. Everything looks exactly the same. The same tired red brick buildings with dirty windows, the same broken signs and potholed car park. The only difference is the newer bikes and fresher faces.

A few smile at me, but most of them just scowl, either

in disapproval or confusion; I don't really give a shit. I'm not here to make friends.

Abandoning my bike, I head straight for my father's office. My heart thunders in my chest as I picture what they might do to her.

If they've got her, is she even still alive?

I remember all too well the ferocity of his anger when he discovered what her father had done. I remember him swearing on his own grave that he would end not only the Collins family but the entire Devil's Brotherhood.

And he did.

Or at least he thought he did.

My hands tremble with adrenaline as I wrap my fingers around the door handle and push it open. I don't bother knocking like I should. Fuck asking for permission, he has something that belongs to me.

I storm inside, expecting to find at least my father behind his desk, pretending to rule the world. But it's empty.

With a storm brewing inside of me, I set about checking every motherfucking room in this place.

———

It's almost an hour later when I get to the other end of the building. I've been through every place I can think of that they might have taken her, and everyone I've questioned all give me the same story—one I was expecting—that they've not seen my father, Cruz, or a girl.

It's bullshit. Utter fucking bullshit.

No closer to having any answers, I find myself back at my bike, still with guys staring at me as if I don't belong here. And I don't. Not anymore. But I need some fucking answers.

Pulling my phone from my pocket, I find a message from Emmie, asking me if everything is okay.

Knowing that she's going to be worried, I hit call and lift my phone to my ear.

"Have you found her?" she asks in a rush the second the call connects.

"Not yet, no."

"Dad." Her voice cracks on my name. "Something doesn't feel right here."

"I know, Em. I'm going to get to the bottom of it, I promise."

"O-okay." She sniffles and it rips my heart in two.

"I'm coming home. I'll see you in a few."

"Dad, no. You need—" I cut off her argument by hanging up.

I look back at the clubhouse, feeling like I'm missing something. She's close, I know she is. But I need more. I can't just keep running around like a headless chicken. My father trained me better than that. I need intel, and I need a solid plan if I'm going to get her out of this alive. Assuming that she still is.

Dread sits heavy in my stomach as I start up my bike and head out of the Reapers compound. Glancing over my shoulder before I pass through the gates, I promise to be back. I refuse to play their little game. They have something that belongs to me, and they can be damn sure I'm getting it back.

"Dad!" Emmie all but flies at me before I'm even through the front door.

I wrap my arms around her and hold her tight. "It's okay, Em. Everything is going to be okay."

"Where is she? People don't just disappear like that."

I debate how much I should tell her. I've always kept her away from that life, and thankfully my parents and Cruz—albeit reluctantly—agreed to play the part to protect her.

"Come and sit with me."

I guide her through to the living room and we both drop to the sofa, but before I get to say anything, I'm reminded of the events that led to all of this in the first place.

"Shit, Em. Your head." I gently take her face in my hands and inspect the wound.

"I'm fine, Dad. It's nothing."

"What happened?"

She cowers away slightly, raising my suspicions.

"Emmie?" I warn.

"Some girls said some stuff. I retaliated. I know I shouldn't have done it," she adds in a rush, before I get a chance to say anything, "but they just rub me the wrong way and I wanted to show them that I won't stand for their bull."

I wrap my arm around her shoulder and pull her into my side. I want to tell her off for fighting, but knowing the levels I'd go to right now to protect Piper, it seems pretty hypocritical.

"Just... please don't let it happen again."

"I'll try, but I really can't promise anything. I've never met such a bunch of vapid bitches. Everyone in my old school was either too drunk or high to care."

I hold her tighter, relief once again washing through me that I'm able to protect her now instead of being forced to leave her with her mother.

"What's going on with Piper, Dad?" she asks, her big, dark eyes gazing up at me and begging for answers.

My heart twists. I can't lie to her. I respect her too much for that.

"Your grandfather..." I start, dread racing through my veins that I'm going to tell her some of the truth.

"Is the Prez of an MC, yeah, I know."

My chin drops in shock.

"How'd you..."

"Mum." She rolls her eyes.

Of course, it makes total sense that all these years I've sworn my family to secrecy, yet that bitch told her everything.

"I overheard, if that makes it any better."

I shake my head. "Piper's father was from a rival MC, and when we first met, first started... dating... it wasn't under good circumstances. Things were complicated. It got very, very messy and her parents ended up..."

"Dead. Dad," she sighs, "I'm a big girl, you don't have to sugar-coat this for me."

I nod, hating that she's so grown up. It's easy to think she's still my innocent little girl, but that's far from the truth.

"I thought Piper died alongside them. I had no idea her father had got her out. It wasn't until we walked into Knight's Ridge that I learned the truth."

"That you still loved her."

"Yeah, that too. Things didn't end well between us, and I won't lie, my intentions when I first saw her again weren't exactly honourable."

"Dad," she breathes.

"Emmie," I sigh. "She'd really hurt me back in the day. She betrayed me and my family. I'd loved her so much in one moment, and then the next I hated her more than anyone I'd ever met before. I was only a little older than you are now. It was a lot to take. Then to think she'd died... It was a mess.

"But I never really hated her, and as the past few weeks have gone on, things have changed."

"You really love her, don't you?"

"Yeah, Em. I do. I always have."

She smiles at me sweetly. "I knew the second you saw her. Your whole demeanour changed. The way you looked at her... I've never seen you look at anyone like that."

"You're too perceptive for your own good, you know that?"

"No, I just want you to be happy, Dad. You've lived here alone for, well... too long. You deserve to find someone."

"You're a good kid, Em," I say, gently kissing her head.

"Yeah, you're not too bad either, old man." She wraps her arm around my waist and silence falls over us for a few minutes. "So the moral of this little story, I'm guessing, is that Pops has her?"

Ice floods my body at the mere thought. I know what he's capable of. I've witnessed what he's willing to do to the people he thinks have wronged him, let alone ones he knows betrayed him.

"Yeah. I'm pretty sure Pops and Cruz have her."

"They can't have too many places they'll have taken her. Do you think they'd hurt her?"

"Yeah, Em. I do."

Pushing from the sofa, I start pacing the living room while her eyes track my movements.

It's over two hours later when my phone pings with an alert. My brows pull in at first, not knowing what the unusual sound is for, but when I pull it from my pocket, I find a notification that makes my heart jump into my throat.

Piper's phone has been turned on.

I open the tracking app and wait for it to load. And, sure as shit, when it does it shows the clubhouse.

"I'm coming for you, you motherfuckers," I mutter to myself. "I'm just going out." I try to make it sound casual when I look at Emmie, who's pushing the dinner I've tried to force her to eat around her plate.

"You know where she is?"

"I believe so. Stay in the house. Do not answer the door," I warn.

"You think they'd..."

"No, but I need to know you're safe in all this. I can't be worrying about both of you."

She nods, a sad smile pulling at her lips. "I'm not going anywhere, Dad. Just... bring her back, please. I... uh... kinda like her."

"Yeah. Me too, kiddo."

Checking that I've got my knife, I head out the door and climb on my bike, ready to start a war if necessary to get my girl back.

24

PIPER

When my body starts to wake again, the first thing I realise is that I'm still trembling. My fingers and toes are numb, and I feel weak as fuck. But the next thing I notice is that my eyes are burning with the bright light that's searing through my eyelids.

It takes all the energy I have just to pull them open, and when I do, I wish I hadn't bothered.

"Piper Collins," the man on the chair before me drawls. "I never thought I'd see the day, seeing as I thought I put a bullet in your pretty little head all those years ago."

Charles Ramsey.

A man I'd recognise anywhere, no matter how grey his hair has turned or how many new wrinkles cover his face.

Despite the changes over the years, his eyes are the same.

The same soulless, cold pits of darkness bore into me with more hate than I think I've ever witnessed before.

"Well, you clearly didn't," I spit, only now discovering that my gag has been removed. I'm not willing to cower down to him like I'm sure everyone else does. If he's going to kill me, I refuse to go down without a fight.

My father taught me better than that.

"Clearly. There will be no doubt this time, though. I'll cut your fucking heart out myself if it's what it takes."

My stomach turns over at the visual. "Fuck you."

"Thanks for the offer, but I don't touch lying, vindictive little bitches. I'm sure Cruz wouldn't need much convincing, though." At that, his youngest son steps from the corner of the room. "He can be quite the evil cunt when he wants to be."

Cruz winks at me, but there's no playfulness to it. It's full-on evil.

Fear skates down my spine, making my trembling even worse.

"That's it, baby girl. Be afraid. It only makes my cock harder." Cruz cups himself through his jeans, and I gag.

"He'll come for me," I breathe, not really meaning to say the words out loud.

I regret it the second both Charles and Cruz begin laughing.

"You stupid, deluded little girl. No one is coming for you. No one cares about you. You. Are. Nothing."

My teeth grind with anger as a storm brews inside me.

"Have you forgotten what I told you?" Cruz starts. "D doesn't want you. You were just his way to a paycheck he needs. How do you think he's paying for Emmie to go to that school, huh? It sure isn't from tattooing. He needed you to get his inheritance. Now, you're nothing to him. He won't come for you. *He doesn't want you.* How could he, after the way you treated him? Treated us all? You dirty little snitch."

Tears streak down my cheeks. I desperately will them

to stop, not wanting them to know that their words affect me. But they do. Every vicious word that falls from Cruz's mouth rips me open that little bit more.

I knew I should have been on my guard with Dawson. And I was, to begin with. But the young, lovesick girl inside me took over and clouded my judgment.

I hate that they're right.

Why else would a man who's hated me for the best part of his life, propose to me after only a couple of weeks of reconnecting?

Of course it was a game. How could it be anything else?

But even still, deep down, I don't want to believe it.

Would he have let me get close to Emmie, knowing this was all fake?

Fuck, my head is spinning.

"Cruz," Charles instructs with a nod of his head.

He reaches into his pocket and pulls out my phone.

I watch as he powers it up and stares down at the screen.

A sadistic smile pulls at his lips before he turns it around. "Cute photo, but look... nothing. He hasn't called, hasn't sent any messages. He. Does. Not. Care. So now he's had his fun, now he's got what he wanted out of you, it's our turn to play."

Cruz reaches behind him and opens a door. Two huge, evil-looking guys step inside the room.

They come to a stop slightly behind Charles like two dogs trained to heel. I almost laugh to myself, because that's exactly what they are.

Puppies. Evil fucking puppies.

Cruz steps up to me and wraps his hand around my

throat, pulling my weak, frozen body from the ground as if I weigh nothing more than a feather.

He leans in close, the roughness of his stubbled jaw scratching my cheek until his lips are in front of my ear.

"You're going to wish I'd killed you in that van." His words are cold, void of any kind of emotion. Nothing like the young boy I remember who was so full of life.

"W-what happened to you?" I whisper.

"You, baby *girl*, and you're about to regret every second of it. When my big brother walked away from his responsibilities, I was forced to step up. I've been trained by the best." He runs his nose down the length of my neck, breathing me in. "Hmmm... you smell sweet enough to eat," he murmurs.

"Stop, please," I don't want to beg, but as his grip on me tightens, I don't know what else to do.

"I think I've changed my mind," he whispers, sending shivers racing down my spine before increasing his volume. "I don't think I want to share."

"Well then, boy. It's a good thing you're not in charge here."

Cruz stands back. His master has spoken, it seems.

I narrow my eyes at him as his stare pins me in place. I desperately search for any hint of that little boy, the one who used to spend all his days playing football in the Ramseys back garden, who had a dream of going pro one day.

His hand drops from my throat and I suck in a deep breath, filling my lungs with the air they're desperate for. My legs just about hold me up.

But I soon realise he's not finished with me. His hand comes to the tie of my wrap dress and he tugs until it loosens and the front falls open, exposing my body to them.

His eyes hungrily slip down the length of me.

"I can understand why my brother decided to take you for another ride. Shame we're about to fucking ruin you."

"Cruz, please."

"Oh, baby girl, please keep begging." He trails his finger from my chin, down over my collarbone and between the valley of my breasts. "Is that how you got Dawson to pop the question? By being his dirty little slut?"

"Fuck you."

"Ah, that's right. It's all fake. You don't even have a ring, do you? He couldn't even spare a few pounds of that impressive inheritance he's about to receive to buy you something to remember him by."

His fingers drop lower and my eyes squeeze tight as I beg my body not to react to his touch.

"You're going to regret ever messing with us, Collins. And you're about to learn a very valuable lesson." He takes a step back, although his eyes remain on my breasts.

"Jinx, all yours."

My eyes fly open just in time to see a wicked smirk pull at one of the guys' mouths.

He's a similar age to us with a shaved head and an angry looking snake tattoo that wraps around his neck and disappears under his shirt. He's not unattractive, but as he takes a step toward me, I wish they'd just hurry up and kill me instead of whatever they're intending on putting me through.

"I've heard a lot about you, snitch," he growls once he's in front of me. I don't get a chance to respond even if I wanted to, because he lifts his arm and backhands me across the face.

Unable to control my body, I crash to the floor in a heap. But it seems that isn't enough for him because he instantly hauls me back up, pinning me to the wall by my throat.

"I'm going to rip this pretty little body in two until you regret the day you were ever born, let alone the day you crossed the Prez," he seethes with so much venom it makes a fresh wave of fear race through me.

My eyes fly to Cruz's but his are dark. There is zero compassion or care in his evil depths. He really isn't the boy I once knew.

"Oh God," I whimper as Jinx spins me around and shoves me hard against the wall. My cheek burns with the force as my dress is pulled away from my arse.

His fingers just wrap around the edge of my knickers, ready to rip them away, when the door flies open.

"Get your fucking hands off her."

My entire body sags in relief.

He came.

Dawson came for me.

25

DAWSON

I'm at the Clubhouse in record time. My heart thunders in my chest as I pull up to the exact same prospect as earlier. He looks shocked to see me again so soon, but he doesn't question my reappearance and lets me through once more without a fuss.

I'm almost disappointed because every single muscle in my body is pulled tight with my need to rip someone limb from limb for thinking they had a right to touch my girl.

I know this is what I'd planned to do.

I was going to make her fall, make her my fiancée and then turn her over and force her to accept her fate.

But that was then, and this is now. Things change, and they change fast it seems.

The thought of my father or Cruz hurting a hair on her head makes me murderous. The only person who should have the power to hurt her is me.

She wronged them, she wronged us all, but she was a kid, just like I was. She didn't have a choice. And looking back all these years later, I'm glad she did. She changed my life in a way I never expected, and although I was heartbroken and furious, I still knew that she was the best thing that ever happened to me, it's what made it all hurt so much. If it was just a bit of fun then I'd have been all for revenge. But it wasn't, and I'm not.

As I pull my bike to a stop in the same place I parked earlier, there's a young prospect watching me from the shadows.

Killing my engine, I hang my helmet over the handlebars and instantly walk his way.

He watches my approach, but he doesn't give anything away. It's too late, though. I already know that he knows.

"Where have they taken her?" I ask, cracking my knuckles ready for his refusal.

A second of silence passes between us as he fights with his conscience.

"I-I don't know what you're talking about," he stutters, only making himself look guiltier.

"I'm not going to ask you again. Where have the Prez and VP taken the girl?"

He averts his gaze for a beat, and I use his hesitation to cock my arm back.

"Argh fuck," he groans, his entire body twisting away from me with the force of my punch.

Reaching out, I have his throat in my grip and him pinned up against the wall, his feet off the ground, in no time. Little fucking weed; he's going to need to bulk up if he thinks he's going to make it around here. Well, that is if he gets to live after this. My taste for blood right now is almost as strong as my father's to get the information I need.

"Where. Are. They?" I growl in a low voice.

"I-I can't."

"Do you know who the fuck I am?" I ask, cringing at myself for using that line. I said I'd never use my father's game to get me anywhere in life. But then I guess I didn't imagine this situation.

"Y-yes."

"Good. Then you know I'm not fucking about when I say that I will kill you if you don't give me what you know, because," I seethe, "I know that you know."

He trembles beneath my hold and I smile at him. But it's anything from joyful. It's evil, sinister. One that I was forced to give over the years but equally hated at the same time.

Pushing my hand into my pocket, I flip my knife and watch as all the blood drains from the prospect's face.

"Please, please, don't do this," he begs like a little bitch. Where the fuck is my father finding these pussies from?

"Then tell me."

I press the blade to his throat with enough pressure that it instantly draws blood. I need him to know that I'm not messing about here.

His wide eyes stare into mine, the fear within them feeding the feral beast inside me. I tamped him down a long time ago, but right now, he's emerging faster than I thought possible. I was trained for this life from a very young age. It comes almost as naturally as riding a bike.

"B-b-b—"

"B-b-b," I mock. "Spit it the fuck out. Or do I need to kill you?"

"B-basement."

"Basement?" I ask, not remembering this place ever having a basement.

"T-the storage room next to your father's office. It has access."

"Good boy," I sneer at him, pulling my blade away and then letting him drop to the floor.

I take off for my father's office, hoping that little shit didn't just lie to me.

I suck in a deep breath as I come to a stop at the door he just told me about.

I wanted a plan. I wanted to know what I was walking into, but I'm going into this blind. She could be down there alone, or there could be loads of guys just waiting for me.

Wrapping my fingers around the handle, I blow out my breath and push through.

Sure as shit, the second the door opens, I find a set of stairs.

As silently as I can, I walk down. At the bottom, there are four doors. I wait, and thankfully, someone's voice tells me which room I'm aiming for.

With my knife still in hand—wishing like fuck it was a gun—I step forward. Without thinking about the consequences, I throw the door open and walk inside.

The sight has bile rushing up my throat and my grip on my knife tightening.

"Get your fucking hands off her," I growl, turning all eyes on me.

"Son, how nice of you to join this little party."

"Let her go," I demand, much to my father's amusement if the curl of his lips and his laugh are anything to go by.

"You always were clueless, boy. It's why you couldn't stick with this life."

"Jinx, back off."

"I don't fucking answer to you. Prez?"

Thankfully, Dad nods and he steps away from Piper a little, exposing her arse to the rest of the room.

I move faster than anyone anticipates and I get a clear shot at Jinx before all hell breaks loose behind me.

My knuckles and the metal that adorns my fingers connect with his eye socket before I flip my knife and drive it into his side.

His eyes go wide as he registers what I just did before I throw him to the side like a rag doll.

I stand in the middle of the room, my chest heaving, sweat dripping from me, tension crackling around us.

Piper is behind me, resting back against the wall. I can hear her shaky breaths. But she's okay. Something settles inside me, but it only lasts a second because Cruz comes at me.

"I've been waiting a fucking long time for this, brother."

He always was slower than me, and it seems that even with the years that pass, nothing has changed. I block his first punch easily then throw a counterpunch that sends him flying across the room instead.

Finding his feet, he flies at me again, teeth bared, ready to kill.

No words are said as he ups his game and gives me a real fight. I know he hates me for the life he thinks I condemned him to after Piper 'died' and I walked away from the Reapers. We all know that being Dad's VP was my job. It was my destiny. But my walking away meant it fell to him, and he gave up everything he had to step up to the plate. It was expected of him, yeah, but he didn't have to comply. It was his choice at the end of the day. Dad might have been insistent, but he could have said no. Dad only had so much power; what was he going to do? Kill him?

"Dawson, no," Piper screams when Cruz manages to get a solid punch in, making my nose explode.

"I'm okay, baby. Get ready to get the fuck out of here," I say over my shoulder before clocking my brother so hard on the side of his head that he drops to the floor like a sack of shit.

Movement from the corner of the room catches my eye, and I turn just in time to watch as Dad's other goon pulls a gun.

He aims it right at Piper.

"NO!" I cry, time suddenly slowing to a damn near stop as I race toward her.

The bang sounds out a beat before I get to her. Everything around us goes silent as I stop in front of her before a burning pain explodes in my shoulder.

"Dawson, oh my God."

"Stay behind me, okay?"

Moving as fast as I can, I reach for the gun sticking out of Cruz's waistband.

Another shot sounds out, piercing the silence in the small room until Piper shrieks. I move just in time so the bullet only grazes my arm.

"Motherfucker," I roar, pulling the safety back on Cruz's gun and shooting off my first round in years. Thankfully my aim is still intact, because it goes straight between the cunt's brows.

He drops to the floor as I turn, slice through Piper's restraints and lift her into my arms.

Standing over Cruz's body, I raise my gun once more and then look to my father, who's standing like a stone, watching these events play out before him.

"I'm pretty sure he's still alive, but I can soon fix that." Dad's mouth opens, but he doesn't get a chance to say anything because I lift the gun and put a bullet through Jinx's stomach instead. "You want your boy to be next?"

"Son," Dad says softly, as if he's trying to get me on his side.

"Right now, I'm not your fucking son, Prez. I'm your fucking enemy. You want your boy to live, you let us walk out of here and forget we ever existed."

"Dawson." Frown lines mar his forehead, but I don't lower the aim I have on Cruz's head.

Family or not, they took my girl. They did this, and they deserve to pay. It's only the thought of my mother sobbing over their graves that stops me from pulling that trigger.

"This is over," I state, ploughing my boot into Cruz's ribs before marching from the room.

Dad doesn't say anything as I walk out with my girl in my arms. I can only take it as him agreeing to my terms.

As I climb the stairs, I hold Piper tighter, hating that I can feel her trembling in fear against me.

"You're safe, baby girl." Her tears soak into my shirt where she's tucked her face into the crook of my neck.

Kicking the main door open, I march us through and out to the car park. Eyes land on us as we emerge, including a set I got very close to out here not so long ago. I nod to him in a thank you. No one dares to say anything to us as I make my way to my bike.

It's wishful thinking, because as much as I can try to convince myself that my shoulder isn't in excruciating agony, I can feel myself starting to slip from both the pain and blood loss.

Deciding against the bike, I force my legs to carry us toward the gates.

Each step becomes harder work, and my head starts to swim, the world going hazy around me.

Got to keep going. Got to keep her safe, I tell myself over and over as I stumble forward.

"Dawson?" I'm vaguely aware of her voice and she pulls her head from my neck. "Dawson. Fuck."

Something hits my back, and then I'm falling.

"I'm okay. I'm okay," I say, but even I know it's a lie.

26

PIPER

"Dawson, no," I scream as we crash back against the outer wall of the clubhouse. His grip on me loosens and I manage to get to my feet before he falls to the ground. With my arms around his waist, I attempt to lower him gently so he doesn't hurt himself any more than he already is.

I run my eyes over him quickly as I wrap my dress back around me. He's covered in blood, but the fabric over his shoulder is soaked from the bullet he took for me.

"Dawson, can you hear me?" I ask in a rush, holding his rough cheeks in my hands.

"I'm okay," he breathes. It's so quiet I almost miss it.

"Fuck." I need to get us out of here. I look around the quiet street. I can hardly call an ambulance or an Uber.

My head spins, my entire body aching, although somewhat relieved that it's warmer out here than it was in that room.

I'm just about to go back to the gate and beg for someone to help us when an SUV pulls to a stop at the curb before us.

"Help me get him in," a guy in a Reapers cut says.

When I look up, I recognise the man, but I can't place him.

He takes most of Dawson's weight while I open the back door of the SUV.

I climb in beside him and cradle his head in my lap.

"Do you have any rags or anything for me to stop the bleeding?" I ask in a rush as he opens the driver's door.

"Fuck." He quickly removes his cut and pulls his shirt over his head. "Here, use this."

I ball it up and press it against Dawson's shoulder as hard as I can in the hope of stemming some of the blood.

"Where to?" the guy asks, his eyes finding me in the rearview mirror. There's a softness in the blue depths that I'm so relieved to see.

"Um..." I know we can't go to a hospital with a fucking bullet wound. Dad used to have a team on-call for whenever shit like this went down. Charles did too. A thought hits me. "Dawson's house." I rattle off the address, but he doesn't so much as punch it into the GPS.

"It's about twenty minutes. He going to be okay?"

Dread sits heavy in my stomach, and my hands tremble in panic. "Only one way to find out."

"Fuck," the guy barks, slamming his palm down on the wheel. "We'll get him there, Piper."

"How do you know my name?" I know it's not important right now, but I feel like I need to know who this guy is. The one who's potentially saved Dawson's life.

"You don't recognise me, do you?" He chuckles to himself. I shake my head, despite the fact that he's concentrating on driving and can't see me. "Well, I guess I do look a little different from the last time you saw me. My brows pull together.

"I... I think I do but..."

"Name's Link. Although, you'll probably remember me as Justin"

"Justin?" I gasp, memories of Dawson's teenage best friend coming back to me. "Well, shit. You've..."

"Changed, yeah? The IT geek look wasn't really working for me so..."

"Wow," I say, looking at the full sleeve of ink I can see from here, and the ripped muscles. "You patched in?"

He doesn't answer. I guess the fact that he took his cut off only moments ago is the only answer I need.

I have so many questions, but now is not the time.

I carefully lean forward, until I can slide Dawson's phone from his pocket.

I unlock it and stare down at the passcode.

"Fuck."

"Try your birthday," Justin suggests.

"W-what?"

"Your birthday. You know, six digits."

I do as he suggests, although it seems crazy. Surely it's more likely to be Em— "Well, shit."

I meet his knowing eyes in the mirror for a beat before I set about finding the number I need.

"He never forgot about you, Piper."

"I..." I start, but I find I don't have any words. I'm so confused right now that words like that don't help.

Finding Dawson's mum's number, I breathe out a shaky breath and pray I'm not making a massive mistake right now.

She answers on the second ring and my heart jumps into my throat.

"Dawson, is everything okay?" she asks in a rush. She

sounds every bit the concerned mum, and it makes my heart constrict for everything I lost.

"Um... i-it's Piper, actually. D-Dawson's hurt. He's been... shot," I force the word out through my clogged throat as she gasps.

Sarah Ramsey was always such a soft and caring woman. The total opposite of her husband. I often wondered how they ended up together.

"Oh my God," she breathes.

"We're heading for his house."

"I'm leaving now," she says before I've even started asking my question.

"O-okay, thank you."

I'm just about to hang up when she says my name.

"Yeah?"

"Thank you, thank you for calling me."

I nod to myself and hang up. I don't want to tell her that I didn't have any other option.

Dawson's breathing is getting dangerously shallow as Justin pulls the SUV to a stop outside his house.

He's pulling open the back door in seconds. "Come on, let's get this motherfucker inside so you can nurse him back to health."

"He's been shot, Justin. I don't think I can just dress up and make it all better," I mutter, wishing that I could indeed do just that.

Justin somehow manages to get him out of the car, allowing me to race around to the front door. I'm about to knock when it opens for me.

Emmie's eyes land on me for a beat before she looks over my shoulder.

All the blood drains from her face as she takes in the state of her father.

"He's going to be okay, Em. Let's move out of the way." We stand aside as Justin gets him into the house. "In there." I point to the living room, pulling Emmie into my arms as a sob rumbles up her throat.

"H-he's going to die, isn't he?"

"No, Emmie. No, he's not. But he needs your help right now. Go upstairs and get all the towels you can and any first aid stuff you can find. Your gran is on her way."

"You called Gran?" she asks, looking a little gobsmacked. "Dad told me e-everything," she manages to get out through her hiccups.

"O-okay. Well, your gran used to be one of the best nurses in the city. She's worked miracles over the years."

Emmie nods before turning and racing up the stairs, while I join Justin, who's trying to make Dawson comfortable on the sofa.

"It's okay, I've got it." I take over and he stands back to allow me some space. "Are you going to be in trouble for this?"

He ignores my question. "I'm assuming you left a mess behind you both?"

"Uh... yeah. Prez was there though, so I've no doubt it's already dealt with."

"I should get back." He walks out of the room but stops in the doorway when I call his name.

"Thank you. I don't know what I'd have—" I sob, cutting off my words.

"It's okay, Piper. I've always got my boy's back. Reaper or not."

I smile at him. "I'll get him to call you when he can," I say, because I can't consider any other outcome than Dawson being okay right now.

"Appreciated. Call me if you need anything, Piper."

"Thank you, Justin. Thank you so much." He nods once and then walks from the house.

"Gran," Emmie shouts as she descends the stairs.

In seconds Dawson's mum appears in the doorway, still wearing her pyjamas and carrying a huge bag. Hopefully, of all the things she'll need to fix her son.

"Thank you," I whisper as she drops to her knees beside me.

Her eyes hold mine for a second. Aside from her obvious concern for her son, her expression is totally unreadable.

"You can fix him, right?" Emmie asks from the doorway, causing us both to turn to her.

Tears continue to stream down her cheeks as her eyes flick from Dawson to Sarah and back again.

"Of course. Why don't you go and make me a coffee while I get started?"

Emmie rushes off and Sarah opens her bag. "Keep that pressure applied," she instructs as she pulls out a pair of scissors and begins cutting down the centre of Dawson's shirt.

"Okay."

"Is this the only wound?"

"Um..." I think back. There was a second shot. Did it hit him too?

"I... I don't know. There were two shots but..." My voice wobbles as everything begins to get too much.

"It's okay, Piper. You did well. Let's get this one looked at and then we'll deal with any others."

I nod—not that she's looking at me—as I lift Justin's shirt from Dawson's shoulder.

Sarah gasps when I pull it away to reveal the bullet

hole in his skin. I'm hoping it's just because it's her son and not because it's really awful or anything.

"You're not squeamish, are you?"

"I think we're about to find out."

With Emmie standing in the doorway, Sarah works her magic on Dawson.

Turns out, the bullet went right through, leaving a clean wound for Sarah to patch up. How it didn't hit me, I have no idea. Guilt begins to swamp me that I should be the one with a hole in my body right now, not Dawson.

That bullet was aimed for my head, it doesn't take an idiot to work that out.

Dawson saved my life tonight. I have no doubt about that.

A sob erupts as I sit on my knees, holding Dawson's hand.

Sarah has given him some pain relief and he's out of it, thankfully unaware of what she's doing.

"This one is just a graze, I'll just clean it and wrap it. Why don't you and Emmie go and get a drink? Have a breather."

"I'm... I'm not sure I can leave him."

"Piper," she sighs, turning her eyes on me. They're now softer than when she first arrived and it makes a fresh load of tears fill my eyes. "He's going to be okay. You saved him."

I shake my head. "He wouldn't be in this state if it weren't for me."

She pulls her gloves off and reaches for my hand. "Everything happens for a reason, sweetie. Now, go and get a drink. I sure could do with another."

"Okay," I breathe, pushing to my feet. I walk around her, stopping to drop a kiss on Dawson's forehead.

"Come on. I make a mean hot chocolate," I say to Emmie as I pass her.

After Emmie points out where everything is in their kitchen, I work in silence until I lower two mugs of chocolatey, creamy goodness to the counter in front of her.

"Thank you," she whispers without looking up at me.

I sit beside her, pulling my mug closer and wrapping my hands around it, relieved to have something warm after being so cold earlier tonight.

We both stare at our mugs, the tension between us growing as the seconds tick by.

When Emmie finally does speak, it rocks me to my core.

"I can't believe you played him. I trusted you."

My breath catches at the pain in her voice.

He really did tell her everything.

"Emmie, I—"

"No," she snaps, her voice suddenly harder and full of hatred. "Do not sit there and try to make excuses for what you did. He loved you, Piper. He loves you, and you..." Her voice cracks. "How could you?"

"I'm not going to make any excuses, Emmie. What I did was wrong, but I didn't have a choice."

"We always have a choice."

I blow out a breath. Did I? Would my father have followed through with his threats if I didn't?

"It didn't feel like I did. But that's not the point. It was wrong, but..."

"But..." Her eyes narrow on me.

"I fell in love," I sigh. "My father set the whole thing up, but he clearly didn't think it through properly. Because in pushing me to Dawson, he changed my life forever. Your dad, he..." I laugh to myself as I think back to our time together. "He was everything to me. When we were together, it was like the rest of my life didn't exist. I wasn't Arthur Collins's daughter. My life didn't revolve around doing as I was told or having to toe the club line. I was just me for the first time in my life. It was... it was amazing.

"I should have told him, I know that now. But I knew he'd hate me, and I knew it would only bring forward the inevitable war between our fathers, and I didn't want to lose him. I was selfish and greedy, but I was in love. We all do stupid things when the heart is involved."

"Amen," Sarah says, joining us.

"Mrs. Ramsey, I'm so sorry," I say, turning to her.

"Sarah, please. I'm not that old yet." She chuckles as she walks farther into the kitchen. "This still hot?" she asks, gesturing to the kettle.

"Yes, but let me," I say, stepping down from the stool.

"No, no. You look like you've already been through enough tonight. At the hand of my husband and youngest son, no doubt."

She doesn't need my verbal answer to confirm her suspicions.

"Emmie, could you give us some privacy, please?" Sarah asks her granddaughter.

"Sure. I'll go and sit with Dad."

Emmie leaves with her mug as the tension thickens around us.

Sarah doesn't come to sit beside me. Instead, she remains standing.

"I knew, you know."

"Knew what?"

"About the two of you."

I suck in a breath.

"My son can't lie, not to me at least. I knew the moment he'd given his heart to a girl."

"Why didn't you say anything?"

"Many reasons," she admits. "Some the same as yours. Charles and your father... their rivalry went on for longer than you probably even realise. Did you know that they went to school together?"

I shake my head.

"They'd hated each other before they even knew the other existed. Because they knew what their names meant. Once they learned the truth, it was only a matter of time before at least one of them ended up in a coffin. I'm surprised it took as long as it did, to be honest. Sorry," she adds.

"He was so happy, Piper. I'd never seen the sparkle in his eyes that appeared after he met you. I wanted to believe your intentions were honourable, but deep down, I think I knew they weren't. I found it hard to resent you when you made my son smile as you did.

"But that all changed when I was forced to watch him drown in pain after the truth was exposed. If I didn't believe you were already dead, I'd have killed you myself back then for the hurt you caused him."

"I'm so sorry, Sarah. If I could change any of it..."

"All of that is done. The decisions have been made and the pain felt. It's what happens from here on out that we can control."

Lifting my mug, I take a sip of the chocolatey goodness, hoping that it gives me some of the answers that I so desperately need. Sadly, no inspiration strikes. Instead, all that happens is my exhaustion hitting me. I really need to be curled up in a bed with this right now, not getting an interrogation from Dawson's mother.

"I knew that you couldn't have been dead the second I looked into my son's eyes when he came to dinner last weekend. I knew that no other woman could put that look on his face. I also knew nothing good could come of it."

"It seems you weren't the only one who knew, because Cruz didn't waste much time."

"He's angry, Piper. He's never forgiven Dawson for walking away, and he blames you for that."

"So I heard," I mutter, thinking of the words he spat at me in that room.

She drinks her chocolate despite the fact that it's still steaming hot and then turns her narrowed eyes on me. Gone is the softness of a few moments ago, and in its place is a warning, one that she ensures I hear loud and clear.

"My son loves you, Piper. I didn't need to tend to the fallout of tonight to know that. My husband, despite his actions, knows this too. If this is what you want, then you need to fight for it. I'll talk to Charles and Cruz and ensure the two of you are left alone. But—and don't take what I'm about to say lightly, Piper— if you hurt him again, I will come after you, and I will ensure that I don't walk away until I see that bullet go through your head with my own two eyes."

My mouth goes dry and I fight to force down a swallow.

"I know things are rarely simple. Take some time to figure out what you want, but once you do, stick to that decision. I'm not my husband, I don't go around ending lives for the sake of it, but hurt those I love and you can be damn sure I'll turn up on your doorstep with only one intention."

I watch her tip the contents of her mug into the sink before placing it into the dishwasher. When she turns back to me, her concerned mum expression is back full force.

"I've given Dawson enough pain relief for about four hours. I've left a box of medication on the coffee table. Two pills every four hours if he needs it. If that's not enough, call me. If you run out, call me. If anything—"

"I'll call you," I reassure her. "He's in good hands, Sarah. I promise."

"I know he is, sweetie. I'm just his mum, I can't help it." She smiles. "I'll just go and say goodbye to them both and I'll be out of your hair."

"Thank you. Thank you for everything."

She nods, squeezes my shoulder gently as she passes, and leaves the room.

I know she's right. I've got a lot to think about. Tonight has revealed a lot of truths, but right now, I'm too exhausted to even remember what they all are.

I listen to their voices before the front door opens and closes, signalling Sarah's departure.

I allow myself two minutes to finish my drink before I walk through to check on them.

"Everything okay?" I ask Emmie, who's sitting on a cushion on the floor beside her dad, holding his hand. My heart clenches at the sight of them.

"Gran is right, you know," Emmie says, startling me. "If you hurt him, I'll be standing right beside her as she puts an end to it all."

"Emmie, it was never my intention to hurt him." My eyes remain locked on Dawson's face. All I ever wanted was to be able to love him. I sigh, and Emmie finally looks up at me.

"You should go shower. You look a mess."

A sad laugh falls from my lips. I haven't looked at

myself, but after what I've been through tonight, I can only assume she's telling the truth.

"Dad has an en suite in his room, second door on the left."

"T-thank you. Do you need anything before I..." I trail off, glancing over my shoulder at the stairs.

"No, I'm okay." I nod, turning away from her and heading for the stairs. "Piper," she calls out, making my steps falter. "I'm really glad you're okay. I'm sorry about my crazy family."

I laugh, this time a lot more genuinely. "I'm glad your dad kept you away from this crazy world, Emmie. You're so lucky to have him."

"I know," she whispers, her voice cracking once more.

Leaving them together, I make my way upstairs to clean up.

I don't want to, but the second I locate Dawson's en suite, I stand at the basin and look into the mirror. My hair is all over the place, my makeup is smeared across my face, and my cheek is still glowing red from where that prick backhanded me. My dress is covered in Dawson's blood and ripped at the shoulder, but thankfully it covers up enough of me that I haven't spent the evening flashing everyone. Lifting my hands, I find marks around them where they were bound with rough rope.

I sigh as I stare into my red-ringed eyes. I shake my head, not wanting the memories of tonight to assault me. Not yet, anyway.

Stripping out of my clothes, I turn Dawson's shower on and step under the torrent of hot water. It runs a murky shade of brown around my feet and my lips curl in disgust.

It was never meant to come to this.

Unable to stop the tears, they fall from my eyelashes and mix with the shower water.

He's playing you, baby girl.

Cruz's words fill my mind, no matter how much I try to force them away. I can't think about them now; I just need to get through the night and ensure Dawson heals, and then I can deal with it. Then I can find out the truth and then make some decisions about my future.

27

DAWSON

Pain. That's the only thing I feel when I begin to wake from what feels like the deepest sleep of my life.

Why does everything hurt—

My eyes rip open as memories assault me one after the other.

Emmie's call to say Piper had gone.

Finding her in that basement.

Dad.

Cruz.

Jinx.

The sound of the gunshots echoes in my mind like they've just happened, and the pain in my shoulder only increases as I remember the bullet piercing my skin.

I remember carrying her out. She's okay. She was alive, and then... nothing.

I look around the darkness of my own living room.

How did I get back here?

Twisting my head to the side, my breath catches when

I find Piper asleep on the floor beside the sofa I'm on, covered in Emmie's pink blanket.

Unable to ignore my need to touch her to make sure I'm not hallucinating from the pain, I reach out with my good arm.

My other shoulder screams and makes my eyes water, but I don't let it stop me. I need to know I'm not imagining all of this right now and the reality isn't that we're both dead, our bodies being taken care of by the team who clean up all of my father's messes.

The second my fingertips connect with her warm cheek, relief like I've never felt before floods me. Emotion clogs my throat and tears burn the backs of my eyes.

She's okay. We're okay.

She stirs from my touch, and I feel bad that my need for her has disturbed her after what she went through because of me.

I stupidly thought my father and Cruz wouldn't find out about this. That we would be safe for a while before I grew a pair and spoke to them about it.

I should have done that sooner instead of burying my head in the sand.

But you didn't care if they got her at the beginning. I swallow down that little thought. It might have been the case, but that all changed somewhere along the line. It might have even happened that first night I fucked her in her kitchen, I was just too deep in denial to admit the truth to myself.

Her eyes flicker open and my breath catches when her tired, violet orbs find mine.

"Piper," I breathe. "Are you okay? Is Emmie okay?"

She chuckles, but it's hollow. "I'm fine. Emmie is fine.

She's asleep upstairs. You were the one who was shot. How do you feel?"

"I'll live."

She scrambles to her knees, taking both of my hands in hers, and stares down into my eyes.

"I didn't think you were going to. Fuck, Dawson. That was the scariest fucking thing I've ever been through."

"I'm sorr—" She presses her hand to my lips to cut off my words.

"I'm not talking about what happened to me. I thought you were going to die in the car on the way here." The tears that were filling her eyes drop. "I-I thought you were going to die because you felt you had to protect me."

"I do have to protect you, Piper. You're my girl."

She shakes her head and averts her gaze. Dread begins to grow in my stomach.

She is still mine, isn't she?

"Whose car?" I ask, needing to fill the gaps.

"Ju... Link's. He pulled up after you collapsed and brought us both back here."

A smile twitches at the corner of my mouth. Of course it was Link.

"And what about this?" I point to my patched-up shoulder.

"Your mum."

"You called my mum?" I ask, astonished.

"I didn't know who else to ask. Do you need any more painkillers? Your mum said—" Releasing her hand, I press two fingers to her lips to stop her talking.

"Let's go to bed."

"Dawson," she warns.

"I can walk up the stairs, baby girl. I refuse to let you

sleep on the floor instead of in my arms." She looks from me to the door and then to her makeshift bed.

"If you're sure it's not too much. I can hardly carry you."

"I'll be fine."

I suck in a breath before dragging up as much energy as I can find to push myself to sitting.

The room spins; I'm not sure if that's the pain or whatever pain relief my mum has given me. She's known to dish out the extra-strong shit like it's sweets.

"You okay?" Piper asks, rushing to my good side and wrapping her hands around my arm.

"Yeah, I'm good."

"You're a really shit liar, you know that, right?"

I laugh at her words and immediately feel lighter as I manage to get to my feet.

It takes what feels like a year to get to my bedroom, but the second I drop down onto my bed, I'm so fucking glad I made the effort.

Piper's footsteps sound out around the room as she faffs about.

"Baby girl, please just come to bed," I demand when she returns with a box of pills and a glass of water.

"I'm just making sure you have everything you need."

"All I need is you, baby. Now get in here."

I watch as she walks around the bed to what I guess is now her side.

This wasn't how I was hoping to introduce her to it.

As she gets closer, I drop my eyes down her body, a smile twitching at my lips when I realise she's wearing one of my shirts.

"You got anything on under that?" I ask.

"Sure do." She lifts the hem, showing me a pair of my boxer briefs.

"Fuuuuck, baby girl. I think I lost too much blood for it all to be rushing south."

"Oh shush, you. There will be none of that."

She lifts the covers back and climbs in beside me. Her arm gently brushes mine as she copies my position, lying on her back and staring at the ceiling.

I can't help feeling like something huge has shifted between us tonight. I guess it's understandable; I still don't know what they put her through aside from what I walked in on. But right now, it feels like there's an ocean between us.

"Piper?"

"Yeah."

"Are we okay?"

She lets out a long breath that does nothing for the concern that's only growing within me. "We'll talk tomorrow, Dawson. Right now, you need to rest."

I want to argue, demand that we talk now, but as I lie there, my body sinking into my memory foam mattress, I begin to lose the fight with my exhaustion.

"Come here," I say, lifting my good arm to pull her over if necessary.

"Dawson, I don't—"

"Please, Piper." I hate the desperate tone in my voice, but I need to know she's here and alive before I pass out again.

The next time I wake, the pain has lessened a little and the sun is brightening the room. But when I turn to look at the other side of the bed, it's empty.

I lie there for two minutes before I push myself up. I make use of the bathroom and brush my teeth before pulling on a pair of sweats and heading out of the room.

I stand at the top of the stairs, contemplating just going back to bed, but the scent of coffee and bacon fills my nose and I start the arduous task of getting down to the kitchen.

"Dad," Emmie squeals the second she spots me. She's off the stool in a flash and by my side, helping me in.

My eyes find Piper's, and what I see there confirms that I was right to worry. She's shut down.

"We had bacon sandwiches; would you like one?" she asks as Emmie directs me to the stool she vacated.

"Yeah, I'd love one." I manage to catch her hand before she escapes around the counter and I pull her into the gap between my legs. Reaching out, I cup her cheek and look into her eyes. "How are you doing?"

"I'll be fine." I raise a brow in question. I hate that she's trying to cover up the seriousness of what she went through yesterday.

"Okay," I say, because even though I know she's lying, I don't want to have the conversation in front of Emmie.

Piper smiles at me but it's forced as she steps out of my hold and sets about making me a coffee and then some breakfast.

"How are you feeling?" Emmie asks, hopping up on the stool Piper left empty.

"I'll be fine, Em. Gran did a good job at patching me up."

"I didn't realise she was such a bad-arse."

"Oh?"

"Yeah, you should have heard her threatening Piper. Even I was scared."

"My mother threatened you?" I ask, ripping my eyes from Emmie to Piper.

"It's okay, Dawson. She has every right to be pi—annoyed."

Emmie rolls her eyes. "You can swear, I'm not exactly an innocent child," she mutters.

"Don't I know it."

"She just doesn't want to see you hurt again. I've already caused you enough," Piper says, ignoring our little father-daughter banter.

"It's not her place to get involved. I'll speak to her."

"Please don't. She has every right, she's your mother and she loves you. I'm just glad she was gentler with her warning than your brother was."

"Did he hurt you?"

She shakes her head and looks at Emmie.

"Em, any chance you could give us a few minutes?"

"Sure thing, old man. I've got homework to do anyway."

"Good girl." She rolls her eyes at me once again before kissing my cheek and disappearing upstairs.

Silence falls upon the kitchen as Piper cooks. The sizzling of the bacon is the only thing that can be heard. I watch her work. She's still wearing my clothes that she slept in last night, and I can't help my eyes from dropping to her bare legs.

She looks unbelievable, making herself at home in my kitchen, dressed like that.

My mouth waters, but this time it's not for the coffee and bacon.

"Here you go," she says, placing a plate in front of me.

Suddenly ravenous, I reach out and lift the first sandwich to my mouth.

I groan around my first mouthful, feeling Piper's stare burning into the side of my face.

"Did he hurt you?" I ask again.

She lifts her wrists and inspects the welts. "It was only Jinx who physically hurt me. Cruz was more about words."

"What did he say to you?"

She opens her mouth to respond when the home phone starts ringing. I ignore it, my need to talk to Piper more pressing than anything anyone can tell me over the phone right now.

"Ignore it," I say when she looks like she's about to move.

"Are you going to get that?" Emmie calls from the top of the stairs.

"No. You're not either."

She mutters something before the voicemail kicks in.

"This is a message for Mr. Ramsey. It's Roger from Partridge Wright solicitors. I'm sorry I missed your call this week. Congratulations on your engagement. If you'd like to return my call when it's convenient for you, we can discuss how to move forward with the money you're now entitled to." He says more, but the blood rushing past my ears makes it hard to discern the words.

Emmie's feet thunder down the stairs until she's standing in the doorway. My eyes don't move from Piper's devastated ones, but I feel Emmie's burning into me.

"It's true," Piper whispers. "What Cruz told me. It's true. You're using me." Her voice trembles and something inside my chest cracks open.

"No, Piper. It's not just that. Please, let me explain." She's already off the stool and backing toward the door to make an escape.

"You were playing me," she sobs, although she doesn't cry. There are no tears in her eyes, just anger.

"No, Piper."

"Stop." She holds her hand up to cut me off. "Just stop lying to me, Dawson. We all heard that. Cruz knows, your father knows. Was it only me who didn't know this was all one big joke?"

"No, I didn't know."

"Go upstairs, Emmie," I demand, but all she does is put her hands on her hips and stand her ground.

"And to think, I stood beside Gran last night because I was worried about Piper hurting you again. But all along, she's not been the one playing games. It's been you. How could you? She loves you, you idiot."

In the time it takes Emmie to rip me a new one, Piper has fled from the kitchen.

"Piper, wait," I call, getting down from the stool and following her. She's already out the front of the house with no shoes on and wearing only my t-shirt and boxers. "Just come back inside. Let me explain."

"No, Dawson. There is nothing you can say to me to make this right. I trusted you. I trusted you with my life, and this is how you treat me. I get that you wanted to hurt me, that you wanted revenge, but I believed we'd moved past that." Another sob rips from her lips, and this time two tears fall with it. "I trusted you," she screams, starting to lose her control.

"Please, just come back inside. Please, Piper. I can explain."

I'm on the verge of trying to drop to my knees to beg her when a car pulls up behind her.

The window drops and the driver says, "Car for Piper Hill."

"Yes, yes that's me," Piper says in a rush, running for the back door of the car.

"Piper, no, please. Just hear me out."

She doesn't look at me as she gets into the back of the car and slams the door.

"NOOO," I cry, racing forward, ignoring the pain that shoots down my body. But I'm too slow; the driver slams his foot on the accelerator and they speed off down the street.

I don't move until the car has turned the corner and is no longer in view.

"FUUUUUCK," I roar into our silent street.

"Come back inside, Dad," Emmie says from the house.

Turning to her, I find her standing in the doorway with her phone in hand.

"You called that car." It's not a question. I already know the answer.

"I can't believe you played her. Who even are you right now?"

"Emmie, I—"

"No, I'm not interested." With that said, she turns on her heels and races up the stairs before the sound of her bedroom door slamming shut makes me flinch even from out here.

28

PIPER

The second the car pulls up at the address I told him to divert to, I fly from the back without a second thought. I should be nicer to him. He put up with me crying all the way here like it was totally normal. He also accepted my new destination with little fuss. Not that I have any clue where he was taking me originally; just the knowledge that it was away from Dawson was enough.

I drag in a shaky breath. My heart still feels like it's been ripped in two as I reach out for the buzzer.

"Yeah?" A sleepy, groggy voice crackles down the line.

"Lisa, it's me. C-can I come up?" My voice cracks, and I hate that he's got the power to do this to me.

"Yeah, yeah," she says in a rush before a buzzing fills my ears.

Pushing through her building's main door, I make my way up to her floor. When I get to her flat, I find the door open and let myself inside.

A fresh wave of tears hits me the second I look at my friend.

"What the fuck did he do?" she asks, coming over and wrapping her arms around me.

"It... it... he..." I stutter against her shoulder.

"Shhh, it's okay," she soothes, holding me a little tighter.

I'm so grateful for her in those few moments. I've been back in London for years now. I've had numerous jobs, but for some reason I never quite clicked with anyone, not just guys. Work colleagues were just acquaintances. But the day I walked up to her reception desk for my job interview, I felt something different between us. Thankfully, we've been close ever since, because right now I have no one else.

Maybe it was my fear of getting close to anyone and getting caught that stopped me from making friends. I don't know. All I do know is that I need her right now like I never have before.

"I'm sorry," I say, pulling back from her embrace when I realise that I've got tears and snot all over her shoulder.

It's not until I look at her that I realise how she looks. Her hair is a mess, her makeup smeared all over her face, and, like me, she's wearing a man's shirt—only hers is a smart button down to my black t-shirt.

"Am I interrupting something? I-I can go," I offer, hoping like fuck that she doesn't take me up on it. I don't think I could handle being alone right now.

"What? No, don't be silly. You're more important. Do you want a coffee? Then you can tell me what that motherfucker has done."

I nod, unable to form words the second I think of the desperation in his voice as I walked away. Of course he was desperate; he needs me for his payout.

A sob erupts and I fall down onto Lisa's sofa and drop

my head into my hands. I drag in lungfuls of air as the scent of coffee surrounds me.

After a few minutes, Lisa places a mug on the coffee table for me before curling herself onto the other end of the sofa and cupping hers in her hands.

"You're hungover, aren't you?" I ask, looking her over once more. Her complexion is pale, and her eyes are bloodshot.

She reaches a hand out and holds her thumb and forefinger a little apart. "Just a teeny bit."

I shake my head at her, glad for the distraction.

"So, go on. What has you knocking on my door this early on a Saturday morning?"

"Lis, it's nearly midday."

"Huh, it must have been a good night." She shrugs, taking a sip of her steaming coffee.

"It's all fake," I whisper, but seeing as she doesn't ask me to repeat it, I assume it was loud enough to hear and understand.

"Nah, Piper. No way. I've seen the way he looks at you."

I shake my head. "Some shit went down with his family last night," I admit, seeing as she already knows how we got to this point. "His brother swiped me on my way to the shop. He—"

"Wait, he swiped you? As in, he kidnapped you?"

"Yeah. He threatened me and told me that everything with Dawson was a lie, that he was playing me to get back at me. That the only reason he proposed was because he was due some inheritance once he was engaged."

"No, that's bullshit. It's got to be."

"It's not," I confirm, forcing the two words out through the emotion clogging my throat. "I might have believed it was if it weren't for the solicitor leaving a very incriminating voicemail this morning."

"Fuck."

"Uh huh." I sip my coffee, barely feeling the burn as it touches my lips and scalds my tongue. I'm too numb. The only thing I can feel is my heart shattering in two as I relive what happened in the past twelve hours.

She's silent for a few seconds as she thinks. "Go back a bit. What happened after you were kidnapped?"

"Do you need to look so excited by this?" I mutter, seeing the twinkle in her eye.

"I'm sorry, I've just never lived through anything like this before. I thought it only happened on the TV."

"Fucking wish it did," I mutter. "He gagged me, bound me and I was hauled to the basement of their clubhouse." I hold out my wrists to show her the damage.

"Holy fucking shit, Piper."

"They chatted some shit. Threatened me. It would have gone a lot further if *he* hadn't turned up and rescued me."

"He rescued you?" She swoons. "Like, full-guns-blazing rescued you?"

"Kind of," I admit. "He was shot."

"Fuck." Her eyes go so wide they almost pop out of her head.

"He's fine. It was a clean shot, in and out of his shoulder. He'll survive."

Lisa lowers her mug to the table and gently rubs at her temples as she tries to process what I've just told her.

"He took a fucking bullet for you?"

"He played me, Lisa. He only wanted me alive to claim what he thinks he's owed." Admitting that hurts like a bitch, but it's the truth. "He wanted revenge on what I did to him all those years ago. So did his father and brother. They should have just killed me and put me out of my misery."

"No," she snaps. "No, don't you ever say that."

"This is such a mess, Lis. I knew when he came back into my life that I shouldn't trust him. Hell, I'm pretty sure he even told me himself not to. Yet I went and bloody fell for him again."

"Did you really ever un-fall?"

"Not helpful," I growl, annoyed that she's right. I've always loved him, and I'm pretty sure I always will.

"So how did you end up here?"

I recount the morning and how I assume it was Emmie who called me an Uber to help me out.

"Smart kid."

"She's the best. She doesn't deserve any of this, which is why he stepped away from this life years ago. One minute she hates me because of what I did, and then the next she discovers her dad is just as bad."

"She'll be fine. You know better than anyone how resilient kids can be."

"She's already lost her mum and uprooted her life. This is just too much."

Reaching back for our coffees, the two of us drink in silence, but Lisa's concerned eyes never leave mine.

"Do you have your stuff?" she finally asks, glancing at the unit by her front door where her handbag sits.

I shake my head. "I haven't seen my bag since Cruz..." I blow out a breath. "I can't even get into my flat," I admit, tears once again pooling in my eyes.

"I've got your spare key, so that's not an issue. You can get a new phone and replace everything else. What matters right now is you." She reaches over and takes one of my hands in hers.

"Thank you, Lis."

"Anytime, you know that. So, what now?"

I blow out a pained breath. "Now? I guess I try to rebuild my life once again." I open my mouth to say more but think better of it. On the journey here, leaving the city crossed my mind. Having a totally fresh start where there's no chance of anyone knowing me. I love city life, but London isn't the only one. I'm sure I'd love others just as much. Manchester, Liverpool, Glasgow... there are plenty of options that are miles away.

But I can't tell her that right now.

She'll tell me it's too soon to make that kind of life-changing decision, and she's probably right. But knowing he's going to be at school with Emmie, knowing that she could walk through my office door at any time and remind me of everything... I'm not sure I can do it.

"Do those hurt?" she asks suddenly, looking down at my wrists and ankles. "I've got some—"

"No, it's okay."

A noise somewhere else in the flat makes me look up at her bedroom door.

It was kind of obvious by the state of Lisa that a man was here, so it's hardly a surprise to hear someone moving about back there. What I am surprised about, however, is how tense Lisa goes the second she hears it.

"Piper, I need to tell you something," she says sheepishly.

"Okaaay." I narrow my eyes at her, wondering what has her so nervous. There's only one man I don't want to see walk out of her bedroom right now, and I'm pretty sure he didn't beat me here, or even know where she lives. I'm not even convinced he likes her.

"It's just that... shit." The door opens, and someone I was not expecting to see emerges wearing just his trousers, his toned, golden torso on full display, and his messed-up sex hair all over the place.

"Henry?" I ask, astonished. I know these two flirt on occasion, but I never thought anything would actually happen between them. Henry is not Lisa's type, as she's pointed out to me time and time again.

"Hey," he says, his voice still rough from sleep. "Is everything okay?" His eyes drop to what I'm wearing, lingering on my new ink, and I want the sofa to swallow me up.

"Um..."

"Piper's got some man trouble," Lisa helpfully points out.

Henry's shoulders tense, his lips pressing into a thin line. His need to protect me is sweet, but it's totally misplaced. "What did he do?" he barks.

"It's a long story. One I'm not repeating again. I just..." I sigh. "Could I get that spare key?" I ask Lisa, suddenly feeling exhausted and needing my own things around me.

"Of course. You want to borrow some clothes too?"

"Yeah, actually. That would be great."

"Come on," she says, waving me toward her bedroom. "Henry, you know where the coffee machine is. Make yourself useful."

He watches the two of us disappear with his brows pulled together.

"I'm so sorry," Lisa says, spinning on me. "I wanted to tell you when you first arrived but..."

"It's fine," I say, dropping down on the end of her bed,

trying to ignore the fact that her bedroom smells like Henry and sex. "There was never anything serious between us. He's fair game."

"We had a little too much to drink last night, and well... this is where we ended up. He's pretty decent; I can't believe you never told me about—"

"Stop, please, I beg you. I said I was okay with it, not that I wanted to swap notes."

She nods and turns to her wardrobe. "These should fit, they're a little tight on me," she says, handing me a pair of leggings. "Aaand... here." She passes me an oversized jumper.

"Thank you. I'm just going to..." I gesture toward her bathroom.

"Take your time, use whatever. I'll be right out there. Would you like another coffee?"

"No, I think I just need to get home."

"Okay." She smiles at me and slips out of the room.

Gathering up the clothes she left me, I take them to the bathroom to pull on.

Despite the fact that I'm almost covered from head to toe, knowing I'm not wearing any underwear leaves me feeling naked and exposed as I walk back out to join them.

Henry is still here. He's made himself at home on Lisa's sofa.

"Here's the key."

"Thank you so much for this."

"You want me to come over later? We could get takeaway? Get drunk?"

I consider my options for a moment. I could do those things alone just to remind myself that I'm once again single while my heart still belongs to a man who stole it when I was eighteen, or I could spend the time with my friend.

"If you don't have any other plans, that would be awesome."

"Whatever you need."

"Hey," Henry says, piping up. "You want a lift home? I need to head out anyway."

"Um..." Do I really want to get in a car with him right now? I guess it's better than a stranger in an Uber. "That would be great, if you don't mind."

"Of course not. Let me just get my shirt back." He looks at Lisa, who giggles like a schoolgirl under his stare, and then turns to the bedroom to change.

Ten minutes later, I find myself sitting in Henry's passenger seat, heading across the city to my flat.

"You want to talk about it?" he asks.

"No, not really." I wrap my arms around myself and curl into his seat.

"Want me to go and knock him out?"

I snort a laugh, and he glances over at me as if my reaction hurt him. "I'm sorry, but you've seen him. You really don't stand a chance."

"Hey, I can hold my own."

"I'm sure you can," I say, hoping it sounds reassuring. Against any other normal guy, he could. But we're not talking about a normal guy here. We're talking about Dawson. I think he already wants to flatten Henry for ever touching me; he doesn't need any more excuses.

"You need to stop at a shop or anything?"

"Henry," I breathe, "I get that you're trying to help right now, and I appreciate it, I really do. But can you please just take me home?"

"Sure."

"And when you get home, you really need to shower, because you've got Lisa's lipstick all over your neck."

His cheeks flame red at my words. "Shit, I'm sorry. Is this weird for you?"

Part of me thinks he wants me to say yes, just to know that what we had actually meant something to me. But I never lied to him.

"Of course not. Just do one thing for me."

"Shoot."

"Don't hurt her." I have no idea if last night was actually a one off, if it was an accident or if Henry was trying to get back at me in some way. I want to say that I'm being delusional, but the way he looked at me when he emerged from her bedroom made my stomach twist in knots. I really hope I'm wrong, but I'm cautious nonetheless.

"Of course. It was just a bit of fun."

"That's good."

"You want me to walk you up?" he asks after pulling into a visitor's space outside my building.

"Thank you for the ride, but I'm fine."

"Okay. I'll catch up with you later, make sure you're okay."

"I don't have my phone."

"Oh... What the hell happened, Piper?"

"Not now." I shake my head. "I'll see you Monday."

Before he can say anything else, I push the door open and end his chance.

Once I'm at the front door, I give him a wave and disappear inside, already knowing that he won't leave until I do so.

As I walk inside my flat, everything feels the same, yet at the same time, everything is different.

When I walked out of here yesterday morning, I thought I was coming back in a few hours to pack a bag and to spend the weekend with my fiancé. How wrong I was.

I turn on the coffee machine and place a mug into it before walking to my bedroom, stripping out of Lisa's clothes as I go.

I walk straight into my bathroom, locking down the thought of him showering right there and the sight of the water running over his body. I turn my back on the glass screen and twist the bath taps before pouring in some bubbles. The scent fills the room immediately, but it does little to make me feel any better. I'm not sure anything could right now.

I retrieve my coffee before sinking into the burning water. But still, I barely feel the sting of pain.

Resting back, I close my eyes and torture myself by replaying the events of last night and this morning through my mind.

I have no idea when it happened, but I must have fallen asleep. I wake with a start, sloshing cold water all over the floor when I sit up too fast.

"Shit," I mutter, pushing myself up and walking straight into the shower. The cold blast helps to wake me up before the warm stream heats my skin.

I reach for my Love Hearts shower gel but think better of it. It might be my scent, but all it's going to do is remind me of him.

In the end, I don't bother. Instead, I just step out and wrap myself up in my fluffy robe, twisting a towel on top of my head.

I tip my now cold coffee down the sink and make myself another before curling up on the sofa and turning the TV on in the hope that I can find something to distract me.

It doesn't work. Nothing works. All I see is him, and it rips me in two.

I barely survived him once. I knew I wouldn't survive him a second time around. What was I thinking?

29

DAWSON

"You're a lucky motherfucker, you know," Link says the second I open the door and find him standing on the other side.

"It was a clean shoulder shot. It was hardly going to kill me."

"Tell that to the poor fucker who had to clean your blood out of the back of my truck," he mutters, following me down to the kitchen. "But that's not what I meant."

"Please, enlighten me."

Link—or Justin, as he used to be known as—and I were always tight growing up as kids. He was the last person I ever thought would show an interest in joining the Reapers and patching in, but a couple of years after I walked away from that life, he walked straight into it. I guess crazier things have happened.

"Piper."

"Oh, yeah."

"What's with the sad puppy tone?"

"I kinda fucked up."

"How? You were unconscious. How'd you manage to fuck shit up while out of it?"

I pass him a coffee and sit beside him with my own. My movements are still slow as fuck, but thanks to the pills my mum left, it hurts a little less right now.

"Wait, you aren't surprised to know she's alive?" He shakes his head, guilt covering his features.

"Link," I growl. This wouldn't be the first time the Reapers have come between us. I fucking hate that my father has his loyalty over me.

"It's not like that. Cruz has been trailing you. He got suspicious and he started looking closer."

"How long?"

"A week."

"He was waiting to strike."

"And you didn't think to fucking say anything?"

"I couldn't. Well, not to you. But I did to him. I told him to let it go, that it was no longer our issue. The two of you seemed happy, and it was as it should have always been."

"But he didn't listen."

"Of course he didn't. He fucking hates her, D."

"I know. He blames her for what his life became." Link doesn't need to tell me that, I've heard it from the horse's mouth enough times over the years.

"You should have warned me."

"What difference would it have made? Last night was always going to happen in one way or another."

My teeth grind, hating that he's right.

"I should have spoken to them."

"Maybe. I'm pretty sure it wouldn't have stopped them."

"So what now?" I ask, dread sitting heavy in my

stomach.

"Your mum's got involved." I drop my head and rub at my temples. *Of course she has.* She's the only one who can talk any sense into my father, and sometimes even Cruz if he's in the right mood. "Prez has called everything off. You should be good to go."

"Just like that?" I ask curiously. After the effort they went to last night, I'm surprised they'd give up so easily.

"I don't think Prez wants to lose any more men to your trigger-happy hands."

"Jinx?" I ask, knowing that I left him with a bullet lodged in his stomach.

"Critical."

"Fucker deserved it. He was about to..." I trail off. Link doesn't need me to paint him a picture of what went down. He's been around that shit long enough to know what happens.

"I get it, man."

"So, what did you do?"

"You mean Cruz hasn't already told you?" I raise a brow.

"All I know is that she's back from the dead."

I blow out a breath. "You know I enrolled Emmie at Knight's Ridge?"

"Yeah. What the fuck is that about? I'm not sure any of us belong at private school."

"She might not belong, but it's what she deserves." He nods. "Anyway, I kinda need to pay for it. I'm due inheritance from my gran, but in order to get it, I needed to be engaged. Piper just appeared at the right time."

"You played her?"

"To start with, yeah. But then—"

"You remembered how pussy-whipped she makes you

and you fell for her all over again?"

"Something like that. I don't give a fuck about the money, really. I just thought I could give Emmie a better start into adult life. It was almost like fate. I needed a fake fiancée, and there she was, like a fucking angel."

"Jesus, D."

I take a sip of my coffee, not really knowing how to respond to that.

"Do you have a plan yet?"

"A plan?" I ask. "I'll find the money somehow. I'm not pulling her out now that she's started."

"I'm not talking about the fucking money, arsehole. I'm talking about your girl. You still love her, right?"

"Never stopped."

"So you need to fucking fight for her."

"She deserves better."

"Fucking right, but are you going to let that stop you?"

Link only stays long enough to drink his coffee before he pulls his phone out, telling me that he's ordering an Uber.

"Wait, how did you get here?"

"How'd you think, motherfucker?" He pulls open my front door and points down the street a little at where my bike sits by the curb.

"You fucker. How'd you do that without the keys... wait, don't tell me. I don't think I want to know."

"Wise choice, man. But just know, she's as good as new now. Piper's bag and shoes are in the top box. Maybe you should take them to her," he suggests seconds before his car pulls up. "That's me, I'm out. You know where I am," he says, turning his back on me and slipping into the car.

Grabbing my keys from the side, I walk down to my bike and get Piper's things.

He's right. I should take them to her. She's going to need her phone and purse.

I place them on the dresser in the hall before making my way upstairs. Emmie hasn't even come out since she slammed her door this morning, I really need to talk to her.

"Em," I call, knocking lightly.

"Go away."

"Emmie, come on."

"No, I'm mad at you."

"I'm sorry, Em."

"Are you?"

"What? Of course. I never wanted to hurt you."

"No, you just wanted to hurt Piper. She betrayed you, I get that, Dad. But she was a kid. I'd like to think that mistakes made at eighteen can be overlooked a little once we're adults. Hell knows I'm gonna screw up over the next few years. She loves you, Dad. Like, really loves you. And you totally destroyed her."

"I know," I whisper, pressing my forehead to her door.

"You love her?"

"Yes."

"You really want to marry her, even if you get nothing but her out of it?"

"Yes."

"Good. Then go and make it right."

I blow out a breath, wondering how on Earth I'm meant to make that happen. Something tells me that she's not going to forgive me easily—if ever—for this.

The second I walk back into my room, I fall down onto my bed, my exhaustion too much to ignore. When I wake again, the sun is sinking, and my room is a warm shade of orange.

The low beat of Emmie's music fills the silence around me, and I push myself up to rest against my headboard.

Reaching over for the water and pills that are still sitting on my bedside table, I take two before heading for the shower, hoping they'll kick in quickly.

I wash as carefully as I can before pulling on a clean pair of sweats and attempting to pull a shirt on, but I give up halfway and grab a zip-up hoodie instead.

"Em," I call through the door once more.

"What?" she barks. Good to know she's still mad, then.

"I'm heading out for a bit. You good?"

"That depends on where you're going."

"Link dropped off Piper's bag, I'm going to take it to her."

"Good. Make her listen to you and bring her back."

"I'll do my best."

Shaking my head at my daughter, I walk away, pulling up the Uber app as I go, knowing that there's no way I'll be able to ride my bike.

It's dark by the time I pull up outside Piper's building. My heart thunders in my chest. I don't know how she's going to take to me turning up like this, but I can't sit at home and do nothing.

Climbing from the car, I look up to her living room window. Her lights are on, but that's the only sign that she might be home.

After thanking the driver, I stalk toward her building, grateful that I don't have to buzz and alert her to my arrival. I pull her keys from the pocket of her bag and let myself in.

For the first time, I make use of the lift instead of hauling my arse up the stairs. The second I step inside, I understand why Piper doesn't use it. It smells faintly of piss.

My lip curls but I stick with it. I don't really have the energy for much else.

Thinking better of letting myself into her flat, I put her keys away and instead knock on her door.

"Who is it?" a female voice that doesn't belong to Piper asks after a few seconds.

"Dawson."

"Fuck off."

"How about we wait for Piper to tell me that."

I swear I hear a growl before the lock clicks and the door is pulled open.

"Good to see that you look like shit," is the first thing that falls from Lisa's lips the second she locks eyes on me.

"Is she here?" I ask, taking a step toward her.

"What do you want?"

"To talk to her."

"Not happening. Thanks for coming by, but we're good without you." She attempts to swing the door closed on me, but I'm quicker and reach out, wincing in pain when it shoots from my shoulder and down my spine.

"I'm not leaving until I've spoken to her."

Our eyes hold, a silent battle of wills ensuing until I hear a voice that makes every single muscle in my body relax.

"Is that dinner?"

"No. Unless you ordered a scumbag."

"Shit, is it—"

"Piper, please. I just want to explain."

"I'm not interested. I thought I made that clear."

Desperate to see her, I push the door wider despite my shoulder's disapproval. My breath catches the second my eyes land on her. She's got her hair piled on top of her head, and she's wearing a white vest with a pair of grey joggers and nothing else. She looks beautiful.

"Please, baby girl. I need you."

"You should have thought about that before you lied to me." Her eyes narrow, daring me to say anything else.

"I never lied about how I feel about you, Piper. It really has always been you."

"Whatever, Dawson. I don't believe you."

My lips part to respond, but I can't find any words.

"That's your cue to leave," Lisa adds.

"Bullshit." I barge past her, much to her irritation, and step right up to Piper. "Piper, I love you," I say, reaching for her hands. "I love you so fucking much."

Tears pool in her eyes, but she doesn't allow them to drop.

"I'm sorry, Dawson. This," she rips her hands from mine and gestures between us, "is over. Lisa is right, you need to leave."

"But—"

"There's nothing left to say." She turns away from me and it splits my heart in two, but I refuse to stand here bleeding out in front of her friend. If she were alone, I might stoop to lower levels.

"I brought your bag. Thought you might need it." I place it on the side and walk backward toward the door. Piper's shoulders tense, but she shows no other sign that she hears me. "I'll give you some time, Piper. But you're wrong. This isn't over. Not by a long shot." With my words hanging in the air, I spin around and march out of her flat.

Lisa slams the door behind me, but she's not quick enough. I hear the sob that rips from Piper before the lock clicks into place.

30

PIPER

I can't say I'm surprised that the first person I see the next morning, aside from Lisa and the other girls in reception, is Emmie.

"I fucking hate him," she huffs, falling down into the seat and crossing her arms across her chest.

"Emmie," I sigh.

"No," she snaps. "Don't tell me how to feel. I hate him for hurting you."

"Things between your father and I have always been complicated."

"I know that, and I also know that *relationships are always complicated,*" she says in a tone that I assume mimics a grownup. "But this fucking blows."

Can't really argue with her there.

After Dawson did as he was told on Saturday night and left, Lisa and I got blind drunk in my need to wash him out of my system. Turning my back on him like that damn near killed me, but I couldn't see any other option. No matter how much my heart wanted him and my body craved him, I was not going to walk straight back into his arms after that.

I was not that girl, no matter how much my heart wanted me to be. My head is stronger.

"I know, Em. I'm so sorry you were dragged into this."

"That's just it, though. I was. If this was fake, he never would have let me get close to you."

"It's my job."

"That's bullshit, and you know it. You were meant to spend the weekend with us. He wouldn't have let you anywhere near me if he wasn't serious."

"You really need to stop overanalysing this. Your dad did what he did. No matter his intentions at the end, at the beginning he knew exactly what he was doing."

"You know what he wanted the money for?"

I shake my head, although I have my suspicions.

"He wanted it for me. For here," she says, gesturing to our surroundings. "He could have found any old woman years ago to claim it if he wanted the cash. We both know that most women would trip over themselves to have a chance to nail him down. But he never did."

"So it was just luck that he found me first?"

"Fate, Piper. It was *fate*."

I want to believe her and think that it was the universe bringing us together once more and making right what went very, very wrong all those years ago, but it's just wishful thinking. I never believed in all that crap before, so why should I start now?

Thankfully, the bell rings and Emmie doesn't have much choice but to head to class, leaving me alone once more with my head spinning.

"Trust me, I hate him as much as you do right now. But you're both hurting. Please, just hear him out."

"I'll think about it," is all I can manage around the giant lump that's formed in my throat.

A part of me wanted to follow Emmie's suggestion and hear what Dawson had to say, but sadly—or maybe not—a bigger part of me was too stubborn to even consider letting him attempt to break down my walls once more. It was bad enough I allowed him to scale them the first time.

As each day passed, I told myself that maybe I'd reach out the next day. But those days soon turned into a week, and that week turned into two.

If I wasn't at school getting harassed by Emmie or out getting drunk with Lisa, then I was at home, curled up on my sofa and still crying over that arsehole.

I wanted to be able to put him behind me and move on with my life. I figured that I should be able to do it again.

A month has passed since that fateful night. Barely a minute goes by where I don't think about Dawson and what happened, but I know that I'm doing the right thing.

Despite what it feels like, maybe the two of us weren't meant to be.

Rolling over in bed, I pull the covers up to my cheek, sighing in relief that today is the start of the school holidays. It's time without worrying about other people and having to plaster a fake smile on my lips every other second to try to convince others that I'm okay. Thankfully, everyone aside from Lisa and Henry are fooled by it. All I have to do is avoid them, and Emmie, and I can almost pretend that none of it happened.

My buzzer goes off, ruining my peaceful lie in. I groan,

rolling onto my back, and then climb out of bed and pull my robe on.

Pressing the button on my intercom, I find Lisa staring back up at me.

"It's too early for this," I moan into the speaker.

"Just let me up and stop bitching. I've got a surprise for you."

"Oh?"

"You won't get it if you allow me to freeze my tits off out here." Laughing at her, I press the button to allow her into the building and then open my front door before heading to the bathroom to freshen up.

"Pack an overnight bag," she calls through to where I'm brushing my teeth.

"What?" I ask, thinking I misheard her.

"Pack an overnight bag," she repeats.

"That's what I thought you said."

"You need a bikini, something nice for tonight, and something casual for tomorrow. Plus your usual shit."

I narrow my eyes at her. "What have you done?"

"I figured that we deserved to spoil ourselves for once, so that's what we're doing. You've got ten minutes. There's a car downstairs waiting for us."

My chin drops. "Right, okay."

I race around my bedroom, packing everything I might need, and, after getting outfit approval from Lisa, she grabs my bag from the bed and all but drags me from my flat.

"I've not even had coffee," I moan as we descend the stairs.

"I've got you covered, don't worry," she calls over her shoulder.

"Lisa, tell me you haven't," I gasp as I walk out of the building and take one look at the vehicle with the engine running before me.

"I told you we were treating ourselves."

She nods at the driver, who climbs out and opens the back door for us.

"It's a freaking limo, Lis."

"I know," she squeals excitedly, poking her head out of the door. "Come on, I picked us up a Starbucks. There are pastries, too."

I have no idea why I'm standing in the middle of the car park arguing about this. My best friend has organised us a limo. This is pretty fucking awesome.

I settle myself on a seat and reach for the coffee waiting for me.

"Where are we going?"

"Surprise." She winks. "Now, sit back, relax, and enjoy the ride."

Immediately, I do as I'm told.

"Wow, I could totally get used to this."

"I know, right? All we need are a couple of billionaire boyfriends and we'd be laughing. Talking of boyfriends. Any word from—"

"I thought we were treating ourselves?"

"We are."

"Then can we please agree not to talk about him? You only asked me yesterday, and the day before that, and the day before that. And my answer is the same. No, I haven't heard a peep."

"That's so weird. I could have sworn..." She trails off when I shoot her a pointed look.

"Okay, sorry. So... any other plans for the break?"

I sigh. I have zero plans. Literally none. I considered booking a last-minute break and just getting out of the city. It was actually what I was going to do as soon as I got up this morning, but Lisa seems to have put pay to that.

"Nope, free and... single." I wince at myself. "You?"

"Not yet, although I'm hoping I might be able to find someone to entertain me for a few nights."

"What happened to Henry? Bored of him already?"

She considers my question for a few moments. "Yes and no. I don't know. He's coming on a little strong."

"By that, you mean he didn't instantly vanish from your life the second you'd come?"

"Something like that."

"Kinda what happens when you dip your nib in the office ink."

"Hey, he was the one doing all the dipping, I'll have you know."

I bark out a laugh, and after weeks of drowning in my own misery, it feels so damn good.

I'm surprised when the limo pulls into a gravel driveway and comes to a stop. The journey was shorter than I was expecting. Leaning over, I look out of the window for the first time.

"Whoa," I breathe, staring up at the impressive manor house before me. "What is this place?"

"It's a hotel with an award-winning spa."

The spa isn't a shock—I kinda guessed it might be something along those lines when she made me pack a bikini—but I wasn't expecting something quite this fancy.

"Come on, we're all booked in for an afternoon of ultimate pampering."

Excitement explodes in my belly, and I realise that it's

the first time I've felt it in a very long time. My life has been a dull mix of grey for weeks, so it's nice to finally have a little colour.

Lisa scoots toward the door as the driver pulls it open.

"Thank you," she says to the driver before waiting for me to join her.

"How much did this cost you?" I ask, staring up at the huge building.

"Not as much as you'd imagine, actually."

"Well, let me know my half and I'll ping it over to you."

She nods at me and we make our way to reception to check-in.

Lisa had organised for us to have an early check-in, so we're immediately handed our room keys and directed to the fifth floor of the building.

"The fifth floor is the top floor," I mutter, hitting the button in the lift. Lisa smiles at me, and my stomach flips. "Tell me you haven't."

"I might have." She winks at me, and I squeal in excitement.

"This is the best start to the holiday ever."

"It was worth it to see you smile, Piper."

Said smile drops slightly at her reminder of why it's been missing for weeks, but I don't dwell on it; I'm too excited to see our room.

"This is by far the nicest place I've ever stayed," I say, spinning on the spot in our suite's living room.

"We're going to get so drunk today," she says, plucking the cooled bottle of champagne from the bucket beside the sofa.

"You can't start that yet," I shriek, but it's too late; she's already shot the cork across the room.

"You only live once, Piper. Might as well make the most of it." She pours it into glasses and hands one over. "To making the most of it." She lifts her glass and clinks mine.

"Thank you so much," I say before lifting the glass to my lips and allowing the bubbles to explode on my tongue. "Mmm, that's so good," I say, taking another sip.

"Okay, unpack and don your bikini. The spa is calling."

With our hotel-supplied white fluffy robes on and our bottle of champagne, we head down to the spa. Lisa confirms our bookings for the afternoon before we're pointed in the direction of the dressing room and pool and relaxation area.

We find ourselves a couple of loungers and drop down. Soft music plays out around us and blends with the trickling waterfall at the other end of the pool.

I sigh, tipping my refilled glass to my lips. "Why don't we do this every weekend?"

"I literally have no idea," Lisa says, resting back and closing her eyes.

As the afternoon passes, we're scrubbed, waxed, polished, buffed, and massaged. I feel like a new woman. It's just a shame none of the treatments magically fix a broken heart.

"I'm not sure I've got the energy to get dressed up and eat," I admit when we stumble back to our suite later that evening.

"Uh-uh, you are not getting out of it. Go shower and shimmy your arse into the little dress you brought. If we're lucky, we might snag those billionaires we're after."

My stomach twists, but I find myself agreeing with her and walking to my room.

I don't mean to do it, but when I get to the end of the

bed, I reach inside my bag and pull my phone out. My heart sinks when I see no messages.

I don't know why I keep torturing myself, expecting that he'll have reached out. It's been a month. It's obvious his warning about us not being over was as fake as our brief relationship.

Throwing it back inside my bag, I march toward the attached bathroom and turn the shower on.

"Wow," Lisa says when I join her in the living room a little over an hour later. "If I were a guy, I'd totally be hard for you right now."

"Because that's not creepy."

"What? I'm just saying. You look hot."

"You could have just said that," I mutter, pulling at the short hem of my dress, feeling a little exposed for a meal in a fancy restaurant.

"Stop it," she chastises, slapping my hands away. "Let's go. I'm starving."

The wine and the food are out of this world, and by the time we're heading back for our suite over three hours later, I've got a nice buzz going on and everything feels a little easier with a stomach full of five-star food and exquisite French wine.

"Go get into something more comfortable. I've got another bottle heading this way."

"You're joking, right?"

"Do I look like I'm joking? We're living, remember?"

"Or dying of alcohol poisoning," I mutter as I make my way to my room.

I make quick work of getting out of my dress and

pulling on something more comfortable. I tell myself not to check my phone, but because I'm weak, I do it anyway. The second I see there's nothing, my need for the wine Lisa mentioned increases tenfold. Is it possible to drink a person out of your system?

31

DAWSON

It took two weeks until I almost felt normal again, but I fear my shoulder is never going to be right. I went back to work last week, desperate to do something other than mope around the house and go out drinking with the guys—something I really shouldn't have done on top of the painkillers. I needed something—anything—to help me numb the pain of walking away from her that day.

I had no idea how much time I was going to give her, but I figured I'd know when enough was enough.

Emmie is still barely talking to me. The most I got out of her was at parents' evening, where she was forced to talk with me and her teachers. I was thrilled to hear that her teachers thought she'd settled in well and was working hard. As far as I knew, she'd had no more fighting incidents since that hockey match, and I was relieved that her teachers didn't have anything to add. It was a great night, aside from the constant death stares I received from Henry. At no point was he brave enough to actually talk to me, though. He just stood there with hard eyes and a smug as fuck grin on his face.

I pull my hood up over my head and drop back into the shadows. Now I'm a little more able to move without wincing in pain, I figure it's time to give my little brother a well overdue visit.

I have no idea if he just thinks I've forgotten about what he did to Piper. He's even stupider than I thought, if he was. He should know I won't let that shit lie.

Mum's checked in on me a couple of times since she patched me up. She came by a few days after to take my stitches out, but I haven't seen her since. I get it. Her loyalty is to my father, just like almost everyone in my life. I roll my eyes at myself. I might have walked away all those years ago, but really, I'll never escape. I might be even more estranged from them now than I was before, but it seems my father still has control of my strings where some of the people I care about are concerned.

Seeing movement up ahead, I press my back farther into the wall and wait to see if it's him. The second I see him, I allow him to turn toward the stairs that lead to his building and then I follow.

I put my foot in the main door to stop it from closing and wait until he has his front door open before I make my move.

I step up behind him, plough my knee into his lower back, and wrap my arm around his throat.

"Ah, brother. I've been expecting you," he growls through the pain.

I push him farther into his flat and kick the door closed behind me. To my surprise, he doesn't try to fight me. As usual, his flat is a fucking mess with beer cans, vodka bottles, and baggies of weed everywhere. I take a closer look at his coffee table to find its glass top covered with powder.

"I thought you'd got off the snow, motherfucker," I growl in his ear.

"Yeah, and here I was thinking you'd got bored of trying to ruin my life."

"Ruin your life?" I bellow, pushing him into the room.

"You and your little bitch... that's all you've done."

"Don't fucking talk about her like that." I fly at him, my hand wrapping around his neck and squeezing enough so he's not likely to forget where it is.

My forehead comes to his, and I angrily breathe in his face. All the while the motherfucker smirks at me.

"I don't control your life, Cruz. Only you have the power to make yourself happy."

"Bullshit," he spits. "You know for a fact that I didn't have a choice after you so selfishly decided to walk away from the life you were born into. You should be the one taking that cunt's orders right now, not me."

"You could have said no."

He laughs at me, but it's full of malice and hate.

"Really? You really believe that?"

"I know he can be a cunt, Cruz, but he's still our father."

Cruz shakes his head at me, sadness creeping into his eyes.

"You've got no idea, do you? No fucking idea."

"No? Tell me. Give me a fucking clue."

But all he does is continue shaking his head at me.

"It's done," he finally growls. "The decisions have been made, and the vows have been taken... well, almost. How did your little woman take the truth?" he sneers.

"Fuck you." Pulling my arm back, I follow through with what I came here for.

My knuckles and rings connect with his cheekbone, and his head snaps to the side.

"You're out of practice, brother." Cruz launches himself from the wall despite the grip I had on his throat. He's not the weak little boy I remember from growing up, the one who would rather be kicking a football around than training inside a fighting ring.

He growls some inaudible warning before he retaliates. Only, much to his annoyance, I'm faster. I block every shot he tries before managing to get a few of my own in.

"You're never going to even look at her again, let alone touch her, threaten her. Do I make myself clear?" I roar once I've finally taken him to the ground. I kneel on his chest as it heaves with exertion. Blood pours from his face, his eyes already swelling, and his lip busted. I can't say I look that much better myself; the taste of copper is filling my mouth and I can feel it dripping from my chin.

"Fuck you, Dawson."

I push from his body and back up toward his door.

"Take this as a warning. The next time you so much as breath around her, I'll put a bullet through your fucking head."

Without waiting for a response, I wrench his door open and storm through it.

Wiping at my lip, I make my way back down the steps and onto the street to find my bike.

Now I've got that out of the way, it's time to get my girl.

I think I've made her wait long enough.

32

PIPER

"I'm not ready to leave," I complain as Lisa and I carry our overnight bags to the door of our suite. "How much do you think it would cost to live in a place like this?"

"More than you'd make in a lifetime, Lis."

She blows out a long breath. "A girl can dream, right?"

I laugh at her as I pull the door open, glancing behind me for one last look at our little bit of heaven. With a sigh, I let the door swing closed as she passes me.

The slight pounding in my temples from the wine last night has almost gone now, thanks to the pills I found in the bottom of my handbag and the incredible breakfast we were served this morning. I'm pretty sure I've never eaten so much in one sitting ever. It felt so naughty, but oh so good. I'll happily eat salad all week to make up for it.

We hand our keys over to the lady sitting behind the desk and thank her for our stay.

"Ready to head back to reality?" Lisa asks as the memories I've been trying to keep at bay since we climbed into that limo yesterday threaten to swallow me whole.

Tears pool in my eyes, and Lisa doesn't miss it.

"Piper," she breathes, taking my hand in hers. "You really need to talk to him. I hate seeing you like this."

"What good will it do? He still lied to me."

"Are you really willing to lose what the two of you had because of a mistake? It's not like you've never made any," she adds quietly.

My stomach twists. I want to tell her that it was different. That I was forced. But at the end of the day, while I might have been young and felt like I had no choice, I didn't need to handle it the way I did.

"Honestly, I have no idea."

"Well, this is just my opinion, so take it as you like. But you need to hear him out at least. Get everything out on the table so you can make this decision with all the facts. Right now, all you've got is hearsay from his brother—who sounds like a right cunt, by the way—a voicemail, and the man's daughter."

I blow out a breath, climbing into the back of the limo behind her.

Before we know it, we're settled in the back of our over-the-top vehicle and heading back toward the city.

"Thank you for this. I really needed it."

"I'm glad it helped," she says, reaching over and squeezing my hand.

"You going out tonight?"

"Yep. My plans are all sorted." She rubs her hands together in excitement. "Hopefully, I can find a man who'll appreciate all of this hard work." She gestures to her body, and I laugh at her idiocy.

I expect her to invite me because it's what she usually does, whether she's heading out with a group from work or others she parties with, but the invite never comes.

I don't dwell on it. I'm more relieved than anything else. After that much pampering and relaxation, all I want to do is sleep.

I decided last night that I'm going to look for a last-minute getaway the second I get home. Maybe Monday to Friday, and then depending on how I feel, I'll bite the bullet and talk to Dawson once I'm back, hopefully with a clearer head.

It must be half an hour later when the limo pulls to a stop. Knowing that we can't possibly be home yet and sensing that this isn't just a pause for traffic, I sit forward and look out of the window.

"What the hell?" I mutter, seeing an empty fairground only a few feet away.

When I turn back to Lisa, I find a weirdly tense expression on her face.

"What?" I bark, confusion rushing through me and damn near twisting my stomach in two.

"I need you to get out of the car, Piper."

"What? This is insane. I just want to go home."

"Piper, just do as you're told," she laughs.

A second later, the door is pulled open and the fresh, late October air comes rushing inside.

I look from her to the open door, my brows pulled together.

"Go on," she encourages, but although she's smiling, I can see her own nerves.

I narrow my eyes at her, but, sensing that she's not going to give me anything, I scoot forward and climb from the car.

The sun makes me squint as I step to the ground, but despite the fact that I can barely see, I don't miss a familiar tingle that races down my spine.

When I look up, the first thing I see is the Ferris wheel in the distance. I gasp, knowing that he's close, my heart thundering in my chest.

I've totally been set up.

Twisting around, I search for the person I know is staring at me. I don't have to look far; the second my eyes land on the entrance to the closed fairground, I find him.

A breath rushes out of me as I take him in.

My eyes drop to his feet, finding his well-loved boots, and I make my way up. His dark jeans are ripped at the knees, exposing his ink, before sitting low on his slim waist, his white t-shirt shows off his ripped abs before his leather jacket covers his arms and shoulders. My body aches, being so close to him after all this time. We've been apart longer than we've been together, but it doesn't matter. The pull is there. If anything, it's stronger than ever.

Steeling myself, trying to prepare for seeing his face and looking into his eyes, I lift my head.

My breath catches at the dark shadows that circle his eyes, but it's the cut lip and eyebrow that really concern me. He's been fighting. I want to look back to his knuckles to confirm what I already know, but the second my eyes lock onto his dark ones, I fall under his spell.

"Piper," he breathes, taking a step toward me.

My head screams run, that being here is a bad idea, but my heart yearns for me to step forward and straight into his body, to feel his arms come around me and for him to tell me that everything is going to be okay.

"W-what is this?" I ask when he's close enough to hear my whispered voice.

"This?" he asks, gesturing behind him. "This is me

trying to make things right, baby girl. You want to go for a ride with me?"

I look up at the Ferris wheel and swallow nervously.

"I'll keep you safe, I promise."

His words threaten to cripple me.

Curling my fists, I press my nails into my palms in a lame attempt to keep myself grounded. It's pointless, I already know it's impossible around him.

A car door closes behind me, and when I spin, I find Lisa sitting in Henry's passenger seat before he floors it out of the car park.

"She... you..." I seethe, looking back at him.

"Don't be mad at her, I gave her very little choice."

A thought hits me. "Last night, the hotel... that was all you, wasn't it?" I don't need the answer, I can read it on his face. "You play dirty, Dawson."

"I just do what I think is necessary to get what I want." His smile almost melts me. He holds his hand out, but, much to his disappointment, all I do is look at it.

His eyes drop with sadness, but he takes a step toward the closed entrance nonetheless.

I walk beside him, keeping a somewhat safe distance. "Are we meant to be going in here?" I ask as he unhooks the chain around the fence and opens the makeshift gate.

"I thought you liked breaking the rules." He winks at me, and it tells me all I need to know. He's organised this.

He doesn't stop walking until we're in front of the Ferris wheel.

"I hope you know that I'm still as scared of heights as I was back then."

"I don't doubt it, baby girl. Come on, time to face those fears."

He gestures for me to step in the car, and I stupidly

follow orders. The car rocks the second I sit down, and my heart jumps into my throat.

I swallow down my fear. It's not the most pressing issue right now. I need to keep my head to hear whatever Dawson has to say to me.

He joins me, sitting so close that the entire length of his body presses against mine, and then wraps his arm around my shoulder.

My mouth waters as his scent fills my nose.

I'm so fucked right now.

A man appears out of nowhere and steps into the little booth to get the ride running.

"I'm sure there was a less scary way for you to make your point," I mumble as the ride starts to move.

"I'm sure there was." He falls silent for a few minutes, and I start to wonder if he hasn't actually brought me here to talk. But then the ride jolts to a halt with us at the very top. The car rocks and my stomach turns, my eyes slamming shut in fear.

"Tell me he knows it's broken. Tell me I don't have to climb down, please."

Dawson chuckles lightly beside me, pulling me tighter into his side.

"He's stopped it because I asked him to, Piper. Nothing is broken, and there will be no climbing." His lips drop to my ear. "Unless you want to climb me," he whispers, setting off sparks of desire throughout my body.

I chastise myself. I'm angry with him; I should not want to do what he just suggested.

With my eyes still closed, I stupidly picture what it's like to be wrapped around his body with his large hands holding me up and driving me crazy.

I shake my head, hoping the thoughts will fall out with the movement.

"P-please, can you just say what you need to say so we can get down?"

"Look at me, baby girl."

I turn to him, but my eyes remain shut.

"Open your eyes," he whispers. "It's just you and me, baby."

After a beat, I do as he says, gasping at the heated look in his eyes when I find them immediately.

"Emmie just turned up at the studio one day, telling me that she was moving in with me. She'd fallen out with her mother, again, and said she was done. It was what I'd wanted for years, but her mother barely let her spend her allocated time with me, let alone move in with me."

"Well, this time was different. When I called her that afternoon, she told me to do whatever and that our daughter was now my responsibility. I still don't know what tipped them both over the edge. Emmie has refused to talk about it, and since that phone call, I haven't been able to get hold of her."

"Anyway, Emmie moved in with me. She's always been a good kid, but her mother didn't exactly give her the best start in life. Despite my almost constant offers to help, they lived in one of the roughest council estates in London, and Emmie was forced to witness God knows what on a daily basis. Those horror stories you hear from inner-city schools on the news? Well, they pale in comparison to what used to go on in her old secondary school."

"We picked up her results—they were as bad as we were both expecting—and I could see the disappointment on her face. She was better than the shit she was forced to put up with on a daily basis with her mother."

"I decided there and then that I was going to do something about it. I know some people on the board for Knight's Ridge, and I reached out to see what I could do."

"They agreed, but they told me there would be no fee subsidy. Not that I really expected one. I'd had some inheritance sitting in a bank account since I was a kid that I'd been adding to. I knew I'd be able to cover the first couple of terms, but after that it was going to be an issue if I didn't do something drastic."

He blows out a breath. His eyes find mine for a beat before he looks back to the blue sky ahead of us.

"When my grandad died five years ago, my gran explained to me that they were leaving everything to me. But that there was a clause. I had to be engaged to get it."

"I laughed at her at the time, thinking it was insane. But the two of them had been married forever and I knew they just wanted to see me happy."

"I never really thought about that money after that day. I wasn't interested in getting married, and I didn't need it."

"But that all changed with Emmie. I wanted to give her the world, to open up possibilities that she'd never have without a decent education. So I decided that I needed to find a woman."

"My intentions were shit, I can't deny that. I was going to use her for what I needed and then dump her. I can't pretend that I was going to do anything else. My daughter was the priority, and that was all I could see."

"Then before I could start putting my plan into place, I found you."

He reaches out and takes my hand in his, tangling our

fingers together. His touch soothes something inside me, stopping me from pulling away.

"I was so angry that morning. Not only did you drag up the pain and heartache that you left in your wake, but you were alive, and you never reached out to me. You never once tried to tell me. I loved you so fucking much, Piper, and you just allowed me to think you were gone."

"I'm sorry, I—"

"No," he says, bringing his eyes to mine once more and shaking his head. "This isn't about what you did. You don't have anything to apologise for."

"I thought it was the perfect revenge. Make you fall for me again and then drop you almost as fast as you did me."

My heart thunders, listening to him talk about this quite so honestly. I want to be furious at him, I want to shout and scream for attempting to treat me so poorly, but I can't. I can see his pain from all those years ago shining bright in his eyes. As much as his actions the past few weeks might have been wrong, I can't ignore the part I played in them.

I was the one who put that pain there. Caused him so much heartache.

"But I forgot something."

"W-what?" I ask when he falls silent.

"I forgot how incredible you were, how you could make me smile like no one else, how just your presence made everything about my life better. And..." he sighs, squeezing my hand tighter and staring right into my eyes. "I forgot how much I love you. I tried to ignore it, to push it aside and keep it in the past where I thought it belonged, but the truth is, I never stopped loving you."

The tears that had been pooling in my eyes finally fall over.

"It was always you, Piper."

"Dawson."

"When I asked you to marry me, I wasn't thinking about the money. The words weren't about deception. They came out of panic, because I knew I could never lose you again. I needed to keep you this time, baby girl. We'd been offered a second chance, and I knew I needed to grasp it with both hands."

"But... y-you never even bought me a ring," I say, feeling ridiculous. Really, a piece of jewellery means nothing, but Cruz's words still ring out in my head.

He laughs. "Of course I did, baby girl. I'd planned on taking you out that Saturday night and asking you properly. We just... never got there."

Releasing my hand, pushing his hand into his pocket and pulling out a small black velvet box.

"Oh my God," I gasp, my hand covering my mouth.

He turns to me, the determination on his face making my heart clench as I wait for what he's going to say.

"Piper... the only thing I've ever wanted is you. I don't care about the past, I don't care about your family, I certainly don't care about the money. It's just you, Piper. Always you. I love you so much. I never thought we'd have another chance, but I'm not letting it slip through my fingers. I promise to get down on one knee the second we're back on solid ground if you want me to, but, Piper Collins, will you marry me?"

He opens the box to reveal the most stunning rose gold engagement ring with a huge diamond in the centre.

"Dawson," I breathe, unable to take my eyes off it. It's perfect, utterly perfect. "You chose this?" I ask.

"Yeah, you used to love rose gold, so..."

I shake my head, hardly able to believe what's just

happened.

"You... you really want this... me... after everything?"

"Oh, Piper." He releases my shoulder and cups my cheek. "More than I can explain. It was always meant to be you and me."

"It was," I sob, unable to contain it any longer.

"So what do you say? Shall we make it official?"

"Yes," I cry, forgetting about everything but this incredible man in front of me.

His fingers twist in my hair as he pulls my lips to his.

He kisses me gently to start with before his tongue slips past my lips and searches mine out.

I have no idea how long we're up there, kissing like a couple of teenagers, but when he pulls back, I realise it was nowhere near long enough.

"I love you too," I blurt. The smile that lights up his face makes our time apart almost worth it.

He sits back, pulls the ring from the box and reaches for my hand.

I watch in amazement as the boy who's held my heart since I was eighteen slides that incredible ring onto my finger.

"What do you know, it fits perfectly." He smiles.

"You knew it would, didn't you?"

"Might have." He winks. "Ready to get back to the world?"

"Yes, please." He laughs at my eagerness, and I can't help but join him.

"We can come down now," he bellows, making me jump.

"Only you would lock me up here against my will to ask me to marry you," I say as the wheel starts to move.

"I needed to make sure you listened to me."

"Still seems a little unnecessary," I mutter, but I can't wipe the smile off my face.

The second we're at the bottom, he pushes the bar away from us and pulls me from the car. I just about manage to shout a thank you to the guy who clearly did us a massive favour this morning, seeing as the three of us are the only ones here.

"Dawson, slow down," I cry, my legs going faster than I can control as he pulls me along behind him.

"Nope, I've got plans."

"Oh yeah?" I ask as we race through the gate toward the waiting limo.

"Yeah, now get in." He pulls the door open and all but pushes me inside before the driver even has a chance to get out.

"I can't believe you got us a limo."

"Only the best for my girl," he whispers as he backs me into the seat and then crawls up my body, giving me no option but to lie back.

His huge body engulfs mine, his hand running from my thigh up to my waist.

"Fuck, I've missed you," he mutters before taking my lips once more in a bruising kiss.

I'm so lost in him that I don't even think to look to see if the privacy glass is up as his hand slips inside my hoodie and up to my breast. I'm only wearing a bralette beneath, and Dawson finds his way under the fabric in no time.

"Ow. Oh God," I groan when he pinches my nipple hard.

He presses his knee between my thighs and my legs automatically wrap around his waist, his length pressing against my sensitive core.

"Dawson, please," I moan, shamelessly grinding against him. It's been entirely too long since he's had his hands on me, and now he's here, I'm damn near desperate.

He rips his lips from mine and looks down at me. His eyes are dark, hungry, and dangerous, and they only make me wetter for him.

"Question is, how many times can I make you come before we get to your place?" His hands wrap around the edge of my leggings and he drags them and my knickers down my hips.

My skin burns with need for him, my temperature soaring.

With his hand around the back of my neck, he pulls me from the bench. My hoodie and bra join my leggings in a heap on the floor before he drops his lips to mine once more as he lowers me back down.

His lips trail across my jaw and down my neck. He alternates between soft kisses and sharp nips to my skin that drive me crazy.

"More," I beg. "More." I roll my hips against him to find some friction.

"My greedy baby girl," he groans against my collarbone before descending for my breast.

His hot lips wrap around my nipple and I cry out as bolts of pleasure shoot to my core. "Can... can he hear us?" I ask, my mind suddenly aware that we're not the only ones in his vehicle.

"Fuck knows. As long as he can't see you, I don't give a fuck."

"Dawson," I scream when he bites down on my nipple so hard I see stars.

33

DAWSON

My mouth waters as I spread her thighs wide and run my tongue up the length of her pussy.

She's so wet for me, so ready for me to push my cock deep inside her, but I need to wait. That time is coming. Right now, it's about her. My fiancée.

I know she has been for a while, but it's official now. She said yes despite everything—and while my cock wasn't inside her—and she's wearing my ring. My fucking ring.

I'm brought back to reality when her fingers slide into my hair and twist until I swear she's about to pull it out.

I tease her clit until she's crying out for more. Lifting my fingers, I give her what she needs and push them deep inside her.

"Oh God," she cries, her back arching off the bench, and I relentlessly rub at that spot inside her that drives her crazy. "Dawson, Dawson, Dawson," she chants, and my chest swells with pride and love.

I had no idea if my words were going to be enough

today. A big part of me thought she'd refuse to even get out of the limo once she learned that I was waiting for her. But she did, and not only that, she allowed me to get her up on that ride and give her all my truths, all of the things I should have told her the second I realised how I felt.

"Shit, I'm gonna..." She trails off as her release slams into her, but I don't stop until she's back from her high. Her body convulses, her juices flood my fingers, and her fingers grip even harder as she rides it out.

Sitting up, I take her with me until I settle back against the bench seat and place her so she's straddling my lap.

Instantly, her lips find mine and she swipes her tongue into my mouth, growling when she tastes herself.

Her arms lock around my shoulders as she finds my hard length beneath my jeans and begins rubbing herself on it.

"Baby girl," I warn, my hands coming to her hips to slow her movement.

Ripping her lips from mine, she stares down into my eyes. Her usual violet ones are dark and blown with lust. They flick down to mine for a beat when I sweep my tongue along the bottom one before she looks back up.

"Fuck me, Dawson. Show me just how much you've missed me."

She circles her hips.

"I was waiting until..."

"If you even think about saying our wedding night, I can tell you now that you won't make it until then."

I want to laugh, but the serious look on her face kills my amusement. The knowledge that she needs me this much is sobering as much as it is a head fuck.

I stare at her, really stare at her.

"Fuck, I love you."

Her hands go for my waistband before my arms even have time to move, and she has the fly undone in record time. I lift my hips slightly and she tugs the fabric just low enough to free my aching cock. Her burning hot fingers wrap around my tortured length. I can't help the growl that passes my lips the second we connect. It's been too long, way too long since I've been inside her.

"Piper," I groan as she jacks me a couple of times.

"Hmm... who's the impatient one now?" she teases.

"Baby, please, just..." I lose my words the second she lifts up and guides the tip of my cock to her entrance. She's so slick from her previous release that I slide deep inside her in one smooth move.

"Oh fuck," I bark. My head falls back for a second, my eyes closing as I revel in the sensation of her body wrapped around me. "So good, baby," I whisper, lifting my head and threading my fingers through her hair. "So fucking good." I crash her lips to mine as she starts to move. It's fucking incredible, but it's not enough.

Taking her hips in my hands, I help lift her so she's almost completely off me before dropping her back down at the same time my hips thrust up.

"Oh, fuck," she screams every time the head of my cock hits her cervix.

Her back arches, thrusting her tits in my face. Leaning forward, I capture one in my mouth and suck hard before biting and laving at the sting with my tongue. I move to the other side and give it the same treatment. All the while her movement becomes more erratic as her release creeps closer.

"Come for me, baby girl."

"Dawson," she moans, her nails raking over my

shoulders. If it weren't for my t-shirt, I've no doubt that she'd be gouging my skin from my body right now.

I move her faster, slamming into her harder.

Her body begins to tighten and I drop my fingers to her clit to give her the final push.

My name echoes around the enclosed space as her body locks up for a beat before pleasure races through her. She clamps down on me so hard I have no choice but to follow. My eyes slam shut as my cock jerks inside her. A groan rips from my throat as my fingertips dig into her hips, holding her in place while we both ride out the final beats of our release.

There's no way the driver doesn't know what's going on back here right now. Not that I give a fuck.

"Oh my God, Dawson," Piper gasps as she looks out of the window and tries to scramble from my lap.

Following her stare, I find that we've stopped and are parked out the front of her building.

"Huh, I guess we're back."

"How long have we been here?" she asks, as I finally allow her to lift off me so she can find her clothes.

"No idea," I say, watching her fight with her leggings in her panic, a smile playing on my lips at her obvious embarrassment.

"The windows are blacked out, baby. No one saw—"

"The driver knows. He has to."

"So?" I ask, finally moving to tuck myself away.

"So? Oh my God." She drops her face into her hands.

"No point in acting all innocent now. I vividly recall you being the one who demanded I fuck you."

"Ugh, what you do to me?" she mutters, pulling her hoodie over her head and shoving her feet into her boots.

I chuckle as I move to the door and push it open. The

second my eyes adjust, I find our driver standing a few feet away with a smirk.

"Great ride. Thanks, man." I pass him a couple of notes I had in my pocket and take Piper's bag from beside him. "Come on, baby," I call back inside, knowing that she's hiding.

"I can't believe you just said that," she mutters to both mine and the driver's amusement.

Finally, she emerges, her cheeks glowing bright red from embarrassment, and I don't make it any better when I throw her over my shoulder and slap her arse.

"I'm not done with you yet," I announce, marching up to her building's main door right as one of her neighbours holds it open.

"Put me down," she demands, her tiny fists hitting my arse but having absolutely no impact. "Dawson, I'm not joking, put me down right now or I'll..."

I can't help laughing at her warning. "Or you'll what?"

"I'll... I'll..."

"Come back to me when you have a real threat to dish out, baby girl."

"I won't have sex with you again," she blurts.

An amused chuckle falls from my lips. "Is that right?"

"Yep, maybe I'll impose the wedding night rule."

"I'd like to see you try. You won't last twenty minutes once we're inside your flat."

"Try me," she mutters.

"Oh, baby. I'm going to be doing more than that."

I rummage around in her bag to find her keys with her still hanging over my shoulder.

"You can put me down now," she huffs.

"Nope."

I push through the door, drop her bags to the floor, and march straight for her bedroom.

"Dawson," she fumes, resuming her assault on my arse. That is, until she squeals as she goes flying through the air and lands in the middle of her bed. She bounces a few times but her eyes remain trained on me.

I shrug off my jacket before reaching behind my head and pulling my t-shirt off in one foul swoop.

Piper gasps and my smirk widens, my fingers dropping to my jeans and popping them open. I toe off my shoes and kick everything off aside from my boxers.

"Now..." I growl, stalking toward her. "Where were we?"

"I was telling you that you were an arse and that we weren't having sex again." I can already see her restraint waning as her eyes run down the length of me.

"Oh, that's right. The only thing is..." I push my hand inside my boxers and grasp myself. Her eyes follow my movement, her teeth sinking into her bottom lip. "That doesn't work for me."

I continue moving but hiding myself from her.

Her eyes get darker, her skin flushing once more.

"Hot, baby?"

She shakes her head, her defiance getting the better of her. It'll only last so long.

"Hoodie off," I demand, my eyes holding hers.

She sits stock still for a beat before she scoots forward and follows orders.

Her hoodie hits the floor and her bra follows before she pushes her leggings and knickers back down. When she stands, she makes sure she's so close to me that her nipples brush up my chest.

A growl rips from my throat before I fist her hair and tilt her head back.

"You're playing with fire, baby. And you will get burned."

Her eyes sparkle as her fingertips tickle down my stomach. My muscles bunch everywhere she touches before she slides both hands into the waistband of my boxers and pushes them from my hips.

My eyes search hers as our breaths mingle. A battle of wills, one that she's already lost, ensues.

Tension crackles between us, the culmination of desperation after so much time apart, the passion that's always simmering on the surface, and the desire that our time together in the limo barely scratched the surface of.

"Fuck it," she mutters, jumping into my arms and wrapping her legs around my waist.

I can't help but laugh into her kiss.

"Just kiss me, Dawson."

I forget all about muttering the words 'I told you so' and instead walk her toward the bed. I lower her down gently before crawling over her.

"Now," I murmur, peppering kisses along her jaw, "let me show you just how much I've missed you."

My lips make their way down her body, much like they did in the limo, but this time, I'm in no rush and I savour every single inch of her.

"Oh God, please," she begs as I trail my tongue down her inner thigh.

"What do you want, baby?"

"You, anything, just... you."

"Good answer," I whisper, trailing my finger through her wetness and dipping it inside her just enough to drive her insane. "But it's not specific enough for me."

"Your cock, Dawson. I need your cock. I need you to fuck me."

As I line myself up against her entrance, she purrs like a fucking cat and tries to suck me deeper.

"How about this?" I surge inside her, shooting her up the bed until her head connects with the headboard, but I wrap my hands around her hips and bring her back down to me before folding over her and brushing my lips against hers. "You get my cock, but instead of fucking you, I tell you how much I love you..." I place a kiss to the corner of her mouth, moving my hips slowly. "I tell you how incredible you are, how beautiful you are..."

"Oh God, Dawson." Her eyes fill with unshed tears as I move inside her with slow, considered movements.

"How I can't wait to spend the rest of my life with you, and make love to you." I don't give her a chance to respond. Instead my tongue slides past her lips and laps at hers at the same slow pace as my hips.

One of my hands wraps around the back of her neck so I can tilt her to deepen the kiss and she hooks her leg over my hip.

"I love you, Piper. I always have and I always will."

"I love you too, Dawson. Always."

34

PIPER

Dawson left me to finish up in the shower five minutes ago, promising to have a coffee ready for when I get out.

I wash the bubbles from my skin and step out, finding both of my towels missing.

"Dawson," I call, coming to stand in the bathroom doorway with water running down my body.

My breath catches when I find him staring back at me, only now, he's fully dressed once again.

"Going somewhere?" I ask, trying to mask the disappointment in my voice.

We might have finally dragged ourselves out of my bed to wash away the sweat of the past few hours, but I wasn't planning on leaving, or even dressing, anytime soon.

"Yeah. Pack a bag, we need to go."

"Go? Go where?" My heart immediately jumps into my throat and I rush forward. "Is everything okay? Emmie? Do... they still want me?"

"Everything is fine," he soothes, pulling me into his

arms despite the fact that I'm going to get his clothes wet. "We just can't be here."

"Why? I ask, my brows pulling together. "Don't you like my flat?" I feel slightly offended. This has been my home for years; why wouldn't he like it?

"It's great. There's just one problem with it."

"Oh?" I quirk a brow.

"It's not our home."

Butterflies erupt the second those two words pass his lips.

Our home.

Piper and Dawson.

A wide smile threatens to spread across my lips, but I contain it for now.

"O-our home?"

"You're wearing my ring, baby girl. Now, pack what you need for tonight. You're moving in."

"But—"

"You really going to argue about this?"

"Um..." My eyes hold his as he waits to see what I'm going to say. "No, just wondering about when we're going to get the rest." The smile I've been holding bursts free.

"I'm going to regret this, aren't I?" he laughs. "Now, put some clothes on before I take you again and you can't walk into our house."

I shoot into action, pulling on some underwear and then clothes. Now he's mentioned being there, it's the only place I want to be. This flat might have been my home, but I've got a new one now, and it's wherever Dawson is. He's always had my heart anyway, so he may as well get my body to go with it.

―――

Thirty minutes later, we're sitting in the back of another car—one without a privacy screen—heading across town.

My hand tenses in his hold and I feel his eyes turn on me.

"You're thinking about the limo, aren't you?"

"What makes you say that?"

"I know your tells, baby. Your cheeks are flushed, your breathing is heavy, and I bet that if I were to dip my fingers—"

"Okay, you've made your point," I say, quickly shutting down giving another driver some entertainment for the day.

"You're no fun," he sulks, his lips curling into a pout.

"Who was on the other end of this?" I ask, running my fingers over the recent cuts on his knuckles. I've wanted to ask since I first saw them, but he's ensured that I've been thoroughly distracted.

"I paid Cruz a visit."

"Oh."

"You don't have to worry about him or my father anymore. It's over, baby."

"H-how?"

"Short version, I told them all to fuck off and leave us alone."

"And the long version?" I ask.

"It doesn't matter. I'm done with them, for good now. It's just me, you, and Emmie from here on out, baby."

"I'm so sorry, I never meant to break up your family."

"Piper, my family has been broken for a long time. This was just the final nail in an already very rocky coffin. I'm just glad no one ended up in one."

"So Cruz is still alive?"

"Sadly," he mutters.

"Dawson, that's your brother," I chastise.

"And you're going to be my wife. That wins hands down every fucking time, baby."

"What about Jinx?" I ask, thinking of him bleeding out in that room after Dawson shot him in the stomach.

"He's fine."

"Okay. That's... g-good, I guess."

"Is it?" he asks, his brows shooting up. "After what he was..." he trails off, not wanting to say the words as much as I don't want to think about them.

"I just meant that the fewer people you've..." I glance to the driver, realising how this conversation must sound to him. "Yeah... just... the fewer the better, you know?"

Dawson laughs, and it makes my chest swell. He reaches out and pulls me into his body. "Yeah, baby. I know." He presses a kiss to the top of my head and we fall silent for a few minutes as London passes us by.

"At least Emmie should start talking to me again now," he mutters.

"What? Why isn't she talking to you?"

"She hasn't since you left."

"But that's been..."

"I know. A long fucking time."

"I knew she was pissed. She used to turn up at my office every day to tell me."

"Every day?"

"Yup. She really needs to start making some friends."

He falls silent. "Did I make the right decision putting her there? I want to do right by her, give her a good education, but equally, I don't want her to just exist."

"You're doing an amazing job, Dawson. She's lucky to have you."

"I don't know about that. But it's not too late to move

her; she could still catch up elsewhere... somewhere... cheaper."

"What are you talking about? You've got that money to pay for her tuition."

"I'm not taking it."

"No, Dawson. Don't do that just because of what happened. Both of you deserve that money."

"I don't want you to think—"

"I don't." I take both his cheeks in my hand and stare deep into his eyes. "Forget about the reason for getting it. It's just inheritance, Dawson. An inheritance that could make your daughter's life. Don't refuse it because of me. Give her everything she's missed out on, everything she deserves."

"You're fucking amazing, you know that?"

I shrug in his hold. "I'm just me, Dawson."

"I know, that's the amazing part."

The car finally comes to a stop outside Dawson's house and we climb out before he grabs my suitcases from the boot.

"Be quiet," he warns before pushing the key into the lock and stepping inside.

I look around at his home. It's exactly as I remember, and I instantly feel relaxed. There's something about this house, although I'm pretty sure it's got nothing to do with the bricks and everything to do with the people inside it.

"Emmie," Dawson calls, "can you come down here please?"

When a loud, "No," comes in response, I have to stifle a laugh. She really is pissed.

"Emmie," he warns. "I think you're going to like it."

There's a loud groan before her footsteps creak against the floorboards above our heads.

We wait silently as she descends the stairs. My heart pounds in my throat as I wait to see her reaction.

The second she registers I'm here, her entire face lights up.

"Piper," she breathes. "Dad, please tell me this is for real."

She looks between the two of us, waiting for confirmation. "It is, Em. She said yes, properly this time."

I hold my hand out so she can see the ring, and Emmie squeals before running at us both and pulling us into a hug.

I look up when I sense Dawson staring at me. "I love you, baby," he mouths over his daughter's head.

"I love you too." Reaching forward, I press my lips to his once Emmie has stepped back.

"Oh, ew. Am I going to have to put up with this all the time now?"

"We'll try to keep it down," Dawson mutters against my lips, not even bothering to attempt to hide his smile.

"Ugh, for Christmas I want better speakers," she announces before turning toward the kitchen. "We need to celebrate. Drinks?"

"Yes," I agree, following her to find her pulling out a bottle of champagne from the fridge.

"I wondered why this suddenly appeared," she says, eyeing her father when he follows me through.

I turn to look at him with wide eyes.

"What?" he says with a laugh. "I was feeling hopeful. And you, young lady, can have one and one only."

"Ugh, keep your hair on, old man, it's not like I want to actually get drunk with you two."

Dawson laughs, taking the bottle from her hands and popping the top.

The three of us raise our glasses.

"To the future, family, and the love of my life."

We both clink as Emmie makes a gagging sound.

Ignoring her, we take a sip before he pulls me into his arms.

"How it always should have been, baby girl."

And in that moment, I'm just an eighteen-year-old girl falling in love all over again.

EPILOGUE

Piper
Two months later...

"I never thought I'd get to do this," Emmie says from behind me, her voice soft and full of emotion.

I look up to the mirror and my eyes find hers. They're full of unshed tears, but she has a wide smile on her face. I know the feeling.

"You look beautiful."

"Thank you, but it's nothing compared to you. Dad's going to lose his shit."

"Em," I warn, but I can't help laughing.

She shrugs, pushing her feet into the heels I convinced her to wear today. She might have got a say on the dress, but there was no way she was wearing a pair of Converse as she requested.

I watch her, the same worried feeling tugging at me that has only been growing over the past few weeks.

I started off believing her when she told me that it was just the pressure of school work. That she wasn't used to having so much and having teachers who cared if it was handed in or not. But as the days passed, I can't help feeling like there's more to the story.

As far as I know, she's not got into it with the girls since her hockey incident, but just because there are no visible injuries, I'd be stupid to think it's just stopped like she's tried telling me it has.

I'm trying really hard not to take advantage of my position at school and dig deeper. I need to trust that if—when—she needs us, she'll ask for help.

"Are you ready? The car's waiting for us."

"Yes," I say, shoving my concerns down and jumping from the stool.

I grab my red shawl to wrap around my shoulders before copying Emmie and sliding my feet into my shoes.

We turn to each other, excitement shining in our eyes.

"You ready for this?" she asks, running her eyes down my vintage ivory lace dress.

"More than ready."

"I can't believe after all these years my dad is finally getting married."

"Tell me about it." I laugh. Stepping up to her, I take her hand in mine. "It just proves one thing," I say to her.

"Oh yeah?"

"Miracles can happen." She shakes her head at me. "Everything happens for a reason, Emmie. No matter how hard things seem, there's always a light at the end of the tunnel."

"I feel like you're trying to say more than you're really saying here," she says, her brows drawing together. She's too damn perceptive for her own good.

"I just..." I trail off, not really wanting to put a dampener on the day. "I'm here for you, Em. Whatever you need, okay? I just need you to know that."

"I know, Piper, and I appreciate it but... do you really want to be late because of this conversation?"

"Come here." I pull her into my arms and hold her for a beat. She returns my embrace and it does nothing for the tears in my eyes.

Straightening my spine and squaring my shoulders, I release her and take a step back.

"Right, let's do this thing."

Her hand slips into mine, and together we make our way across the little bridge that connects mine and Dawson's bedroom to the main cabin and out to the front door to greet the driver.

Dawson took charge of organising the transport, so I'm not surprised to find an old muscle car waiting for the two of us.

"Oh wow, that's gorgeous," Emmie says, running her eyes over the sleek black vehicle.

"Anyone ever tell you that you're your father's daughter?" I ask with a laugh.

"Yeah, all the freaking time. I'm not sure how I feel about it, if I'm being honest."

"Take it as a compliment. Your father is the best person I know."

"Hey," she complains, pointing to herself.

"You come a close second."

"I should think so too."

As we get closer, the driver pulls the back door open for us. Emmie lifts her floor-length red gown up and steps inside, and I follow.

The drive to the registry office is short, but by the time

we pull up outside, my hands are shaking and my palms are sweating.

"You do know you only saw him like two hours ago, right?" Emmie asks me, looking a little too amused by my nerves.

"I know but..." I blow out a breath. "This is a big thing. A once in a lifetime thing. You'll understand when it's your turn."

"Yeah, we'll see."

"You might think that now, Em. But one day, someone will come barrelling into your life, like it or not, and steal a part of you that they'll never give back."

Something flashes across her face. Understanding? Pain? I'm not quite sure, because as quickly as it appears, she locks it down.

"Come on, it's time to turn you into my new mum."

"Em, you know I'll never rep—"

"Don't even think about giving me that speech. My mother is a piece of shit, you're more than welcome to take her place."

I stare at her with my chin dropped. "O-okay."

The driver opens the door once more, and we step out and quickly make our way inside. It's mid-afternoon, but it's so cold that frost still coats the ground around us. It almost makes it look like we've pulled off the perfect white Christmas wedding. Almost.

In seconds I'm standing outside the door where I know Dawson is waiting for me, and my nerves quadruple.

I shake my arms out, trying to rid myself of the anxiety as Emmie once again laughs at me.

The music changes behind the closed doors, and one of the assistants gives me the nod before opening them.

I blow out a breath in preparation for seeing him. Emmie is right—I only saw him this morning—and seeing as we've gone against almost every wedding tradition, we slept in the same bed last night. But still, my stomach is a flurry of butterflies as I lift my foot from the ground and take a step toward him.

Every head in the room bar Dawson's turns my way and I swallow, my mouth suddenly as dry as the freaking desert.

Lisa beams at me as she wipes a tear from her eye while all of Dawson's Rebel Ink family—who are very quickly becoming my own—smile at me.

Ripping my eyes from them all, I look at my man—or rather, his back.

One second I'm standing at the back of the room, desperate for him to turn around, and the next, I'm stepping right up behind him.

Knowing I'm there, he turns, both of our breaths catching as we look at each other.

"Piper," he breathes, his eyes running the length of me.

My vintage, strapless lace dress hugs every one of my curves before falling straight to the floor. It's simple, classic, and stunning. I knew it was the one, the second Emmie, Lisa and I walked into the shop a few weeks ago.

"You look..." His voice cracks, and it threatens to tip me over the edge. "Wow."

"Not looking so bad yourself," I say, trying to keep it together. I can't cry before we've even started.

Exactly as I knew he would be, he's wearing a white shirt, open collar and sleeves rolled up to his elbows, exposing his ink, and a smart pair of black trousers. The whole look is mouth-watering.

I stand before him as the officiant starts the service. I

don't see anyone else in the room. I barely even hear the words she's saying because I'm too lost in a pair of brown eyes that I never thought I'd ever get to look into again, let alone vow to look into for the rest of my life.

"I love you," I mouth, totally ignoring whatever is being said to us.

"I love you too."

We say our vows and exchange our rings in the flash of an eye. But the second Dawson has permission to put his lips on me, everything grinds to a halt, for a few seconds at least.

Still unaware that we've got a roomful of friends, and Dawson's daughter, staring at us, when his tongue slips out to tease mine, I eagerly deepen the kiss. Much to everyone's amusement when we finally pull back.

But he doesn't pull away from me. Instead, he leans into me, his beard brushing my cheek and his lips tickling the shell of my ear.

"As it was always meant to be."

Emmie

"Does anyone else think it's kinda weird that Spike's girl and Emmie are closer in age than she is with the rest of us?"

Kas's eyes lock with mine before rolling back in her head. I like Kas a lot. She gets me in a way most people don't. And that's not mentioning that she snuck me up a joint when my dad was too busy entertaining his new bride last night.

"Shut the fuck up, Titch," various voices call from different places in the huge open plan room we've all spent our Christmas Day in together. We've been here two days now and Dad's already given up trying to chastise them about their language. I get that he's trying to protect my virtue or whatever, but it's kinda pointless. I've heard, and seen, a hell of a lot worse than these lot can throw at me. I've known these guys almost all my life; they're like those weird uncles every kid has that they can never quite escape from.

When Dad first suggested I spend the holiday with him, Piper, and all his friends, I can't say I was all that thrilled, but his eyes lit up in that way they do now Piper is back in his life, and I could hardly say no. I also couldn't exactly send him off and opt to spend the time with my mother, seeing as she has still vanished from the face of the Earth.

"What? I'm just saying," he sulks, lifting his beer can to his lips. "And, while I'm at it, this is nice and all, but it's not exactly Vegas."

"Yeah, well, not all of us are stupid enough to get so drunk we have a shotgun wedding," Spike points out.

"It's time for you to get planning, you know. Aside from Emmie, you're the only unmarried one left," Titch adds.

"Whatever, man," Spike says, flipping his friend off and pulling Kas into his side. The way he holds her, looks at her, I've got a feeling he already has a plan. He's certainly not letting her go anytime soon.

"So Emmie, how are the boys down at the posh school? You managed to find yourself a trust fund knight yet?" Titch asks, turning his inquisition on me. My stomach churns as one face pops into my mind. One that doesn't belong there, but one that appears more often than it should nonetheless.

"No, Emmie is banned from boyfriends until she's at least twenty-five. Isn't that right, Em?" Dad says with a shit-eating grin on his face.

"Whatever helps you sleep at night, old man."

"I'll take that as a yes, then. Come on, give us all the gossip. How big is his—"

"Titch," Dad barks.

"Trust fund. How big is his trust fund? Fucking hell, D. I'm not about to ask your daughter how big her boyfriend's cock is." He rolls his eyes like the mere idea is ludicrous, but I think everyone in the room would expect no less from him.

"I don't have a boyfriend," I say with a sigh. It's the truth, I don't. And if I can help it, I'm going to escape that hell hole of a school without one, too. All the guys are entitled, pretentious pricks who think every girl should bow at their feet, and the girls? Pfft, they're just a bunch of stuck-up bitches who follow them around like lost fucking puppies. Pathetic.

I knew before I stepped foot on Knight's Ridge soil that I wouldn't fit in there. But sadly, it seems I underestimated just how much of an outcast I'd be. I have no idea why, but it seems I walked into that place with a target on my back that very first morning and the shots have been coming my way ever since.

Most I can handle. Most I can ignore.

Their teasing and name-calling rolls off me like water off a duck's back.

All but one of them.

Because there's something about him. Something that makes me think it's personal, despite the fact that I have no fucking clue what it is. And I have a feeling that if he carries on the way he is then I'm not going to make it through my time at that godforsaken school alive.

But I won't make it easy for him.

I'm a fucking Ramsey, and we don't break easily.

Even for rich, privileged arseholes like Theo Cirillo.

Want more of Emmie?

Add her book to your TBR now and keep your eyes peeled for news!

ACKNOWLEDGMENTS

I can't believe we're at the end of the Rebel Ink series. I spent so long with Zach begging me for his own story, and now, not only did he get exactly what he wanted but the entire series is done.

I have loved these boys and their girls so much. Their stories have taken me to places I never expected to go, and they've kept me on my toes throughout the entire journey.

I hope you've enjoyed spending time with my bad boys as much as I have. It really feels like the end of an era with this final release, but I have so many ideas for what's to come and with a little bit of luck, this won't be the end of my boys! I'm sure I'll have plenty of future characters who'll need some ink along the way!

Should I mention Emmie? That girl has utterly stolen my heart. From the first second I wrote her in Defy You I knew she was going to be something special. So is she getting a story? Hell yeah! She won't stop screaming at me. I don't know when yet, but all the ideas are there, I just need a few more hours in the day to get it out, but just like Zach, I can't imagine she'll pipe down anytime soon.

As always, I have a huge amount of people to thank for supporting me and helping bring not only this book but the entire series to life. I couldn't do all of this alone and each one of them along with all the bloggers, bookstagrammers and you, my readers, make this happen. So thank you for being on this crazy journey with me. This might be my last release of 2020 but I promise you there are so many more to come.

Until next time,

Tracy xo

ALSO BY TRACY LORRAINE

Falling Series

Falling for Ryan: Part One #1

Falling for Ryan: Part Two #2

Falling for Jax #3

Falling for Daniel (An Falling Series Novella)

Falling for Ruben #4

Falling for Fin #5

Falling for Lucas #6

Falling for Caleb #7

Falling for Declan #8

Falling For Liam #9

Forbidden Series

Falling for the Forbidden #1

Losing the Forbidden #2

Fighting for the Forbidden #3

Craving Redemption #4

Demanding Redemption #5

Avoiding Temptation #6

Chasing Temptation #7

Rebel Ink Series

Hate You #1

Trick You #2

Defy You #3

Play You #4

Inked (A Rebel in and Driven World crossover)

Rosewood High Series

Thorn #1

Paine #2

Savage #3

Fierce #4

Hunter #5

Faze (A prequel to #6)

Fury #6

TBA #7

Ruined Series

Ruined Plans #1

Ruined by Lies #2

Ruined Promises #3

Never Forget Series

Never Forget Him #1

Never Forget Us #2

Everywhere & Nowhere #3

Chasing Series

Chasing Logan

The Cocktail Girls

His Manhattan

Her Kensington

Co-written with Angel Devlin

Hot Daddy Series

Hot Daddy Sauce #1

Baby Daddy Rescue #2

The Daddy Dilemma #3

Single Daddy Seduction #4

Hot Daddy Package #5

B.A.D. Inc. Series

Torment #1

Ride #2

Bait #3

ABOUT THE AUTHOR

Tracy Lorraine is a M/F and M/M contemporary romance author. Tracy has just turned thirty and lives in a cute Cotswold village in England with her husband, baby girl and lovable but slightly crazy dog. Having always been a bookaholic with her head stuck in her Kindle, Tracy decided to try her hand at a story idea she dreamt up and hasn't looked back since.

Be the first to find out about new releases and offers. Sign up to my newsletter here.

If you want to know what I'm up to and see teasers and snippets of what I'm working on, then you need to be in my Facebook group. Join Tracy's Angels here.

Keep up to date with Tracy's books at
www.tracylorraine.com

INKED SNEAK PEEK
A DRIVEN WORLD / REBEL INK CROSSOVER NOVEL

INKED
CHAPTER ONE

Harlow

"What the hell do you think you're doing?" Bailey, my best friend and roommate, asks the second she finds me sitting on the couch with a blanket over my lap, a tub of ice cream in hand and a rum and Coke on the coffee table.

"Err... Friday night in?" I say, my brows drawing together, trying to figure out if I've forgotten something. The look on her face and the way she's standing impatiently with her hands on her hips sure points to that.

She's just finished a twenty-four-hour shift at The House, caring for her boys, so I was expecting her to take up residence on the other couch with her wine while we caught up with *The Bachelor*.

"It's Austin's birthday," she says with a roll of her eyes.

"Right."

"We're going out. We're meeting everyone at Rush in..." she pulls her cell from her back pocket and looks at the time, "in like... an hour, so we need to get our shit together."

Before I have a chance to argue, she's standing before me and pulling the ice cream from my hand.

"Come on, H. Move that sexy ass and go and find a hot little dress to wear."

After depositing the tub on the coffee table, she rips the blanket from my lap and attempts to pull me from the couch.

"Really?" I sulk. "Austin won't care if I'm there or not, I barely know the guy." We might work for the same company, but it's not like we spend any actual time together, other than the odd night out.

"I told him you'll be there."

"But you didn't think to tell me," I mutter, eventually going easy on her and standing.

"I could have sworn I'd mentioned it."

"When could you? You've hardly been home this week."

She shrugs. "Well, you know now. It's going to be a great night."

She ushers me out of the living room—thankfully after I grab my drink. I have a feeling I'm going to need it.

When we get to my room, she allows me to get ready alone, which is a relief. The last thing I need is a Bailey makeover for tonight.

Smoothing down my silk top, I add a layer of gloss to my lips and slip my feet into my shoes.

Bailey's still sitting in front of her mirror when I join her in her room thirty minutes later.

"How are you ready al—no, no, no. You can't wear that," she says looking at me over her shoulder in the mirror. I look down at my skinny jeans and black blouse.

"Why not? It's perfectly fine."

"Yeah, for an afternoon with your aunt."

Minus the height of my heels, I can't argue with her.

She spins on her chair, and I get a look at her dress—if it can even be described as such. It's fire-engine red; I swear I've got underwear that covers more skin.

I run my eyes over her, suspicion beginning to stir in my stomach. "I feel like I'm missing something. This isn't just a night out for Austin's birthday, is it?"

"His cousin's coming."

And now, it all starts to make sense.

"The British one?"

"Yes! I can't wait to hear him say my name," she swoons, getting this far-off look in her eye.

I shouldn't be surprised—she's been telling me about him for quite a few weeks now and trying to convince Austin to introduce them.

"You mean moan your name," I mutter.

"Harlow, I'm not some easy piece of ass, you know."

"Really?" I ask, my brows lifting, my lips curling in amusement.

"Okay, so maybe I am, but only for the right guy."

"Riiight."

I watch as she gets up from her seat and walks toward her wardrobe, thankfully pulling her ridiculously short dress down in the process so I don't have to see her easy ass.

"Now, let's see what I've got."

"Oh no, B. You're not getting me in one of your dresses. They barely fit you, they'll never cover my ass and tits."

"Have faith, girl. Have faith."

Sadly, I have very little. I love Bailey, but at times she has questionable taste. Our styles are opposite in every way, not just with how much skin we deem acceptable to expose.

"Yessss..." she squeals, and my stomach drops into my heels. "This will look killer on you."

She pulls out a scrap of navy fabric and holds it up in front of me with a wide smile on her face.

"B, you won't catch me dead wearing that."

"Just try it on. It's a little big for me." I don't see how that's possible, seeing as it looks like it's a size zero from this distance, but I keep my mouth shut. "It'll be perfect. And," she adds, an idea hitting her, "it might help with that little situation you're in the middle of."

"I'm not in the middle of anything," I say, swiping the hanger from her because I already know that fighting with her on this is pointless. I may as well just try it on, prove it doesn't fit, and then hope she'll allow me to revisit my wardrobe for a dress that will cover what God gave me.

"It's been what? A year since a guy so much as touched you."

It's been almost a year and a half since my last failed attempt at a date, but I refrain from correcting her.

I shimmy my jeans down my legs and carefully pull my blouse off before laying them out over Bailey's bed. "What?" I ask when she shakes her head at me.

"You know it is okay to sometimes leave clothes in a pile on the floor, right?"

"I'm a neat freak. You could have to deal with a hell of

a lot worse than me following you around and tidying up after your messy ass."

She rolls her eyes and hands me the dress once I'm in only my underwear. Deciding that pulling it up might be the easiest option, I step into the fabric and attempt to drag it over my hips. The material has more stretch than I gave it credit for, because it skims happily over my curves. I pull the straps up my arms and put them into place over my shoulders before looking down.

"Okay, you are *so* wearing that. Have you seen your ass?"

"Weirdly, no," I sass, looking over my shoulder at the mirror behind me. I nod, because I can't deny that the fabric hugs it pretty nicely.

"You gotta lose the bra though."

"Nope. Not happening."

Bailey's hip juts out and she rests her hand on it as she stares at me in a 'go on, try and argue' stance.

"There's enough support in the dress."

"I'm sure it'll hold them up just fine, I'm more worried about flashing someone."

"Making your mission a sure success."

"I'm not on a mission. I'm perfectly happy as—"

"Nope. You need a man-induced orgasm. End of."

I know I've been a little uptight recently, but it's not my lack of male attention that's causing it, and I doubt a night with one will solve the issue.

Bailey must see my shoulders drop, because she walks over and takes my hands in hers. "I know you're worried about her. I am too. But sitting around the house feeling guilty about not being able to do more isn't going to help in any way. No matter the results, you still have a life. You may as well at least attempt to enjoy yourself."

"I guess." I don't feel all that enthused, but I know she's right.

"Now, drink this," she says, handing my glass back to me. "Then let the girls free, and we're out of here."

I tip my glass to my lips and swallow what's left before doing as I'm told. I'm soon following Bailey out of the house toward the awaiting car. Despite my earlier disinterest, tingles of excitement start to ignite in my belly. I can't deny that the dress looked good once I turned and got a proper look at myself in the mirror. I also can't deny that I'm currently showing more boob than I have to anyone outside the bedroom in a lot of years.

Shaking thoughts of my past from my head, I climb in the car as Bailey begins flirting with the driver. Just because I'm dressed up and showing a little skin, it doesn't mean I'm going back to a time in my life I'd rather forget. I'm just going out for a night of drinking and dancing with my best friend. It's exactly what I should be doing. I'm young with no ties, a Friday night out for a colleague's birthday should be a normal thing to do.

Pushing aside my worries, I look at Bailey, who flashes me a wide smile, and I try to relax.

"Tonight's going to be great. Did I tell you that Rylee managed to secure the VIP section for us thanks to her… connections," she says, wiggling her eyebrows. I groan as I think of her boss, Rylee and her famous boyfriend.

My heart starts to race. "A-are they going to be there?" I try to ask as casually as I can.

"Please don't tell me you're still scared of being in the same building as him?"

"I'm not scared, B," I argue, although I'm not entirely sure that's true. "I just always make myself look like an idiot every time I'm anywhere near him. I turn into a fumbling teenager with one glance in his direction." My cheeks heat at my admission. I don't need to tell Bailey this—she's witnessed my mortifying behavior, time and time again when it comes to him. Colton Donavan. My teenage heartthrob, incredible Indy driver, and all-around nice guy. It should be illegal to be that good looking, kind and generous. I was obsessed with him in my former years, thanks to discovering a trashy magazine on the coffee table after school one day with him on the cover. No matter how many years have passed, it seems the second I'm in his vicinity, I return to that time in my life where I had no idea how to control my raging hormones or to keep a leash on my mouth.

"Oh, I know. Why do you think I demanded you come? You're tonight's entertainment," she says with a laugh.

"B," I squeal, swatting her shoulder playfully as she teases me. "I've no idea what's wrong with me."

"I get it. He's... captivating." Her eyes darken as she relives the one moment of her past that she'll never let me forget. "And his kiss," she says on a sigh.

"Oh, get over yourself," I chuckle. "You know full well that you got passed up that night for Rylee and haven't stood a chance since."

"I know, and I still stand by the fact that I rocked his world so much that night that he lost his mind a little after. I mean, why wouldn't he want more of this?" She gestures to herself with a pout.

"No idea, B. No idea."

"Well, I'm over it." I laugh; with the number of times she brings it up, I beg to differ, but I'm not going to point it out again. "I've got my sights set on a British banger tonight."

I bark out a laugh. "Do you even know what this guy looks like?"

"Only in my imagination."

"So he could be an old cockney with a beer belly and a bald head?"

"Yes and no. He's still in his twenties, so I'd like to think he's not bald."

"Still leaves a lot to go wrong, don't you think?"

"Nah, it's all good. I can feel it in my blood."

"I'm pretty sure that's the wine."

"Meh, tonight is my night, H. Just you wait and see. I'm gonna snag me a Brit, and I'm not letting this one out of my sight."

"If you say so," I whisper, looking out the window and seeing the neon lights of the club coming into view.

After saying the right words in the bouncer's ear, he stands aside and allows both Bailey and I to enter the club, although not before he gets his fill of her scantily-clad body.

"You offering up sexual favors again, B?"

"Not necessary this time. Come on, stop dawdling, the bar and the Brit are calling."

She grabs my hand and together we make our way through the crowd and toward the roped-off stairs that lead to the VIP section.

As we move, the loud bass from the music vibrates through me, and even though being here tonight was the last thing I wanted to do after a long week at work, I can't help a little excitement and the desire to get up on the dancefloor creeping in. It's been a long time since I've let go with my best friend and forgotten about the world for a few hours.

After sweet-talking the second bouncer in as many

minutes, we're climbing the stairs and away from the masses of people.

We're only three-quarters of the way up when I first see him. My nerves hit me like a sledgehammer and my body starts to tremble. It doesn't matter how many times I see and talk to him. It doesn't matter that I hear stories from Rylee about what a 'normal' guy he is. To me, he's still the man I had pinned to my teenage bedroom walls and said goodnight to before falling asleep.

I focus on my feet as I climb the stairs, the gems on the front glinting in the spotlights above and giving me a distraction from the man I'm walking toward.

I've got one more step to climb. Thinking I'm safe, I look up, but the second I meet his piercing green eyes, my feet falter. The platform of my shoe connects with the step, and I go tumbling forward.

Closing my eyes, I reach my hand out in the hope that it connects with something to break my inevitably painful collision with the tiled floor. Thankfully the pain never comes. Instead, my hand hits something warm and soft.

Finding my feet, I drag my eyes open to see what stopped me.

The second I see what I used to stop my fall, I gasp in horror and stumble backward into someone else. Large hands grip onto my waist to steady me as I keep my eyes locked on the floor. My cheeks flame so hot I swear they're going to catch fire any moment.

"Jesus, Harlow, that was some entrance," Colton says with a laugh as I continue to die a thousand deaths at embarrassing myself once again.

"Are you okay?" A deep, smooth voice washes over me from behind, making me wish the ground would just swallow me up. I nod, but not before I hear the laughter of my best friend behind me.

"I'm fine. I'm fine," I mutter, looking up but only so I can see which way the bar is so I can get a drink and hopefully wipe this disaster from my memory. "T-thank you," I whisper to the man behind me who's still holding me upright, probably thinking my legs don't work correctly.

"Anytime." I push to move away, but his voice makes me pause. It's deep, rough, and his accent is... I don't have time to try to figure it out. I just need to get away from him and Colton's green eyes that turn me into a fumbling moron.

"Oh my God, Harlow. That was classic," Bailey howls beside me as I wait for the bartender to notice me. "I mean, Colton's used to women falling at his feet, but using his cock to save yourself from breaking your nose on the floor? That was fucking—"

"Enough," I bark. "This is all your fault." Turning to her, I narrow my eyes in the hope it'll shut her up.

"Me?" she asks, innocently pointing to herself.

"Yes. I should be on the sofa right now with my second tub of ice cream and watching others falling in love on some shitty reality TV show."

"Oh yeah, that sounds like a winning way to spend your Friday night, H. I'll call you a cab right now to return to your evening of fun."

"Really?" I ask hopefully, missing her sarcasm.

"No. Harlow. No. You embarrassed yourself, so what? Colton doesn't care, so neither should you." She waves and the bartender comes right over—of course he fucking does. One look at her and he's like putty in her hand. Me?

He barely even saw me standing here. Rolling my eyes at myself, I listen as Bailey orders us four shots of tequila.

"Tequila?" My lip curls in disgust.

"Yes, hopefully it'll give your confidence a boost and loosen you up a little."

"Here's hoping," I mutter, more to myself than her as I pick up the first one and knock it back before immediately going for the second. The alcohol burns my throat, but it's only seconds before it starts warming my belly. Maybe it will have the effect Bailey intended.

"Oh, the birthday boy's here. Let's go and wish him a happy birthday." I look over to where Bailey's focus is and see both Rylee and Colton standing before Austin.

"It's okay, you go. I'll order some more drinks."

"He's just a guy, H. You can talk to him like any other."

"I know. And I will talk to him... them. I just... I need another drink first. I can only embarrass myself so much every hour."

Shaking her head at me, she takes off across the room, her heels clicking against the black polished tiles and her mile-long, tanned legs eating up the space. I don't need to look around to know she's got the attention of at least a handful of men as she moves. Bailey has this aura surrounding her, one that turns all attention on her. Something that I most definitely don't possess. I'm just the best friend who makes an idiot of herself as often as possible and only helps to make Bailey look so much more desirable.

Blowing out a long breath, I turn back to the bar, only to find that the bartender has once again vanished to serve someone else. Sitting myself up on a stool, I watch as he gets farther and farther away from me before turning to play on his cell.

Fantastic.

Thinking that I'll just order a cab home, I turn to slide from the stool but come to a stop when I find a guy standing before me. One side of his mouth curls up in an unsure smile.

"Hey, how are you doing?"

His deep voice is immediately recognizable. My eyes drop to his hands that are tucked into the pockets of his pants, but as I do that, I feel the warmth of one of them against my waist from not so long ago.

"Oh yeah. I'm sorry about that. I'm a bit of an id..." My eyes run up exposed forearms that are covered in ink. I find the rolled fabric of his white shirt and my mouth waters when I discover his muscular biceps beneath. It's open one button too many at the neck, showing even more art, but it's when I find his light blue eyes that it feels like my world tilts slightly.

His lopsided grin turns into a megawatt smile, exposing perfectly straight white teeth beneath, and my entire body sighs.

"Can I buy you a drink?"

It takes me a few moments to register that he's said anything, but once I do, I tilt my head to the side and look at him once more.

"Y-you're the Brit?"

That lopsided smile returns, but this time a dimple pops up in his cheek.

"What gave me away?" I bite down on my bottom lip and his eyes drop to focus on it. "It's Corey. And you are?"

"H-Harlow."

"Well, it's a pleasure to meet you, Harlow. Shall we?" he asks, gesturing toward the bar before lifting his hand to call the bartender over.

Ignoring the vacant stool beside me, he chooses instead to stand next to me. Just close enough that his warmth heats my side and his scent fills my nose. This guy knows what he's doing. It should be a turn off, but I can't help but fall for his charm. Maybe Bailey was right. I bite down on my bottom lip as I attempt to remember what it feels like to be touched by a man.

Bailey's going to kill you for talking to him first, I think as I look up at him once more, my cheeks burning with my previous thoughts. When I glance over my shoulder, I see she's still preoccupied with Austin and a few of the other counselors from The House along with Rylee and Colton. That's enough to tell me that I'm not heading over there anytime soon.

INKED
CHAPTER TWO

Corey

Tonight is my first night out—night off, actually—since setting up the studio over here. But Austin gave me little choice about it. He first mentioned it a few weeks ago, and, assuming he'd forget about it, or at least forget about me, I pushed it aside. But when he called again at the beginning of the week and told me that I had to be here and reminded me that he'd given me prior warning, I didn't stand a chance. Part of my moving here was so that I could spend time with this side of my family, something he used against me to ensure I attended. Turns out though, he didn't need to try quite so hard; all he had to do was mention the quality of the women who would also be here, and I'd have followed orders in a heartbeat.

I realised just how right a decision that was when I found myself following a curvy redhead up the stairs to a

VIP area that's been reserved for my cousin tonight, courtesy of his famous friend.

I've been so busy that women haven't been on my radar all that much since I arrived in LA. I mean, I've spent my fair share of time inking them, but that's about as close as I've got. And my lack of action hasn't been more obvious to me than those few seconds of watching her arse sway before me as she climbed the stairs.

"So, you know Colton?" I ask once we've given the bartender our orders. A pint for me and a rum and Coke for her. I must admit, I was surprised. I was expecting her to order a glass of bubbles like I've seen the other women drinking, or at least a glass of wine, but it seems this woman has been sent to surprise me tonight. First, her fine arse, swiftly followed by her damn near falling into my arms not long after, and now this.

"Thank you. I need this," she says, swallowing a generous mouthful before turning to look at me. "I work with Rylee. I've spoken to Colton several times."

"Same. Although from the number of hours I've spent watching him fly around a track, I like to think I know him quite well."

"Hmmm..." she hums, her cheeks flaming almost as red as her hair.

"So you work for Corporate Cares? Are you a counsellor?"

"No, no." Her eyes go wide like the idea in itself is shocking. "I support the organisation wholeheartedly, but me and kids don't mix." I open my mouth to tell her that that can't possibly be true, but she beats me to it. "I'm in charge of fundraising."

"Sounds like fun."

"I love it. It's important for me to give back."

I nod at her, finding myself lost in her chestnut eyes as she stares back at me.

She coughs, clearing her throat and breaking the tension between us after a few seconds, and I'm forced to look away.

"So what is it you do?"

"Harlow, there you are. I thought you were coming to talk to the birthday boy," a high-pitched voice says from behind me before a blonde wrapped in the smallest dress I've ever seen stands so close to me that I have to take a step back.

"Yeah... I... uh..."

"Oh, are you still embarrassed about that? I'm sure Colton's already forgotten." She waves her friend off with a swish of her hand, and my eyes widen in shock. "Who's your new friend?" She turns to me, her eyes running over my face as what I guess is supposed to be a sexy pout appears on her lips. She falls a little too far from the mark for me. That and all the effort she's putting in to look so good.

"Corey," I say politely, holding my hand out for her.

"Oh, my Brit." *My Brit?* My eyebrows rise at her assumption. "Austin didn't say you were here yet." Ignoring my hand, she steps right into my body, pressing her breasts into my chest and stretching to drop a kiss to my cheek. "I've been so looking forward to meeting you."

"Oh really?" I ask, placing my hands on her shoulders and trying to remove her from me. "I'm not sure Austin's ever mentioned you."

Harlow snorts a laugh and when I look up, I find the most breathtaking smile lighting up her face.

"Oh, that can't be true. I'm sure you've just forgotten. I can only imagine that you've met so many new people since you arrived. I'm Bailey. I work with your cousin. He's told me all about you."

"Is that right?"

"Sure is. So tell me about yourself, I can't wait to get to know you better."

"Well, actually, I was in the middle of a conversation with your friend here."

Bailey stands back and looks over her shoulder. "Oh, okay, well…" She sounds dejected, making me wonder how many guys turn her down. Not a lot, I'm guessing.

"Would you like a drink, B?"

"I'd love one, thanks." I stand and watch both of them as Harlow orders Bailey a sauvignon blanc. They're both stunning, Bailey more so now I don't have everything thrust in my face, but to me, Harlow stands out by a mile. Her soft red hair, her large dark eyes that just ooze innocence… I bite down on my bottom lip as I study her while she talks to her friend. She must sense my stare, because her eyes flick to mine and she startles when she finds me looking back. Colour hits her cheeks, and it only makes her more alluring. It looks like coming here tonight was more than worth it.

My cock stirs behind the fabric of my jeans, desperate to end the evening with a little action.

Bailey lifts her drink from the bar and takes a sip while looking between the two of us suspiciously.

"So… I'm just going to go…" she trails off before disappearing off into the crowd.

"Good friend of yours?" I ask once I'm confident she's well out of earshot.

Harlow laughs and excitement shoots through me. She is exactly what I need tonight.

I take a step closer, her perfume filling my nose and making my mouth water.

"Yeah, actually. My best friend."

"Really? You seem so..."

"Different?"

"Yeah," I say, relieved that I'm not the only one who sees how opposite they are.

"Don't let her front fool you. She's a great person. She just comes across a little—"

"Desperate?"

She laughs. "I was going to say full-on, but desperate works too. Everyone around us seems to be coupling up. Austin, Colton," she says flicking a look over to where they're standing with their girls. "She's just feeling left behind."

"And she thought I might get her up to speed."

I watch her lips, enthralled as she purses them to take a sip of her drink. "You've no idea. She's been going on and on about meeting you since Austin told her you'd first moved here."

"Why? She's never met me. I could be a right arsehole." A smile curls at her lips.

"The accent," she says like it should be obvious. "She was hoping you'd talk all sexy to her." Harlow rolls her eyes at her friend's insanity. "So, are you?"

"Am I what? Going to talk all sexy to her?" I drop the tone of my voice and delight when the roughness of it makes her pupils dilate. My brows pull together as I cast my mind back over our previous conversation, trying to figure out what she's asking me.

"No. An *arsehole*," she says, adorably trying to mimic my accent.

"Some would probably say I was. Others not so

much."

"Cryptic."

Closing more of the space between us, I reach out and tuck a lock of her hair behind her ear. "Maybe you'll just have to find out for yourself."

Her lips part but no words come out as my fingertip brushes the shell of her ear. "I... um..." I search her eyes, trying to read her. She seems reluctant, yet there's something in her eyes. Something wild that I know is screaming to get out.

Our connection holds before she sucks her bottom lip into her mouth and my gaze drops to watch.

"Harlow," that familiar voice calls from somewhere. "We're going to dance. You coming?"

My eyes jump back up to hers. I want to ask her to stay here with me, but I've just met her; I've got no right to even suggest keeping her away from her friends and colleagues.

After another second, she rips her eyes from mine and looks at Bailey, who holds her hand out.

"Yeah, just coming."

I stand back, allowing her some space. She downs her drink before giving me a small smile and walking towards her friend.

Her arse sways as she makes her way over, and my trousers suddenly seem a little too tight as I imagine what, if any, underwear she's got on beneath. When I look up, I find Bailey watching me. Her eyes are narrowed, and I'm not sure if it's jealousy or a warning.

DOWNLOAD now to keep reading Corey and Harlow's story

Printed in Great Britain
by Amazon